A BU

'UNCONSCIOUS INFLUENCE'

Author of
The Rebecca Rioter and *Chloe Arguelle*

A BURGLARY
OR
'UNCONSCIOUS INFLUENCE'

by
AMY DILLWYN

In Three Volumes

Edited and with an introduction by
ALISON FAVRE

HONNO CLASSICS

This edition © Honno Ltd 2009
'Ailsa Craig', Heol y Cawl, Dinas Powys,
South Glamorgan, Wales, CF64 4AH

First published in Great Britain by Tinsley Brothers, London in 1883

© Introduction, Alison Favre

British Library Cataloguing in Publication Data
A catalogue record for this book is available from the British Library

ISBN 13: 978-1-906784-07-2

Published with the financial support of the Welsh Books Council.

Cover design: www.giselles.co.uk
Cover image: © V&A Images, 'Spring' by Frederick Walker
Printed in Wales by Dinefwr

CONTENTS

Introduction

Alison Favre

Until Honno's popular re-edition of *The Rebecca Rioter* in 2004, E. A. Dillwyn of Swansea, otherwise known as Amy Dillwyn, was one of the great 'underread'. John Sutherland, who coined this term in 1996, identified 878 out of some 3500 'underread' Victorian novelists.[i] Of these 878, 312 were women and 113 were spinsters, many using pseudonyms or otherwise disguising their gender, and many publishing five or more novels. Amy Dillwyn conforms to Sutherland's analysis of the typical 'underread' novelist, but she, for one, certainly did *not* deserve to fall into oblivion: her writings cast a fascinating light upon an otherwise under-represented facet of history – the life of the Anglicised upper-class gentlewoman in Victorian Wales. In both her literature and her life, she challenged the expected gender norms of her class and epoch.

Biography
She was born in 1845 into the Welsh gentry, the second daughter of Lewis Llewellyn Dillwyn, industrialist and long-time Liberal M.P. for Swansea, and his artistic, supportive wife Bessie de la Beche. On both sides of the family, they were unconventional. The Dillwyns were Anglicans, but of Quaker stock, with a reputation for business acumen, an open-minded attitude to boys' *and* girls' education, women's fulfilment and the fight for the abolition of slavery. The De la Beche side was unusual too. Though, unlike the Dillwyns, the family had gained its money through the slave trade, Bessie's young life was spent

accompanying her father Henry, travelling Europe including Wales, studying geology, entomology and sanitary concerns. Both families shared scientific pursuits, such as an interest in the fossils and shells in the Gower area; it was through these activities that Lewis and Bessie first came to meet.

Amy had a very free childhood and was particularly close to her brother Harry, her elder by two years. Bookish but sporty, she loved to romp with him in the Glamorganshire countryside, tree-climbing, fishing, ice-skating, boating and horse-riding, among many other outdoor activities. As her family belonged to the 'Upper Ten Thousand', that is, those members of the gentry and aristocracy who 'did the London Season', Amy was presented at Court as a debutante at seventeen, and was fully expected to make a good marriage. Tomboy as she was, she enjoyed the balls, opera, theatre, concerts and outings of the Season. She was soon engaged to a young acquaintance singled out for her from an early age, the wealthy Llewellyn Thomas of Llwynmadoc. Despite some misgivings about marriage, she was numbed when she learned of her fiancé's sudden death from smallpox in Paris in 1864. Although she continued the Season almost each year, she subsequently remained single. Tempted to enter an Anglican sisterhood, she seemed doomed to a life of abnegation, caring for her family and doing the 'good works' typical of spinsters in the Victorian period.

It was during her late twenties and thirties, when Amy despaired of leading a worthwhile life and had become a semi-invalid, that she began writing. First she wrote religious allegories to interest her Sunday school pupils, and then started publishing short stories in periodicals, and book reviews in the *Spectator*. Of her six known novels, her first, *The Rebecca Rioter* (1880), is based on first-hand accounts by her grandfather, father and uncle of the arrest of Rebecca rioters in Pontardulais in 1843.[ii] The next two, *Chloe Arguelle* (1881) and *A Burglary*

(1883), are both concerned with resistance to the hypocrisies of upper-class society, while *Jill* (1884) and *Jill and Jack* (1887) continue the critique of the upper classes from below stairs, as the heroine escapes the stultifying role of an inactive young lady by becoming a lady's maid, then a courier. Dillwyn's final novel, *Maggie Steele's Diary* (1892), returns to *A Burglary*'s topic of theft among the gentry.

By this time, however, with the death of her brother in 1890 and her father in 1892, Amy was at last free to lead a life of her own. But her circumstances, on the face of it, did not seem propitious: she was turned out of the family home, Hendrefoilan, when it was inherited by a nephew, and faced debts incurred by her father's zinc works at Llansamlet. This proved an 'opportune misfortune', however: Amy at last had a purpose in life, namely to rescue the jobs of over two hundred employees at the Spelter Works and save the family name. Her invalid state forgotten, she worked for four years, living on a bare minimum, to claim the Dillwyn Company from Chancery and make it a going concern. She became a household name in Swansea and was known nationally and even internationally as a cigar-smoking businesswoman, feminist and supporter of charities. Once more physically active and energetic, she lived to be ninety, dying in December 1935.[iii]

The Novel

First published by the Tinsley Brothers in 1883, *A Burglary* was doubtless conceived at the same time as two short stories on similar themes published by Dillwyn in *Tinsley's Magazine*. In *A Comet's Tale*, the male hero and first person narrator is out at night to observe a comet when he is spied by two burglars and ignominiously tied up and gagged before managing to make his escape. The second, *One June Night: A Sketch of an Unladylike Girl*, deals with a Welsh adolescent who, startled by a strange nocturnal noise, quits her shocked governess and takes on a poacher. Helped by the game-keeper, she manages to capture him, only to relent and release him after hearing his tale of family poverty that has occasioned his misdemeanour.[iv]

A Burglary, the full-blown, three-volume development of these fictional explorations in transgression and unconventionality, has a circular structure, in that it begins and ends with an elder brother chaffing his sister. Its parts echo the same pattern: the first volume starts and ends with moth-hunting, volume two begins and ends with a question and volume three with an adventuress planning and achieving marriage to a member of the nouveaux-riches. The novel's structure is also clarified by its series of parallels and oppositions set up to compare and contrast characters, situations and themes. It is written mainly in the third person and told by an omniscient narrator, who intervenes to analyse, explain and help the story along by means of flashbacks and foreshadowing. Ostensibly a broad-ranging novel of manners in the style of Thackeray's *Vanity Fair*, it has recourse to the sensation genre, yet is also inventive and anticipatory of later developments in fictional styles.

The tale is set mainly in Wales: until the tenth chapter of the second volume all its scenes take place at or near Llwyn-yr-Allt, home of Mr Rhys, the magistrate, and his two children, Ralph, seventeen, and Imogen, sixteen. Nearby is the town of Cwm-Eithin, a thinly-disguised Swansea, whose municipal inaugurations, slums, and incompetent police force are vividly evoked. The Rhys's neighbours and acquaintance include Sir Cadwallader Gough, the local M.P., Trevor Owen, the barrister son of Lord Llyn, as well as Polly Thomas, the domestic, Jones the bailiff, and Richard Richards, a local collier and poacher. Welsh is the language spoken in the Richards' household and the children are bewildered when addressed in English.

Idiosyncratic dialect versions of English, clearly marked by the influence of the speakers' first language, Welsh, are effectively employed to indicate the indigenous culture of the area. Wales, here, is 'Wild Wales' in that it affords a natural context of liberty and joyous anarchy in which the Rhys youngsters evolve. They can be *uncivilized* 'barbarians' or regular 'Red Indians' to their hearts' content, pursuing such activities as night-time 'bug-hunting'. On the other hand, in the upper-class London society in which scenes from the later chapters are located, the context changes to one of restraint and *civilized* humbug. The taming influence of that society is especially noticeable in Imogen, the tomboy. Initially she dreads the thought of taking her place within society as a debutante, but is gradually seduced by its charms and snares. Despite her determination not to be wed, she is courted by two admirers, the honourable Sir Charles Dover and the villainous William Sylvester. The latter is a gentleman burglar who steals the prized jewels of Imogen's cousin, the heiress Ethel Carton, while she is staying at the Rhys's. Fearing he may have been recognized due to a missing finger, he allows Richards, who has a similar handicap, to be accused instead.

Themes and Leitmotifs

The title and subtitle *A Burglary or 'Unconscious Influence'* suggest the book's concerns with issues of transgression and power. Before the narrative begins, Sylvester, its complex villain, has embezzled the funds of his employers, the financiers Messrs Glass of Cwm-Eithin, a transgression which he attempts to hide by thieving to make up the loss. Manifestly dishonest, he yet manages to dissimulate his evil action through the gentility of his demeanour; he is a veritable wolf in sheep's clothing. Other more minor characters amongst the gentry, such as Elise Bolyn and Trevor Owen, could also be considered as transgressing against the social code in that they adopt underhand methods of seeking advantage and marrying for money; both are veritable 'gold-diggers'. Imogen, on the other hand, breaks the codes of her class by refusing to appear genteel. Wearing workmanlike clothes, a 'strong serge dress and jacket, Welsh flannel petticoat…[and] thick greased boots', she hardly looks like a child of the gentry, and provokes a passing gipsy to comment, "Queer lot some of those gentry be!" Nor is her behaviour ladylike, as she roams the countryside freely at night in her chase after moths, tearing her clothes, scratching her limbs, and revelling in the freedom of her rough apparel. She has no vanity and is the despair of her maid, who complains that if her mistress were left to her own devices her clothes would be "put on with a pitch-fork." 'Fiercely intolerant of fashion and conventionalities', Imogen has resolved to live 'in single blessedness', a resolution in itself a transgression of the Victorian codes since spinsterhood carried social stigma: when she proposes to her brother that she should keep house for him, he demurs, telling her, "Take my word for it you'll be a failure if you don't marry." All in all, Imogen is a rough diamond or 'a nugget of gold' which has 'not yet shed its mud coating'.

As well as transgressing against the social codes of dress and conduct, Imogen also infringes on the spatial dimensions proper to her caste. When the novel opens, she is on the threshold of a new life, about to cross the limit or boundary between childhood and adulthood. Her favoured position, however, is not within the home and within the bounds of propriety, but outside, in the dark, catching moths with her brother. From that vantage point, she observes other young women, the 'social butterflies', in the light of the front door setting off for a ball: for the time being she has not 'crossed the Rubicon'. The outsider fears becoming an insider caught within the nets of her prescribed society, yet her first words, musing about the next ball, are "I suppose I shall be going too." Ideally she wishes to combine the two worlds, outside and in, 'catching huge and marvellous moths to the sound of enchanting music'. At the same time, for all her headstrong ways, Imogen has the sensitivity to dread appearing to intrude upon the private space of others, whatever their class. She is reluctant to offend by words, hiding her real feelings by slang expressions or brusqueness, and she hesitates to enter the Richards' hovel and advise on improving their life-style. This shyness and fear of intruding is a characteristic she shares with her first suitor, Sir Charles Dover. Such scruples are not present in Trevor Owen, who is invasive in his officious inquiries into the burglary and in his rude intrusion into the Richards' household, or in Sylvester, who intrudes by monopolizing Imogen at every ball and whisking her away from other company.

But transgression of the spatial dimension is most obvious, of course, on the night of the burglary. Sylvester trespasses on the Rhys property, thanks to a window left unfastened by Imogen and Ralph. As a gentleman insider, he knows the house and finds the heiress's room easily. When he realizes that Ethel's slumber is feigned, he feels obliged to adopt a poacher's accent to intimidate and confuse her, before he binds and gags her. The transgression is not immediately detected, for he leaves by the same unfastened window. During that same night, the Rhys youngsters have been guilty of their own spatial transgression, pilfering food from the family kitchen and taking fruit from the kitchen garden, before letting the pigs loose to chase them across the property of their aunt and uncle. But while Sylvester's trespass is legally culpable, the Rhys's remains in the family and is but high-spirited play. Interestingly, the text also considers the interim position of another act of spatial transgression, that of Richards the poacher. He and his wife can never accept that poaching for food is illegal trespass on the gentry's land and theft of another's property, as worthy of punishment as stealing jewels. For them, rather, poaching is 'fair game', as it was for generations of peasants, in Wales as elsewhere.

What Dillwyn is most interested in exploring, however, is not the transgression itself but what it leads to: the corrosive, dehumanizing effects of deceit and dissimulation, and the manner in which they alienate the culprit from his fellows. Her complex portrayal of Sylvester focuses on his acting skills; indeed, theatre images are a leitmotif in the novel. Sylvester is the prime hypocrite, masking his guilt by taking on the assumed role of a poacher during the burglary itself, and then adopting the pose of sophisticated gentlemanly integrity as he moves within the local high society. Small wonder that his talent leads him to play 'the villain of the piece' and adopt the same poacher's accent in the 'Theatricals' organised at the height of the London Season. Ethel, the victim of his transgression, is herself not without acting skills and a vivid consciousness of the drama of her situation: she imagines the face of her maid discovering her trussed-up body 'as good as a play'. Even Imogen imagines cleansing the Richards' hovel 'like a transformation scene in a pantomime'. Another leitmotif running throughout the novel is the image of moth, tempted by the light which attracts but destroys, just as abundant wealth attracts but ultimately destroys the dispossessed. A moth flutters through the 'Theatricals' scene, turning and seeking to escape burning its wings on the lights. It can be taken to symbolize Imogen's yearning for liberty, in the face of the attraction she feels towards the glamour and glitter of her social destiny, or Sylvester's attraction to Imogen which imperils his capacity to maintain his false façade, but it also prefigures the ensuing fire which is about to engulf many of the 'social butterflies' Imogen had earlier admired.

The transgression topos of *A Burglary* is matched by the power topos of the subtitle, *Unconscious Influence*. As noted on several occasions in the novel, Imogen develops an adolescent infatuation with her older cousin Ethel. Her idol is quite unaware of Imogen's feelings, but by precept and example is able to wield power over her. Ever since her religious confirmation, Imogen has been eager to be 'of real use in the world, and make some solid difference to it'. Ethel's slight rebuke concerning the poor state of the Richards' cottage and the need for reform, together with her easy benevolence towards cottagers, influences Imogen to act on their behalf, and involve herself in their need for better sustenance and healthier living conditions. By extension she is also influenced to act for justice, hotly defending Richards' cause, ironically in front of the real culprit. But even as she does so Imogen in her turn becomes in herself an unconscious influence on Sylvester. From the moment when he first overheard it, Imogen's clear peal of joyous laughter had struck Sylvester's ear as a curious echo from his own early days of innocence. Subsequently his strange attraction to this 'queer girl' leads to the undermining of his stronghold of evil. His unchivalrous behaviour 'in a coat of mail of selfishness' is gradually transformed. Under her unconscious influence, he first forgets to 'look after number one' and acts for the good of another, as in the 'Mad Dog' scene when he protects Imogen from harm. In order that she should have her wish and prove Richards' innocence, he is then nearly tempted to confess his crime and give himself up. Finally, in the scene of the 'Croesus pyre' or fire at the Croesus-Hoggs' house, he is influenced to act in accordance with her desire and try to save others, recognizing as he does so that 'he does not feel so absolutely severed from her now, as he has always done heretofore'. If 'a burglary' leads to alienation and dehumanization, 'unconscious influence' leads to the desire to merge with the beloved and adopt the virtues they are perceived as embodying, even if, as in Sylvester's case, it also leads to death.

Literary Techniques

Limits, intrusion, transgression and power are probed and anatomized in the novel, but they fail to account for its cleverness, charm and comedy. The tone of the writing is sophisticated: its readers are clearly expected to be familiar with a wide range of English literary references and a cosmopolitan array of continental languages. Moreover, the author's love of things entomological is evident in her references to various varieties of moth and butterfly, and her assumption that the reader too can distinguish rare specimens from the common breed. Such expectations, along with the tendency to expound on such matters as rational dress theory or the necessary distinction between blameless and blameworthy dirt and untidiness, might be considered didactic or proselytizing. However this 'preaching' is never invasive for it is moderated by charm and comedy. The charm of the wild, hoydenish Imogen is undeniable. She is a fully rounded, complex character, and so is Ethel who, for all her apparent indolence, is aroused to action and to fine moral discernment when she needs to prove her worth. Sylvester too is a convincingly delineated and ultimately appealing villain, whose psychological motivations in performing extreme acts are at least as open to the reader as they are to himself, while Sir Charles Dover's initially comic attempts to gain Imogen's approbation are balanced by his evident appreciation of her unorthodox virtues.

The charm of the more minor 'society' characters lies in their very absurdity; with her quick eye and ear for humbug, Dillwyn entertains us with the gushing 'quite too awfully tremendous' exclamations of Lady Elise Bolyn, the magpie eye and 'Paul Pry' manner of Trevor Owen, and the prancing, 'St Vitus' Dance' movements of Guelf Crœsus-Hogg, who as his name indicates, hogs his riches. Onomastics, or the art of describing characters by their names, is much used by Dillwyn, and adds both to the novel's comedy and to greater understanding of its characters. If Imogen means 'beloved girl', all three of her cousin's names have noble connotations – Ethel from 'aethel' (noble), Percival (from the knight of the Round Table) and Carton (from *A Tale of Two Cities*) – while Sir Charles Dover can only evoke quintessential Britishness. Dillwyn's sense of fun is also evident in the description of moth 'public houses', where moths become drunk on sugared rum and are easily captured unlike their teetotal friends. It is present too in the word play, especially with polysemic words, like 'skate' (the ice sport and the fish), 'grub' (larvae, digging or food), 'maggot' (a larva or a whim), or indeed 'humbug' (a boiled sweet or social hypocrisy). High comedy, based on wit, word play or the deft use of irony, is matched by low comedy, based on physical humour, as in the scene in which Dover ineptly tries his hand at butterfly-hunting in order to impress Imogen, and ends up in a duck pond with a broken net and no fritillary. Dillwyn's love of language, and her understanding of the way in which literary devices can 'roughen up' habitualized expression and defamiliarize it for the reader, is also evident in her frequent use of alliteration, in such phrases as 'terpsichorean twisting and twirling', 'poor as a peer' or 'last will…be lost', for example. Most strikingly, perhaps, she uses the present tense unexpectedly but to great effect, to heighten and render more immediate and vivid her depiction of such scenes as the climactic ballroom fire episode.

The cumulative effect of its literary techniques and intertwining themes and leitmotifs is to produce in *A Burglary* a novel which is in itself both transgressive and capable of exerting an influence on the reader. Because of the pleasurable reading which the text offers, with its comedy, charm and sensational episodes, its moral influences may be imbibed by the reader unconsciously, but their inclusion was by no means an unconscious act on the author's part. As Dillwyn's diary entry from as early as 1863 suggests, "...I always have a sneaking kindness for the villain, because he gets so abused..." , it was from the first her conscious intention to develop her reader's capacity to feel sympathy for her villain.[v] Through no fault of his own Sylvester has been brought up to be a gentleman without a gentleman's means, a situation which he attempts to correct through his acts of embezzlement and theft: he is damaged by the class system just as surely as the Richards' family is, and is morally unhinged by its impositions and expectations. The pressure to 'act the gentleman' takes away the innocence and honesty of the upper class male, as surely as it traps his women in a golden cage and leaves the exploited labourer impoverished at his gates. Imogen's protestations throughout the novel against the manner in which middle and upper class gender roles atrophy female energy are also transgressive; coming as they do in advance of the 'New Woman' novels of the 1890s to which in a sense they look forward, they add to the novel's critique of the class system as ultimately destructive of human potential.

Dillwyn has in effect 'burgled' the typical English bourgeois novel of the period of its more attractive features, its comedy of manners, for example, or its sensationalist thrills, to construct a novel which uses its influence to expose and destroy the social structures which such novels reflect. The seductive glamour of the English class system, as adopted by her aspiring Welsh Victorians, goes up in flames at the end of her novel, but in that fire the struggling soul of those corrupted by the system, such as Sylvester, will be forever purged and redeemed.

That a text which reflects in such unexpected yet convincing ways the complex experience of the Victorian Welsh should be left to lie forgotten in the ranks of the 'underread' does seem an anomaly; one can but warmly welcome the Honno editors' decision to give it a new life in their republished Classics series.

Endnotes

i   See John Sutherland's 'Foreword: The Underread' in Barbara Leah Harman and Susan Meyer eds., *The New Nineteenth Century: Feminist Readings of Underread Victorian Fiction* (New York and London: Garland Publishing, Inc.1996), pp. xi-xxv.

ii   For a further account of the Rebecca riots and the part the Dillwyn family played in defending the Pontardulais Turnpike gate, see Katie Gramich, 'Introduction', in Amy Dillwyn, *The Rebecca Rioter* (Dinas Powys: Honno, 2001), pp. xi-xiii.

iii   For more biographical information, see David Painting, *Amy Dillwyn* (Cardiff: University of Wales Press, 1987).

iv   See E.A.Dillwyn *A Comet's Tale* and *One June Night: A Sketch of An Unladylike Girl* (London: Tinsley's Magazine, Volume 32, January-June 1883). I am indebted to Kirsti Bohata for providing me with copies of these stories.

v   I am indebted to David Painting for generously allowing me to consult Amy Dillwyn's diaries and other documents at the University of Swansea Archives and most grateful for his constant efforts to answer my numerous questions. Many thanks also to Jane Aaron, as Honno Classics series editor, for her help in revising this introduction, to Mr and Mrs Richard Morris for sending me copies of photographs of Amy Dillwyn and the diary of her father L.L.Dillwyn, and to Moya Jones, of the University of Bordeaux, for speaking to me about Amy Dillwyn in the first place. Lastly, I must thank the National Library of Wales for allowing the republication of *A Burglary or 'Unconscious Influence'* from the copy they hold.

VOLUME I

Contents

CHAPTER I
Entomological

It is about half-past nine o'clock on a fine night early in September, and the darkness is illuminated outside the front door of Mr Rhys's house, Llwyn-yr-Allt, by the flashing lamps of a couple of carriages that are waiting to convey that gentleman and his guests to a ball at the neighbouring town of Cwm-Eithin.

'Do look at those two little lights glimmering in the plantation!' exclaimed Lady Elise Bolyn, as she issued from the house, cloaked and shawled, and was assisted by her host to enter one of the carriages. 'Whatever are they?'

'Oh, they're only Ralph and Imogen's dark lanterns,' returned Mr Rhys. 'My boy and girl have got a fit of rabid entomology on them, and persecute the poor moths and butterflies by night and day; and that's what takes them out now. They're a regular pair of wild Indians, I often think. Is there room for another in this carriage? No—not comfortably, I think. Ethel and I and Sir Charles Dover will follow in the next, then.'

So saying, he proceeded to offer his arm to his niece, the great heiress, Ethel Carton. The carriage doors were shut— the footmen jumped up beside the drivers, and away rolled the ball-goers to their entertainment, leaving Mr Rhys's son and daughter, aged respectively nearly eighteen and nearly seventeen, to pursue their occupation of encouraging dissipated habits amongst the moths of the neighbourhood by the process denominated 'sugaring'.

For this purpose, the entomologist sallies forth shortly before dusk, and establishes moth public-houses by smearing trunks of trees with an intoxicating and sticky compound of beer, rum, brown sugar, and treacle boiled together. When it gets dark he equips himself with a gauze net and a lantern, and visits these 'sugars,' where he probably finds some thirsty moths sucking in the liquor greedily, and a few more lying on the ground below in a state of thorough intoxication. To catch these is, of course, easy, for he has only to pop whichever of them he wants into a pillbox or bottle, with a drop of chloroform. But there are others whose capture will be less inglorious—moths that arrive at the delicious tap at the same moment as the collector, dart shyly off at the approach of his light, and need a quick hand and eye to follow their flight with the lantern, and dash the net over them before they are lost in the surrounding darkness. Whether Sir Wilfred Lawson[1] and his teetotallers would consider 'sugaring' as a strictly moral proceeding may perhaps be doubted, but Ralph and Imogen Rhys had no scruples on that score ; and on the night of the opening of this story they were enjoying themselves thoroughly amongst the 'sugars', whilst their rival moth-hunter, the nightjar, whirred sociably about close to them, and thought none the worse of a moth as a delicate morsel, when it was full of the heady, sweet liquor to be imbibed at these drinking-places.

The brother and sister had seen the carriages come to the door to convey the ball-goers to their destination, and had suspended their operations to watch the departure of the party. The bushes and grass were dripping from a heavy dew, and to defy the wet the entomologists were dressed in Welsh flannel, corduroys, thick boots, etc., which rough and carelessly put-on costumes were in strong contrast with the silks, laces, jewels, flowers, and altogether elaborate get-up of the gentlemen and ladies starting to the Cwm-Eithin ball. Well aware were the boy and girl of their own untidiness, and much inclined to glory in it, and to look down contemptuously upon a daintiness of attire which was associated in their minds with the restraints of high civilisation and the artificial life of society. Restraints of all kinds they detested, and were of opinion that the greatest happiness to be found upon earth consisted in being at liberty to run wild from morning to night. Both alike were disposed to be fiercely intolerant of fashion and conventionalities; but though this feeling was stronger and more active in Imogen than in Ralph on the whole, yet in her it was at times modified by a mingled sentiment of curiosity about and hankering after the mysterious epoch of her life which lay close before her, called 'coming out'.

The time when a young lady is first regularly brought into society is naturally an era of great importance to her ; and there is hardly any girl who does not speculate to some extent beforehand as to what she will find on the other side of the boundary, when she shall be emancipated from school-room thraldom, and enter the world inhabited by her elders. Of this world Imogen had, of course, already seen something. But as yet her insight into it had only been from, as it were, an outsider's point of view. When older girls, who had crossed the Rubicon, had admitted her into their company, she had suffered from a shy dread of being thought to wish to thrust herself out of her proper sphere, and had never been able wholly to divest herself of the feeling of being with them on sufferance only, and to some extent an intruder. But she knew she would regard the matter very differently when she should be 'come out,' and entitled to take her place amongst them by right. Her *mauvaise honte*[2] would vanish away of itself as soon as she should be conscious of being no longer a mere ignorant postulant, but a free member of her order, and equal to all others thereunto belonging.

In some ways, therefore, she certainly looked with satisfaction at the prospect of entering speedily into possession of the full privileges which were her birthright. But then again she would feel a vague fear lest at the same time she might find herself deprived of any part of that independence which seemed to have penetrated to the very core of her existence, to have become a necessary part of her, and to be almost dearer to her than anything else. She would declare that no chains would ever be to her taste, however richly ornamented and softly padded they might be, and that it was better to be free than to be broken into harness of any kind.

'Next time a ball's coming off, I suppose I shall be going, too,' she said, as she watched the starting of the carriages ; and then she gave a little sigh, and wondered what made her do so.

'Ah, and precious slow you'll find it, I expect,' returned Ralph. 'Just see if you don't get bored to death in no time amongst all the nobs, and then you'll be ready to give your eyes to be skylarking out here instead! Do just look at all those swell clothes being bundled into the trap! Do you think you'll like being got up within an inch of your life, like those poor coves are? Fancy seeing a great big moth that you didn't know fly past, and you not daring to stir after it for fear of rumpling your hair, or spoiling your shoes, or disarranging the creases of your dress, or some rot of that kind! Pah! I never did see anything so senseless as what women wear of evenings—gowns with nothing over their shoulders, so as to catch their deaths of cold, if possible.'

''Tisn't only at night people wear such silly, good-for-nothing clothes either,' replied his sister. 'They're every bit as foolish about their day things, and always *will* find some reason, that's no reason at all, why anything that's sensible and fit to keep out wet or stand a bramble shouldn't be worn; either it's not the fashion, or not becoming, or different from what other people wear, or something absurd of that kind that doesn't really matter one pin. There goes Ethel getting in now; I know her by the opera cloak. Did you see what splendid jewels she had on to-night? She's got such a lot, and all so handsome that she always cuts out everyone else in that line wherever she goes; I suppose she will to-night as usual.'

'And quite right that she should, too,' observed Ralph. 'What's the fun of being such an heiress as she is, and rolling in riches, if you don't show off your tin a bit sometimes? She isn't half a bad sort, Ethel isn't, and not more than four or five years older than me either. I declare, if she weren't my cousin, I shouldn't at all mind having a try for her myself by-and-by; but it don't do to marry one's first cousin unluckily, you see.'

'Not half a bad sort, indeed!' exclaimed Imogen indignantly, for she had been smitten with a romantic admiration for Ethel Carton, and resented Ralph's tone of cool patronage of her idol. 'Why, she's just the very nicest girl in the world, and you talk as if it would be condescension on your part to so much as look at her! I *do* think your impudence beats everything.'

Ralph chuckled. Knowing his sister's *penchant*, he had intended to excite her ire, and had succeeded.

'Thought I'd get a rise out of you there, Im,' he returned. 'Well, there go the carriages off at last. I wonder if the people in 'em are thinking of us at this moment, as we are of them?'

'The odds are they don't think about us at all,' answered Imogen. 'If they did, probably they'd think us "young barbarians all at play," in their benighted state of ignorance as to what constitutes true enjoyment. Hie! there goes a big moth!'

Dashing off after the insect at full speed she got another glimpse of it, made a swoop at it with the net, and at the same moment rolled over into a small open ditch that lay just beneath her feet. Her upset was scarcely to be wondered at, seeing that the whole plantation was a network of open ditches, which it was not always easy to avoid even in broad daylight. The sudden disappearance of the light she carried informed Ralph of what had happened to her.

'There you go, stupid!' shouted he, with a feeling of righteous indignation lest the fall should have caused the loss of the moth. 'I thought you knew your geography better than that by this time! Have you got him?'

'Not quite sure, but I *think* so,' she answered, struggling up out of the ditch. ''Twasn't forgetting my geography that upset me, for I remembered well enough the ditch was there; only I should inevitably have lost him if I'd shirked a cropper just then. Give us a light, now, and let's see if he's in; ha! yes—I spot him here in the tip of the net among some old thistle-heads.'

'What is he—new, or not?' asked Ralph anxiously.

'I *think* so, but can't quite make out,' she replied, after inspecting the capture carefully through the transparent gauze of which the net was formed. 'He's some kind of fine big *Noctua* at any rate, and we'll keep him.'

So saying, she proceeded to transfer the insect to a pill-box, with a small dose of chloroform.

'Mark!' shouted Ralph, leaping up into the air, and striking wildly with his net at a great *Geometer* flying swiftly past overhead. 'Bother! I've muffed him, and he looked rather a good one, too! He was making for the scabious-bed, I daresay—let's go there—we haven't been there at all to-night yet.'

This scabious-bed was a favourite haunt of moths. It was situated in a low-lying, swampy field, and near by bloomed wealth of thistles, honeysuckles, and other sweet-scented flowers beloved of moths, who flitted to and fro in numbers, and stayed their flight now here, now there, to buzz lovingly in the very heart of some plant, and sip its honey. But with the advent of Ralph and Imogen the blissful enjoyment of the insects was at an end. Shining lights betrayed their presence; nets snatched them up; they were held close to the lanterns and examined critically; some were set free again, and others kept, according to their respective rarity, and to how many of their kind had already been secured for the collection. The sport went on merrily, for the two young people deemed chasing rapid-winged moths by lantern-light amongst ditches, trees, bushes, and brambles a most exciting and fascinating occupation, and recked nothing of what bruises and scratches might ensue as they rushed hither and thither in the soft, odoriferous, delicious air of the summer night. Many moths have a way of flight that is peculiar to themselves, and easily to be recognised by the practised collector, who is thus saved from wasting time in pursuing the commonest ones. But the most experienced entomologist may be deceived at times; and even Ralph or Imogen were now and again led away into hunting a *Plusia Gamma*, or some equally common insect, which seemed to have suddenly assumed an entirely new kind of flight for the express purpose of annoying them. For how provoking it was when a brilliant catch had terminated an exciting chase, to find nothing in the net but some worthless moth ; and how unmercifully was the captor sure to be chaffed for having been thus taken in like a mere tyro[3]! At last the two hunters thought it time to give up sport for that night, and returned to the house dirty, wet, and a little bit tired, but thoroughly healthy and happy. There the contents of the numerous pill-boxes and bottles were emptied out, and the chloroform-stupefied insects were inspected. Those thought worth keeping were shut up again with an extra dose of the anaesthetic to put a painless end to their existence, and the others were turned out into the fresh air to recover themselves and fly away at their leisure.

'I wonder how they feel in the morning,' remarked Ralph, as he put a batch of those not wanted out of window; 'they must be uncommonly chippy[4] and headachy, I expect, and not in any great hurry to get up. By-the-bye, we've got to make an early start to-morrow morning, if we mean to have a go at those tench and eels at Gwern pond; it's quite a mile and a-half off, and we ought to be there at daybreak.'

'Ah! yes,' returned Imogen, yawning. 'We must mind not to oversleep ourselves; we ought to try and wake at about two or three o'clock, and whichever wakes first will have to call the other.'

'Well, then, we'd best be off to bed now, or there'll be precious little chance of either of us waking,' replied Ralph. 'I say, just think of those poor fellow-creatures of ours shut up in a stuffy, hot room at this moment, in nasty, uncomfortable, dry clothes, and having to 'do the civil' no end. Don't you pity them? *I* do.'

CHAPTER II
Intruders

Imogen woke early next morning with a vague consciousness that there was some special reason for arousing herself instead of settling off to sleep again, as she felt inclined to do. With a heroic effort she overcame the temptation to give way to sleepiness, and began trying to recollect what it was that had made her want to wake early. The projected fishing expedition soon came to her mind, and she remembered, too, that Ralph would have to be called. It was pitch dark, so she struck a match and looked at her watch. Only half-past one, and that was still too soon to be moving; so for another hour she allowed herself to sleep lightly and fitfully, occasionally waking up altogether and looking at the watch.

Even the most energetic of mortals cannot tear themselves from their couches while still sleepy, without a pang. But when half-past two had arrived, she hardened her heart, jumped out of bed rubbing her eyes vigorously, and emerged into the passage without troubling to carry a candle, as she knew every inch of the house too well to need one. Groping her way to Ralph's room, she went in and shook him till he was too thoroughly awake for there to be much danger of a relapse into slumber, and then returned to her own room to plunge into a big bath of cold water, and perform her toilette. This was quickly accomplished, and when she issued forth into the passage for the second time, she was attired in a strong serge dress and jacket, Welsh flannel petticoat turned up at the bottom with waterproof lining, thick greased boots that had never known blacking, and leglets, i.e., short leather gaiters reaching from the top of the boot to halfway up the leg. It was a costume that was, no doubt, more serviceable than elegant; but it was eminently workmanlike, and showed clearly that its wearer meant business in the matter of wet, mud, and briars.

The ball-goers had returned early from Cwm-Eithin, and were already in bed, so the house was perfectly still as she proceeded gently downstairs to join her brother, who had already got out the fishing rods and tackle, and was waiting for her.

'I say, Im,' whispered he, 'I'm frightfully hungry; ain't you?'

'Yes, pretty well,' she answered in the same tone. 'Let's go to the larder and see what's to be had there.'

To the larder, therefore, they went, and found disappointment in store for them. They had fully anticipated that the door would be locked and the key taken away, but had never doubted that they would be able to rout it out from wherever it might be hidden, as they had done on sundry occasions previously.

The cook, however, had been too many for them this time. She strongly objected to their surreptitious visits to the provisions, and had endeavoured to baffle them by concealing the larder key in all kinds of unlikely and out-of-the-way places. But as she found that they invariably unearthed it from the remotest hiding-places she could devise for it in the kitchen, she had at last determined to secure herself from future incursions by taking it to her own room with her. This was a measure which she only adopted unwillingly as a last resort, because, as no power on earth would ever have made her think she could sleep safely in any house unless her bedroom door were locked or bolted, it followed that when she kept the larder key in her own possession at night, she was obliged in the morning to leave her comfortable bed in order to hand it out to the kitchenmaid earlier than was at all agreeable to her. But even this hardship she would endure sooner than not preserve her larder inviolate.

'Wot bizness has they young limbs got to come a-helping of theirselves to things in my kitching in the middle of the night?' grumbled she to the butler. 'But I 'ont put up with it—that I 'ont! To 'ave a missis come in once a day at a reg'lar hour, as one can prepare and 'ave things straight for, is quite as much as *hany* cook's temper can be hexpected to stand—and more too, sometimes—and I'm blessed if I bears more hinkisitions than that into my privit haffairs. So there! '

The hungry intruders, however, had no suspicion of this malice on the cook's part, and began ransacking the kitchen in search of the precious key.

'Have you looked under the mat in the passage?' asked Ralph; 'it's put there sometimes.'

'Not there now though,' returned Imogen, lifting the mat and shaking it. 'Try if it's in the drawer of the pepper-grinder—I found it there once. Or perhaps it may be hanging under the round-towel in the scullery—or else stuck upon the ledge under the tap in the sink.'

But after these and various other possible hiding-places had been explored in vain, the invaders came to the unwelcome conclusion that some new and undiscoverable receptacle for the key had been hit upon. In foraging, however, they had come upon the relics of a peach tart that had been put into a cupboard and forgotten, and with this they managed to take the rough edge off their appetites.

As the last crumbs of the tart were being demolished, Imogen suddenly remembered that they had not provided bait for the fishing the evening before.

'Whatever shall we do about bait?' she exclaimed; 'we ought to have got it ready last night. There isn't half such a good place for getting it down at Gwern as there is here, but I'm afraid it's too dark yet to see to dig worms. Shall we wait a bit till it's lighter, before we start, and get the bait first?'

'Oh, bother! No; I vote we don't do that,' answered Ralph. 'I'm not going to be dawdling about doing nothing after I've had the grind of getting up, I can tell you! Tell you what! there's crams of worms in the stables' manure heap, and if we take our mothing lanterns there, I back it we'll be able to get as many as we want in no time.'

This seemed a good idea. The lanterns were fetched and lit, and then the brother and sister went into the smoking-room, which was on the ground floor, opened the window, and jumped over the sill and out into the fresh, sweet morning air.

Outside the window lurked a man to whom their exit at this unexpected hour caused considerable discomposure. When he heard them unbolting the fastenings inside he drew back hastily behind a projecting corner of the house and crouched down, making himself as small as possible, and wondering who they were and what could bring them there at so strange a time. What should he do if they chanced to turn their lanterns so that the light should reveal his presence? Should he try to account for being there? or should he take flight? or—the look on his face was not a pleasant one as he contemplated the third alternative that occurred to him, and felt for the butt of a revolver that was in his pocket.

His alarm was needless. The couple closed the window after them, and walked off happily towards the stables, talking and laughing as they went, and all unsuspicious of danger, though they passed so close to the man that he could have touched them by putting out his hand.

'A boy and girl, by Jove!' muttered he, staring into the darkness after them with the utmost astonishment; 'I can tell that by their voices, though I can't see them. What can they be up to? Their going out is a good job for me anyhow, for as they've left the window unfastened, I sha'n't need to use any tools to get in.'

Just then Imogen was laughing at some small joke, and as he listened to the joyous, innocent laughter, his face softened, and a half-wistful expression came into it. The sound still rang in his ears after she had gone out of hearing. There was something in her tone that affected him strangely, reminding him of the time when he, too, had been unstained by evil, and making him feel almost ashamed, in spite of himself, of the difference by which he was now removed poles apart from such as Imogen.

But he despised that feeling as mere sentimental weakness; and as soon as the coast was clear, he lost no time in lifting up the sash by which she and her brother had issued, climbing on to the sill, and so by stealth making an entrance into the house.

CHAPTER III
A Function at Cwm-Eithin

The day on which this story opens had been a glorious one for Cwm-Eithin, there having taken place a grand inauguration of something or other which was, for the time, regarded by the townspeople as of first-rate importance. It was indispensable to their well-being, would develop their trade, ensure their lasting prosperity, supply all future needs, put their town on a par with every metropolis in Europe, be a magnificent success, a beautiful object to behold; the only wonder was how the town had ever managed to get on at all without it. In a couple of years again it would probably be very differently considered, as by that time those who now upheld it would have got some fresh maggot into their heads, have tired of this present fancy, and become supremely indifferent to it, or perhaps have taken to grumble at it as a mistake, a failure, or an eyesore, which was far from impossible. But just now any suggestion of such a change of opinion would have been scouted as absurd. There was a regular epidemic of admiration for, and intense excitement about the all-important subject, an unlimited amount of fuss and expense was bestowed upon it, and the day of its inauguration was made the occasion of extraordinary demonstrations of rejoicing.

There was an imposing procession, a ceremony, military escorts, bands, a public luncheon, toasts, flags, bell-ringing, firing of guns, singing, illuminations, fireworks and enthusiasm. All classes with any claim to consideration, were represented at the function—lords, commons, clergy, soldiers, sailors, volunteers, dissenters, railway directors, friendly societies, and tradespeople. Immense efforts had been made to secure the presence of as many notables and school children as possible—the former to make speeches, be gazed at, and regaled upon salmon, chickens, pineapples, champagne, and similar delicacies ; and the latter to swell monster choruses in the open air, and enjoy the magnificent feast of one plum-bun apiece. Some magnates of very first-rate importance, indeed, had been induced to attend from a distance, and all local grandees were present as a matter of course. Wealth in every shape and form was conspicuous in all the best places, whilst poverty was graciously permitted to stand and stare wherever the police thought it would not be in the way of its betters; and might further look forward to the high privilege of sharing with them in bearing the burden of additional taxation, which would fall upon all ratepayers as a necessary consequence of the costly decorations and entertainments in which the town thought fit to indulge.

When the question of how much money should be spent upon the proceedings had been mooted, one or two individuals had been daring enough to wish to reduce the amount proposed, but had been promptly snubbed into silence. They had been told to remember the enormous advantages that were going to accrue to the town; they were reminded, too, that there would be large profits to be made out of an influx of visitors consuming quantities of meat, bread, wine, beer, poultry, milk, butter, etc., and were told that what with that, and the high prices at which seats in windows and gardens would be sure to let, whence views of the procession, ceremony, or fireworks could be had, the townspeople would be easily able to recoup themselves for the extra rates they might have to pay. In reply to this, it had been urged that such arguments were not exactly applicable to the case of anyone who did not sell provisions, or whose house happened to be situated in some out-of-the-way back street through which the procession would not pass, and whence no view of anything attractive was to be had. On this the objectors had been told severely that a selfish, mean, grudging spirit was most unbecoming to great occasions like the present one; that it would be ridiculous to allow the wishes of a whole community to be interfered with on account of a few petty interests; and that minor considerations must always give way to what was for the good of the majority. And as the final decision of the matter rested with municipal rulers and influential merchants, whose shops and residences lined the route of the procession, and who were sure of reaping an abundant harvest from visitors to the town, it need hardly be said that the open-handed way of looking at things prevailed, and that public money was lavished in the most liberal manner.

The day's festivities culminated in a ball, on an unusually large scale, given to the town and its distinguished visitors by the borough member, Sir Cadwallader Gough. It was given in the Town Hall, as being the only building big enough to accommodate the crowd of guests, who came in shoals—and their best clothes. Everyone was asked who had the slightest pretension to local standing—even though it might be no more than was afforded by the possession of a good-sized shop; and tradespeople and nobodies had the gratification of finding themselves, for once in their lives at least, fellow-guests with individuals of exalted rank. A ball to so large and mixed a collection of people naturally partook more of the nature of a state function than a dancing assembly. Everyone's chief object was to show themselves and their smart attire, to stare at everyone else, and to enjoy the supper, which was understood to be going to be 'very well done indeed,' and was consequently looked forward to as one of the most important features in the evening's proceedings.

Under these circumstances, terpsichorean twisting and twirling became quite a secondary consideration, and there was a far greater number of spectators than of dancers.

The company occupied itself chiefly in promenading solemnly round the hall, criticising one another's appearance, discussing the events of the day, and displaying their wit by ridiculing the speeches that had been made—taking due precautions, of course, to ascertain before doing so, that the speakers and their families were safely out of earshot.

Those who considered themselves as the *crème de la crème* of the ball found 'quizzing the vulgarians' a very amusing occupation. Anything in dress, style, or manner that was at all different from what they were accustomed to see, was unhesitatingly condemned as vulgar, absurd, and outlandish. Satirical remarks upon the lower orders were received as the height of wit. This was quickly perceived by that acute observer, Mr John Scriven, who had come with the Duke of Clanthistle's party, and thereupon he devoted himself for the rest of the evening to hunting out peculiarities that had, as yet, passed unnoticed, and pointing them out to the fashionables and aristocrats with whom he consorted, pluming[1] himself as greatly on being the first to draw attention to any oddity, as though he had achieved some clever and valuable discovery.

The objects quizzed, meanwhile, blissfully ignorant of the sport they were affording, gazed to their heart's content on the great people to whose company they had the felicity of being for once admitted on apparent terms of equality; and pointed out to one another any of the swells whom they knew by sight, with a proud consciousness of the extra importance which that knowledge conferred on them in the eyes of their own set. What dignity did it not give to be able to say, —'Oh! that young lady with the magnificent jewels is Miss Carton, the great heiress, whose jewellery is so celebrated, you know;' or else, 'the tall gentleman with a short chin and grey hair is the Marquis of Scilly,' etc.

Thus both upper and lower classes gave mutual satisfaction in one way or other, and proved the truth of Miss Burney's saying in *Cecilia*, that *'Pleasure given in society, like money lent in usury, returns with interest to those who dispense it.'*

And mixing freely amongst all in the throng, moving hither and thither with a smile and pleasant word for everyone, affable, genial, agreeable alike to high and low, were to be seen local M.P.s and their wives, and whoever had an eye to political interests, present or future, in that part of the world.

The much-expected supper took place as soon in the evening as could be managed, and proved sufficiently sumptuous fully to justify the anticipations that had been formed about it. It was a stately and ceremonious banquet to which the long string of guests were marshalled in due order of precedence, as though at a state dinner-party. As soon as it was over, aristocrats and democrats alike seemed to feel that there was no particular reason for staying any longer. Carriages rolled up to the doors and departed in rapid succession, and the great hall was speedily emptied.

And thus the Llwyn-yr-Allt party returned home much earlier than is usually the case from a country ball; and this was how it came about that the whole household was already in bed and asleep at between two and three o'clock in the morning, when Ralph and Imogen set off for Gwern pond, and the stranger entered the house by the window they had left unfastened.

CHAPTER IV
A Pig Hunt

Digging for worms by lantern light in the manure heap was a successful operation, and the tin box in which the bait was carried was soon full. Then the brother and sister extinguished their lanterns, deposited them beneath a bush, and set off for Gwern, which was the residence of an unmarried uncle and aunt of theirs, and where there was a pond well stocked with tench and eels. The roads were deserted at that early hour, and the only people they saw were some gipsies moving camp, who stared with surprise at meeting a young lady and gentleman striding along in the dim grey dawn, and carrying fishing rods and basket.

'Queer lot some of those gentry be!' said one gipsy, turning to look after them. 'What should make they, that might sleep in the night, be waking, and they that might ride, be tramping afoot?'

But the surprise which they excited was quite unsuspected by either Ralph or Imogen. They were merely doing the thing they liked; since it was pleasant to them, it seemed to them natural and reasonable for it to be the same to every one else; and it never entered their heads to suppose that their tastes were in any way peculiar as judged by those of the majority of the world.

On reaching the pond, the rods were at once taken out of their cases, and the reels and lines adjusted. Live bait was prohibited as cruel, so the worms were killed by sprinkling with salt before being stuck on to the hooks and flung into the water, and as soon as this was done, the two fishers settled themselves down at the edge of the pond, and fixed their attention on their respective floats.

How delightful is it to a sportsman to watch his float when there is a fish about the hook! First comes an unsteady quivering, just strong enough to send tiny ripples circling away from the cork. Is it an indication of a nibble, or is it merely caused by the wind? No; it is certainly a fish, for now one end makes a hasty curtsey into the water that can only have resulted from a tug at the end of the line. Then the float relapses into quietude and remains motionless for perhaps a minute or so. Why doesn't the stupid thing move again? Wouldn't it be well to pull up the line and see if the fish has sucked off the bait and gone away? for of course it is mere folly to go on fishing with a bare hook. Only then supposing the fish to be still there, a premature pulling-up might frighten him away altogether. Hurrah! he's still on, for there go a couple of unmistakable ripples shooting away from the float. What sort is he likely to be, and how big? Two or three very decided dips downwards come next, and then all of a sudden away rushes the cork at a tremendous rate, bobbing violently as it goes. This tells the fisher that the time has come to strike sharply, and he presently lands in triumph an eel, tench, or fish of some kind or other. But great as his satisfaction may then be, it is not quite equal to what he felt whilst looking at the antics of the float, and waiting for the right moment to strike.

In watching that bit of wood writing on the water what is going on below, there is a keen, subtle enjoyment of anticipation, which disappears as soon as the uncertainty is over, the fish in his power, and he knows all about it.

Ralph and Imogen had good sport at first, but by-and-by it appeared that the breakfast hour of the fishes was past, for neither tench nor eel gave a sign of further appetite, and matters threatened to become slow. The fishers, however, were not unprepared for this contingency, and had provided themselves with a book a-piece. The author whom they most affected was

Captain Mayne Reid[1], and they were soon perched upon some rails that bordered the pond, and deep in *The White Chief* and *The Scalp Hunters* respectively, only raising their eyes from the pages at intervals to make sure that the floats were still undisturbed.

At last Ralph put down his book, stretched himself, and remarked,—

'I don't fancy cold tart is very feeding; anyhow I know I feel just as peckish as if I hadn't had anything to eat all the morning. What if we make a raid on the garden? The fish don't seem like biting now, and the rods'll take care of themselves till we come back if we stick 'em into the ground.'

'All right,' replied his sister, jumping off her perch; ''tisn't six o'clock yet, so there'll be no one about. I wonder if we'd best get into the garden by the *japonica* over the wall, or shove back the rusty old lock of the further door with a nail as we did last week?'

'Oh, picking the lock will be safest, I think,' returned Ralph; 'if we were to slip in climbing the *japonica* and smash some of its precious old boughs, we should get into awful hot water. Come along; I'm just starved, and I know there's plenty of morella cherries left still.'

The lock of the kitchen-garden door was easily opened from the outside and shot back again from the inside, so that all might appear right on the arrival of the gardeners; and then the famishing couple hurried to the cherry-tree and fell upon the beautiful black berries, glistening temptingly in the early sunlight.

These proved eminently satisfactory, and it was not long before the well-covered tree was stripped of every cherry within reach, and the earth beneath strewn with an abundance of shining stones. Then a few supplementary peaches, nectarines, and greengages were disposed of; and as by this means the fishers felt their inward cravings somewhat appeased, they scaled the wall with the help of a pear-tree, dropped down on the other side, and began returning towards the pond.

'Ah!' said Ralph, with a sigh of satisfaction, 'no one knows what the flavour of morellas really is until he's been to the garden like this to breakfast on them—picking them straight off the tree.'

'I guess the gardeners'll be a little puzzled to account for their sudden diminution, though,' observed the girl; 'they'll think the birds were uncommonly hungry for fruit last night. I say, let's go and turn out the pigs and have a jolly good hunt, whilst there's no one about to see us.'

This seemed to Ralph a capital idea, and they at once turned their steps towards the pig-sty, which was at that time inhabited by two pigs, who had already given them several excellent runs on previous occasions, though unfortunately they could only enjoy this sport by stealth, as it was one of which they felt grave doubts whether the authorities would approve. A pig is a first-rate runner if not too fat, and these two had been effectually prevented from putting on a superfluity of flesh by the attentions paid them during the last few weeks by Ralph and Imogen. Not only were the animals kept thin by the actual exercise involved in being hunted, but there was also to be taken into account the anxiety of anticipating the chase beforehand and meditating upon it afterwards. For if you put yourself into the pigs' place you will see that the mental wear and tear, resulting from such harassing thoughts, would certainly be enough to interfere with the digestion of the most well-regulated pig that ever grunted, and hinder him from duly concentrating his energies on that faculty for getting fat, which distinguishes him from the rest of creation.

No sooner was the door of the sty opened than its inmates, recognising the voices of their persecutors and knowing what was in store, rushed out with many expostulating grunts and squeaks, charged at full speed down a hilly field, forced themselves through a wire fence at the lower end, and got in a small lawn beyond. Here there was a check in the pursuit, for as Imogen took a flying leap over the wires, she caught her foot in the top one and rolled over like a shot rabbit. Ralph stopped to laugh at her tumble, and this gave the pigs time to cross the lawn and a hedge on the other side, enter a little plantation, and ensconce themselves panting in some bushes. Consequently when the hunters went on again and jumped over the hedge, they could see nothing of their game, and were at fault.

'Where in the world can the brutes have got to?' exclaimed Ralph, after searching for a few minutes in vain. 'I'm positive they didn't go further than this plantation, for I've been keeping my eye on the other side whilst I ran, and should have seen if they'd gone on that way. What a cracking pace they went! They must be rather blown, I expect, wherever they are.'

'They've stowed themselves away pretty snugly, at all events,' said Imogen; 'we must beat the bushes regularly and see if that'll rout them out.'

Thump, thump, whack, whack, went the sticks upon every tree and thick place in the copse; but it was to no purpose. Piggies lay close, and their pursuers emerged from the plantation looking blankly at each other.

'Well, they're *bound* to be in here somewhere,' cried Imogen, 'for they certainly can't have vanished into thin air! But what's become of them, passes me to find out.'

'Let's try through again more carefully,' suggested Ralph. 'We only beat the tops of the bushes that time. Suppose we see what's to be done by poking our sticks right into every hole and corner.'

This mode of drawing the cover was successful. When the clump in which the pigs lay had merely been shaken and struck with a great deal of noise that did them no harm, they had been too cunning to move. But when a random thrust through the leaves prodded them sharply in the ribs, they thought it high time to make an effort to save that bacon which there seemed at present but a very remote chance of their ever becoming. Uttering vigorous and indignant protests, they quitted the plantation, again took to the open, and rushed helter-skelter up and down a field.

Next to this field lay a small flower-garden, enclosed by a trim, well-made hedge. Being very closely pressed, they presently charged the hedge wildly, broke a gap in it, careered over the flower-beds beyond, to the destruction of many a cherished geranium and other plant, forced a way out at the opposite side, and burst into the carriage drive leading to the house.

Here the fun came to a premature conclusion, for, as the hunters came dashing after them, they found themselves suddenly face to face with the bailiff on his way to the farm, who stood in amazement at the unexpected apparition.

Nothing was further from the wishes of Ralph and his sister than that their pig-hunting exploits should be discovered and reported to their uncle and aunt. For the first moment, therefore, they were considerably taken aback at thus meeting the bailiff with appearances so much against them, but promptly recovered their self-possession, and were quite equal to the emergency.

'Oh, good-morning, Jones,' said Ralph, with the utmost *aplomb*. 'You'd better see to getting those pigs back to their proper place. They were in the upper flower-garden just now, so we've been driving them out.'

Which statement, though strictly true, was not calculated to give the hearer an altogether accurate impression of what had been taking place.

'In th' upper flower-garden, sir!' repeated Jones, in extreme surprise. 'Why, how the dickens was they get there, I wonder? I'll take my oath as they was safe in the sty last thing last night, with the door fast upon 'em. And the fence round the garden is as sound as can be, without no gap in it not nowhere—at least there wasn't none yesterday, whatever!'

'Well, there's a pretty big one there now, at all events,' answered Ralph. 'However, as you've come, you can see the pigs out of mischief, and there's no need for us to trouble about them any longer.'

So saying he and his sister left the road and returned to the pond, congratulating themselves on the fortunate accident of the creatures having broken into the garden, and thus furnished them with an excellent and truthful excuse for the unlawful occupation at which they had been caught.

Jones meanwhile went on his way scratching his head, and not a little mystified. He was not really as confident as he pretended to be that the pig-sty door had been properly fastened overnight, for he had an uneasy consciousness of having neglected to go and see to it, as he ought to have done. Yet, even if their escape from the sty might possibly be explained in this way, he was still utterly at a loss to imagine what attraction they could have seen or smelt in a garden full of nothing but flowers to induce them to make a gap through a stiff fence in order to get into it. Past experience of pig nature gave him no clue to solving the problem. But some slight knowledge of former pranks played by Ralph and Imogen made him generally inclined to suspect that, if anything went wrong when they were in the neighbourhood, it was by no means unlikely for them to have had some hand in the mischief; and the poor man was beginning, too, to have a hazy kind of idea that, somehow or other, the Gwern pigs never *did* seem able to get fat in holiday time!

CHAPTER V
Imogen's Ideas

The interlude of fruit breakfast and pig-hunt, which had served to relieve the monotony of fishing, had taken some time; and on returning to the pond, it was found that Ralph's bait had been carried off without catching anything, and Imogen's hook had been swallowed by a fine eel, which had subsequently twisted itself into an almost inextricable knot with the line. Disentangling the creature was a difficult and slimy operation; but it was at last accomplished successfully, and then the two hooks were re-baited, and again cast into the water, while the fishers settled themselves comfortably on the rails as before.

Imogen's energetic nature was a somewhat curious compound of ardent love of running wild, with genuine desire to do right, and vague aspirations after something more elevated than the merely savage existence which she found so delightful. Some accidental circumstance now happened to set these aspirations stirring within her, and she felt a sudden longing to get her brother to sympathise with her. But it was by no means easy to her to express the inner self that she was conscious of and wanted to make him understand; for she was intensely shy of giving vent to any sentiment that sounded at all high-flown, and if ever she did want to utter anything noble, chivalrous, romantic, beautiful, or exalted, was apt to conceal it in slangy and common-place language. Many was the time that she had thus, when really in her best moods, laid herself open to the charge of vulgarity from those who could detect nothing of the beautiful thought that was underlying the coarse outer wrapping of speech that she had used. For it is not everyone whose perceptions are keen enough to discover a nugget of precious metal when it is enveloped in a coating of mud; and, therefore, people should beware lest they set up as diggers for gold, either physical or moral, without having the requisite qualities to fit them for that office.

'This sort of life's awfully jolly,' remarked Imogen, by way of leading up to what she wanted to say; 'but I suppose it wouldn't do to have it go on always.'

'I don't see why not,' replied Ralph, a little astonished at her remark. 'However, it can't—worse luck! for as soon as the holidays come to an end, I shall have to go on grinding at my work again. I haven't the gift you have of escaping lessons, and being let to be as lazy as you please. Let's see. How many governesses was it you managed to turn out of the house in the last six months before the article was finally discontinued as hopeless? Were there four or five that went in that time?'

'Oh! I'm positive there weren't more than four, at any rate,' she answered quickly; 'but you needn't say it was all my doing. Two of them gave notice of themselves, so their departure was no work of mine, you see.'

Ralph laughed.

'But if you made their lives so unbearable in one way or other that they positively declined to stay, that comes to much the same thing, doesn't it?' said he. 'There was old Mrs Brown, for instance. You couldn't suppose she would consent to stay at a place where her false brown front was occasionally found to have been dipped in the ink, and her rouge-pot had a trick of disappearing mysteriously, to say nothing of the strange frequency with which dust accumulated in the wards of her keys and choked them up.'

'Nasty, painted bewigged old thing!' returned Imogen. 'What did she go and get herself up like that for, I should like to know? Much good anyone would get from associating with such an old sham. I'm sure it was no loss when *she* took her departure.'

'Well, then, there was Mademoiselle Peyron,' continued Ralph ; 'she used rather to amuse me with her readiness to make eyes at any male creature whatever, and get up a flirtation with him. Why, she wasn't above keeping in her hand even on me when there was no one better to be had. *I* shouldn't have minded her in the house for a bit, but you were too much for her, as usual; and you know she vowed she wouldn't stay with a pupil who never walked with her, sat with her, except during lessons, or did anything whatever to amuse her. The situation was too *triste*[1] to be endured.'

'Mademoiselle Peyron, indeed!' cried Imogen, scornfully. 'It wasn't likely that I'd spend more time than I could help with a woman like her, who was more cut out for a ladies' maid than a governess. She hadn't an atom of pluck, was always collapsing and being *abîmée*[2] or *désolée*[3] about something or other, and could never talk of any subjects but making love and dresses. Such a pig as she was too! You wouldn't believe the state she'd let her things get into before she'd think it necessary to change them or have them washed. There wasn't any possible pleasure or profit either to be got out of *her* society.'

'Somehow or other that seemed to be the conclusion you arrived at in regard to all your governesses,' said Ralph, 'so at last papa had to give it up as a bad job, and determined not to inflict any more of them on you—or not to inflict you on any more of them would perhaps be the properest way of putting it. And the consequence is that now you can be just as idle as you please. You really have been uncommonly leery about shirking work, Im, and I only wish I could learn the dodge of it from you.' The charge of laziness was not very pleasant to the high-spirited, energetic girl, who felt that she did not really deserve it.

'I never tried to shirk work at all!' she exclaimed; 'it was quite accidental that the governesses didn't happen to stay— they were such a wretched lot that I'm sure *no one* could have got on with them. And it's not fair to call me idle when I'm doing just as much work by myself as ever I did in the schoolroom. I'm translating *Silvio Pellico*[4], and trying to learn Italian, because I want to read Dante, and I'm writing a résumé of *Menzel's Geschichte der Deutschen*[5], and doing lots of other things as well. So there! But to go back to what I was going to say when I started: it *is* awfully jolly, and no mistake, to live as we do now ; but yet, I can understand that it may be as well not to be able to keep on doing it always. You see mothing, and fishing, and larking, can't do any real good in the world—"it don't get no forrarder[6]" for them, as the farmer in *Punch* remarked, *à propos* of drinking claret. When one feels what a stunning lot of go there is in one, it seems as if there's bound to be something to sop it all in somewhere or other. And if every chap's got some sort of work cut out for him to do, I calculate we must have it too. I wonder what ours is?'

' *You* needn't bother your head about the matter though, at any rate,' answered Ralph, with an air of more superiority than his twelve months of seniority entitled him to assume, in her opinion. 'A man's got to do something, of course; so he goes into the army or navy, or some other profession. But a woman can't have any profession except to marry, and it's absurd of her to go taking up some particular line when she doesn't know what her husband'll be like, or what sort of position she'll have to fill. Didn't I see in some book the other day—*Felix Holt* I think it was—that *"a woman's lot is made for her by the love she accepts"*? That's about what *my* idea of the matter is.'

This was a sentiment to which Imogen objected strongly— as Ralph very well knew. The popular idea that it was the natural destiny of all women to get married if possible, seemed to her to be an insult to her sex, and she was always ready to oppose it fiercely whenever it was brought forward in her presence. To marry without being in love was a thing which, she felt vaguely convinced, must be wicked; and falling in love she regarded in the light of a piece of folly—a thing not exactly wrong, but a sort of contemptible weakness of which, she was convinced, she would herself never be guilty. Probably the Shaker colony described by Mr W. D. Howells[7] in *The Undiscovered Country*, would have corresponded pretty well to her ideal of the proper mutual relations between the male and female sex—a relationship to be characterised by absolute equality and independence.

'That's just so much stuff and nonsense,' she replied, positively. 'Lots of women never marry at all, and I've quite made up my mind that *I* won't, for one. I'm sure there's no one in the world that I should stand having to live with all my life long—unless,' she added, as a sudden thought struck her— 'unless it were you, Ralph, perhaps. You see I'm pretty well used to you by now, so perhaps I might not dislike keeping house for you by way of an occupation. What should you think of that plan? '

'What gracious condescension!' said her brother, laughing. 'I'm sure I feel immensely flattered, old lady. But then, what if I were to get a wife some fine day? It's a thing fellows have a trick of doing, you know; and whenever that happened, "I dinna ken how ye'd agree, lassie," as the gentleman in *Huntingtower*[8] observes, when there is a question of introducing a second wife into the house, where there's one established already.'

Imogen's proposal had been made in perfect seriousness and good faith, and she was a little bit nettled at Ralph's indifference to the distinction conferred upon him.

'Well—I'm sure *I* don't want it if *you* don't,' she replied, tossing her head. 'If I were to try, it would be just as likely as not that I should find you too great a plague to put up with after all—and I wouldn't be too positive about the wife either, if I were you! No one'll have you, perhaps. But this isn't the point I'm driving at. What I'm wondering is, what we've got to do with our lives to make 'em "something real, something earnest," as some fellow says—how we're to go ahead so as to be of real use in the world, and make some solid difference to it ?'

'Why not let things slide, and see what'll turn up?' returned Ralph. 'That's what I guess people in general and girls in particular had best do. Only I suppose that's not sensational enough to satisfy a soaring ambition like yours. I see clear enough that you're hankering to cut a tremendous dash, and become a public character, and get well talked about.'

'How provoking you are!' exclaimed Imogen; 'I don't want anything of the kind, and shouldn't care if no one were ever to hear a word about me. All I want is just what I say, to be of some real use in the world. It's my belief that every man-jack of us is meant to do that, and that the coves who don't, are failures.'

'Take my word for it you'll be a failure if you don't marry,' returned her brother sagely. 'However, if you really want me to suggest something marked and desperate for you to do, I'll endeavour to assist you. Let me see—what is there? What do you say to cooking? You'll be none the worse for that whoever you may chance to marry. Even if a man is too great a swell to require a wife who can cook his dinner for him herself, yet he'll probably approve of her having some practical knowledge of the art to bring to bear upon the cook.'

His sister had caught readily at the suggestion, and not attended to the last part of his speech.

'Cooking!' she repeated, thoughtfully. 'Yes—I'm not sure that's not a good idea. If some of the poor women about here knew a lot about it, I daresay that would help them to save money and make their homes very comfortable. I don't know any poor people, it's true; but still I might start a cookery class, and—'

'Oh, but that's not at all what I'm recommending,' interrupted Ralph, who enjoyed teasing her a bit at times; 'I said—learn yourself for the benefit of your future husband; I never said a word about classes for cottagers. Of course, though, a woman who could feed her husband upon *soufflés*, creams, *bouchées*[9], and all that sort of muck would be no end of a treasure for a farm labourer—we mustn't lose sight of that fact on any account!'

'Oh, Ralph, you see I'm not chaffing,' cried Imogen; 'please do talk seriously for once, like a good fellow. I do want—'

Here she hesitated. There was in her nature a frank, fearless, speak-truth-and-shame-the-devil sort of feeling which impelled her not to be ashamed of saying out the real thought that was in her, be it what it might; but this feeling was now held in check by her great aversion to say anything that could be regarded as fine or 'goody' in any way. After pausing for a moment, however, honesty carried the day, and she went on speaking— flushing and hurrying as though saying something very dreadful.

'You see I was confirmed this year, and somehow I don't think one can go on just the same after that as one did before; and I do want to keep straight, and be on the square, and do what's got to be done. I don't think so always, I know, but I do so sometimes. There's a couple of lines by a chap called Arnold, saying—

"*Tasks in hours of insight willed,*
May be through hours of gloom fulfilled."[10]

And I expect he's about right there. If one were to fix up what one's got to do some time when one's in a pretty tidy humour, I daresay one would find it easier to stick to the thing afterwards when one's in a bad humour, and not feeling good a bit. If one was to be always staring up at something miles overhead, I suppose almost any one might turn out tolerably creditable at last. I say—do you think you see what I mean, old boy?'

It had been a great effort to her to get over her shyness enough to say so much as this, and her voice shook a little with nervousness as she ended. There was, too, a wistful, half-pleading tone in it which told her eagerness to have in her occasional cravings after higher things the same companionship which she required in her lower amusements. As she worked herself up in this appeal for Ralph's sympathy, she fancied her need of it to be greater than it really was, and pictured to herself how nice it would be if he would agree with her, and how helpful too—for, of course, it would be ever so much easier to be good if some one else were trying to be good also! Whether or not he would take the same view of the matter as she did, she did not at all know; but, at all events, it was worth trying for, she thought.

Ralph was a good deal astonished, and a little bit aggrieved at this sudden fit of earnestness and moralising, and his response to her appeal was not very satisfactory or sympathetic. Although he was a year older, more sophisticated, and less enthusiastic than his sister, yet in his secret heart he by no means disputed the correctness of the sentiments she had uttered, and, indeed, rather approved of them than not. But then it did not at all follow that he should want to have them put into words, and, as it were, flung plump[11] at his head when he was not in the humour for that sort of thing. Consequently, at the present moment he felt a good deal inclined to give her a decided and sharp snubbing, just to teach her not to go blurting out moralisings at inappropriate and unexpected seasons in this sort of way. His conscience, however, did not allow him to go quite as far as that, so he contented himself by answering shortly,—'H'm—oh yes— I see!'

Having delivered himself to this effect, he proceeded to take up the fishing-rods, and examine the state of the bait, in order to introduce a diversion both into the current of her ideas, and also into the conversation. His plan succeeded. For a few minutes she felt a little quamp[12] and disappointed, and then that and all her other sober feelings were forgotten as she gave her mind to the consideration of whether it would be best to throw a line under the big ash, or beyond the blown-down oak; what could be the cause of her bait going so fast although the float never gave a single bob; by what route the otter had reached the pond last week; and other similarly weighty matters.

An eel or two was caught at intervals, but the sport was not as good as it had been at first. Before long the hoarse sound of a hooter at some distant works was heard.

'There goes the workmen's breakfast hooter,' said Imogen, 'and that means half-past eight. We may as well reel up, I should think, for by the time we've got home and tidied ourselves, I expect the swells will be beginning to come down after their ball, and there'll be a chance of getting breakfast. I'm powerfully hungry in spite of those snacks of cold tart and fruit—aren't you?'

'Just *ain't* I?' returned Ralph, with emphasis; 'and then I mean to spend the rest of the day trout-fishing on the Dŵrwen. I shall take a couple of biscuits for lunch, and get off as quick as I can after breakfast, for it's good three miles to the nearest point for striking the river. Will you be able to come too, or do you suppose you'll be wanted to 'do the civil' at home?'

'Of course I'll come, and bring the butterfly net too,' she replied promptly. 'Catch me losing a jolly day's outing to stay at home! Thank goodness I'm not old enough for papa to reckon on me for going pottering about after company yet, and he's got Aunt Sophia to attend to this lot for him. I shall hate when I come to have to do that sort of work, I know. There won't be much jam about being bound to spend the day dowagering in a carriage with fine ladies, talking pretty to visitors, picking one's way through the mud in one's best clothes because the guests must be taken for a gentle constitutional, or some other abomination of that kind, when all the time one's dying to be free and out of doors, and doing as one likes. Ugh!'

Ralph grunted sympathetically at this moving picture of horrors; and then they collected together and counted the fish they had caught. The eels had been killed at once and lay scattered here and there in the long grass with their throats cut, but the tench were to be kept alive, and had therefore been put into the covered fishing-basket and sunk into the water, with their prison made fast to the shore. The total catch was found to be fourteen tench and eleven eels.

'Not a bad morning's work, after all,' remarked Ralph complacently, as the fish were arranged carefully in the basket with an abundant supply of wet leaves and grass to keep them fresh. 'We'll take the tench straight to the garden and put 'em into the little tank so that we can fish 'em out with a net as they're wanted. And now for home and respectabilising ourselves.'

The basket of fish was no light weight, and they sometimes slung it between them and sometimes carried it by turns, as they stepped out briskly up the hilly road leading from Gwern to Llwyn-yr-Allt. When they reached the house they kept carefully out of sight, and sneaked in quietly by the back way, having a vague idea that they would be held guilty of some grievous breach of manners if 'company' were allowed to behold them in their present condition.

Their over-strained sense of the iniquity of being muddy and dishevelled was due to often-reiterated condemnations of that condition which had been dinned into their ears from earliest childhood by prim authorities, such as nurses and governesses, who regarded all untidiness as being alike reprehensible. Wherein, however, the aforesaid authorities were mistaken; since there are unquestionably two kinds of untidiness, which are distinctly different from one another; the one kind is slovenly and therefore legitimately blameable, being an untidiness that never was nor could be anything else; whereas the other is blameless, having made its original start in good order, and only become disarranged by subsequent honest wear and tear. And between these two there is obviously a marked difference which ought to be recognised in the language that is applied to them, especially in the case of children.

No such distinction, however, had ever been taught to Ralph and Imogen, and so they now fully believed themselves to be unpresentable in polite society till they should have removed as far as possible all traces of their occupations of the morning. Indeed, they were not altogether sure whether it was quite becoming on their parts not to feel ashamed of the rosy cheeks, robust and healthy looks, bright eyes, scratched hands and faces, and tremendous appetites, which were so many indelible symptoms of what they had been about, and must inevitably accompany them when they should enter the dining-room and join the visitors at breakfast.

But on this particular morning they might have spared themselves all anxiety about the matter. During their absence from the house an event had occurred so startling as fully to engross the attention of the whole household, and they might have presented themselves in any fashion they chose, without fear of having any peculiarities of their appearance noticed or commented on.

CHAPTER VI
An Heiress

Ethel Percival Carton, cousin to Imogen Rhys, heiress to very great wealth, and possessor of more splendid jewels than any other spinster in the kingdom, must have a chapter of introduction all to herself, since she is obviously a personage of too much consequence to be brought into a story in the casual sort of manner that does very well for girls with nothing worth mentioning a year.

The precise amount of her heiress-ship was not known definitely, but it was popularly estimated as being somewhere between eighty thousand and a hundred and twenty thousand a-year; for when people talk of sums of that magnitude they are apt to become vague, and to regard twenty thousand pounds, more or less, as the merest trifle. She was an only child, and had inherited from her parents, who were both dead, a very large fortune. And besides this she was the chosen inheritor of Mr Carton, her father's brother, who was a childless old widower of immense property, and with whom she lived at Carton House. A Mrs Grey, who was a poor relation of the family, also resided there, and officiated as her chaperon; but as Mrs Grey was a nonentity, and as Mr Carton hardly ever interfered with his niece, Ethel was virtually mistress of the place, and did pretty much what she liked with herself and every one and thing connected therewith.

The affairs of an heiress are of course far more worthy of attention than those of an ordinary young woman who has nothing to recommend her except her own merits, and therefore the world at large had always taken a lively interest in Ethel and whatever concerned her. Consequently she had from childhood been made much of, flattered, smiled upon, and deferred to on all sides, till she had come to regard her own importance as a sort of matter of course, and only what was strictly her due; though she might perhaps have been a little shaken in this opinion if it had ever occurred to her to notice and try to account for the striking contrast between the deference which was invariably paid to herself and the very inferior amount of consideration bestowed upon the majority of other girls of her own standing.

The continual homage that she had received all her life would have been enough to spoil many characters completely; but, fortunately, she was endowed with sufficient sterling good sense and simplicity to save her from being much the worse for such treatment. The fact was that she was not altogether a young lady of the everyday type. Neither she nor anyone else had yet discovered that fact, but there it was, all the same. An ordinary good-natured, pleasant, unaffected sensible girl, graceful and rather pretty, but with nothing very remarkable about her one way or other, was the verdict that would have probably been pronounced upon her had she had no special golden charms to recommend her. That was all true as far as it went; but, furthermore, she had a shrewdness of judgment, and sundry other latent talents and good qualities, for which no one gave her credit, because she was too indolent, and too entirely satisfied with her position, to take the trouble properly to develop them or make them apparent. On account of her costly setting, people would behave to her as though she were rare china, while all the time, in their secret hearts, they sneered at her as nothing but common ware; yet, could they have perceived all that was hidden within her, they would have been forced, greatly to their surprise, to acknowledge that she was in very truth the valuable porcelain which they affected to consider her to be.

The easily obvious good points which would have earned her the verdict just mentioned, would have sufficed to procure her an average share of social success, whatever her station in life might have been; but, nevertheless, if left to find her own level in society, not as the representative of great riches, but simply as Ethel Carton and nothing more, there would certainly have been a vast difference in the sort of reception that she would have met with, and the change would not have been a flattering one. Various charms and accomplishments of hers upon which she was now continually complimented in the most gratifying manner, would then have been passed over unnoticed; little jokes that now received the applause due to high-class witticisms, would then often not have been honoured with even a smile; the interest that was now taken in her likes and dislikes, and the eagerness shown to do her any service and to anticipate her wishes, would then have ceased; her goings and comings would no longer have attracted the same attention that they did at present, nor would her opinions about things have been considered equally important; it was possible that she might have had to undergo the mortification of being neglected, and even snubbed, by those who now appeared to be entirely devoted to her, and firmly convinced that it was out of the question for her ever to be in the wrong, or her company otherwise than in the highest degree acceptable. Some dim and hazy idea she had of the possibility of a state of affairs of this kind existing in regard to other people, but by no means realised how completely it was the case as regarded herself. Indeed, it was a matter into which she had no wish to examine too closely; for she did not see what gain it would be to her to have the unpleasant certainty that no one liked her for her own sake, when there was obviously no remedy for it; since it was impossible for her to alter her circumstances, and divest herself of her gilded setting, even if she should desire to do so,—which she certainly did not.

She was quite aware that constant intercourse with dependants, toadies[1], and people more or less servile, could not be exactly wholesome, and must necessarily prevent the mental atmosphere from being bracing and healthy. But she did not care to open her eyes too wide in order to try and discover reasons for thinking that all the people surrounding her were to be included in that category, and thought it better to acquiesce contentedly in the existing state of things, than to be ferretting and routing about merely on chance of finding out what would make her dissatisfied with it. This was not to be wondered at, for few people find it unpleasant to be paid court to; and if continual deference and artistic toadying fall to anyone's lot as naturally as the air that is breathed, it is too much to expect of human nature that the favoured individual should, of his or her own accord, turn away from these things or quarrel with them. Everyone would rather be welcomed than received with indifference, agreed with than contradicted, looked up to than despised, held in honour than slighted. And this is not only because of the actual gratification afforded by being thought well of, but also because of the great extent to which people's opinion about themselves is affected by that which they believe others to entertain about them.

If a man meets with black looks on all sides, he probably feels as if he had done something wrong, however innocent he may really be; whereas, when the world manifestly thinks him a fine fellow, he is almost sure to enjoy an exhilarating conviction that he is one, even though unconscious of any particular act of virtue to entitle him to that credit. The spectacles through which we regard ourselves are very apt to be of the same tint as those through which our companions regard us; and so the fact that other people seemed to think Ethel all she should be, was a great assistance to her having the same opinion about herself as a general rule. A very comfortable opinion it was, too, and one which produced a tranquil sensation of content, and an idea that things in their present condition were so eminently satisfactory, that it would be a pity to disturb them; and hence the good sense which she undoubtedly possessed did not make her at all object to spend her time chiefly in the company of persons who had more or less interested motives for being agreeable to her. Some of these were toadies of the common, vulgar type; whilst others were specimens of a higher and more refined class of the same article—people who, if accused of being so, would have rejected the imputation indignantly, and would certainly have scorned to occupy the position of paid companions, but who, nevertheless, were ready enough to do all that in them lay in order to become habitual hangers-on at any house where the loaves and fishes were to be found in abundance, and were not very nice[2] as to the means by which that end was to be attained.

Ethel's willingness to let these individuals associate with her, however, never seemed to lead to her being very intimate with them; and this imperviousness of hers was a source of great disappointment to some who had been encouraged by her accessibility to imagine that they would have no difficulty in attaining to the coveted post of toady-in-chief. For this important situation there had been various candidates of both sexes who had aspired to be either bosom-friend, husband, confidential adviser, or something of the same kind which might give the aspirant a permanent influence over her; but somehow she had eluded them all, and not one had managed to become attached to her in the desired capacity.

In her treatment of these people, she always displayed great skill and tact. When civilities were offered her, she received them placidly, profited by them as far as might be convenient, and never worried herself on the subject of what motives might have prompted them. If she found people agreeable, she was quite ready to enjoy their society for as long as she and they might be thrown together, and seemed to be thoroughly happy and contented with them; yet when circumstances happened to drift them away from her again, she made no effort whatever to prevent it, and those who had flattered themselves they were becoming necessary to her, would find suddenly that they had passed out of her life and left no more trace there than does an arrow on the air which it has cleft. She never committed herself to people, or behaved so that they could have just cause to complain of her as unkind or fickle whenever she might chance to drop them; nor was she ever known to snub any one harshly; but for all that she would not let herself be taken possession of. Invariably pleasant, amiable, and polite towards all who came in contact with her, she nevertheless carefully avoided giving anyone really good reason for supposing that he or she was indispensable to her; and she seemed to understand, as though by instinct, exactly how to behave so as to keep herself to herself when she chose, and gently to shake off whoever showed symptoms of too burr-like a character.

Her disposition was an indolent one; but she was charitable, good-hearted, and conscientious, and had a religious belief which was very genuine and firm, and a real support to her on critical occasions, though at other times it may perhaps have been somewhat sluggish. She had a high opinion of masterly inaction as being almost always the best policy to adopt; because, as she said, 'If things get into a mess, they generally seem to come right by-and-by, if they're let alone; and if they're not in a mess, why, of course, there's no reason for meddling with them at all.' And this doctrine was evidently eminently well adapted to gratify the natural inclination to laziness that was characteristic of her. Add to all this that her gracefulness, prettiness, and pleasantness had completely captivated Imogen, who had fallen in love with her as a girl in her teens sometimes does do with one a few years her senior, and then Miss Carton will have been described sufficiently for the requirements of this story, and in order to do justice to the position which she occupied in the world's estimation.

CHAPTER VII
A Burglary

On the night of the Cwm-Eithin ball, Ethel Carton the heiress, famous for her wealth and her jewellery, returned to Llwyn-yr-Allt with the rest of Mr Rhys's guests. Having been assisted to undress by her maid Green, she went tranquilly to bed, and was very soon fast asleep. But she was not destined to pass the night undisturbed. Her slumbers had lasted but a short time before some sound partially awoke her, and she wondered drowsily what it was. Any unwonted nocturnal sound has a tendency to suggest the idea of robbers to most people, even though it is not at all a necessary consequence for them to suppose that the particular noise which they hear at that moment is caused by a thief; and so there was nothing remarkable in her thoughts having turned vaguely, for an instant, in the direction of some one breaking into the house. But the idea merely glanced across her mind in the haziest way, and then altogether vanished.

Being of a placid disposition, and not given to nervousness, or a habit of fidgeting about imaginary dangers, she regarded burglaries as very remote possibilities. No doubt they occurred sometimes; but *she* had never been bothered with them, and did not see why she ever should expect to be. She remembered that before going to sleep, she had been conscious that somewhere within hearing there was an ill-fitting window which rattled in its frame, whenever the wind blew. Of course it must have been that that woke her, and she wasn't such a silly as to be alarmed at a common, every-day sound like the rattling of a window, which was a thing she had heard all her life long.

44

Besides, even if there were anything wrong, it was clearly not her affair, but her uncle's, since the house belonged to him and not to her. One couldn't be expected to wake oneself wide up, just to go listening to stupid noises, and worrying about visionary evils, in other people's houses. That was obviously the owner's business; and it was quite nuisance enough to feel bound to bother oneself in that way in one's own house, without wanting to go and do it in other places as well. And after such an unanswerable argument as that, it would be quite ridiculous for her to trouble herself any further about what sort of noise she might have been disturbed by.

A dreamy half-doubt did indeed cross her very sleepy mind as to whether this argument would appear quite equally satisfactory in a wide-awake condition; but the doubt departed as quickly as it came, and the reasoning seemed to her conclusive in her then drowsy state; so she turned comfortably on to her other side, and closed her eyes with a sweet consciousness of having thoroughly fulfilled her duty, and done all that any one could possibly expect of her.

She had not, however, had time to get quite sound asleep again, when something else aroused her. She fancied she heard footsteps come softly up to her door and stop there in the passage outside. This gave her a momentary feeling of surprise, as she knew that neither of the rooms near hers was occupied. But then she immediately jumped to the conclusion that one of the gentlemen must have been sitting up late to smoke, and had mistaken his way to bed. Yes, evidently that was it; for there was her door handle being turned, and a light shining into the room. How excessively stupid of whoever it might be.

'Who's there? Can't come in!' she called out.

'Oh, beg pardon—made mistake,' was muttered by a male voice in reply. Then the door, which sounded as if it must have been opened pretty wide, was shut gently, the light disappeared, and everything relapsed into silence.

'I wonder who it was?' thought she with as much wrathfulness as was compatible with her sleepiness. 'It really is too idiotic of people not to know the look of their own doors!'

And with that reflection she again snuggled down into the bedclothes, and composed herself to resume the slumbers that had been thus twice interrupted.

She was not long in dropping off into a doze; but was once more aroused, and this time by a sound of something rustling close at hand. Very soon she was broad awake, and frightened in good earnest. Round part of her bed a curtain was drawn, and on the other side of this appeared a glimmering light, which cast the shadow of some one moving stealthily across the room. In a moment or so the caster of the shadow came within range of her eyes, and she saw to her horror that it was a man whose face was covered by a black mask.

At this terrifying sight she felt an immediate and not unnatural inclination to scream, but controlled it with an effort, having presence of mind enough to perceive that the wisest thing she could do, would be to simulate sleep at all events till she should have time to think over the situation, and determine what else there was to be done. Keeping her eyes shut, therefore, and continuing the regular breathing proper to a sleeper, she hurriedly revolved in her mind all the courses of action that were open to her. Supposing she were to scream, what use would that be? Directly she did so, she would probably be silenced by violence; and even if she should resolve to take her chance of that, yet she felt sure her voice would not penetrate far enough through thick walls, and closed doors, to be of any avail in bringing assistance, for unluckily her room was some distance off from that of any of the other inmates of the house. There was a bell to have recourse to, of course; but as it was near the fireplace, and quite out of reach from the bed, she did not feel disposed to try and get at it to ring it; and so altogether she quickly came to the conclusion to abandon any idea of summoning help by making a noise.

The next thing to suggest itself was, whether flight was anyhow possible. Could she not manage to slip quietly out of bed, get safely as far as the door, rush into the passage, hold the door against the enemy from the outside, and shriek till she should succeed in attracting some one's attention? But then, as bad luck would have it, the execution of such a manoeuvre as this was rendered impossible by the situation of the bed, for it was a long way off from the door, and had one side jammed close up against the wall, whilst the other side faced right into the middle of the room. It was hopeless to think of leaving the bed without being seen immediately, and so that idea also had to be dismissed as impracticable.

The only other plan that presented itself to her was, that she should do nothing at all, but remain perfectly quiet, just as she was. It has already been mentioned that she upheld a policy of masterly inaction as usually the best to be pursued, and by staying quiet she would evidently be carrying out this cherished principle, and avoiding all risk of committing herself to anything decisive which she might, perhaps, afterwards have reason to repent of. Masterly inaction carried the day with her. What are principles worth if they do not assist one at critical moments? And how are they to have a chance of doing that, unless one sticks to them steadily? So the end of the pros and cons of various plans which had passed swiftly through her brain was, that she determined to lie still, and go on feigning sleep. The intruder might help himself to whatever he chose unmolested, and then the instant he was safe out of the room she would lock the door, and proceed to ring, scream, and arouse the household by every means of clamour in her power.

A few words will suffice to account for the burglar's presence there. Miss Carton's jewels were renowned, and there could be no doubt that any woman who owned such things would be sure to bring the most costly to display at an occasion like the Cwm-Eithin ball, when there would be so very favourable an opportunity to show them off to a large number of people, and eclipse a great many of her own sex—some of whom she might even hope to see turning green with envy at the sight. Her jewels, therefore, had attracted the burglar to the house where it was known that she was going to stay. It was a place of which he had some previous knowledge, and by means of a short and apparently careless conversation with one of the servants, he had discovered what bedroom she was to occupy. He had expected to have to break into the house, but the exit of Ralph and Imogen had saved him that trouble, as he had simply pushed up the window which they had left unfastened, and thus easily effected his entrance. Knowing his way about inside, he had had no difficulty in reaching Ethel's room; and the opening of the door, which she had attributed to a mistake on the part of one of the other visitors in the house, had been his doing. Having opened it wide enough to admit him, he had slipped in before closing it, and had at the same time hidden the light of the dark lantern that he carried. After that he kept perfectly still for a short time, until her regular breathing made him believe her to be fast asleep; and then he advanced cautiously towards the dressing-table in search of the booty which was the object that had brought him there.

Her quickly-formed resolution to pretend sleep made her continue the steady breathing of a sleeper unbroken, save for just one momentary check that occurred at the first discovery of his presence. Short as the interruption in the sound was, it had not escaped his quick ear, and he went softly up to the bedside, and turned the light full on her face to try and ascertain if she were really sleeping or not. She felt him close to her, felt him touch the bed, felt his breath upon her face, and could hardly retain her self control. It was well-nigh impossible to lie there, acting peaceful repose, and not having an idea of what he might be going to do. All kinds of horrible thoughts and fears rushed across her mind. Perhaps he was armed with a knife or pistol, and was about to take her life; perhaps each breath she drew might be her last.

How would death feel? Would it be very terrible? Would it be quickly over, or would each fraction of a second seem a long-drawn hour of agony? In that dreadful moment of suspense and feeling of utter helplessness her faith came to her assistance. Religion was a living factor in her life—a real belief, and not a mere empty form of words—and she now with a sort of desperate mental effort grasped and held fast the knowledge that God was with her always, that He loved her and was watching over her, and that she was as much under His care at one time as another—now in her solitude and danger, as when she was in apparent safety and surrounded by friends. The thought was comforting and restful, and it gave her will strength enough to conquer the almost ungovernable nervous eagerness of the body to take action of some kind or other.

Yet the longing she felt to look and see what might be impending was very nearly irresistible; and the difficulty of forcing her eyes to remain shut was increased by the flashing of the light close to them. She did all she could to keep her eyelids closed in a natural manner; but the rebellious muscles would twitch a little in spite of all her efforts to keep them still, and a tremor quivered over them for an instant, which did not pass unobserved by the robber, and which made him increasingly doubtful as to the genuineness of her slumber. He hesitated, and watched her attentively. Certainly she had every appearance of being sound asleep, and in that case there was no need for him to take measures to keep her quiet. He would much prefer not proceeding to extremities, if it could be helped, and desired nothing better than that she should sleep through the whole business. But, of course, his own safety must be his first consideration, cost what it might; and what if she were shamming after all?

After pausing for about a minute—which appeared to her at least an hour—he left the bedside as if satisfied, and went to the table. He appropriated her purse, which was lying there, and then began noiselessly opening the drawers to hunt for her jewel-case. To abstain from looking at him when his back was turned was too much to expect of human nature, so she ventured to open her eyes and watch his movements. This was exactly what he had calculated she would do, if not really asleep, and had accordingly set a trap for her, into which she now fell unsuspectingly. By skilfully tilting the looking-glass, he had so arranged it as to make it reflect the lantern-light straight into her face; and thus a glance into the mirror immediately showed him the gleam of her open eyes. He took no notice of this at first, but went on quietly ransacking the drawers till he had found what he wanted, and also a few valuable rings and other trinkets which had been left carelessly lying about. All these he pocketed, and then began to return to the bed; and it need hardly be said that her eyes were re-closed with the utmost promptitude directly he turned round in her direction. Her fond hope of having imposed upon him with her feigned slumber, however, was rudely dispelled by these words; and as she listened to them they conveyed to her mind a vague impression of some kind of incongruity, as if the speaker's voice was an assumed one, and as if the vulgarity of his accent and manner did not sit upon him quite naturally.

'Stop quiet and yer safe enough; but if yer speaks so much as vun single vord, I'll dash yer brains out vith this 'ere life-perserver! Oh, it ain't no use yer pertendin' to be asleep any longer; I knows better, for I seed yer in the glass ven yer wos a pryin' at me.'

Perceiving the uselessness of carrying on her attempt at deception, she opened her eyes and looked at him, with a decided feeling as to her tenure of life being unpleasantly frail. Her fright, however, did not prevent her from remembering the importance of making such observations as might enable her to give some description of him, and to recognise him hereafter, and she rapidly took in as much as she could of his appearance. The black mask which he wore kept any part of his face from being visible. In the left hand he held a lantern, and by its light she noticed something that might perhaps be an assistance to his identification, she thought. This was that one of the fingers was missing from the right hand. In this hand was grasped a short, wicked-looking bludgeon.

'A life-preserver, does he call it?' thought she, with a shudder; 'it looks a deal more like a life-destroyer, to my mind.'

'Now,' continued he, deliberately, and with the same manner as before, as to which she was quite puzzled to determine whether it were natural to him, or put on for the occasion, 'don't yer speak nor move, as yer valleys yer life, young ooman. I've a-got all as I wants, and I'm a-goin'; and no doubt as yer be thinkin' to wait till I've cut my stick and then raise the 'ouse upon me. Werry purty indeed—and don't yer wish as yer may get it? But I 'asn't no wish to 'arm yer, so before I goes, all I'll do is to make yer safe, so to say. Now don't forget wot I tell'd yer at fust, and keep quiet for yer life, 'cept jest to do as I tells yer.'

Depositing his lantern on a small table, he produced some cord from his pocket, and ordered her to put her hands out of bed. She dared not disobey, and with the middle part of the rope he tied them together securely; next he made one end of the rope fast to the foot and the other end to the head of the bed so as to prevent her moving away. Then he took one of her own pocket-handkerchiefs and tied it round her mouth, stuffing it in so that she was unable to call out, and could only breathe through her nose. When he had finished gagging and imprisoning her in this fashion he drew back a step and surveyed the performance critically.

'*Might* still wriggle yer 'ead down to yer 'ands and get loose that way, though I don't think as it's likely,' he observed. 'I'd best tie back the 'ead too, and then yer can't get free without 'elp—not unless yer be a meedyum, or one o' they Davingport[1] brothers as I've 'eerd tell on. Don't be afraid now, yer won't be strangled if yer keeps quiet.'

So saying he made a running noose in a piece of rope, passed it round her neck, and secured it behind her so that it would not hurt her as long as she lay still, but would choke her if she pulled at it. As soon as this was done he remarked facetiously that he should be sorry to disturb her any longer, and advised her to go to sleep again now; and then he departed with his spoils.

Her first thought was one of genuine and profound thankfulness at being still alive and unhurt after the peril to which she had been exposed; then as his parting words recurred to her they set her ideas off in a fresh direction.

'Advises me to go to sleep again, does he?' thought she indignantly. As if that could be possible when one's had such a thing as this to excite one, and when, too, one's fixed tight in one place by his nasty ropes! Oh dear! Don't I wish I were free, and could jump up this moment, and give the alarm, and have him caught and punished as he deserves, and made to give me back my things. It's quite horrid to lie here and do nothing to interfere with him, while he's going about as he pleases. I wonder if he's satisfied with what he's stolen already, or if he's doing any other mischief in the house? It's *too* provoking to lie here tied up by the head like a horse in the stables—can't I by any possibility manage to get free?'

A vague idea occurred to her that perhaps if she could anyhow bring her feet to bear upon one of the fastenings, that might help her to regain her liberty, and so she began to contort and writhe about her body in hopes of accomplishing this. But it was to no purpose. The thief had not bungled his job of making her safe; and after she had nearly throttled herself with the noose round her neck, she perceived that there was nothing for it but to wait till her maid Green should come in the morning to release her. How astonished Green would be! Her face of horror when she got to the bedside would be as good as a play. Green would have a bit of a triumph over her too, for before leaving home they had had a grand discussion as to what set of jewellery to bring for the ball, and she had finally brought her best diamonds and sapphires in spite of Green's advice, the latter having wanted her to wear another and less valuable set which, in her opinion, matched best with the ball-dress. Ethel now devoutly wished she had taken Green's advice, for the stolen set was a particular favourite of hers. Would she ever see it again she wondered?

Then her thoughts went off in another direction, as she remembered with no little amusement her drowsy conviction a short time ago that it could not possibly be her business to trouble herself about burglars when staying in another person's house. It really was a disgustingly lazy, selfish way of reasoning, which nobody ought to have accepted contentedly even in the very sleepiest condition. Well, she had been nicely paid out for it anyhow, and it was quite ludicrous to think how promptly retribution had overtaken her.

She was usually disposed to take a fair, and, for a woman, an impartial view of events; and as her habitual tranquillity and disinclination to fuss gradually resumed their sway and calmed down her first excitement, she began to think that the retribution part of the affair was rather a joke, even although it had resulted in her own discomfiture; and she could not resist a smile at the recollection of the selfish and absurd logic which had so completely satisfied her half-awake condition, and for which she now had to suffer.

Then she thought of nothing very particular for a few minutes, till it suddenly occurred to her that she was not quite sure but what she might be getting sleepy; but she was so thoroughly convinced of that being impossible that she dismissed the idea immediately; she was quite positive that she must inevitably lie awake till morning, and that her rest was hopelessly spoilt for that night.

Lying awake was dull, and she would pass the time by speculating about the burglar, and what likelihood there was of her knowing him if ever she should see him again. She did not at all want to lose her diamonds and sapphires, to say nothing of sundry other valuable articles which he had carried off, and she greatly hoped he would be caught. There had been something about him which was not altogether what she should have expected such a man to be like in one or two ways, and no doubt he had taken pains to disguise his real identity on purpose to avoid recognition. That would account for the sort of unnaturalness that had struck her in his voice, way of speaking, and pronunciation, and also for the indefinable impression of incongruity which he had given her, so that she could almost have fancied he was acting a part. Of course this was caused by the constraint he put upon himself in order to seem as different as possible from what he really was; and it would make it all the harder for her to know him again. She had often noticed how apt people were not to correspond to preconceived ideas about them, and she certainly thought that this man was a proof of the truth of that observation, for he hadn't been exactly an embodiment of her idea of a burglar.

She had always taken it for granted that such a person would be sure to have coarse, rough hands, harsh to the touch, and brown and dirty in appearance; whereas his had seemed to her to be smooth and fine-textured when they had rubbed against her face in gagging her, and she could have almost declared, too, that they were white, and looked like those of a gentleman.

Yet there was not anything very surprising in that either, when she came to think about it; for as anyone who was a thief would have especial need for suppleness in hands and fingers, he would be likely to keep them constantly oiled, greased, or something of that kind which would probably make them soft and white. Besides, she had been in a great deal too much of a fright to have noticed such things carefully, and could not really feel at all certain of anything connected with his hands except that there was a finger off the right one. Indeed, as far as touching her face went, she was by no means positive that he had done so at all, and that it might not have been only her own soft handkerchief that she had felt rubbing against her cheek. Since she was a handkerchief, then, she supposed she might as well—

Good gracious! Whatever could have made her fancy herself a handkerchief? Could she possibly have been going to sleep? She would be only too glad to do so, for she cordially detested lying in bed awake. But then, unluckily, sleep was impossible just now, she knew very well, and she was doomed to watch through the remainder of the night.

How uncomfortable it was to have one's mouth stuffed full of handkerchief like this! Still, matters might have been worse; for what if she had happened to have a cold in her head which would have stopped up her nostrils, so that she could not breathe through them? In that case she really could not imagine what would have become of her, with neither mouth nor nose able to act as air passages, she must certainly have smothered. He would have been obliged to take that into consideration, and leave her mouth open; only then she would have been able to scream and make a noise when he was gone. Altogether it was a very perplexing question to settle, and she could not think what he would have done.

Further than this, her reflections did not continue. Her repeatedly broken slumbers returned to her again, and she was conscious of nothing more till it was time to get up in the morning, and she woke to find Green standing beside the bed with a look of horrified amazement on her face, and a cup of tea in her hand.

CHAPTER VIII
An Aristocratic Toady

When Ethel had been invited by her uncle, Mr Rhys, to stay at Llwyn-yr-Allt for the Cwm-Eithin function and ball, she had asked if she might bring with her Lady Elise Bolyn, who was paying her a long visit, and whom she could not very well leave alone; and as the request had been assented to readily, Lady Elise, also, was amongst the number of Mr Rhys's guests.

She was the eldest daughter of the Earl of Bolyn, was a few years older than Ethel, and had no very great affection for her own home. Her father was of old family, and possessed a creditable stock of ancestors; but he was poor for a peer, and she greatly disliked the various petty economies that were practised in order to keep up the semblance of wealth considered necessary for the Earl of Bolyn. As, furthermore, she did not get on well with her mother, she took care to be at home as little as possible, and was always on the look-out to make friends with anyone who rejoiced in the possession of money and the comforts which it can procure, with whom to establish herself for good long visits.

In return for such hospitality, she was quite prepared to sink her own individuality, and would lay herself out to be agreeable to uncongenial natures amongst rich hosts with an amount of complaisance which would not have been displayed towards other people. Not that she allowed to herself that she was a mere toady, or put the motives for her actions before her own mind in a broad, coarse way that would have been derogatory to her self-respect. She was above being dependant, she thought, proudly; an earl's daughter, indeed! Was it likely that she should ever humiliate herself so greatly?

But for all this pride of aristocratic birth, she was certainly never guilty of the folly of quarrelling with her bread and butter in any way, and had a quite surprising natural aptitude for accommodating herself to the angles of anyone who had the power of giving her the enjoyments that she hankered after. To such a person as Lady Elise, therefore, Ethel was of course extremely attractive, and her ladyship felt ardently impelled to become the bosom friend of the heiress. For this purpose she had of late been taking much pains to ingratiate herself with Ethel, and appeared to some people who did not know Miss Carton well to be in a fair way to attain her object, seeing that she had been a good deal with Ethel in London during the last season, and when that was over, had been invited to stay at Carton House, without any limit for the visit being fixed, but with a sort of tacit understanding that she was to stay as long as she pleased. Thus, as has been already mentioned, it had come about that she had gone to Llwyn-yr-Allt in Ethel's train for the grand ball at Cwm-Eithin.

When her maid brought her the news of the burglary, she lost no time in leaving bed and attiring herself, in order to hurry off to the heiress's room, and condole with her. Here was an event which might, it seemed to her, prove an invaluable opportunity for advancing towards that close friendship which she was so anxious to see established between herself and Ethel. The nerves of the latter could not fail to be unstrung, and her whole system upset, by the shock of what had taken place. She would be sure to be in a state when a little petting, cherishing, mental propping-up, and sympathy would be particularly acceptable. It was quite likely that she would be inclined to hysterics, shrinking from general society, unfit to be worried about business, perhaps unable to leave her room.

How welcome at such a moment would be a faithful and zealous friend to soothe the agitated nerves, and to be a comforter, supporter, and medium of communication with the rough outer world! And how delighted would Lady Elise be to perform that part on the present occasion. She would devote herself heart and soul to her friend's interests, spare no pains for her service, save her from all necessity of coming in contact with other and less sympathetic individuals; be, in short, even as a sister unto her. And in regard to this last simile, it may be observed, that when it passed through Lady Elise's mind, it must have referred rather to the conventional ideal of that relationship than to any personal experience of her own, as to the feelings to which it gave rise. For though she had sisters, yet she had never shown any eagerness to fly to their assistance when they got the measles, or fell into any other kind of trouble, either mental or bodily; and had, to say the truth, always been much more ready on such occasions to consider her relations as nuisances, and to grumble at them, than to make the slightest effort to help them, or to put herself out of the way on their account.

Anticipating, then, that the burglary would have given her an unexpectedly good opening for making herself necessary to Ethel, Lady Elise hastened to Miss Carton's room, knocked at the door, and was told to come in.

'My *dearest* Ethel! What *is* this that I hear? Can it possibly be true? It seems quite *too* horrible? You poor, dear thing; how you must have suffered! Are you really still alive after it all?'

Such were Lady Elise's exclamations as she opened the door and entered the room, eager to render all the devoted attentions which she made sure her friend must be in urgent need of. But the sight that met her eyes when she was well into the room was not at all what she had been prepared for, and made her feel decidedly disappointed. Instead of being in a condition of hysterics and general collapse, Ethel seemed no more nervous and fluttered than if she had spent a night of unbroken repose. With Green's assistance she was calmly performing her toilette as usual, and gave no indication whatever of being likely to prefer shutting herself up with a sympathetic friend, to going downstairs to breakfast with the common herd.

'Well,' answered Ethel, smiling, 'of course I can't say what you may have heard, but, at all events, I'm altogether uninjured and alive. Though I've been robbed, yet the thief was a gentlemanly creature, who, notwithstanding his threats, used no brutal violence, and accomplished his purpose with as little barbarity as was possible. But if he spared *me*, he didn't do as much for my jewels. There's my favourite set of diamonds and sapphires gone, amongst others, and who knows if I shall ever get them back again. Isn't it heart-breaking?'

'Oh, it's awful! Quite too altogether awful!' cried Lady Elise. 'And I can't tell you how I pity you. That great stone in the centre of the pendant was simply the veriest love of a sapphire that I ever *did* set eyes on. But, *of course*, you'll have them back some day or other, you know; all the jewellers will know of their being stolen, and so the thief won't venture to take them for sale to anyone, and then, sooner or later, they are certain to be found in his possession, and brought back to you.'

'I only wish it may be so,' answered Ethel; 'but I don't feel very hopeful in the matter when I remember what stories have been told of the ease with which jewels can be taken out of their settings, and disposed of abroad, so that all trace of them is lost.'

'Ah, quite true!' returned Lady Elise. 'I'd forgotten all about the foreign jewellers; I haven't such a memory as you have. You really never do forget *anything*, I think! But I'm quite surprised to find you out of bed already, for I felt positive you wouldn't think of getting up just yet. You know, dearest, that after such a shock as this fearful robbery must have given you, a little extra care of yourself is *most* indispensable, for fear that else you may be the worse for it afterwards. *Surely* you aren't thinking of going downstairs as usual, now, immediately, are you? It would be *far* more prudent to have your breakfast quietly up here, and not expose yourself to the fatigue and worry of society till your poor nerves have had time to recover themselves a bit. I'm sure *no one* could wonder, or think it anything but the most natural thing in the world for you to do. And I shall be only *too* delighted to be of use to you in any way possible, so you needn't be bothered about business affairs, if only you'll accept my humble services, and let me see people for you and act on your behalf. It'll be no trouble, but a real *pleasure* to me to be able to help you at all.'

It had certainly never entered Ethel's head that there was a possibility of her being expected to remain secluded, and assume the part of an invalid, merely because her trinkets had been stolen, and her first impulse was to laugh at the notion, and declare that she had never felt better in her life. But when she found that Lady Elise seemed seriously to regard it as a matter of course that she should not be equal to mixing in society just yet, she was troubled by a momentary qualm of doubt and uneasiness. It was always her ambition to do whatever would be generally considered the right thing. Indeed, her anxiety on this point was carried to an extent which was quite remarkable in a person possessing as much originality and strength of character as she did. At the present moment, therefore, though she did not feel the very smallest inclination to stay upstairs, and was, on the contrary, stirred by a faint curiosity to witness the sensation created amongst people by her adventure; yet the idea that to eschew society for a while was, perhaps, in the eyes of the world, the correct course to be pursued by a lady who had been robbed, made her pause and hesitate before replying to Lady Elise.

A very few seconds of reflection sufficed to bring her natural good sense to the front, and show her the absurdity of affecting to be an invalid when she was really as well as possible. But she would on no account run any risk of being thought wanting in due decorum, so she was careful to give no sign of the surprise and inward amusement she had felt, as she answered with the utmost sedateness,—

'Thanks, very much indeed; but I think, on the whole, that I shall come down as usual. You see the man didn't do me any bodily damage; and besides, I slept very comfortably after he was gone. I didn't think that I should have, but I did after all. Furthermore, I'm uncommonly hungry this morning—though I don't suppose any of us have a right to any appetite, after the tremendous supper Sir Cadwallader gave us last night — and I never think breakfast's half nice when one has it in one's own room; do you?'

Evidently the burglary was not going to prove the splendid opportunity to Lady Elise which she had hoped. Her little castle in the air had crumbled away promptly, and it only remained for her to make the best she could out of the situation as it was,

'You don't mean to say you actually went to sleep again!' she exclaimed, with enthusiastic admiration. 'Why, you dear, brave creature, I can hardly believe it possible.'

'Yes, but I did though, really,' answered Ethel. 'You can ask Green if I wasn't fast asleep when she came to call me.'

'Oh, of course I believe it if you really say so, without wanting any further evidence than your word,' returned Lady Elise; 'but, upon my word, Ethel, your pluck is something *too* extraordinary, and your nerves must be simply of iron. I'm *convinced* that not one woman in a thousand, and very few men, would have been able to sleep the rest of the night after such a dreadful affair. And yet you did; and here you are this morning just as quiet and composed as if nothing out of the common had happened to you. You're perfectly *wonderful*; isn't she, Green?'

Green simpered and coloured at this appeal to her, and felt a little embarrassed. When amongst her equals she did not hesitate for a moment to express her opinion freely about Miss Carton, or any other individual who might chance to be mentioned. But to do so in the presence of her superiors was quite a different matter, and appeared to verge on a breach of etiquette. If, on the present occasion, she should assent to the proposition that her mistress was wonderful, she had doubts whether it would not imply a free-and-easy sort of criticism that was unbecoming to her station to indulge in, and might be considered as taking a liberty. Still, it would obviously never do to ignore an earl's daughter who had condescended to ask her opinion. So Green replied with a solemnity that was intended to show how far she was from treating the subject with any approach to undue levity,—

'I think so, my lady. And I only 'opes as Miss Carton mayn't come to feel it too, by-and-by, when, perhaps, there may come a rehaction.'

To find oneself considered heroic by other people is always gratifying; and from the glimmer of gentle complacency which passed over Ethel's face, a physiognomist would have rightly inferred that the tribute of admiration she was receiving was not unacceptable to her. But yet her satisfaction was a little spoilt by the fact that in some secret recess of her soul lurked a faint uncertainty as to whether, perhaps, the composure with which she was credited was not owing as much to her being of an easy-going, unemotional, and rather lymphatic temperament, as to her having any heroic pluck or power of self-control. It might be so or not. She really did not know; and determined that some day, when she had leisure, she would set to work to think the subject out carefully, and find out the truth about it.

This was an excellent resolution; only, unluckily, it eventually never came to anything; for the very good reason that directly after being made it went completely out of her head, and never returned there afterwards. None the less, however, at the time of making it she had been quite in earnest about meaning to put it in execution, for she always wished honestly to know the real truth about herself and her qualities as far as might be possible to do so. Any self-deception of which she was guilty was really not her own fault so much as that of the *entourage* and position, which seemed, as it were, to thrust it upon her in spite of herself. Considering how habituated she was to be treated as though she were of different clay to average mortals, it was hardly strange that she should be gradually learning to consider it an indisputable fact; and it certainly spoke well for her character that she should still be capable of entertaining any doubts on the subject.

On the present occasion there were so many important things to occupy her attention, that it was not surprising for her speedily to have forgotten the self-examination which she had determined upon. Every detail of the robbery had to be related; the jewels, and the robber had to be described as accurately as possible, and all particulars had to be gone into over and over again, for the benefit of people who, either as a matter of business, or else from mere idle curiosity, wanted to know exactly all that had happened. Indeed, she got very tired of repeating the same thing so often before she had done with it; but yet found some amount of compensation for the annoyance in the novelty of the sensation which she was creating. It was so absolutely different from anything she had ever done before. There was, of course, nothing new to her in attracting attention, and feeling herself to be a central figure in whatever society she might be; but on no previous occasion had she been able to feel that she had such a really fair claim to the position as now.

To begin with, she had been robbed of many thousand pounds' worth of jewellery, which was a sufficiently uncommon occurrence to be in itself almost a distinction. Furthermore, she had, for the first time in her life, taken part in a genuine, sensational adventure. And as she looked back on the events of the night, she could reflect with satisfaction that her fright had not been immoderate, and that even though she might not have so acted as to deserve all the extraordinary amount of glory that Lady Elise and others sought to attribute to her, yet at all events she had got through her adventure without disgracing herself in any way, or giving way to unreasonable terror.

CHAPTER IX
Imogen Hears of It

The burglar had departed with Ethel's jewels without committing further depredations, and as his entrance and exit were made through the window that Ralph and Imogen had left open, no trace of his presence was to be found anywhere in the house, except in Miss Carton's bedroom. Consequently no one knew or suspected anything of what had occurred, until such time as Green went to pay her usual morning visit to her mistress, and found her gagged and bound as has been told.

The moment Ethel was released, she despatched Green to Mr Rhys, and as soon as he heard of the burglary, he sent off a messenger post haste to communicate with the Cwm-Eithin police. But by that time several hours had already elapsed since the thief's departure, and as the town was some miles off, there was a yet further loss of time before any pursuit was commenced. All this delay gave him a good start, and his chances of escape were increased by the fact that the local constables were not remarkable for detective talent, promptitude of action, or fertility of imagination. It was in his favour, too, that the best description Ethel could give of him was but a vague one; for the loss of one finger from the right hand was not much to go by, and yet that was the only really definite mark of identification that she could furnish.

Meanwhile, by means of valets and ladies'-maids, the news had quickly spread through the whole household, and of course created universal excitement.

When Imogen and Ralph returned from Gwern pond, they sneaked in and upstairs to their own rooms by the back way without meeting any one; and as soon as the girl was in her room, she rang the bell for her maid Millet, to assist in that 'respectabilising' process which had to be gone through before descending to the dining-room for breakfast. On occasions of this kind, it was Millet's wont to put on a highly aggrieved air at beholding the torn and sodden condition of the petticoats, stockings, boots, and other garments whereof she was the appointed guardian. But on this particular morning she quite forgot to give her customary signs of disapproval, and was in an irrepressible state of fluster and excitement which was plainly visible to her mistress when she answered the bell. Millet was an individual of whom Ralph had once remarked with much truth that she 'regularly wallowed in rapture whenever she could be the first to tell a bit of news;' and the more sensational it was, the more she enjoyed relating it. Now that the intelligence of the burglary had been diffused so widely through one establishment, it was an unhoped-for piece of luck to meet with someone who was still ignorant of it, and a sort of spasm of joy thrilled through her, when in answer to her remark,—

'I s'pose hin corse, miss, as you've 'eard what 'ave 'appened?'

Imogen made answer,—

'What has happened? I've not heard of anything particular, or likely to put you into such a state of commotion as you seem to be in.'

'There 'ave been a burglairy, miss,' replied Millet; and as she spoke her face and manner expressed alternately the intense relish which she experienced in telling such a startling piece of news, and the grave horror which she thought would be the fitting frame of mind in which to approach the subject of so heinous a crime. 'Oh, it's reely quite shocking to think of! And you not to 'ave 'eard of it yet—just look at that now! Which it was the very remark as I passed to Mrs Lamb when she come to my hapartment for to talk it hover with me.' " 'As my young lady gone to pore Miss Carting, says I?"—those was my own words to 'er. But Mrs Lamb, she's one of them that'll halways try and snap one hup has hif one 'ad said something foolish, so she said, says she, as short has you please,—"Ow should she 'ave gone there, or 'eard hanything hat all hof the matter, and she hout of the 'ouse hall the time, and not come back to this blessid minnit?" But no matter for 'er a snapping of me hup like that—I mortified 'er hafterwards, I did — I mortified 'er hat the breakfast-table.'

'Well, never mind about all that,' said Imogen impatiently, cutting short the account of how Mrs Lamb had been mortified that seemed impending. 'What about the burglary? and what about Miss Carton?'

'Yes, that's jest what I am telling you hof, miss, as fast as I can hutter the words,' replied Millet, without the faintest consciousness of having been in any way led aside from her original theme. 'Hit's quite dreadful as such people can be in the world, I do declare. To think as this 'ouse 'ave been broke hinto, and Miss Carting's room hentered, and hall 'er lovely jools took, and she seen the man 'er hown self, and 'e tied 'er 'ands and feet together, pore thing! and put an 'anker-chief in 'er mouth, and fastened 'er down in bed so as she shouldn't move nor hutter a sound while 'e got clear hoff! And there she was this morning fast hasleep, if you can believe it, miss, when Miss Green took 'er in 'er cup of tea. Least-ways, so Miss Green says. But Sir Charles's gentleman says as 'e reely *can't* believe that— and hindeed it seems so haltogether himpossible that I can't 'elp 'aving some doubts myself as to the haccuracy of the statement.'

'Was Miss Carton hurt in any way?' asked Imogen quickly, with a rush of colour to her face that showed her anxiety lest any harm should have been done to her cousin.

'Oh no,' replied Millet; 'she's totally huninjured, Miss Green says — not a scratch, nor a bruise, nor nothing.'

This assurance relieved Imogen's mind, and she proceeded without further remark to change her clothes and get ready for breakfast. An elaborate toilette was a thing which she looked down upon as frivolous and ridiculous, for she had not yet attained to that love of dress which most women have from their earliest childhood. Consequently the style of dressing which she preferred was more rapid than elegant; and when left to her own devices in the matter, she was apt to appear with her hair parted all awry, the edge of her petticoat protruding below her gown, the front and side of her skirt twisted so that each had usurped the place of the other, and a general look of having had her clothes 'put on with a pitchfork,' as Millet expressed it.

Of course when the maid was with her, that official never allowed such untidiness; but as the extra time that was taken up by her carefulness was always a sore trial to Imogen, whilst, on the other hand, the young lady's want of vanity, and indifference to her personal appearance, were a continual source of grievance to Millet, therefore it naturally resulted that the periods devoted to dressing were generally rather purgatorial times to both mistress and maid.

'It's my belief,' Millet would declare to a sympathising audience of other maids, 'that I might send Miss Himojin down with 'er glove on top of 'er 'ed, and she wouldn't know it! No; nor yet hif 'er gown was made wrong side up, and put on wrong side in front! She don't know a bit what clothes she 'ave, and don't never think as a thing's wore out so long as it'll 'old together some'ow or hany'ow. I never see the like of 'er in hall my born days before. She'll take and read hall the time I'm dressing 'er 'air, and never give so much has one single look in the glass to see what I'm doing hof. She's a good young lady enough in many ways, and I will say for 'er as she hisn't that mean, and nasty tempered, and spying as many is. But still, to a maid as takes a proper pride in 'er purfession, it's 'art breaking to serve a lady like that as 'asn't a scrap of hinterest in 'ow she looks. When I see 'er sometimes hafter she've been dressing hof 'erself, I feel that hashamed hof 'er that reely it's as much as I can do to bring myself to hac-knowledge 'er as belonging to me hat hall!'

On this particular morning, Imogen found it even harder than usual to remain tranquil during the time required by Millet to perform her office; for the girl was longing to rush off to see if she could do anything for Ethel, and to satisfy herself personally as to her cousin's safety. It had been her first impulse to do this directly she had been told of what had happened; but she had been restrained by the fear of not perhaps being wanted just then, and of appearing to be over-fussy; for the sort of adoration which she had lately begun to feel for Miss Carton was mingled with a considerable amount of awe.

Imogen, on the verge of the line dividing her present from her future condition, when she should be 'come out,' had, as it were, looked across the boundary to reconnoitre the inhabitants of that other sphere which she was shortly to enter, and which was so different from the careless, unconventional, running-wild state of existence she had hitherto known. Upon the male denizens of the new country she had bestowed no attention, feeling perfectly certain that she should never care to marry, and being absolutely devoid of that inclination for flirtation which nature commonly implants in a woman's breast. But it had been different in regard to those of her own sex; these had seemed more interesting to her, and now and then, as occasion offered, she had observed them with a closeness that was quite unsuspected by the objects of her study. The result of her observations had been unsatisfactory, and she was disgusted with what she believed to be the characteristics of the whole body of those who were to be her future female companions.

Petty vanities, silly little airs and graces, recognised conventional insincerities, and other similar small matters were things of which she was intolerant with the intense intolerance of a child; and as she had frequently detected these failings amongst 'come out' young ladies, she had come to the hasty conclusion that they were all alike, that they were but a poor and despicable set of creatures, and that the more essentially feminine they were, so much the more thoroughly contemptible were they likely to be.

Proof of the over-hastiness of this conclusion, however, was not long in coming to her, for she suddenly began to discover that one of the despised class had a strange fascination for her, and it was soon evident that one who was pretty, graceful, and feminine, had nevertheless been able, without effort on her own part to quicken into life the capacity for romantic attachment which exists somewhere or other in the composition of most people, but which in Imogen had till now lain dormant. The person who had unconsciously performed this feat was Ethel. Her money had had nothing to do with it, for Imogen was as yet too innocent of worldly-mindedness to be in any degree mercenary; it was something in Ethel's own self that had captivated her, and begun to evoke in her breast a feeling that she had not before experienced.

Any kind of devoted friendship or attachment that could possibly be called sentimental, had hitherto been made fun of mercilessly by Imogen because it had seemed to her unreal. She had never had such a feeling herself, and did not, therefore, believe that other people had it either. But now she began to look at the matter differently, as personal experience taught her the necessity of admitting sentiment to be a real component part of human nature. She looked up to Ethel enthusiastically, as a being for her to worship from a position of wide inferiority without any expectation of reciprocal affection. For Ethel to care about her and be friendly with her in a cousinly fashion was, of course, no more than the natural result of their relationship to one another; but Imogen would have deemed it the height of presumption for her to think it likely that she could call forth any warmer feeling than that from one so far above her as Ethel. To belong to the same family as Miss Carton was to Imogen a source of happiness, because she was thereby enabled naturally to be on a more intimate footing with her idol than if they had been unconnected by any tie of blood. But this pleasant sense of cousinly familiarity was not strong enough to overcome the shyness which, on the present occasion, withheld her from hurrying off to Ethel the instant that she heard of the burglary, as she would have dearly liked to do.

Imogen reflected that every one else would be likely to do that, and to go clamouring for an account of what had happened, and making a tremendous fuss and bother. She herself had always had a horror of making a fuss about things, or indulging in special demonstrations of excitement; and this tendency to undemonstrativeness had been encouraged by noticing the habitual placidity of Ethel's demeanour, which she had attributed to Ethel's being of the same mind as herself in the matter. It would never do, she thought, for her to be as ridiculously fussy as the majority of man and woman kind, and to cause herself to be ranked amongst them as such in Ethel's mind.

So she controlled her impatience, and would not allow herself to stir in the direction of the person whom she was longing to see, until Millet's ministrations were at an end, and she was fully attired in her best clothes in honour of the company staying in the house.

Then she set off towards her cousin's room; but paused after a few steps, debating in her own mind whether it might not be even better to wait till she should meet Ethel downstairs in the ordinary course of events, rather than to pay an unwonted bedroom visit which might, perhaps, be thought to betoken an undue disposition to fussiness, and so lower her in the esteem of the individual whose good opinion she most desired to win. She was standing in the passage, considering this important question, when the matter was settled for her by the appearance of Ethel and Lady Elise on their way down to breakfast.

'Good morning,' said Imogen, brusquely, and manifesting not the least symptom of being in any particular manner interested or excited. 'So there you are, Ethel! Is it true you've been burgled?'

'Yes, indeed, alas!' returned Ethel, with a look of comically exaggerated woe. 'A whole lot of my treasures have been carried off, and amongst them one of my favourite and most valuable sets.'

'What a horrid bore for you,' replied Imogen, laughing at the deplorable face Ethel had assumed. 'However, you look all serene after it, so I conclude you didn't get any way damaged, did you?'

'Oh no, not a bit,' responded the heiress; 'you shall hear all about it by-and-by; only I want my breakfast before I do much talking, for the robbery, or the ball, or something or other, has given me a sharp appetite this morning.'

'Come along then—I've ditto,' answered Imogen. 'Grub's bound to be in by now, for the bell went some time ago.'

And with these words she and the other two ladies descended to the dining-room, each one of them presenting an aspect of being unemotional that was peculiar to herself, and different to that of her companions. Imogen was so in appearance only; Lady Elise, on the contrary, was inwardly indifferent though she thought fit to make a great show of excitement in order to be credited with the sympathetic interest of devoted friendship; and Ethel was calm and unmoved both inwardly and outwardly, because it was her nature to be so.

CHAPTER X
An Inspection of Fingers

Amongst the visitors staying at Llwyn-yr-Allt was a barrister, named Trevor Owen, who, like Lady Elise Bolyn, thought the burglary might possibly prove a very opportune misfortune, and hoped to reap some profit to himself from it. His father was a peer more blessed with children than with materials to support them; and Trevor, being a younger son with his own living to gain, had adopted the law as his profession. Briefs, however, are apt not to rain very plentifully upon a man who has no family connection amongst attorneys, and whose brains and general capacities are in no wise above those of any other average specimen of humanity; and Trevor soon arrived at the conclusion that the simplest and most expeditious means of providing for himself would be to marry a rich wife.

Could he have chosen his parentage, he would unquestionably have preferred to be the son of a rich commoner who could give him an ample portion, rather than that of a poor viscount from whom he derived little except a handle to his name. But as this misfortune of his birth was evidently irremediable, he did not waste time in fruitless lamentations over it, and set himself wisely to make the best of such advantages as had been afforded him. Though the honourable prefix which was his birthright would certainly not of itself suffice for food and clothing, yet still, by skilful management, he thought it might be made to conduce to the attainment of those necessaries. It was inferior to money, no doubt; but yet it could justly be considered as an article of marketable value, since it conferred upon its owner a precedence and position which many women find irresistibly attractive, and which might greatly assist him in the wooing of such a helpmate as he desired. In other respects, also, he had qualifications to make him agreeable in the eyes of society in general, and women in particular. He was an excellent dancer, and, being only twenty-eight years of age, was not yet too old for a keen enjoyment of that amusement—and a good partner is always an acceptable individual. Besides this, he invariably had plenty to say for himself, dressed well, was tall, and by no means ugly, even though not to be called positively handsome.

The chief drawback to his personal appearance was a peculiar air which he always had of wanting to know more of everything than other people did. This air is generally inseparable from the wearing of eye-glasses, and renders their indiscriminate use undesirable—since even the least curious of mortals with an eye-glass stuck in his or her eye must infallibly look as though anxious for an undue share of information about things. But though Trevor Owen wore no glass, none the less had he the inquisitive look which that appendage conveys; and no one who had once seen him could doubt his being a bit of a Paul Pry[1]. There was really nothing that he did not want to know; and when he had ferreted out all he could about anything, he seemed always to be troubled by a conviction that the most valuable and interesting part of the information still remained untold. He took good care, however, that his curiosity should never stand in his light, or give offence to those by whose displeasure he could be injured; and altogether he seemed as likely to be a successful suitor for a woman's hand as the majority of men going about the world in search of wives.

Such an heiress as Ethel was, of course, a most interesting individual in his eyes; but though he knew her by report well enough, he had never had a chance of becoming acquainted with her until the time of his present visit to Llwyn-yr-Allt, when he was greatly rejoiced to find that she also was amongst Mr Rhys's guests.

Determined to make the most of the opportunity, Trevor, ever since his arrival, had been doing everything he could think of that seemed likely to produce a favourable impression of him on the young lady's mind; and the moment he heard of the burglary, he began to reflect on how to turn it to good account.

In the first place he sniffed a brief. If he could contrive to display advantageously what legal knowledge he possessed, and give her a good opinion of his ability, zeal, and sagacity, there would be a reasonable chance of her instructing her solicitors to employ him for the prosecution whenever the burglar should be caught. Besides that, it was an affair that was sure to attract public attention and be very much talked about, so it would be a good advertisement to him to get his name mixed up with it as much as possible from the very beginning. And finally, supposing she could be induced to trust him as a lawyer, might not the professional connection lead eventually to a yet closer and more tender tie between them? Such things had happened to other barristers before now; so why not to him as well as another? Feeling convinced that he would be an idiot if he could not manage to profit in some way or other by the robbery, he lost no time in placing his services at Miss Carton's disposal, and offering to assist in investigating into all that concerned the loss of her jewels.

His offer was accepted readily. The police had not yet had time to arrive; and it seemed to Ethel as if a barrister would be the next best thing to a policeman under the circumstances. It gave her a vague sense of confidence to know that there was on the spot some one acting for her, whose professional experience made him likely to know all about the detection of crime and criminals. The only other representative of the law who was in reach at that moment was her uncle, Mr Rhys, who was a magistrate. But she knew that he was by no means active in his magisterial duties, and thought it extremely probable that whatever knowledge of legal matters he had ever had, was become rusty through want of practice; therefore she was inclined to think that the wide-awake looking young barrister, fresh from the law courts, was more likely to be of use to her at present than any other person who was available, and she was gratified to have his energies working on her behalf.

This he was quick to perceive, and at once proceeded to act in such a way as should make it impossible to doubt that his whole heart and soul were in the case he had undertaken, and that he had identified himself with it as completely as though his own interests had been involved. Having asked leave to cross-examine her as a necessary preliminary, he performed that operation in a manner that was a happy combination of the sympathising friend with the hard-headed, practical man of business, and thus elicited all the information she could give as pleasantly as possible. Next he explored the whole house thoroughly, and examined rooms, staircases, passages, windows, doors, and fastenings without end—which looked business-like at all events, even though it did not bring to light anything more than was already known about the robbery. Then he went to the smoking-room window, which, having been wide open, had naturally been supposed from the first to have been the thief's way in and out of the house; upon this window Trevor concentrated his attention for some time—standing with his head stuck on one side like a magpie, viewing the place from both inside and out, and taking notes of every dent, notch, or scratch that was to be discerned on paint, wood or stone near the window. Furthermore he asked innumerable questions (many of which appeared to the uneducated minds of those who were not lawyers to be utterly irrelevant) of every member of the household; and altogether he left no stone unturned to demonstrate the devouring eagerness that he felt to hit upon some clue that might lead to the detection of the villain who had robbed Miss Carton.

One of the thief's fingers was missing from the right hand. Well; that was a very important point to start from, and would throw grave suspicion upon anyone who might be discovered in the vicinity in that maimed condition. It could do no harm to make absolutely sure of the innocence of every one who was within immediate reach, and with Mr Rhys's permission, Trevor proposed at once to pass in review the hands of every person then in the house—whether visitor or servant—in order to investigate their number of fingers. Mr Rhys stared, and hummed and hawed, being in truth not quite pleased at having the command of affairs in his own house thus taken from him by this extremely energetic young man, whose ideas were so much more ready than Mr Rhys's own. As, however, he could not think of any valid objection to the proposal, orders were given to carry it into effect, and the whole establishment was speedily paraded before Mr Owen. So suspicious of everyone was that gentleman, and so determined to do his work quite thoroughly, that ocular evidence alone was not enough for him, and he insisted on submitting every finger to the test of being pinched and pulled by him before he would be satisfied that it was real, live, flesh and blood.

'Supposing a robber to be short of a finger, he'd be very likely to have a sham one,' he observed knowingly; 'and if so, he'd wear it as a rule, so that no one should know of his deficiency; then he could take it off by way of a blind when he wanted to do business, you see.'

The finger-inspection produced a great sensation amongst the servants—especially the maids—and gave rise to mingled feelings of wrath and mirth. It was both insulting and ludicrous to have a gentleman prying into and feeling their hands, and supposing that one of them might possibly have been Miss Carton's robber; and the females resented the supposition all the more because it of course involved also the belief that they were capable of having donned male attire—which idea was an immense shock to the sensibilities of most of them.

"Ow dare 'e heven *think* such a thing!' said Millet indignantly; 'but there—they barristers is mostly a low lot, as it stands to reason they should be when you think of the hinferior sort of parties has they be halways coming in contack with. And though Mr Howen is by birth a Honourable and a reel gentleman, yet when 'e demeans 'imself to take up with a purfession like lawyers, why, in corse, 'e soon comes down to the levil of the rest of 'is trade.'

All the maids had a strong sense of the 'horkardness' of the position which caused them to be much oppressed with shyness; and this found expression and relief in foolish simpers, blushes, suppressed giggles, or uneasy contortions of the body, according to the temperament of the individual under examination. Mr Owen, however, was quite superior to feeling awkward or bashful about anything whatever that had to do with collecting evidence for a case, and proceeded as calmly with his hand-researches amongst total strangers as if he was in the habit of conducting such things every day of his life. He was drawing near the end of his task, and had discovered no deficiency of fingers anywhere, when he was struck by a look that came into the face of a heavy-looking girl whose hands he had just examined. A gleam of intelligence came into her eyes, her stupid face partially lighted up, and her mouth opened. From these signs he inferred that some bright idea had invaded her mind and was about to issue from her lips, so he paused to hear what would come. But to his disappointment the mouth merely gave vent to an inarticulate sound, and was then again shut up tight.

'Well, what were you going to say?' he asked sharply; 'out with it.'

That a thought had suddenly struck the girl was perfectly true; but yet she had no wish or intention of communicating it to the strange gentleman. Ideas being of rare occurrence in her mind, when one had actually come there it had quite taken her by surprise, and she had been on the point of blurting it out at once as freely as she would have done if in the company only of friends in her own station of life. But before she could so, her slowly working brain had evolved a second thought which had checked the impulse to speak.

What if the thing she had thought of was to bring Richard Richards into trouble? Indeed, it would be a pity to do that. If so be as 'twas he as was the thief, she'd no wish to save him, not she; but still it didn't seem right to go and put this gentleman as she didn't know after a neighbour, neither. If Richards was the man they wanted, they'd be sure to find him out for themselves fast enough without her help,—and serve him right too!—but she shouldn't like to think as *she'd* been the one to set them on his heels.

The result of her meditations was, that she held her tongue steadily, though becoming extremely red and confused as Trevor Owen repeated his question several times in the vain hope of extracting an answer.

'Who's that girl?' said he, turning impatiently to the butler, who was assisting him. 'Make her answer me, can't you? I'll swear she's got something to say. I saw it in her face just now, only she's shy, or frightened, or something, and won't let it out.'

'Polly Thomas, sir, that is,' replied the butler. 'She don't belong to us reglar, but comes in now and again to wash up a bit when the work's in any ways extry, such as comp'ny staying here. Why don't you speak, Polly, and answer the gentleman, like a good girl?'

In Polly's eyes the butler was a person of almost more dignity and consequence than anyone else in the house—even including Mr Rhys—and to disobey his orders was an act of daring hardly possible to contemplate. Still she could not bear to go against her sense of what was due to a neighbour who was on friendly terms with her and hers; therefore she remained silent, shuffling her feet to and fro, blushing, rolling and unrolling her apron round her hands, and giving other similar indications of the excessive nervousness and discomposure which she was experiencing.

This reticence was by no means approved of by the bystanders, who were greatly excited on the subject of the burglary, and caught eagerly at anything which seemed to offer a chance of throwing fresh light upon the mystery. Further pressure was put upon her, not only by the butler and Mr Owen, but by the other servants also, and on all sides she heard whispers of 'Speak you, Polly.' 'What is it?' 'Tell, girl, tell,' etc. This pressure was more than she could stand, and she finally gave way before the potent engine of the public opinion of her own class.

It came out at last, therefore, that all the fuss about fingers had suddenly reminded her about Richard Richards, for she knew there was something looked odd about one of his hands. She hadn't never taken no notice of what it was, not she, and wasn't sure but what it might be a finger gone from it as he had. That was all as she'd been thinking of.

This was deemed by Mr Owen quite worth inquiring into further. Who was Richard Richards? he asked immediately. And where did he live? Trevor soon learnt that Richards was a collier with a wife and children, that he lived not far beyond Mr Rhys's property, and that that gentleman held him in abhorrence and believed him capable of any iniquity, because he was a notorious poacher.

The next step to take, in Mr Owen's opinion, was to proceed at once to Richards' cottage, find out if he had a proper complement of fingers, and if not, try to ascertain where he had spent the preceding night. Would it be too much to ask Miss Carton to accompany this reconnoitring expedition, if she were equal to that amount of fatigue after the terribly trying events of the night? Her presence might be of great advantage, as, perhaps, they might be fortunate enough to see the man himself; and if she were to be able to pronounce positively either for or against him, waste of time over a false scent might thus be avoided. Perhaps Mr Rhys would be able to spare a carriage to take her?

She replied graciously that she felt quite equal to going to the cottage, and should prefer to go on foot, as she always liked to have a walk on the morning after a ball, if possible; and with that she went to put on her things without loss of time. As soon as she was gone Mr Rhys and Mr Owen had a slight sparring match as to whether or not the former gentleman should be of the party going to the cottage. Trevor wanted to manage everything himself and let Miss Carton see how well he did it, and he feared that Mr Rhys's coming might relegate him to the second place; therefore he tried to impress upon his host the importance of staying in the house in order to give any directions that the police might require, and made every suggestion he could think of that might induce Mr Rhys to remain at home.

Mr Rhys, however, had no intention of doing anything of the kind. As being a magistrate for that district, Ethel's uncle, and also master of the house where the burglary had been committed, he felt that he was in every way entitled to take the lead in all that was done, and to decline being pushed aside by this meddlesome young fellow who seemed to think no one knew anything but himself. So he announced positively that he meant to accompany his niece to the cottage and make the necessary inquiries as to Richard Richards, in such a manner as to put an end to further discussion of the matter; and Trevor Owen had to resign himself to a companion, whose presence he would gladly have dispensed with.

He had not done badly so far, however, having, undoubtedly, contrived to show himself to be a very energetic young fellow, and to display an ardour on Miss Carton's behalf which disposed her to regard him favourably. For few people dislike to feel that their interests are being looked after by a sharp, active, business-like person, who may be relied upon not to let the grass grow under his feet; and that was just the impression of his character which he had managed to give her.

CHAPTER XI
The Superiority of Red Indians

It may be remembered that Ralph had announced his intention to spend the day in trout-fishing, and that Imogen had made up her mind to accompany him. Accordingly, they went off as soon as they could after breakfast to prepare the fishing-tackle for the proposed expedition; but whilst they were in the midst of their preparations, they were interrupted by their father. The general commotion produced by the burglary, and a vague sense that he ought to do *something*, but did not quite know *what*, had by this time worked Mr Rhys into an uncomfortably fidgety condition, and he was inclined to be annoyed at anyone's supposing it possible to go on in the same way as usual without regard to the important event that had occurred.

Where were Ralph and Imogen off to now? Fishing in the Dŵrwen? Oh, nonsense! It was out of the question for Ralph to go away from home to-day; he must stay and make himself useful. There would be the police coming presently, and inquiries to make, and directions to give, and fifty things to do and see to in consequence of all this bother about the robbery; and then there was the ball party staying in the house to be looked after and entertained as well, and altogether the fishing must absolutely be postponed to some other day when the boy could be spared. He was wanted to help about something at that very moment; and so the son was carried off then and there by his father to assist about some trifling matter or other, which would, on ordinary occasions, have been considered quite unimportant, but which was caused by Mr Rhys's present state of fussiness to assume unnaturally large proportions.

Thus Imogen, to her great annoyance, found herself suddenly deprived of her companion, and also of the day's outing to which she had been confidently looking forward. She began to think it was decidedly a mistake to be in a house where a burglary had just taken place. It was liable to interfere with one's plans, however unconcerned one might be with it; and besides that, it put every creature except herself into a state of flutter and excitement which was simply intolerable. She was quite sick of all the nonsense she had heard talked about the all-engrossing subject, and could not imagine how people could care to go on making the endless, ridiculous, and unpractical surmises and suggestions that were re-sounding in all parts of the establishment. And all the effusive sympathy and condolences that were poured in upon Ethel, too! Imogen did not in the least believe in the sincerity of the greater part of them, and could not understand how anyone had the patience to listen to such humbugging stuff quietly. Of course these strangers couldn't *really* care so very much about her cousin's loss, and so whatever was the use of pretending such a lot of rubbishing, good-for-nothing interest? She regarded all the commotion with a lofty contempt, and wondered how people could condescend to allow themselves to be so easily moved, and to behave in such a foolish manner.

What was the good of civilisation, if civilised beings made such gushing, affected fools of themselves? Having recently read *The Last of the Mohicans*, she knew perfectly well that those admirably brave and stoical people, the Red Indians, deemed all violent demonstrations of excitement undignified, and thought that 'Wagh!' was an amply sufficient expression of opinion under all circumstances. Well! and quite right too. It seemed to her that these savages were out and away superior to the silly, chattering, emotional products of civilisation amongst whom she lived, whose sentiments were all on the surface and wanted for show. Such people could not ever feel things really, genuinely, and deeply at all; since when a feeling was frittered away and spread about in all directions it must lose its power as a stick would do if cut up into little bits—it would be simply worthless! she was glad to think that *she*, at all events as yet, hadn't been caught and tamed and made just like all the rest of the world; she still had enough of the barbarian in her not to want to talk when she had nothing but intensely stupid and meaningless words to utter; nor yet to affect exaggerated, unreal feelings because other people did so, or because it might be thought the right thing to do. Wagh! was a most impressive remark if grunted in a properly expressive tone; and Red Indians had altogether the best of it, in her judgment.

Having thus worked herself up into a highly intolerant and misanthropical (as far as civilisation was concerned) frame of mind, she began to reflect upon what she should do with herself at the present moment, and how she should spend the day. Staying indoors in fine weather was, of course, a thing not to be contemplated for an instant; nor yet would she remain within reach of any of these fine, civilised folk whose senseless chatter provoked her. She would take her beloved butterfly-net, put a book in her pocket, get right away where she would be able to be by herself, and pass her time in mothing or reading as the fancy took her. There were nuts to be had now, and she loved nuts. She might gather a handful of them, climb up to the tree-sofa, and lie there contentedly eating nuts and reading for as long as she liked without the least fear of being disturbed by objectionable fellow-creatures, for no one knew of the place except herself and Ralph. And here it may be as well to remark for the reader's benefit, that what she and Ralph denominated the tree-sofa, was a place at the top of a tree where the boughs crossed and intercrossed one another so as to form a sort of rough couch whereon a person could recline at full length. It was much frequented by Imogen in hot weather, and she would often lie there for hours in perfect satisfaction with an amusing book to read, whilst the birds flew close to her, twittering and singing but never heeding her presence, and the wind gently swayed the boughs beneath her, and blew to and fro the over-hanging leaves, so that the sunlight now came dancing over her face and book, and now left her in the shade.

The first thing to be done was to go and pick the nuts. Armed with her butterfly-net, she was about to sally forth, when she remembered that she had not got the book which she meant to take, and which stood on a shelf in the front hall. She was proceeding in search of it when she met Ethel, who had just come down stairs with her walking things on, ready to set out for Richard Richards' cottage.

'Oh, so you're going out too, are you, Im?' said Ethel pleasantly. 'There's some poor man near here whom uncle Rhys and Mr Owen think may possibly know more than he should do about where my stolen jewels are, and we're going to inspect him; come with us, won't you?'

Imogen hesitated. At that particular moment she was eminently out of charity with civilisation in general, and it appeared to her that to go walking with some of the 'swells' when she had intended to go nutting and tree climbing, would be inconsistent with her principles, and a dangerously near approach to consenting of her own free will to be, as it were, caught and tamed—that is to say, reclaimed from the condition of running wild that she delighted in, and knew to be abhorrent to all her friends except Ralph. Had the invitation to join the party come from anyone except Ethel, she would have refused it promptly; but could she say no to anything that Ethel proposed?

'I don't know about that,' answered Imogen, rather ungraciously. 'I'm going mothing.'

'Well, never mind the moths for once,' returned Ethel, without being at all offended at the grumpy manner of one whom she knew to be somewhat eccentric, and was inclined to like, notwithstanding.

You can catch them another day; besides, perhaps there'll be some where we are going. Do come; I want you to.'

Imogen's savagery was not proof against this persuasion from a person whom she regarded with that extreme admiration and veneration sometimes felt by a girl of sixteen or so for one a few years older, and with which, as has been already said, Ethel had unconsciously and involuntarily inspired her young cousin. Imogen felt it deliciously flattering to be thus pressed to accompany the object of her worship, and after pausing in indecision for an instant, she replied,—'All right. I'll come then. I daresay I'll be able to kick up a moth or so somewhere or other on the way.' Might not being caught and tamed be differently regarded, and even possibly considered as endurable, provided that Ethel were to be the captor?

There was also in the front hall a third person, who had listened with interest to the short colloquy between the cousins, and whose own movements were affected by Imogen's decision to accompany Miss Carton. This third individual was a young man named Sir Charles Dover, who was amongst the visitors invited to Llwyn-yr-Allt for the last night's ball. He had been loitering about for the last ten minutes, feeling acutely conscious that he had nothing very particular to do, and wondering how he should dispose of his time. What he wanted was to go out to play lawn tennis, walk, ride, or take some exercise or other; only he did not care about going alone, and could not find anyone of the same mind to be his companion. No one seemed to have any present intention at all of going out except the three who were going to the cottage; and he was shy of joining them unasked, because their errand seemed to invest them with a sort of important, private, business-like halo which he feared to break in upon; besides, he had never met the heiress till the evening before, and held her in no little awe.

But if Imogen were going to accompany the party, that quite altered the aspect of affairs. He thought she seemed rather a jolly girl, and certainly not in the very slightest degree awe-inspiring. He did not at all object to her outspoken straightforwardness; was amused by what he had seen of her wildness and hoydenishness; and had an intuitive conviction that there would always be some chance of a bit of fun going on at any place where she might be present. Since she had been asked to go to the cottage, it was evident that those who were going there as a matter of necessity and business did not regard the visit as a thing requiring any special privacy; therefore, he might safely venture to propose himself as an addition to the party without fear of being considered an intruder.

'May I come with you?' said he to Mr Rhys, who just then joined them. 'I was on the point of going for a stroll, and should greatly prefer your company to my own, if I sha'n't be in the way.'

'In the way? Oh, not a bit of it—delighted to have you, my dear fellow, if you care to come,' returned Mr Rhys. 'Shouldn't have thought of suggesting it, though, if you hadn't proposed it of yourself, for you won't find it very lively, I'm afraid. Business is a great bore sometimes, but of course it has to be done; and you see that I, as a magistrate, am bound to take active steps immediately in an affair of this kind. People expect it of people in our position. Ah! Here's Owen. Are you ready to start, Ethel?'

'Yes, quite,' answered Ethel. 'I wonder if we shall make any very important discovery at this cottage after all—find my set of diamonds and sapphires in the oven, or one of my rings in the teapot, or something of that kind? '

'Ha! Ha!' laughed Mr Owen; 'what an exquisitely amusing idea! But seriously, you know, though I wouldn't have you too sanguine, yet it seems quite possible, from all we have heard, that this Richard Richards may turn out to be *minus* a finger on the right hand as your robber was. And in that case it'll be a very fishy circumstance for a man of notoriously thieving proclivities, unless he should be able to prove quite satisfactorily where he was during the whole of last night.'

'That's true enough,' interposed Mr Rhys; ' but remember that it's a great mistake to go rushing to hasty conclusions in the way that all you young men like to do. The mere fact of a man's having lost a finger from the right hand is, in itself, not even a ground for suspicion, unless accompanied by other suspicious circumstances. Why, I know a gentleman who was paying me a visit here not long ago, and is maimed in just the same way. Yet to charge him, merely on that account, with having committed this crime, would be evidently absurd and preposterous.'

'Some one staying here with a finger off one hand, papa?' exclaimed Imogen. 'How funny that I never noticed it—who was he?'

'I'm not sure that you've ever met the person whom I mean, my dear,' replied Mr Rhys; 'no—now I come to think of it, I'm pretty certain you've not, for I remember that you were away when he was here. It's that young Sylvester who is with the Messrs Glass. But come, come; we must be off and not stop talking here. Excuse my hurrying you all, but it'll never do for me to allow waste of time in the prosecution of the inquiries that have to be made. We magistrates are in a position of much responsibility, and must remember that it's to us the country looks in an emergency of this kind, and that it behoves us to act accordingly.'

CHAPTER XII
A Cottage Visit

The party did not take very long in reaching the place whither they were bound, which was situated at a short distance outside the Llwyn-yr-Allt grounds. Neither Mr Rhys nor any of his family had ever yet set foot in the cottage; but for all that he knew perfectly well where it was, for the same reason that the more a thorn pains one, the more certain one is to be able to lay one's finger precisely on the spot where it lies. For the proximity of so evil-disposed and ill-regulated a person as a poacher was a sore trial to him; and he was resolved that if ever that cottage should be in the market he would purchase it, whatever it might cost, in order to have the satisfaction of ridding himself of his objectionable neighbour.

Though Mr Rhys was naturally a most amiable and benevolent individual, yet his prejudice against poachers was inveterate; and in spite of the warning he had given Trevor Owen against coming to hasty conclusions, he himself had in his secret heart a strong, and by no means unwelcome, impression of the great probability there was that Richard Richards would turn out to be the burglar.

Ethel was the most at ease of either of the five visitors as they entered the cottage. To go into a place of that kind seemed to her a perfectly natural and every-day action, because she had been brought up from her earliest childhood to visit amongst the villagers and poor people living near her as a matter of course. But to Imogen, on the contrary, it was a strange and novel sensation, as she had seldom done such a thing before in her whole life; and she looked about with a mixture of curiosity, shyness, and feeling that they were all being horribly rude, when they had attained their destination and walked into the house, after knocking at the door.

An untidy, uncared-for looking place the cottage was, with a mud-floored, roughly-furnished kitchen, wherein Richards' wife, Ann, was engaged in kneading dough, whilst children of various ages and stages of dirt surrounded her, and from time to time amused themselves by poking little holes in the dough with their filthy fingers. She was evidently a thorough slattern—unwashed, unkempt, and with dishevelled hair that looked as if it might have been done about a week ago, and not since taken down or brushed. The appearance of the children, furniture, and whole place corresponded to that of the mistress; and Imogen, unfamiliar with cottage interiors, and rather fastidious about her eating, wondered with a shudder how near to starvation she would have to be reduced before it would be possible to her to touch food prepared by that woman and in that house.

The unexpected arrival of the gentlefolks—of whom only Mr Rhys and Imogen were known to her by sight—disquieted poor Ann Richards not a little. Such people had never visited her before, and she could not imagine what brought them now, and was disposed to be distrustful—as all people are who know they have something to conceal—of whatever was out of the regular course of things. She knew that her man was fond of poaching, and had been out all the night before, though she did not know what he had been doing, nor where he had been. Could it be that he had got into some fresh trouble with the keepers? The fear of that happening was constantly on her mind, and the sight of Mr Rhys was particularly calculated to suggest the idea, because his detestation for poaching was very well known, and made him an object of especial suspicion to all that class of evildoers. She felt a good deal alarmed, therefore, and being uncertain what particular point might most need to be guarded, was prepared to stand on the defensive all round, and commit herself as little as might be in any direction.

To be entrusted with the exclusive management of the cross-questioning which would have to be done at the cottage was a thing which Trevor Owen coveted greatly. On the way there he had given plenty of hints to that effect—had held forth on the skill required to ask effective and judicious questions, and had expatiated on the impossibility of any person's possessing that skill unless they had acquired it by dint of legal training and practice. But his hints had produced no effect whatever on Mr Rhys, who, having been once roused to act magisterially, did not dislike the feeling of importance it gave him to take a leading part in connection with so serious an affair as this was, and had no idea of allowing anyone—least of all a strange young man of no local standing—to take the bread out of his mouth in the matter. There could be no doubt that he was in the right about this, and that in virtue both of his local position and of his relationship to Miss Carton, he had the first claim to conduct the inquiry that was now about to be made as to the peculiarity of Richard Richards' hand which had attracted the attention of Polly Thomas, and also as to what the man's movements might have been during the preceding night. But though Trevor could not deny the truth of this, and had no option about deferring to the older and more influential man, none the less did it cost him a bitter pang to yield the point, and to have to sit silently listening to 'cross-examination for his side performed by a bungling ignoramus,' as he inwardly termed Mr Rhys's questioning of the woman.

'Good morning, Ann,' said Mr Rhys. 'Is your husband in just now?'

Ann was perfectly well aware that he was not, and had not been since nine o'clock on the evening before. But she saw no reason for at once imparting all this information to people who might, perhaps, have hostile motives for wishing to know where he was, and so declined to gratify their curiosity too promptly by giving an immediate answer.

'My daughter shall see now just, sir,' she replied, and then continued, turning to the eldest child, 'run you, Sairerrann, and see if dadda's in the garden.'

The child addressed had been hitherto standing motionless since the strangers appeared, staring at them with great, wild, brown eyes, that looked half-fierce and half-frightened. When told to go and look for her father, she did not at first move an inch, but only turned her eyes wonderingly towards her mother, and opened her mouth as if about to make some observation. The mother, however, guessing that the child intended to remonstrate against being sent on an errand that she knew to be a fruitless one, nipped the impending protest in the bud, by giving her daughter a slight shove, and adding peremptorily, 'Quick now!' Whereupon Sarah Ann at once departed.

A somewhat awkward silence ensued, which was broken by Ethel's making advances towards friendship with some of the children. This seemed suddenly to suggest to Mrs Richards that the nose of the second boy was not exactly in a condition that was suitable for the reception of company, so she pounced upon him unexpectedly, and hastily pinched and wiped it with a corner of her apron. This attention was hardly received with the gratitude it deserved by the recipient, who evidently regarded the proceeding as quite uncalled for. He acknowledged it by wrinkling up the offending member impatiently and twitching himself out of her grasp as soon as the operation was concluded, with an air of only having tolerated it at all because he knew it to be—though utterly mistaken —kindly meant.

When this was accomplished, Mr Rhys thought it time to resume the inquiries that were the object of his visit.

'By-the-bye, how came Richard to hurt his hand?' asked he. This was a question that greatly astonished Ann.

'Hurted his hand, sir, have he?' returned she cautiously, wondering how her husband might have contrived to damage himself since last she had seen him, and what row he could have been getting into during the night. 'Indeed, and 'tis like enough; what with drams[1] slipping, and stones falling, and one thing and another, there be always something wrong at them colleries. I don't suppose as it be very bad though, neither, for he haven't a said nothing of it to I.'

'Oh! but Mr Rhys means a long time ago,' interrupted Trevor, finding it impossible to keep silence any longer. 'He meant that time when your husband lost his finger—or—let me see—wasn't it two fingers that he lost?'

''Twas only one, whatever,' answered Ann quickly, astonished at this stranger's knowledge about her husband, and surprised into forgetting her determination not to give an atom more information about him than could be helped.

The barrister felt that he had scored a point in thus discovering certainly that Richards was short of one finger, and continued at once, with a glance of triumph, before Mr Rhys had a chance of interfering again,—

'To be sure! Of course it was only one. Stupid of me to have fancied it was two. And it's off his right hand that it's gone, isn't it now?'

But Ann was not to be entrapped into making any further admissions, and answered curtly,—

'Indeed, and I can't speak as to that. I didn't never take no nottice which hand it be.'

She was becoming more and more mystified as to the object of this visit. What possible interest could the gentry have in Richard's loss of a finger? for that had taken place years ago, and could certainly not be referred to any poaching or other disturbance that might have taken place last night. Whatever the drift of their questions might be, however, she would at all events keep on the safe side and let her visitors get as little as possible out of her.

The return of the child now effected a diversion; and Ethel, feeling interested in the wild-looking little thing, and wishing to make friends with her, said kindly, 'Did you find your father, Sarah?'

Perhaps the girl did not recognise herself when addressed only by one Christian name, or perhaps she did not understand English readily, when it was spoken without the familiar Welsh accent. Be that as it may, at all events she paid no attention to the question, and stood silently and stolidly staring as before, without giving the least sign of knowing that anyone had addressed her. Mr Owen seeing this, thought it incumbent on him to interfere on Miss Carton's behalf, and reprove the child for rudeness.

'Where are your manners, you rude little girl?' said he severely; 'you must answer the lady directly.'

His severity, however, produced no more effect than Ethel's gentleness had done, for the child remained immovable till asked by her mother, 'Did you find dadda, Sairerrann? Tell now.' To which she responded, 'Noo!' and then returned to her former occupation of staring.

While all this had been going on, Imogen had watched the proceedings curiously. She did not feel in any way specially drawn towards this dirty, slovenly woman and her equally untidy children; but for all that she was aware of some intuitive feeling of sympathy with them which enabled her to guess pretty confidently at the thoughts that were likely to be passing through their minds. And she observed, too, with some surprise, how completely at home Ethel seemed to be, and how much less awkward she was in her manner of addressing the cottage inmates than any of the rest of the party.

Mr Rhys lost no time in going on with his interrogations, so that Trevor Owen might not again have an opportunity of putting in his oar.

'I'm very sorry Richards is out,' said Mr Rhys, rather stiffly, with a vague sort of impression that the man's being out of the way when he was wanted to be interviewed, was an additional proof of the iniquity of his disposition. 'Do you know at all where he is likely to be found?'

'Well, no sir, indeed and I can't say as I does,' returned Ann.

'Humph, that's unlucky, as there's something that I particularly wish to see him about,' answered the gentleman. 'However, perhaps you can tell me part of what I want to know, and that is, whether he was here during last night, or whether he was away at all?'

At this direct question Mr Owen groaned internally. 'Oh, what an idiot the man is!' thought he; 'but it's just like an unprofessional to go blurting out leading questions like that, and showing the witness—who is evidently very suspicious of us—exactly where to be specially on her guard. Dear, dear! Why *couldn't* he have left the examination to me? If people did but know what fools they make of themselves when they will go meddling with what they don't understand.'

Ann affected not to have heard or comprehended the question, so as to gain a moment's time for considering her answer.

'Er?' she inquired, with a look of absolute stupidity.

'Was your husband out anywhere last night, I want to know?' repeated Mr Rhys, in a rather louder tone.

'Out of here, sir, is it as you do mean?' returned Ann, innocently.

'Yes, of course; where else should I mean?' returned Mr Rhys impatiently.

She had by this time reflected upon the situation sufficiently to perceive the futility of denying what would be easily discoverable from other sources, and replied,—

'Why, no sir; you see as this be his night-week. The colliers always do take it turn about, working one week by day and the next by night, as you do know, in course; and so this being his night-week, he has to be away to work every night.'

'Oh, then he was *not* here last night,' answered Mr Rhys. 'Thank you; I wanted to know about that; well, we must be going now, and won't disturb you any longer. Good day.'

With that he left the cottage, followed by the rest of the party. Ethel, Imogen, and Sir Charles Dover all took leave with more or less courtesy of the mistress of the house as they departed; but Mr Owen stalked out without taking any notice at all of her.

'He didn't even hitch his head at her,' remarked Imogen afterwards, when giving Ralph an account of the visit. 'He might have done that much, I think. It ain't *my* notion to go into any one's house, whether it's a rich person's or a poor one's, and behave as if the owner were a bit of stick that hadn't the right to turn one out if he or she chose. One's only on sufferance, as it were, in other people's diggings, whoever they may be.'

As soon as Mr Rhys had reached the road, he said, with considerable complacency,—

'Well, we didn't go there for nothing, and have found out something of what we wanted to know at all events. So far, I shouldn't say it seems at all impossible for Richard Richards to be the man we want. Eh, Owen?'

'It's hard to say anything positive about the matter yet one way or other, as far as I can see,' answered Trevor, who spied an opportunity of triumph and of showing Miss Carton that her uncle had blundered in managing her affairs. 'Shall we go straight on now to the colliery the man works at, or will it be too far for the ladies, do you think?'

'The colliery he works at!' echoed Mr Rhys, in surprise; 'what should we do that for? and besides, how am I to know which it is?'

'Oh, I beg your pardon for speaking then, sir,' returned Trevor, with the faintest possible accent of sarcasm to be detected in his tone; 'I took it for granted you must know that, as you didn't ask the wife about it. I should have thought there could have been *no* doubt of the importance of going to the colliery at once in order to verify her statement that he was working there last night; but of course you know best what to do, and have probably some better scheme.'

To be able to administer this rebuke to the man who had been trampling for the last some time upon his professional feelings was a comfort to the barrister, and afforded him some slight compensation for what he had undergone.

Mr Rhys was discomposed to perceive the omission of which he had been guilty. 'Bless my soul!' he exclaimed; 'yes— of course—I believe I did think of it once, only then it slipped my memory again. Just go on without me, and I'll step back and find that out, and overtake you in two minutes.' And with these words he hurried back to the cottage, leaving the rest of the party to saunter slowly along till he rejoined them.

'Poor Ann! that means more pumping for her,' observed Imogen. 'I don't expect she will be particularly pleased at his return, for she's had more than she wants of us already, unless I'm very much mistaken.'

'She wasn't pumped to much purpose though,' said Mr Owen with a sigh. 'I do wish Mr Rhys had allowed *me* to conduct the examination. It stands to reason that no amateur can ever understand that sort of thing as well as a lawyer does, and I feel little doubt of having extracted a good deal more information out of her if the case had been left in *my* hands.'

'I'm very glad it wasn't then,' said Imogen bluntly. 'Poor people are one's fellow-creatures after all, and it seems rather a shame to go and bully them in their own homes like that, when they can't get away from one.'

'You're right there, Miss Rhys,' said Sir Charles, who was amused at the way she had snubbed the barrister; 'but then can you fancy living in such a pig-sty as that cottage, and dignifying it by the name of *home*? And don't you think, too, that it's a grave question whether pocket-handkerchiefless children with colds ought to be allowed to exist? I'm inclined to think that it's a proper subject for legislation, and that they ought either to be cured or else done away by Act of Parliament.'

At this stage Ethel joined in the conversation. As she had all her life been familiar with the cottagers residing near Carton House, and been on the best of terms with them, it seemed to her that it was the right and natural thing for the inhabitants of all country houses always to exercise a gentle, kindly, and beneficent influence over their poorer neighbours, and took it for granted that Imogen would think the same, and act accordingly. Considering, therefore, how near the abode they had just left was to Llwyn-yr-Allt, Ethel had been quite astonished at the dirty, squalid condition of the Richards' dwelling, and its inmates; and was disposed to take her cousin mildly to task for tolerating such untidiness.

'I don't wonder at Sir Charles's criticism, Im,' she said, turning to Imogen with a laugh. 'Certainly the Richards' *ménage* isn't very creditable to have in one's immediate neighbourhood, and I know I should be dreadfully ashamed if I had one even a quarter as bad at Carton. Are those Richards' only just come here? or are they very unusually unmanageable? or how is it that you haven't managed to reform them?'

Imogen opened her eyes wide in surprise at an idea which had certainly never before entered her head. She regarded poor people as belonging to a weaker class than her own, and was on that account chivalrously disposed to sympathise with and stand up for them. But it was quite another thing to think of going about amongst them in their own homes, and trying to convert them to the same ideas of comfort, cleanliness, and morality as were entertained by herself and her equals. She had not been brought up, as Ethel had been, to do this. Therefore, whereas Ethel regarded it as simply a matter of every-day duty, Imogen, on the contrary, esteemed it to be a sort of irksome, out-of-the-way, eccentric proceeding which was only fitting for clergymen, and such individuals as were extra good and anxious to be saints.

'Reform them!' she echoed; 'why, I never tried to—they're no earthly business of mine.'

It was now Ethel's turn to be somewhat surprised.

'Aren't they? Well, I should have thought they were, living so close to you,' she answered. 'However, of course you know your own business best. But don't you think it would be an advantage to get them to be a bit cleaner, and civilise them a little? Surely you might do something towards it if you were to try.'

'Oh no! it's quite out of my line,' replied Imogen, who did not at all take to the notion. 'I've no turn for that kind of thing, and never have an idea what to say when I'm in a cottage. Besides, I don't see what right I should have to go interfering with a poor woman, and telling her she isn't clean enough. I should feel all the time that she must be wondering internally why I didn't mind my own business, even if—not being as rude as me—she didn't say so right out. I'm sure I wouldn't stand her coming to tell *me* that I ought to wash—and so why should I expect her to put up with my doing it to *her*?'

'That's not badly put, by Jove!' remarked Sir Charles, 'and I don't know that I ever looked at it in that light before. My mother and sisters at home are perpetually pottering after the cottagers, and I always took it for granted that it was the kind and proper thing to do, and that the people liked it. But I wonder if they really do, after all?'

'Of course they do,' said Trevor Owen; 'or if they don't they're ungrateful brutes! It's absurd, begging Miss Imogen's pardon, to reason about poor people just like ourselves; they're altogether different from us, and can't be treated in the same way. Don't you agree with me, Miss Carton?'

'Indeed, I don't,' answered Ethel; 'I don't altogether agree with Imogen's point of view either; I but it's true enough what she says about their being our fellow-creatures, and having just the same human nature as we have; and I can't bear for people to ignore that.'

Trevor entertained the utmost contempt for the lower classes, and regarded anyone in whom poverty and ignorance were combined as belonging to a very inferior order of being from himself. But at the present moment it was of much more consequence in his eyes to get into Miss Carton's good graces, than to air any private opinions of his own. Finding, therefore, that the sentiment he had just expressed was objectionable to her, he immediately applied himself to modify and explain it away, and was thus engaged until Mr Rhys rejoined them, and the conversation turned into another channel.

CHAPTER XIII
A Fritillary

Imogen's mind was beginning by this time to revert to her favourite pursuit of entomology, and she paused, looking attentively at a hedge they were passing which was thickly overgrown with brambles, ivy, and an abundance of hazel bushes. Sir Charles Dover, who regarded her as the most lively and interesting member of the party, stopped because she did, and the others went on without them—Mr Owen still zealously devoting himself to the heiress, and endeavouring to do the agreeable to her.

'Anything particular in that hedge, Miss Rhys?' inquired Sir Charles.

'Yes, very likely,' she answered. 'I was just thinking what a capital place for moths to be lying in it looked.'

'You don't say so, now?' he returned, not quite knowing what other remark to offer, and inwardly wondering what possible attraction she could find in this 'bug-hunting,' as he disrespectfully termed mothing. He was sure *he* could see nothing to be so fond of in it; only, it need scarcely be said, that that was an opinion which he did not judge suitable to be imparted to his companion.

'Yes I do, though,' she replied, without any suspicion of the irreverent thoughts passing through his mind. 'I shouldn't wonder if it was full of 'em.'

'Well then, why don't you catch 'em?' asked he; 'and why don't they fly about if they're there?'

'Why they're mostly asleep, of course, at this time of day,' returned she; 'and they'd have to be beaten out before one could catch 'em. I expect 'twould take no end of a good beater, too, to get out all there are in such a thick place as that.'

The day was very hot, and Sir Charles did not feel particularly inclined for thumping his stick upon bushes. Still there was nothing much else for him to do, and he thought he would be good-natured to this queer girl. So he said condescendingly,—

'Look here! I don't mind doing beater for you a bit.'

Having made certain that she would jump eagerly at so magnificent an offer, he was rather staggered at the cool manner in which she received it, as if the favour would be rather more on her side in allowing him to help her, than on his in exerting himself for her services.

'*You*!' said she, with an emphasis on the pronoun that was anything but flattering. 'Do you know how to?—did you ever do it before?'

He was amused at this unexpectedly scornful reception of his well-meant proposal, but just the least bit ruffled by it also.

'Well, no,' he answered; 'I can't say that I ever did. But I don't see how that can matter. I don't imagine there's any very great art required.'

'Ah, that just shows how little you know about it,' she replied, 'for the fact is there's a deal of skill in beating. First, the bushes ought to be touched quite gently to knock out any moths that are awake or sleeping lightly; then you get harder by degrees, till you come to routling about amongst the roots with all your might to wake up the heavy sleepers. And nothing but a deal of practice'll ever make you know exactly the best places to poke a stick in at. Of course I don't mind your trying if you like—but you won't find it as easy as you think, *I* know.'

The young man felt nettled at this low opinion of his capabilities, and resolved to show her she was mistaken. It was absurd to suppose he couldn't wake up a stupid moth and make it fly out of a hedge; why, any fool could do that much! However, he kept this sentiment to himself, and set to work at his task.

She was not in the best of tempers, having still not altogether got over the annoyance of losing the day's outing she had meant to have with Ralph, and at first she criticised Sir Charles's performance so unsparingly that he began to come to the conclusion that it was impossible to please her. If he beat hard, that was wrong, and when he struck softly, that was no better; if he hit at the leaves he was told he should rout in the roots, and when he routed in the roots he was asked why he had left the top branches untouched? But by-and-by the moths took to emerging from their hiding-places in sufficient numbers to keep her fully employed in running after them, and amongst those she captured were several that she wanted. This caused her first severity to relax considerably, and she even went so far as to tell him patronisingly that he was not doing so badly for a beginner.

This was all very well no doubt, and ought to have stimulated him to redoubled efforts; but he was getting tired of the hard, hot, dusty work of beating, and besides that, had taken it into his head that he should like to try his own hand at wielding the net.

'I should think you must be getting tired with so much running about,' he said cunningly; 'let me have the net and do some of it for you.'

'Oh, dear no! thanks all the same,' was the answer; 'I don't find catching is any harder work than beating, and it's much better fun! Go on; you haven't half worked through that hollow yet.'

But Sir Charles did not obey. He thought he had sacrificed himself long enough in her service, and that it was high time for him to have a share in the more amusing part of the performance.

'I've a great fancy to try how I should get on with a net,' he remarked insinuatingly.

This was a tolerably broad hint, but Imogen failed to see it.

'Well, if Ralph doesn't want his net this afternoon,' said she, 'I daresay he'll lend it you, and then you can try. Now then! I'm all ready for you to go on.'

'Oh ! but I should like to try now,' urged Sir Charles. 'Couldn't you lend me your net for a minute, and let me do the catching, whilst you beat instead of me? It isn't fair for me to work so hard and not have any of the fun at all; is it now ?'

There was a justice in this claim which she could not deny, however loath she might be to surrender the net.

'Well—no—I suppose not,' she replied, reluctantly. 'But then you see you've had no practice at it. Only fancy if you were to miss catching some first-rate rare moth that we want awfully; perhaps it might be one that we should never have the chance of again, you know.'

The loss of a rare moth would evidently be a serious calamity in her eyes, and the perfect gravity and businesslike earnestness with which she threw herself into her hobby diverted him considerably.

'True—very true,' he answered maliciously. 'I hadn't thought of anything so dreadful as that. Perhaps, after all, it may be wiser not to risk such a misfortune; and, of course, there can't be the *least* chance of its happening as long as the net is held by a practised hand like you, who never by any accident miss the moth you're after.'

This was an unkind speech on his part, for it referred to what had happened a few minutes before, when a moth which she had been especially anxious to secure had suddenly emerged from the hedge. The insect had several times been within her reach, and she had struck at it more than once without success, but it had at last defeated her ignominiously, to her no small disgust. She had rather hoped that her companion had perhaps not noticed the failure, and was now, therefore, considerably irritated to find that such was not the case. What business had a person who was such a slight acquaintance as he was to twit her with her mischance? Decidedly he must be a very rude young man! For it never occurred to her that the lack of ceremony with which she had treated him, took from her the right of complaining when he retaliated upon her in the same way.

Colouring angrily, she held the net out towards him.

'Oh, well, you can try if you like,' she said, ungraciously; 'but I daresay you won't catch a thing. You must give me your stick instead, for I've nothing else to beat with. Now then! look out! I'm going to beat that lump of ivy at the top.'

Her efforts speedily drove out a moth of some kind or other, and Sir Charles struck wildly at it as it whizzed past him; but he failed to get it in the net. He ran a few steps after it without getting another chance to strike, and then it disappeared from sight, and he returned, rather annoyed, to his post, quite aware of the scornful looks that Imogen was casting upon him, though she did not say anything.

With the second moth that appeared he was more successful, but was disappointed to find that the captured insect was only a common thing, which was turned out of the net to fly away again as soon as Imogen saw what it was. He was standing at some little distance away from her, watching for another to emerge from the ivy, when suddenly he heard her shriek out to him,—

'Hi!—look there! That big butterfly! Catch him—don't lose him on any account! Keep him in sight! Run—*do* run! Mark him down! Now—now! Ah! you've muffed him! Give *me* the net; *you're* no good with it!'

This excitement was caused by a splendid reddish-brown fritillary that came sailing along in the brilliant sunshine. Sir Charles ran after it, got near enough to strike at it, but unfortunately missed it.

Imogen, indignant, contemptuous, and reproachful, was dashing up to recover the net which he was wielding so unskilfully; but before she could get within reach of him and snatch it out of his hands, he had set off in full pursuit after the insect. It seemed as if her enthusiasm had at last infected him, for at that moment he certainly felt as if there were no possible alternative between securing the creature he was in chase of, or else running after it for ever.

Away it went like a flash of lightning; then, circling round, again came pretty near. He swooped at it with the net, furiously but ineffectually. Once more it darted away, with him after it, and Imogen following a little way behind. As she ran she kept shouting out instructions, more or less coherent, adjuring him to keep it in sight whatever he did, and ordering him to give up the net to her directly she got within reach of him. This, however, he was privately resolved that nothing on earth would induce him to do till the chase should be over. His whole soul was in it by this time, and he was burning to retrieve the disgrace of his two unsuccessful strokes, and to cover himself with glory by bringing the butterfly in triumph to Imogen. Without that fritillary he felt that life would be not worth the having, and his future existence hopelessly blighted.

Bother the brute, what had become of it? He could swear he had never taken his eyes off it for an instant, yet now it had vanished! He stood still, perforce, and stared around, stamping with vexation, and in an agony lest the check should give Imogen time to overtake him, and insist on the restoration of her property. She had almost got up to him when his eye caught a twinkle of something red, a little way off, on the ground; and there, sure enough, was the fritillary sitting calmly on a white stone, with its great wings stretched out broadly in the sun and motionless, save when now and then a sort of rapid flap quivered through them.

Calling to Imogen to keep back and not frighten the quarry, he advances cautiously; still it remains quiet. A step nearer and he will have a chance; he prepares to strike; Imogen stands watching with breathless interest. No use! away glances the insect like a flash of light, and the chase begins all over again.

What a splendid beauty a fritillary is; but oh, gracious! what a tiresome thing to have to keep one's eyes on. Its manner of going on is too erratic for its course to be reckoned on with any certainty for two moments together; now it shoots along as straight as an arrow, and now zigzags about from side to side, gleaming and glancing hither and thither with a swiftness that makes it hardly possible for mortal eyes to follow the flight.

Keeping the insect in view as best he could, Sir Charles went on in frantic pursuit till he came to a low bank dividing two fields from one another. He heard Imogen shouting something to him but paid no heed to what she said. Of course she was only going on ordering him to give her back the net—give back the net, at such a moment, indeed! As if that was likely!

Turning a deaf ear to her words, therefore, and never taking his eyes off the butterfly, he sprang to the top of the bank and down on the other side. Just as his foot quitted the earth on the top he became aware of the glint of water beneath, and on looking down saw a pond underneath him. It was too late to draw back, for he had already taken his spring, and next moment he was sprawling on his face in a stagnant duck-pond, half full of filthy green mud and water! Dripping, unsavoury, disgusted, but yet undaunted, he rose immediately to his feet, vigorously spluttering out the foul stuff that filled his mouth, and looking eagerly around for the butterfly, in hopes that he might still perhaps be able to retrieve his credit. Alas for his hopes! He had fallen with the net underneath him and completely smashed it; consequently all chance of capturing anything more till a fresh net could be procured was now at an end.

In Imogen's mind there were two contrary inclinations struggling together. On the one hand she felt disposed to laugh at his ridiculous and dismal appearance; and on the other, to lament the loss of the fritillary which she took quite seriously to heart. On the whole her disappointment predominated, and made her too serious to indulge in much merriment just then; she only said mournfully,— 'I wonder if it was *Argynnis Lathonia* or *Argynnis Euphrosyne*! It must have been one or the other of them, because they're the only two fritillaries that are out in September. I wanted it either way; but, oh dear! How *awfully* provoking if it should have been *Lathonia*, which is so rare!'

The poor young man had never before heard these formidable names, and had not the remotest notion of what either *Lathonia* or *Euphrosyne* were; but, anyhow, he perceived that something very disastrous had taken place, and as it had evidently been caused by his over-great ambition in aspiring to the management of the net, he felt very small indeed as he sneaked home by her side in a crestfallen and uncomfortable condition of both body and mind.

Such was the enthusiasm for entomology with which his short experience of it had inspired him, that the loss of the fritillary seemed to him even more to be deplored than his own ducking; and it was an additionally bitter drop in his cup to reflect that that loss was his own fault, and would very probably have been avoided if the net had been in the hands of its rightful owner.

Ah! If only he had let the net alone!

Then, perhaps, a *Lathonia* (whatever that might be) would on this day have been added triumphantly to the entomological cabinet at Llwyn-yr-Allt, and he might himself have had the distinguished felicity of beholding its capture!

VOLUME II

Contents

CHAPTER I
Is This The Man?

The Llwyn-yr-Allt party had not been long gone from Richard Richards' cottage before he arrived there himself, announcing that he should want his 'grub' before long, as he had not had much of a breakfast, and was 'uncommon peckish.' Of course Ann lost no time in telling him of the visitors she had had, the interest they had manifested as to where he had been during the preceding night, and the unlooked-for knowledge possessed by one of the strangers as to the maimed condition of his hand. On hearing all this, Richard became much discomposed. He put down the pipe which he had just lighted, and stood in a state of evident uneasiness, scratching his head and swearing as he meditated, without vouchsafing any response to his wife's questions. As she required a couple of onions and cabbages to stew with the bit of meat she was going to prepare for his dinner, she went into the garden to fetch these vegetables, expecting to find him more communicative by the time she returned. She was delayed, however, longer than she anticipated by the reprehensible greediness of a stray cow that had got in amongst the cabbages, and deemed their flavour vastly superior to that of the dusty grass on the hedges which constituted the bulk of her every-day diet,—she being the property of a poor man who did not consider that the not owning a rood[1]of land of his own was any drawback to keeping one or two animals to subsist, as they could, upon road-side pickings and incursions into the domains of richer neighbours. The cow in question highly approved of her newly-found quarters in the cabbage bed, and had a decided objection to quitting them. Consequently it was a matter of extreme difficulty to induce her to perceive the situation of the garden gate; and when, at last, Ann had conquered this pertinacious obtuseness, procured the things she wanted, and got back to the house, she found that her husband was no longer there. Supposing that he would soon be back, she went on with her cooking for him; and as he had not yet made his appearance when dinner-time came, the meat and vegetables were put in the oven to keep hot, and she and the children dined contentedly upon what was their customary midday fare when he was not with them, i.e., tea without milk, and backstone[2] bread and butter. In vain, however, did she expect his return; for the afternoon and evening wore on, and still he did not appear.

Meanwhile inquiries that were made at the colliery where he worked, had revealed the damaging fact that he had not been there at all for the last day and a half. Where, then, was he whilst the burglary was taking place, since he had not been either at his own home nor yet at his work at that time? Again was he sought for at his cottage; but neither there nor elsewhere was he to be found, and public opinion felt itself greatly confirmed in the suspicions which it had already begun to entertain concerning him. Why should he keep out of the way so carefully, if he was not troubled by a guilty conscience? Everyone agreed that he ought to be brought to trial; so a warrant was issued for his arrest, and he was hunted for far and near, whilst all other investigations relating to the robbery grew slack in consequence of the strong feeling that prevailed that he, and none other, must undoubtedly be the criminal.

For nearly a fortnight he remained undiscovered; and then he was at length found, solacing his retirement in orgies with low and disreputable companions in some of the worst slums of Cwm-Eithin. His capture created the greatest possible excitement; and when he was brought before the magistrates for examination, he was so much the hero of the hour, that the local newspapers thought it worth while carefully to chronicle even the smallest details about his personal appearance for the benefit of their readers, who found themselves accurately informed about such things as the colour of his hair, the number of pimples on his face, the droop of his eyelids, the twitching of his mouth, the muddiness of his complexion, the state of his clothes, etc., etc.

On being interrogated as to his proceedings during the night when the jewels had been stolen, he was unable to give a satisfactory account of himself, and had shown signs of confusion, which were fully reported and expatiated on by the Cwm-Eithin press, in big type, and went far to increase the prejudice against him that already existed.

When told what the crime was with which he was charged, he asserted his innocence of it vehemently and unhesitatingly; but the prejudice against him was none the less strong for that. For people were of opinion that no weight should be attached to the protestations of a man like Richards, who would, they said, be of course as little likely to stick at a lie as at stealing a rabbit, a hare, a pheasant, or a set of jewellery, breaking into a house, or committing any other misdeed.

Ethel having by this time gone back to her own home was sent for post haste to see if she could identify him. This, however, she was unable to do. After being in the same room with him, looking at him carefully, and hearing him speak, she declared that it was impossible for her to give any opinion at all as to whether he was the person who had robbed her or not. He was not altogether unlike; yet he certainly did not correspond to her recollection of the burglar with sufficient exactitude for her to say positively that he was the same man. The great point of similarity lay in the loss of a finger from the right hand, in which respect Richards undoubtedly resembled the thief. As regarded height she was inclined to think that that of Richards was pretty nearly that of her assailant; but was by no means sure about it. As regarded speaking, on the contrary, she pronounced her opinion confidently that Richards' voice was quite different from the robber's. The value of this declaration in Richards' favour was, however, considerably lessened by the impression which she had always had, and which was well known to everyone, as to the burglar's having disguised his voice and not spoken naturally. Richards himself appealed to the fact of none of her property being found in his possession as a proof of his innocence; but then there was but little weight to be attached to that, when it was remembered that ample time for concealing the things had elapsed since the robbery. The upshot of the examination before the magistrate, therefore, was that Richard Richards was committed for trial at the next criminal assizes on a charge of theft and burglary at Llwyn-yr-Allt; and that his guilt was generally considered throughout the neighbourhood to be almost an established fact.

CHAPTER II
The Trial

In situating Trevor Owen at Llwyn-yr-Allt at the time when the burglary occurred, and giving him a share in the very earliest investigations that took place relating to it, fortune had afforded him an opening of which he was not slow to avail himself. The robbery served as a peg whereon to hang many more communications with Miss Carton than would have been otherwise possible; and the activity, zeal, and interest which he displayed in the affair were no bad methods of ingratiating himself with the person most nearly concerned in it.

Of course it is not to be supposed that he was so injudicious as ever to vaunt his legal skill openly to her, or to say anything to make apparent the anxiety to secure a heavy brief by which he was actuated. Oh dear no! There was nothing of that kind to be seen; only he couldn't help taking an uncommon interest in the case, both in his professional capacity, and also as having happened to be on the spot just when the robbery took place. Then, too, as a friend of the sufferer, he was still further interested in it, and was only too happy to give Miss Carton any assistance and advice in his power.

Thus he had a very plausible excuse to account for the way in which he busied himself in the matter. But though he never told her plainly that she could not possibly do better than allow herself to be represented at the assizes by so clever a barrister as himself, none the less did he contrive imperceptibly to instil the idea into her mind, and to imbue her with a considerable amount of belief in his legal talents and acumen.

'I rather think I should like to have Mr Owen employed for us in this business,' said she, in talking the matter over with Lady Elise. 'It seems as if it must be an advantage to me to have a lawyer who was there from the very beginning—knows exactly what the house is like, and where the rooms are, and when we got home from the ball, and what o'clock the robbery first became known, and what immediate steps were taken, and generally all about everything. You see, when a barrister *knows*, to start with, what details are trivial, there's no danger of his wasting misdirected energies upon them (as is constantly being done in trials), under the impression that perhaps they're going to turn out of great importance. And I should think that whatever a man knows by his own eyes and ears, he *must* take in and understand better than if it had been got at through the eyes and ears of, perhaps, stupid and reluctant witnesses. Mr Owen seems to have plenty of wits, too; and altogether I don't think we could do better than have him—do you? '

Lady Elise had quickly detected that Trevor was concerning himself in the burglary from interested motives, and had been watching his progress anxiously, that she might know how to shape her own course regarding him. She had fully made up her mind that marriage was the object he had in view, and was prepared to favour or oppose that object according as he seemed likely or not to be ultimately successful. If possible, she would have liked for Ethel neither to marry nor yet to have any intimate friend except herself, so that there might be no one to share with her the benefits that would accrue naturally to whoever should be the constant companion of so much wealth. But she knew well enough the absurdity of hoping for such an exclusive possession as that of the gold mine which she desired to profit by, and so was ready to pay early court to anyone who appeared likely to become eventually its proprietor.

If, then, Ethel regarded Mr Owen with total indifference, it might be advisable to take every opportunity of speaking ill-naturedly of him, and endeavouring to break off all further connection between them. Supposing, on the other hand, that her affections were beginning to be seriously engaged, then it would be very impolitic to say a word against him. For, even if Ethel did not resent it herself, yet she would probably repeat it to him sooner or later, and then he would be offended; and so it might lead to Lady Elise's being looked upon with disfavour by one in whose good graces she might desire to stand. Or, as she put it to herself, 'not for anything in the world would she wish to be on bad terms with the husband of her dearest Ethel.'

At the present moment Lady Elise was completely in the dark as to how much of an impression Trevor's attentions had succeeded in producing upon the heiress, and inwardly sighed over the impossibility of ever discovering whether 'her dearest Ethel' really cared for anyone or not. Under the circumstances, therefore, she thought it safest to give a diplomatic reply, which would not commit her either for or against him.

'My dearest Ethel, what's the use of asking poor *me* about a legal matter like that?' she exclaimed. 'I should be afraid to give an opinion that would necessarily be as worthless as mine is. Of course, I'm like all women, who always think that a man who's a good dancer, and a personal friend, must inevitably be preferable to anyone else for *any* employment. But what does Mr Carton say to it? I suppose it's he that'll have to settle it, won't he – he's your guardian, and all that.'

'Yes; but I've not mentioned it to him as yet,' answered Ethel. 'I think I'll go and see if he's in now, and if so, make the suggestion to him at once. The worst of it is, that he's so wrapped up just at present in that wonderful electrical copying machine he's concocting, that he can hardly give his mind to anything else; and it's quite as likely as not that I sha'n't get an opinion at all out of him, one way or other. However, I can but try.'

And, so saying, she took herself off to her uncle's room to see if he was there, which astonishing promptitude of action on the part of the habitually indolent heiress, made Lady Elise open her eyes wide, and think that Mr Owen must really have succeeded in producing an impression on Ethel's hitherto obdurate heart.

Ethel's uncle, Percival Carton, was a person whose natural tastes had adapted him far more to be a college professor than the owner of a large property. Science of all kinds was his hobby. He took the keenest interest in everything connected with it; had more than once composed and read at the meetings of learned societies papers which had attracted a good deal of attention; and spent almost all his leisure in trying to find new methods of utilising recent scientific discoveries, by applying them to the ordinary wants of domestic life. Nothing gave him greater pleasure than to succeed in an attempt of this kind; and the sort of life he would have preferred to lead, would have been one passed entirely amongst the studies and experiments in which he delighted. But he fully recognised the fact that Percival Carton of Carton had an active part to play in the world—a place which he was bound to fill, estates and affairs for which he was responsible, and whose management he ought not to delegate to other people; and that, therefore, he was not at liberty to seclude himself in his study and devote himself solely to whatever happened to amuse him most. He was too conscientious to wish to shirk the duties of his position, and strove faithfully to discharge them, however uncongenial they might be. But, notwithstanding his virtue and high sense of duty, it cannot be denied that 'business' was to his mind the most odious word, and the one he most dreaded hearing, out of all that the English language contains. Now and then his patience would give way, and he would indulge in a whimsical grumble to Ethel after this fashion:—'It's really too bad!

Whenever I'm particularly happily engaged, some one or other is sure to come bothering to see me "on business." And then when I've disturbed myself to see what the business may be, it invariably resolves itself into the same old story—money—some one wants money, takes it for granted that I shall give it, and is quite aggrieved if I don't. Upon my word I sometimes think people must believe I was put into the world for the sole purpose of signing cheques! Just to write my name below cheques, and nothing else! What a magnificently elevated idea of a person's destiny, isn't it?' But when he had worked himself up as far as this he would suddenly bethink him of the similarity of his niece's position to his own, and the importance of encouraging business-like ways of thinking in her young mind, and would therefore wind up with a homily upon the duty of finding out, before signing any cheque, that the purpose to which it was to be applied, whether to pay a bill or be given in charity, was a legitimate and proper one; from whence was readily to be deduced the wholesome moral, that even the apparently mechanical and unreasoning action of cheque-signing was not so easy to do as it seemed, since it evidently could not be performed aright unless both brain and understanding had first been brought to bear upon it, in order to acquire that knowledge which ought to be regarded as an indispensable preliminary.

He had for the last several weeks been busily engaged in endeavouring to carry out an idea that had occurred to him as to the construction of a new copying machine. Its motive power was to be electricity, by means of which a person writing with one particular pen, should be able simultaneously to set going a number of other pens which would exactly follow the motions of the one held by the writer, so that innumerable facsimiles might thus be produced of any letter, piece of music, or other writing, with no more labour than was required to make a single original. But he found considerable difficulty in executing his idea in a practical, working form, and was in all the agonies of invention when Ethel came to consult him as to the expediency of employing Mr Owen as her counsel.

Mr Carton had spoilt his niece all his life, and never thought of complaining of her for disturbing him, whatever he might be about. But when he heard what had brought her to see him on the present occasion, he could not refrain from a gentle sigh at having been interrupted in a crisis of his calculations for such an inadequate cause as to settle what barrister should be engaged about the burglary case. What did he know about one barrister more than another? And besides, was not the matter one for his solicitors to settle?

'Owen! Owen!' he repeated absently. 'Who's he? What! That young fellow who lunched here yesterday, is it? Oh yes! I know who you mean now; he's been here several times lately, hasn't he? His father, Lord Llyn, was at Eton with me. What a muff he was, to be sure. He and I did some chemistry together once, and you wouldn't believe what a bother it was to make him recollect that a chlor*ate* and a chlor*ide* weren't the same thing. However, of course, it doesn't follow that this young man must be a muff because his father was. He looks sharp enough, at any rate. But we've nothing to do with appointing our own counsel, you know; the solicitors settle all that, and choose whom they like. They know much more about it than you and I do, of course. Perhaps, if we were to interfere, they might set their backs up, and say they wouldn't be dictated to by their clients. Much better leave it all to them.'

Ethel was perfectly aware that when her uncle spoke like this, she had only to affect to give way to him at once, in order to ensure his prompt consent to whatever she desired. Therefore she answered, as though agreeing with him entirely,—

'Oh yes then, certainly, Uncle Percival. I wouldn't be guilty of a breach of etiquette in the matter on any account. I'd only fancied that perhaps we might have dropped a hint as to liking Mr Owen to be retained on our side without giving any offence to the solicitors; but I quite see now that it'll be better not to say a word about it, as you say.'

Mr Carton was completely mollified by this ready deference to his judgment, and his thoughts had already begun to revert to the beloved copying machine, from which they only had been diverted by this trivial matter of detail.

'Oh! Well, I didn't quite mean to speak so strongly as that,' he returned. 'Do just as you like about it; there can't be any great harm after all in letting them know there's a man we should rather like to have engaged. I'll leave you to please yourself about it. You can send them a line if you wish, you know. Anything else you want me for?'

Ethel answered in the negative, and withdrew from his room; whereupon he speedily became again absorbed in nice calculations relating to the machine he hoped to invent, and thought no more of the interruption from which he had suffered, or of its cause. And thus it came about that Ethel quietly got her own way (as she generally did do), and that Mr Carton's solicitors received an intimation which resulted in Trevor Owen's having the much-coveted brief to appear for the heiress in the great burglary case which was to be tried at the forthcoming assizes at Cwm-Eithin.

It was no wonder that he should have rejoiced greatly upon receiving this brief, for the case had been sensational enough to attract a good deal of attention, and was as favourable an opportunity as could be desired by a young barrister who was anxious to bring himself to the notice of the public in general, and attorneys in particular. Trevor knew this well, and when the trial came off he devoted all his energies to endeavouring to acquit himself so as to produce a favourable impression, first upon Miss Carton, secondly, upon the attorneys, and thirdly, upon spectators who might possibly become clients at some future time. The result was that he did not do at all badly in any respect, and certainly succeeded in advertising himself fully, though it cannot be denied that his anxiety to ingratiate himself with the heiress caused him to bestow more time and care upon belauding her conduct in the encounter with the robber, than was necessary from a strictly professional point of view.

As he described graphically what had taken place and warmed to his subject, he managed to magnify her into a heroine little short of Joan of Arc, Bradamante[1], or any other female paragon of chivalry, either historical or fictitious. So glowing, indeed, were the colours in which he depicted her, that *The Times*—it being a dull time of year, and subjects to write about somewhat scarce—took her as the text for a leading article upon pluck and cool courage regarded as inseparable attributes of the British people.

That these two things and all the other inestimable qualities involved in their possession, said the article, were markedly characteristic of every Briton, was evidently a lesson to be deduced from the burglary that had occurred recently in the neighbourhood of Cwm-Eithin. There it had been shown how even our women, high-born and lapped in luxury though they might be, could be confidently relied on not to shrink like cowards in the presence of danger, but to comport themselves with an undaunted calmness of which no bronzed and scarred veteran need have been ashamed. And surely, therefore, we might with justice congratulate ourselves upon being a nation that need never dread loss or diminution of supremacy amongst other nations whilst our national backbone continued as stiff and unflinching as it was at present.

Of this and much more to the same purpose was the article composed, and was very widely read and approved of, notwithstanding a paragraph, sneering at it as pompous and gushing, which appeared in next day's *Pall Mall Gazette*. But *The Times* article was the more popular of the two. For when we read that good qualities are so inherent in our race as to make it well-nigh impossible for any member of it to be destitute of them, we naturally receive the statement as a personal compliment, and experience a thrill of proud gratification which is a very pleasurable sensation. And every editor of discrimination bears this fact in mind, and knows better than to be niggardly of articles tending to the national glorification, which will put his readers into a good humour with themselves.

Thus Ethel, to her surprise, suddenly found herself elevated by means of her counsel's eloquence into a sort of heroine whom the country was called upon to admire and feel proud of. It was a situation which she had neither anticipated nor desired, and would greatly have preferred avoiding if possible. But she was thrust into it so unexpectedly that she had no option in the matter, and was obliged placidly to accept the homage which she had no power of refusing. It amused her, however, to have thus discovered, by personal experience, how extremely simple a matter it might be to achieve celebrity; since, in her case, she knew that it had been attained solely by that policy of masterly inaction of which she was so fond, and which had been her guide in her adventure with the burglar. And what could possibly be more simple than to do nothing at all?

Richards was defended by a barrister named Herbert, who commenced by stating that the prisoner was most certainly innocent of the crime whereof he was accused, for the very excellent reason that, during the whole of the night when it had been committed, he had been at a place miles away from Llwyn-yr-Allt. Mr Herbert regretted to be obliged to add, that the pursuit in which Richards had been then engaged was not exactly a legitimate one, seeing that it had been nothing less than a nefarious appropriation of sundry hares and rabbits. The consciousness of the illegality of his occupation had been the cause why Richards had concealed himself when he heard that he was being inquired after, and had also been, at first, unwilling to say where he had been on the night in question; and it was not till he had fully realised how much more serious a charge than poaching had been brought against him, that he had confessed to the unlawful expedition just mentioned.

Here a juror inquired if there were any witnesses who could prove the truth of this statement? To which Mr Herbert replied that unfortunately there were not, as the poaching excursion had been a solitary one. From this he proceeded to attack the evidence that had been brought against the accused, insisting, strenuously, that it was totally insufficient to justify any jury in bringing in a verdict of guilty. Because a man did not happen to have witnesses who could prove exactly where he had been at any given hour, was that a reason for suspecting him of whatever crime might chance to be committed at that particular hour? Would the jury like to have such a rule as that applied to themselves, and their own families? Then, as regarded the lost finger, on which so much stress had been laid, let them remember what numbers of soldiers, sailors, and others had been thus maimed in the service of their Queen and country. Was each one of these men, merely on account of his wounds— wounds which he felt he might safely call glorious wounds—to be held guilty of having robbed Miss Carton unless he should be able to prove the contrary ? Surely not! What justice, then, was there in singling out one unfortunate individual from amongst the number of the maimed to make a victim of? If the mere loss of a finger from the right hand were to be deemed sufficient evidence of having committed the Llwyn-yr-Allt burglary, then, at least, in common fairness, prosecute all alike who were in that condition, and not one poor wretch alone!

The jury remained long in deliberation before they could come to any conclusion. Richards had said nothing about this poaching business till after he had had plenty of time to concoct any number of stories, and as there was no evidence whatever to support the statement, they thought it seemed uncommonly like a lie. Altogether, in their judgment, the circumstances looked to be very much against him; but yet, on the whole, they could not feel quite satisfied of having enough evidence to convict him on, either. So, finally, they determined to acquit him in a spirit much akin to that of the jury who brought in the well-known verdict of, 'Not guilty—but don't do it again!' And as that was the view entertained by almost every one else also, there was hardly a soul, except Richards' wife Ann, who believed the man to be innocent, notwithstanding his acquittal.

CHAPTER III
A First Ball

It is now January. The assizes are over; Miss Carton's jewels have not been recovered; no clue has been found to any better solution of their disappearance than that they were stolen by Richard Richards, who is generally supposed guilty of the crime, which it is hoped that some future evidence may eventually bring home to him. The great burglary case is still a favourite topic of conversation at all social assemblies in the vicinity of Cwm-Eithin; and a ball is about to be given at a house not far off from that town, whereat Imogen, having by this time reached the age of seventeen, is to make her first public appearance as a 'come-out' young lady.

A girl's first ball is almost invariably a source of some trepidation to her beforehand, and gives rise to considerable flutterings of anticipation, both anxious and pleasurable, in her breast. Imogen was no exception to the rule, though she strongly disapproved of the excitement which she yet could not help feeling, and strove hard to conceal it under an appearance of extreme nonchalance. She believed firmly that the young and inexperienced were held of less account than the old *habitués* in the great world she was on the verge of entering, and she did not at all mean to be looked down upon if she could help it. Besides that, the making of this decided advance towards womanhood gave her a sudden and alarming new sense of dignity, and she was prepared to fire up indignantly if she should detect even the slightest indication of any intention of patronising her, or treating her as a child, on the part of the elders, to whose ranks she was now promoted. Therefore she took the utmost pains to assume such a stately and dignified demeanour as should forbid anyone to suppose it possible for her heart to be beating an atom faster than usual in her novel situation. But it cannot be said that she was very successful in her attempt; for her expectation of keen enjoyment, just tempered by some uncertainty as to what things were going to be like, and the general state of excitement in which she was, were to be read pretty plainly in the sparkling eyes, quick, involuntary glances around, and flushed cheeks, which contrasted oddly with her efforts at dignified indifference. It was no hard matter to read her secret; and to see her shrinking from being supposed to be in a state of youth and innocence, to which most of those whom she envied and sought to resemble would have gladly returned if possible, was certainly a spectacle to amuse any cynical observer. Her condition of unwonted excitement and anxiety to conceal it, had the effect of greatly throwing out and enhancing that wonderful charm, sometimes called the *beauté du diable*[1], which is inseparable from youth in its opening bloom; and thus she was looking her very best, as, dressed entirely in white, relieved only by one or two sprays of a delicate pink flower, she entered the ball-room with her father.

Amongst the guests there assembled was Sir Charles Dover, who had returned to his own home on the day after the disastrous fritillary chase, and had not seen her since. That was more than four months ago; and in the interval she had grown and improved in appearance so considerably that, what with the alteration that had taken place in her and the different way in which she was now dressed, he did not at the first moment know who she was. Seeing her with Mr Rhys, however, helped him speedily to recognise her, and then he stood for some moments gazing at her in mingled astonishment and consternation. *That* girl Imogen Rhys? Where could his eyes have been when he saw her before? for he had certainly not had an idea that she was so pretty and so striking-looking. Was it possible that he could ever have ventured to regard that stately creature in the light of another 'fellow', and to treat her accordingly—expecting her to beat out moths for him to catch, and refusing to surrender her own net to her when she demanded it? Good heavens! What presumption, what insufferable insolence on his part! The mere recollection of it made him colour with shame and vexation, and he wondered if he had a right ever to expect to be forgiven for such fearful rudeness. Really it seemed quite doubtful; but at all events it would do no harm to go and find out how she seemed disposed towards him; so, though not without many misgivings, he went up to where she was standing, and asked if she would give him the pleasure of the next dance.

His nervousness as to how she would receive him was quite uncalled-for. She had never borne malice for his behaviour about the net, and at the present moment there was no room in her head for any recollection whatever of the matter. Eager to dance, delighted to have found a partner so quickly, particularly pleased at its being some one she already knew, with whom it would be much less formidable to make a beginning than with a total stranger, she accepted Sir Charles's invitation with an unhesitating readiness which partly reassured him. Still, however, the memory of his past misdeeds troubled his conscience sorely, and the unnatural dignity with which she was endeavouring to comport herself gave her manner a stiffness that was anything but hopeful, after the frank and evident pleasure of her first reception of him had passed away. About half of the dance was gone through without either of them uttering anything except the most frigid and uninteresting remarks about the weather, the heat of the room, the state of the floor, and similar conventional subjects. Then the young man, plucking up his courage, began to offer the apologies which he said he ought long since to have made to her for the breach of good manners of which he had been guilty on the day of the unlucky butterfly hunt, and to express the penitent horror with which he regarded his behaviour on that occasion.

She had not been thinking of the circumstance till he alluded to it; but when he did this the comical memories evoked were too much for her dignity. She seemed to see the whole scene over again,—the disputed possession of the net, the chase terminating in his ducking, his subsequent discomfiture; and the recollection made her forget her present ambition to be stately, and she laughed out loud with the fresh, joyous, pleasant laugh that was natural to her.

Near where they were standing was a gentleman, who had not yet taken the trouble to procure himself a partner, and was leaning against a wall, watching the crowd of dancers with a face wherein might be detected by a close observer occasional gleams of quiet satire at sundry of the little ball-room incidents that occurred. At the sound of Imogen's laugh he started slightly, and looked at her attentively. Surely, he thought, he had heard that laugh before; not only that, but it seemed connected in his mind with the idea of some unwonted emotion. Strange, too; for the more he looked at the girl, the more certain he felt that she was a complete stranger to him, and that he had never before set eyes upon her. But then how could he have heard her voice? That he *had* done so he was convinced; and that it had impressed itself indelibly on his memory, and had some peculiar association connected with it. But what the association was, when he had heard the voice, and why he should have remembered it so particularly, were things which he could not for the life of him recollect; and for some minutes he stood perplexed, vainly endeavouring to solve the mystery. At last, however, the memory he was searching for suddenly came back to him, and the puzzle was cleared up. After that he leant against the wall, looking on at the dancers as before; only his eyes turned more often upon Imogen than upon anyone else, and when the dance concluded he began to make his way towards Mr Rhys.

That good gentleman was by this time deep in conversation with Sir John Smith, an old crony whom he had not seen for some time, and whom he had greatly rejoiced to find at the ball. The two had quickly commenced discussing the famous burglary case, and Mr Rhys had at once stated his very decided opinion that Richard Richards was the burglar.

'Of course,' he added, 'I don't say that there was evidence enough for the jury to have convicted him—that's quite a different matter, and I don't dispute that they did all they could do. But for all that you may depend upon it he's the man; and so we'll find out some day.'

Sir John was not quite so positive.

'Do you think you will?' answered he. 'Well, I don't think it's unlikely; but I don't feel by any means *sure* of it either. You see the being short of a finger was the only thing against him that was what one would call very definite; and, as Herbert said, it would be deuced hard lines to convict a fellow upon that alone. Why, I have spoken to two men here to-night, in this room, who have each lost a finger; but that doesn't make any one suspect them of having burgled Miss Carton.'

'No, of course not,' returned Mr Rhys. 'But then look at Richards' character and position, and see how against him they are also. He's been a poacher for years, it's well known. And you don't tell me that a man who's got the habit of helping himself to other people's things at pleasure, will confine his thefts exclusively to one kind of property. It isn't likely. So I stick to my opinion as to Richards' guilt—a nice sort of neighbour for me just outside my grounds, isn't he? But, by-the-bye, which are the two fingerless men here to-night whom you mentioned?'

'One of 'em's Tompkins of the Onetieth,' replied Sir John; 'you know he got his finger shot off in Africa or India, or one of those places, fighting against some niggers or other—I forget their names. The other man is that young Sylvester who's with the Messrs Glass, and doing so wonderfully well, people say. He can't be above thirty, and brought no capital to the business; but he's altogether in Messrs Glass's confidence, I believe, and quite like one of the firm—sure to be a partner before long. Ah! Here he is coming towards us now.'

As he finished speaking, they were joined by the gentleman who had been so curiously affected by hearing Imogen's voice.

'How do you do, Sylvester?' said Mr Rhys, greeting the new-comer. 'We've just been talking about the burglary. Very little doubt in my mind as to Richards having done it—don't you agree with me?'

'Indeed I do,' answered Sylvester, 'and so do most other people too, I fancy, for one hardly ever hears a contrary opinion, go where one will. If the police don't relax their vigilance because of the acquittal, but go on watching him steadily, the chances are that they succeed in bringing it home to him sooner or later.'

'Very true,' returned Mr Rhys—'very true indeed! And then, perhaps, I shall get the fellow out of that house where he lives—just under my nose, as I may say. I must speak to my brother magistrates, and see that the police keep their eye on him, eh?'

'You can't do better, I should say,' replied Sylvester. 'I had an opportunity of doing something in that way myself a few nights ago, when I met some of the authorities at dinner, and this affair was talked about. I said all I could about the danger of the attention of the police being taken off upon false scents; and I hope my words may have done some good. But, Mr Rhys, my object in coming to you now is to ask you to introduce me to your daughter. She was away when I was staying at Llwyn-yr-Allt, so I have not yet had the pleasure of making her acquaintance.'

'Oh yes, I'll introduce you to her with pleasure,' was the answer. 'She's sure to be back soon now the dance is over. I see her coming this way now.'

The ceremony of introduction between Imogen and Mr Sylvester was soon performed, and then Mr Rhys returned complacently to his conversation with Sir John Smith.

'I like to know who Imogen's dancing with,' observed Mr Rhys, 'for fear else she might have some partner whom I shouldn't approve of. It's her first ball to-night, and of course she hardly knows anyone yet. My sister Sophia offered to come here with her and chaperon her instead of me, but I thought I'd better do it *myself*. You see it's never *quite* the same thing to a girl if she doesn't go out with her own parents; no one else is so sure to look after her sharply, and take so much trouble about her as they do. And it would be such a nuisance to have one's daughter make any disreputable acquaintances! Well, Imogen seems all right for the present, and doesn't require any more looking after just now, so come and sit down, Smith. I want to tell you about a poor-law case which bothered our union lately so that they begged me to come and help them decide it, though I don't generally go in for that sort of thing, or attend the meetings of guardians. But it seems to me a most exceptional case, and I should like to hear your views about it.'

So he and his crony were soon immersed in the intricacies of the poor-law, whilst Imogen was whirling around the room with Mr Sylvester. His capabilities as a partner were undeniable, and she found valsing with him gave her a fresh insight into the poetry which it is possible to find in motion. Apparently he found her as satisfactory a partner as she did him, for, instead of taking her back to her father when the dance was over, he took her to have some coffee, and managed to keep her in the tea-room till the next dance commenced. Finding she was not engaged for it, he asked her to dance it with him, which she was very ready to do, being delighted to have found so good a partner. At the end of the dance he took her for a turn in the passages and conservatory, loitering about outside till another dance had commenced; and then, by repeating the former process, he managed to secure a third dance in succession.

This monopoly of her was observed with extreme disfavour by Sir Charles Dover, who wanted to dance again with her himself, and hung about near where her father had established himself, watching for her to return, and fretting and fuming that she did not do so. It seemed quite extraordinary to Sir Charles that she hadn't got tired by now of that fellow who was sticking to her so pertinaciously. Perhaps he knew something about that wretched 'bug hunting' that she was so fond of, and that was what made her go on talking to him and dancing with him so long. But, anyhow, it was really very odd of her father not to insist on her coming back to him after every dance. Most girls were expected to do it, Sir Charles knew; and though he thought the rule quite a needless one in many cases, still, with a girl just out, and a partner she'd never set eyes on before—in short, with things exactly as they then were—he was quite convinced that the rule ought to be strictly enforced. If it had been *he* that had been Imogen's partner, it would have been quite a different matter; but then *he* had met her before, been staying in the house with her, and was altogether a different person. In his impatience he made one or two attempts to give Mr Rhys a hint that he was neglecting his duties as a chaperon. But it was to no purpose. The poor-law argument had become more and more interesting in the process of being detailed and explained to Sir John Smith, and Mr Rhys had quite forgotten the need of bestowing any particular care upon looking after a young and utterly inexperienced girl at her first ball.

'Where's Imogen, did you say?' he returned, in answer to Sir Charles's inquiries. 'Oh, she's dancing with someone or other— was here just now—be back again directly, I daresay. — Well, to return to what I was telling you, Smith, about that pauper receiving out-door relief,' etc., etc., and thus he chatted away contentedly, while poor Sir Charles alternately inwardly anathematised Sylvester, and wished that entomology had been included in his own education, in order that he might have been thoroughly well qualified to make himself agreeable to Imogen.

It was not until the small hours of the morning that Imogen got home from the ball, and had leisure to look back upon the events of the night. When she did so, she at once came to the conclusion that she had never before had such a thoroughly jolly evening in all her life. It was even better fun than the best night's mothing she had ever had. She had had no idea that balls were so delicious. If they were all like this first experience of them, she was quite sure she would like to go to one every night regularly. Everything had been delightful from beginning to end; she had danced every dance, and not had a single bad partner for the rounds. Then came the question of which partner had been the best. Well, on the whole, it was Mr Sylvester; and somehow, in reviewing all that had taken place, he figured more prominently than anyone else in her thoughts. Certainly he had made himself very agreeable to her. Yet, still, now that she came to think quietly over all that had passed, was she *quite* sure of that? One or two of the things he had said seemed capable of two interpretations, and might have been intended either in a complimentary or a sarcastic sense by the speaker. She had never noticed the possible *double-entendre* at the time, and had taken them all in perfect good faith. But as she remembered them now, she suddenly perceived the possibility that she might have been placidly allowing a sneering, supercilious stranger to play with her, and amuse himself by patronising and laughing at her under pretence of paying her compliments. The mere idea of such a thing made her furious. She only wished she had suspected it sooner, and she would soon have shown that she wasn't going to stand being made fun of, and condescended to more than anyone else, now that she was come out, and could associate as a matter of right with the grown-ups! It was all the fault of that ridiculous youth and inexperience of hers which had prevented her from seeing what he meant directly, as anyone else would have done, and replying to it properly.

But presently her vehement wrath cooled down again, as her good sense showed her that perhaps, after all, there might not really be anything for her to be offended at, and that there might be some danger of her extreme horror of being thought childish making her over-sensitive. It was absurd to take offence where none was intended; and, after all, whatever he had said might quite likely have been meant in earnest, and been really as nice and pleasant as it had seemed at the time. Of course it would be intolerable to think she had been played with and treated like a child. But then, if he hadn't done it—why, then there was no use in worrying herself about it as if he had!

One thing she was quite sure of, at any rate, and that was that she had certainly never before met anyone who was at all like this Mr Sylvester, and that she would have been very much puzzled to have to pronounce an opinion upon him. She did not quite know whether to call him likeable or unlikeable. Now and again, even when he was making himself most agreeable, he had given her a momentary impression that was strange and unpleasant—an impression of being enigmatical, hard, impenetrable, self-contained, and somehow something she didn't like. She could fancy him to be clever, strong, and a man whom it would be easier to be afraid, than fond of. Yet there was no doubt that she had thought him charming most of the time; and then he certainly did dance exquisitely! She wondered what

Ralph would have thought of him. Ralph generally liked jolly people—and jolly was a term that certainly didn't seem as if it ever could be applicable to Mr Sylvester.

And then she thought no more about him, but said her prayers, got into bed, and went happily to sleep, and enjoyed delightful dreams of mothing with Ralph, and catching huge and marvellous moths to the sound of enchanting dance music.

CHAPTER IV
A Gentleman Burglar

That a man should be a gentleman, and yet stoop to commit burglary, will, doubtless, seem to many people an absurd and impossible idea. Yet, since there have been known gentlemen swindlers, gentlemen murderers, and gentlemen card-cheats in real life, it can scarcely be considered an unwarrantable stretch of imagination for a novelist to suppose it possible also for such a person as a gentleman burglar to exist—more especially when he is not represented as making burglary a profession, but only as having resorted to it on an exceptional occasion, and under great stress of circumstances. And with this justification of our hardihood in having ventured to introduce such a character, we proceed to bring before the notice of our readers the man who was really guilty of the robbery of Miss Carton's jewels, and who, nevertheless, stood high in the world's opinion, and was trusted implicitly by his employers. It was none other than the William Sylvester to whom Mr Rhys had so unhesitatingly introduced his daughter, and who had pronounced so confident an opinion as to the culpability of another man in the matter of the burglary that he had himself committed. Destitute of principles as he evidently is, a glance at his past history may do something to account for his present condition of depravity.

His father had been an officer in the army, of good birth, poor, and wild, who had fallen in love with a young lady at school, and persuaded her to make a runaway match with him. In doing this she mortally offended all her own family, who agreed to ignore her from that time forth as though she had never existed. Within a year and a-half after marriage she died, leaving a boy, William, only six months old, to the care of a selfish, indifferent father, who never gave a thought to the wants of anyone else, so long as he himself was satisfied. He regarded the child as a sort of inevitable appendage, which he could not help keeping and providing for; but when he had done that much, he considered that he had fully discharged all parental obligations, and had not the remotest intention of bothering himself as to the brat's education, or of allowing his own amusements to be interfered with on its account.

At the time of the mother's death Captain Sylvester's regiment was quartered abroad, and continued there for some years, moving about to various military stations. Thus little William's early life was spent in knocking about from one foreign town to another in charge of a wide variety of nursemaids—usually all of indifferent character—without any particular care or training being bestowed upon him; and in that process he learnt to be self-reliant by dint of bitter experience, which taught him that there was no one else for him to rely upon.

Presently Captain Sylvester married again, and a stepmother appeared upon the stage of William's young life. She was a foreigner, every bit as worldly and selfish as her husband, and quite as incapable of attempting to befriend or understand any creature that was not necessary to her in order to contribute in some way or other to her gratifications. She had no objection to her stepson as long as he kept out of her way and did not interfere with her; but otherwise—woe betide him!

Not long after this second marriage his father died, and during the time that the widow wore her weeds she allowed the boy to remain under her nominal care as before, because that was less trouble than taking any active steps to get rid of him. But it was different when, as soon happened, she took to herself another husband. Then the unnecessary boy in the house became an encumbrance and a nuisance to her, which she determined not to tolerate any longer; so she communicated with his father's family, asking what was to be done with this boy for whom she declined to be further responsible. The reply was that she had better send him to a school in England, and the address of the school recommended was given; thither she at once despatched him, and thus washed her hands of him for the future.

At school he spent the next years of his life almost exclusively. Nobody wanted the bother of a strange boy coming into their homes, so when holidays came, and other boys went away, it was always arranged for him to stay on at school, or else to go abroad with some master who might be meditating a foreign trip and glad of a companion so well versed in foreign languages, manners, and customs as was William Sylvester. He certainly did well at school. Resolute, clever, fearless, unscrupulous, and rarely failing in anything he undertook, he seemed to have an aptitude for success, which was little short of marvellous in the eyes of those who failed to perceive the force of his character. Whatever he wanted, that he would get; wherever he might be, his individuality was sure to predominate over and dwarf down that of others; whatever opposition he met with, he would infallibly crush it down by some means or other; and he had never been known to make an intimate friend of anyone, though he was on civil, and apparently amiable terms with most people. Such was the opinion entertained about him by his companions when his school days were over, and he was entering upon manhood. And when the desultory and neglected nature of his bringing-up is taken into consideration, will it not go far to account for much moral obliquity of character?

Left continually, from earliest childhood, to his own resources, to knock about hither and thither as he pleased, and do the best he could for himself provided he did not get in other people's way, it was but natural that he should have soon grown accustomed to depend only upon himself.

The people with whom he had had most to do, and to whom had been directed the instinctive admiration and veneration felt by a very young child for the men and women with whom it lives—these people had been hard, selfish, and worldly; and he had dwelt with them and become imbued with their spirit, till he had grown like unto them. Affection he had never experienced. His mother had died when he was too young to remember her, and since her death there had never been any one to love him and whom he might have loved in return. He had no near and dear relations belonging to him as he saw that most other people had, and he had long ago realised that he stood alone in the world—that there was no one he could trust to except himself, and that if he hoped to succeed in life, it was to himself and none other that he must look for the means of that success.

Just about the time he was leaving school, and when the relations who had put him there were wondering what was to be done with him next, it happened that an opening came to one of them for placing a young man in the great business house of Messrs Glass. This opening having been offered to and rejected by the son of the relation in question, was passed on to young Sylvester, by whom it was willingly accepted. Having thus got his foot upon the ladder, he proceeded at once to make the most of his opportunities, and rose with extraordinary rapidity to the confidential position which he now occupied in his employers' concerns. By what means he had risen, whether always fair or not, is a matter which need not be inquired into too closely here—at all events, he *had* risen, and that fact is quite sufficient for present purposes.

Notwithstanding the swift rate at which he was advancing towards fortune, his progress was still not fast enough to content his ambition; and consequently he was continually dabbling in speculations whenever he thought he saw a likely chance of making money. He loved the excitement attending these ventures, and the greater the risk the more fascinating he found them; but he was careful to keep them as strictly secret as possible, lest they should become known to the Messrs Glass, by whom he knew they would be strongly disapproved of. His speculations had more than once reduced him to great straits for ready money; and when this occurred he had not hesitated to avail himself of his position of trust, in order to embezzle his employers' money and utilise it for his own purposes. At last it unluckily happened, that shortly after one of these surreptitious withdrawals of funds belonging to Messrs Glass, a sudden and totally unforeseen occurrence made it necessary for him either to restore what he had taken sooner than he had expected to have to do so, or else to face inevitable detection of his peculations. Many thousand pounds were required to replace the deficiency in the accounts, and unless he could procure the money by a certain early date, he knew that he must be found out. He racked his brains to see if there was anyone else who could be made to appear guilty of the embezzlement instead of him—but to no purpose; circumstances had so fallen out, that if the crime were discovered the blame of it would unavoidably fall entirely upon his own shoulders. He had no option but to restore in time the large sum he had appropriated, or else be ruined.

Where was the money to come from? He had no rich friend to apply to. Money-lenders would not lend to a man who had no security to offer; or if they did, it would be only at the most exorbitant rate of interest, and besides, he knew that his prospects with his present masters would be at an end if they should hear of him as having had recourse to the Jews. Just when he was in this dilemma he happened to be with some people who mentioned that Miss Carton was going to stay at Llwyn-yr-Allt for the forthcoming grand function at Cwm-Eithin, and then they went on to talk about her famous jewellery, and to speculate as to its immense value. As he listened to their idle gossip the idea suddenly flashed upon his brain that if he could possess himself of this treasure he would be saved. Why should he not do it? He could find his way about in Llwyn-yr-Allt perfectly, for he had been visiting there, and his memory was singularly retentive for any place that he had once stayed at; therefore when he should have got into the house he would have no difficulty if he knew which room she slept in; and he anticipated little trouble in finding out that through some servant. Never having met the heiress he was personally unknown to her, and there was no danger that she would recognise him; besides, he would disguise himself thoroughly. He was fond of acting, and had a considerable turn for it; why should he not now turn this talent to account, get up a little comedy of his own, play the part of a burglar, and carry off jewels that were not the mere stage shams that usually figure at theatricals, but genuine, costly, and (to him) salvation-bringing precious stones? The risk and novelty of the proposed comedy, and the possibility of its turning at any moment into tragedy, made it all the more attractive and exciting to him. The more he reflected upon it the more feasible it appeared, and finally he put the scheme into execution in the manner that has been already shown.

He had previously asked his employers for, and been granted, a week's leave of absence; as soon as he had secured the jewels he went abroad without a moment's delay, and there managed the breaking up and sale of his spoils,—a business which he transacted by aid of certain low and infamous foreign jewellers, of whom he had already some knowledge. Then, returning home in triumph with the sum he required, he paid back the loan that had been borrowed without leave, before any one had detected that there was anything missing. But it had been a nearer shave than was altogether pleasant, and he had been only just in time to save his credit.

He had been quite delighted to find another person accused of the burglary. The precautions he had taken made it impossible, as he believed, that he himself could ever be suspected of it; but, of course, the more false scents there were the better; and when people felt convinced that the real criminal was safe in prison, they were naturally apt to discontinue searching for him elsewhere. Sylvester had no principles of morality to prevent him from hoping earnestly that the accused would be pronounced guilty by the jury; and it would have given him complete satisfaction, unalloyed by a single twinge of pity or remorse, to know that the crime he had committed was being expiated by an innocent man. Provided the law got hold of some one to punish, then Sylvester knew that it would be quieted; and all he cared for was, that the victim should not be himself. Therefore he had been greatly disappointed at the acquittal of Richard Richards. Still, it was satisfactory to see what an intensely strong feeling still prevailed against the man; and never did Sylvester lose an opportunity of strengthening and encouraging that feeling, since it evidently conduced much to his own security.

Security! Sometimes in his solitary musings he would wonder whether, after all, absolute security was really as great a good as people in general deemed it to be—whether any state of existence so tame, monotonous, and unstimulating as the idea that was presented by these two words, could possibly be a happy and desirable one. As far as he was concerned, the sensation of absolute security was a thing which he had long ago determined to do without—indeed, he was by no means sure that he should care about it now, even if he could have it. An element of change and danger gave existence a spice that was not unwelcome; and there was nothing better adapted to develop what resources and capacities a man had in him, than the being really hard pressed—the being driven to save himself or perish. Absolute security meant dulness, too, and he hated being dull unless some very great advantage were to be gained thereby. What fun he had enjoyed out of this burglary—and did so still, for the matter of that! For what a joke it was to hear the affair discussed and speculated upon in the most ridiculous manner, by people who little dreamt that the real criminal was amongst them, and taking part gravely in their absurd conjectures! And how amusing to mix in society, and find himself respected and welcomed by those who had no more idea of his real self than an unborn baby! Good Lord! If they only did know him as he was, what a fearfully black sheep he would be considered! How promptly they would expel him— what a commotion would take place — how tremendously shocked they would be!

Yet what right had they to be shocked—or to pretend to be so? People had been fools enough to set up an absurd standard, and to choose to assume that everyone lived according to it. But what rubbish that was! It was clearly the right of each man to live his life in any way that seemed good in his own eyes—and it was nonsense to try and interfere with that right. Obviously the wisest course of action that was open to a human being, was to prey upon his fellow-creatures to whatever extent their folly might allow him to do so. Therefore why affect surprise when any one did this? One man's chance was as good as another's, provided that his brains were equally good. And supposing that they were *not*, then that was an unavoidable, inborn defect to which he must resign himself; in that case he must make up his mind always to come off second-best in the world, just as much as though he had gone into a battle suffering from blindness, deafness, lameness, or other bodily deficiency.

Of course Sylvester knew something of what he termed contemptuously 'the rotten old conventional ideas' about religion, morality, etc.; but they had made little or no impression upon him apparently, and he reflected complacently that all such stuff had soon been knocked out of his head by the rough process of making his way in the world. He was aware that some people professed to believe in these ideas as being true; but to his mind such people must either be fools who believed what they did not understand, or else liars who did not really believe what they said they did. In either case their professed belief was a thing with which he had nothing to do—a parcel of rubbish about which he never troubled his head. The sole standard of duty he recognised was to advance his own interests under all circumstances. And it seemed, too, to him, that even supposing it possible for there to be any truth in that absurd theory of some future state of existence following when the present one is ended, then whoever had done well by himself in this life, would stand a very good chance of doing ditto in the next also; since he would have acquired an invaluable habit of self-advancement which he would never lose as long as his individuality was unchanged, and which must certainly prove useful to him wherever he might be. The best possible maxim to live by was, take care of number one; and if a man did that thoroughly he would never be guilty of the foolish weakness of troubling himself about whether other people went to the wall or not. Consideration for others, and all that sort of thing, was sentimental bosh; and it was an article that he neither wanted, nor yet would give. His own hands should keep his own head; and let other men look out for *them*selves as he was prepared to look out for *him*self.

And with this exposition of the sentiment and principles of action, grim rather than amiable, of our gentleman burglar, we will close this chapter.

CHAPTER V
A Sunday Call

Wrapped up in a coat-of-mail of selfishness; untouched by the softer, more elevated emotions of human nature; secretly setting at nought and despising all recognised standards of morality, Sylvester now gloried in his own hardness, and superiority to what he deemed the common weaknesses of humanity. Yet he had not always been so; and there had been a time, long years ago, when he would have shrunk with horror from such a person as was his present evil self. That had been when he was a little, lonely fellow, before yet his training had had time to harden him altogether, and when he was still childishly innocent enough to be credulous. It was but very seldom that anything of religion or goodness had been mingled in the instructions of his neglected childhood; yet still, now and then from some nursemaid or chance person there had fallen a stray scrap of better teaching, which had at the time been readily accepted by him as true, and believed in implicitly.

In some inexplicable way the recollection of those early, innocent days had been brought back to him suddenly and forcibly by Imogen's voice and laugh, as he had heard it whilst hiding outside the window through which she had just emerged, on that night when he had stolen Miss Carton's jewels. For a moment there had rushed over his soul a wave of strange, wistful yearning that seemed about to suffocate all other emotions within him. But then it had disappeared immediately, and the subsequent stirring events had caused him to forget all about it till he happened to hear her talking and laughing at the ball with Sir Charles, just as she talked and laughed in the early dawn outside Llwyn-yr-Allt with her brother. That made him remember the extraordinary impression her voice had produced on him before, and for an instant he half thought that it was going to affect him again now in the same way. The feeling passed away, however, and he began to wonder what could have made him notice her voice more than that of anyone else, and why it should have had this odd effect upon him. It was a pleasant voice, certainly; probably the key in which it was pitched was one that chanced to be peculiarly adapted to the resonance chamber, or the auditory fibres of his ear—that would no doubt account for its having struck him so strongly.

Having got introduced to her to see what she was like, he had been much amused with her. The half-repressed excitement by which she was animated, and the three elements of childish simplicity, tomboyish love of enterprise, and innocent womanliness which were struggling for the supremacy within her, had imparted to her conversation a quaint flavour that he found refreshing, and he had contrived to draw her out for his amusement without much difficulty. In order to do this it had been necessary to dance with her a good many times more than had seemed at all fitting in the eyes of Sir Charles. And thus it was not unnatural that when the ball was at an end, and Sylvester had returned home and settled himself comfortably in front of the fire for a last smoke before going to bed, she should have occupied a conspicuous place in his thoughts.

She certainly wasn't one of your die-away, insipid misses; and somehow there was something decidedly attractive in her—though what made her so he found it hard to say. Of course any real union of interests between two human beings was a thing both undesirable and impossible; yet had it been otherwise he really did believe that such an infliction would have been more nearly tolerable with her than with anyone else he had ever seen. The whole world, as far as he came in contact with it, was clearly intended for him to prey upon; yet if by any concatenation of circumstances he had found himself compelled to exempt some one individual from the general category of victims, and identify that person with himself as the object whereon to bestow the spoils of which he had deprived the others, then he could almost imagine himself selecting her to be the favoured exception.

It must not be supposed from all this that his thoughts were turning in the slightest degree towards matrimony. Being hampered with a wife was an idea which he had never been able to contemplate without a shudder of horror. He regarded marriage as an intense nuisance—a yoke from which he fully intended to keep clear. That people should marry for any other reason than that of advancing their interests was incomprehensible to him; even then he thought it the most distasteful of all means for attaining the desired end, and was resolved not to have recourse to it in his own person unless it should be the only road possible to success. But a little flirting was a very different affair, and he had not the least objection to enjoy himself in that way with any woman who might take his fancy. You did not commit yourself to anything in a flirtation; and directly you grew tired of the amusement you could drop it and be off again, free and unfettered as the winds.

Well! He thought on the whole he should go and call at Llwyn-yr-Allt in the course of the next day or so. And having arrived at this conclusion, and finished his tobacco, he proceeded to get into bed.

The ball had taken place on a Tuesday; and as some unexpected business, which could not be neglected, occupied him entirely during the remainder of the week, it was Sunday before he found himself at leisure to pay his proposed visit to Llwyn-yr-Allt. Having no wish to attract special attention to his proceedings by any sort of singularity, he always made it a rule to conform outwardly as far as possible to the moral code by which society chose to be governed—however much he might secretly and really set it at defiance. This habit now made him reflect upon the likelihood that he might shock prejudices if he went calling on a Sunday; and he debated with himself whether it would not be wiser to delay his visit till another day. There was another drawback about Sunday calls, too; and that was that there was always a chance of finding people gone to church—which was a bore when one wanted to see them. On the whole, perhaps it would be best to wait, and then go on some week day.

Yet for the matter of being at church, he doubted that Imogen was of a turn of mind to find church an interesting place; and the more he thought of it, the more convinced he felt that she would probably consider an attendance at the regular Sunday morning service quite enough of that sort of thing for one while, and not care to repeat the performance till another seven days should have elapsed. Then as far as offending prejudices were concerned, it was really only the most rigid of Sabbatarians who were likely to be shocked so easily; and he felt pretty sure that the Rhys family were not to be reckoned amongst that class. For, after all, there was nothing at all out of the way in paying a visit on a Sunday afternoon, provided it was done on foot. Lots of people did that unhesitatingly who would on no account have taken out horses and carriages for the purpose; and so no one could see anything remarkable in his doing the same. And thus the end of his deliberations was that he decided to go and make his call on foot.

The pedestrian part of this decision was no light sacrifice to appearances for him to make. Llwyn-yr-Allt was some distance off, and he contemplated the prospect of the long, dull walk before him with anything but satisfaction. In his stables stood his horse Crambo—an animal of whom he had good reason to be proud, since it was unusually handsome, and as perfect in qualities as in appearance; Crambo was pining for a gallop, and on Crambo's back the journey would be performed in far less time, and with far more ease and enjoyment than on his own feet. But then if he were seen riding about the country on a Sunday, there would be the danger of scandalising his employers, whom he knew to be somewhat puritanical in their ideas; or if not them, perhaps he might offend some other narrow-minded bigot, and thus risk losing that character of being a pink[1] of propriety and respectability which he now bore universally. And the less he desired to have his life looked into, the more it behoved him to be strictly circumspect in all his behaviour; so he resigned himself to the uninteresting walk, and set off.

Before he had quite reached his destination, he was disgusted to behold Mr Rhys and Imogen coming along the road towards him in attire which clearly proclaimed that they must be bound for church. Then he had had this long grind all for nothing, and would just have to grind back again without accomplishing his object, after all; how provoking!

'I was on my way to see you,' he said, after the first greetings had been interchanged; 'I was coming to inquire whether Miss Rhys had recovered from the fatigues of the ball the other night.'

'Were you, indeed?' returned Mr Rhys, hospitably; 'how unlucky! Should have been so glad to have been at home to receive you—so sorry you happen to come just as we are going to church. I tell you what! why shouldn't you come too, and then return with us when service is over? Imogen'll give you a cup of tea, if you like; won't you, Im—eh? Or if you'd prefer something better than slops after your walk, you'll only have to say so and you shall have it. Yes, yes! That'll be the best thing for you to do.'

Sylvester acquiesced willingly. The society of the person who was the object of his visit would be a compensation for the bore of going to church; so he turned back, and accompanied the Rhys's thither, looking as demure, decorous, and altogether unexceptionable a young man as anyone need desire to see.

It was a church in which there were no pews or appropriated places, so that the congregation was at liberty to sit where it pleased, and his companions went into a vacant seat, where there was room for him to follow them if he chose. This, however, he did not do. If he were where Imogen could see him, he would feel bound to make himself uncomfortable by kneeling down for the prayers, in orthodox fashion, lest he might perhaps otherwise incur her displeasure; so he established himself close behind her, where he could hear her voice when she sang, and see her without being seen in return. He watched her curiously during the service, and amused himself by speculating as to what the motive was likely to be which had brought her there for a second time in the day; for he had discovered from something she said, that she had been at the morning service also.

'Funny sort of way for a girl like her to care about spending her time,' he reflected. 'I know lots of people do it because it's *the right thing*; but, unless I'm greatly mistaken, she's not the one to trouble herself about regulating her actions by that rule as much as most do. No; I bet she's got some private reason of her own for coming here. Can't be mothing, since she wouldn't be able to hunt a moth, even if she saw it. Possibly it's the music that fetches her. Or, perhaps, it's the curate that she's after. I've a fancy to know what it is, at all events.'

By way of sounding her on this point, he thought he would criticise the service a little when it was over, and see how she took it. He had a fine opportunity for saying what he liked during the walk back to Llwyn-yr-Allt; that careful chaperon, Mr Rhys, having engaged in a delightful gossip with two

acquaintances as soon as he was outside the church door, called
to his daughter and Sylvester to go on in front, and he would
overtake them directly; and as he gossiped on happily, without
thinking of the flight of time, the other two had a good long *tête-
à-tête* without interruption.

'What childish rubbish they do put into hymns,' remarked
Sylvester. 'Did you notice that absurd bit in the last hymn we
had? I mean those lines speaking of a bodily resurrection, just as
if any one believed in all that now-a-days.'

Imogen looked at him in astonishment.

'I don't know why not,' she replied; 'it's in the Apostles'
Creed, so people who say *that*, believe in it, anyhow.'

He raised his eyebrows with an amused look.

'You don't mean to say,' said he, 'that you suppose whoever
says the Creeds believes every word of them to be true?'

His supercilious smile, and the scornful tone in which he
spoke, showed her that, if she should confess to this belief, she
would be set down in his mind as a mere ignorant, credulous
child, who knew nothing of the ways of men and women. This
would be a terrible blow to one who had just begun to become
ambitious of being considered a woman of the world, and for a
moment she was strongly tempted to deny what she really
thought, in order to save her dignity. But to be ashamed of herself
was far more undignified and humiliating than anything that
another person might think of her; and the truth was the truth,
come what might; so she answered bravely, with her head held
high, and her cheeks flushing,—

'Yes, I do. I may be a great fool for thinking so; but I do, all the
same. If people didn't mean the words, what should they say
them for, do you think?'

He had observed her closely, and succeeded in guessing part
of what had just passed through her mind; still he could not
make her out altogether.

'How can I tell?' he replied, shrugging his shoulders carelessly. 'Possibly they do it because everyone else does; or because they're used to it; or because they don't think at all about it. No doubt they are satisfied that it doesn't much matter—one way or other.'

'I don't see how they can possibly feel satisfied of that,' she returned quickly. 'A lie *always* matters, and of course it must matter most of all when it's said out solemnly in church like the Creeds are.'

It amused him to irritate her a little and see her warmth in condemning lies. Was that warmth wholly genuine, he wondered? or was it assumed for the sake of some private object of her own which he had not yet fathomed?

'You're still very uncompromising in your ideas, I see,' he said; 'at your age it's to be expected, you know. But when you get a little older you'll find that everyone isn't so very particular about being accurate as you now imagine. Take the hymn singing, for instance. You may be sure there's plenty of notions that a congregation wouldn't agree about in the hymns; but no matter for that—start any hymn you like that has a rousing, popular tune to it, and see if every soul doesn't join in it full cry without bothering about its meaning.'

'Well, I can prove that *that's* not quite so certain, at all events,' returned Imogen triumphantly, 'however young and foolish you may think me. I expect everyone else does the same as I do myself in the matter, and that is, whenever I'm singing a hymn, and come to any sentiment that I don't think I agree in, I just shut up till that bit's past. Why, I should be merely uttering a lie else – for whatever's untrue doesn't become a lie any the less if it happens to be sung instead of said.'

Was the girl a hypocrite or not? If so she acted her part of perfect simplicity with wonderful ability, and he must look upon her with increased respect and admiration for the future.

But it would not do to let his inclination to think well of her lead him to credit her with what she had no claim to. And there was a horribly honest-sounding ring about her words and manner that made him fear lest she might not be deserving of the platform of esteem to which he was prepared to elevate her—lest, after all, she might be only saying what she really thought!

Anyhow, as she chose to take the subject so much to heart, in appearance at all events, he thought he had better not dwell upon it any longer; so he adroitly turned the conversation in another direction, and applied himself to extracting so much information as to her plans and engagements as would enable him to arrange his own movements with a view to meeting her occasionally. It was not very difficult to him to draw her out, as he had already discovered at the ball, when she had responded to his efforts in that way by confiding many of her hobbies to him readily. Thus he knew her abhorrence of the popular opinion that all women ought to marry in order to find their proper sphere of life, and also had been given some idea of the grand, though vague, desires which she entertained for being useful in the world. He now easily found out which were her favourite walks and rides; when Ralph was to leave home to read for the army; what parties she was going to; that she was going to Carton House before long to pay Ethel a visit; and sundry similar pieces of information which it might, perhaps, be convenient to him to know. Amongst other things he thus learnt that Sir Charles Dover was to stay at Llwyn-yr-Allt for a couple of days' shooting in the course of the ensuing week—which announcement he received with perfect tranquillity notwithstanding that he had a shrewd suspicion of how greatly Sir Charles was smitten with Imogen. The feeling of some peculiar interest in any person or thing always endows one with a preternaturally keen nose for detecting symptoms of the same disposition on the part of anyone else; and the attraction which

she had for the baronet had been pretty evident to Sylvester on
the night of the ball. But he thought that this other man had not
much chance of making an impression upon a girl who was at
all out of the common run, as Imogen seemed to be. Personally
he did not know Sir Charles, and had never seen him at all
except at the ball. He had, however, observed him to some
extent on that occasion, and the result of that observation was
that he summed up the baronet as being a mere healthy, well-
grown, good-looking, young fellow, with nothing in him—a
youth with no brains to recommend him, and who was destitute
of any means of captivation save what might lie in the fact that
he was a finely-developed specimen of humanity—in short, the
kind of young man described by one of Mrs Oliphant's Scotch
characters as, 'just a long-leggit lad.'[2] And Sylvester would have
curled his lip contemptuously at the idea that 'just a long-leggit
lad,' was ever likely to prove a formidable rival in anything to
a man who was equally unhandicapped by bodily defects, and
who had the advantage of a good intellect to boot!

CHAPTER VI
Ethel's Unconscious Influence

It has been already mentioned that Imogen was going to stay at Carton House, and this visit came off in February.

It is no uncommon thing for a young girl to fall violently in love with one a few years older than herself, without any particularly apparent reason; and whilst the fancy lasts, its object is worshipped with romantic devotion. This passion is generally a short-lived, one-sided affair, seeming at first sight an absurd and lamentable waste of energy on the part of the worshipper. Yet let it not be condemned too hastily. A fierce flame helps to clear rust out of the grate in which it burns, even if it does nothing else; and possibly the girl's ardent attachment may have some similarly beneficial effect upon her character, and may not therefore be so altogether useless as it seems at first.

Into a passion of this kind, Imogen's admiration for Ethel had developed; and the love-sickness was just at its height at the time of her visit to Carton House. Ethel was utterly unconscious of the feeling which she had inspired, because Imogen's horror of gushing young ladies led her to eschew demonstrations of emotion, and incline rather to the opposite extreme of never appearing to care much about anyone. None the less, however, did her thoughts at this period of her existence run continually on the object of her attachment, to whom she looked up with profound reverence as to a superior being who could do no wrong. And it would delight her to imagine all kinds of possible and impossible situations wherein she might picture herself as winning Ethel's approval by some tremendous self-sacrifice, or saving Ethel from injury by some heroic act—generally involving the loss of her own life.

Under these circumstances it may be imagined that Imogen had accepted rapturously the invitation to go and spend a week at Carton House, and had looked forward to that week eagerly. But though when the time came she enjoyed her visit very well on the whole, yet still it certainly did not prove altogether the period of unmixed bliss that she had anticipated, as her pleasure was considerably interfered with by the presence of Lady Elise who was staying there also. Love usually brings jealousy in its train; and Imogen spent much of the week in alternate fits of felicity or misery according as she did or did not fancy that she could discern some marked preference for herself on the part of her idol. To have Ethel all to herself for a ride or walk, or to be chosen as her assistant in any occupation, was no doubt perfect happiness; but then that delight was liable to be succeeded by agonies of jealousy if Lady Elise Bolyn were known to have sat up talking in Ethel's room after everyone else had gone to bed, or to have been honoured with any other mark of distinguished favour.

Every house has its own traditional ways of going on, and of course in Imogen's lover-like frame of mind she was peculiarly open to be influenced by those of Carton House; for such things must necessarily be intimately associated with the place's mistress, and whatever bore the stamp of Ethel's approval was, in Imogen's eyes, at that time necessarily admirable. Amongst the Carton House manners and customs by which she was especially impressed were those which prevailed in regard to the neighbouring villagers and poor people. To exercise some kind of supervision over the district seemed to form part of the daily routine of the establishment; the wants and ailments of the poorer neighbours were discussed and provided for quite as a matter of course; and medicine-chest, advice, cellar, and kitchen were all freely at the service of the sick. From time immemorial this had been the custom at Carton House; and Ethel, who had been brought up to it, and thoroughly approved of it, had never dreamt of making any alteration.

To be thus working naturally and without effort in a right groove, was just the thing to suit her conscientious, but indolent, nature. For though she would have certainly felt uneasy if she had not known herself to be taking some steps to share her worldly advantages with other and less favoured mortals, still, it would have been a sore trial to her to think she ought to strike out a new line of her own at home, and to take upon her shoulders the responsibility of inaugurating an innovation in any way.

On Imogen's previous visits to Carton she had not taken any particular notice of this interest taken in the villagers by the big house; but in her present unwontedly impressionable condition she was struck by it all of a sudden as if it had been a quite new idea. Nothing of that kind was done at *her* home—but for all that it appeared to be an admirable thing. The more she reflected upon it, the more it commended itself to her approval. In the first place Ethel did it, which was alone a proof that it must be right and wise. But apart from that, Imogen was convinced that trying to do good to one's fellow-creatures must certainly be a highly laudable proceeding. She had often wished honestly that she had something to do that would be *real* work for the world—something that would save her from feeling as perfectly useless as she did now; and perhaps if she were to do as her cousin did, and go amongst poor people, she would thus find the gratification of her desires.

She was too shy to mention the subject to Ethel, who had not a notion of the temporary absolute power which she possessed over her young relative, and who would have been very much astonished if she had known the meditations that occupied Imogen's mind as she journeyed homewards when her visit was over, and while the influences of the week just past were working strongly within her.

She began to ask herself whether she should try her hand at going to see poor people. True, she did not feel any special inclination or qualification for the employment—but what did that matter if it was right? Then, too, Ethel did it; and she would like to do the same as Ethel. To endeavour to follow in her footsteps was to offer her a sort of homage. It was most improbable that the adored one would ever come to know of the offering of that homage, no doubt. But it would, for that very reason, be all the more a worthy tribute to pay, since it would be impossible to deny the true loyalty and sincerity of spirit which could bring an offering without looking for any return whatever—not even for so much as a word or thought of gratitude.

As these thoughts passed through her mind Imogen realised that she was in an unwontedly high-flown, exalted, and virtuous mood, and knew also that she would do well to make the most of it while it lasted. Experience had taught her that such moods were not to be reckoned on with certainty, either for duration or recurrence—(a proof of the depravity of her nature over which she had often sighed, and which had sometimes even troubled her quite seriously until some fresh idea had come into her head and made her forget it again). The matter that seemed to her of most immediate importance now, therefore, was at once to make some definite plan of action, so as to lose no time in beginning to carry out her good resolutions before they should cool down. But then came the difficulty of how to make a first start with this new task that she was thinking of setting herself—or at all events of experimenting upon. Here she felt very much at sea. She was not like Ethel who had visited amongst poor people all her life, and knew them, and their families, and all about them—even to the very names and ages of many of their children! When Ethel walked into a cottage and asked after the asthma, rheumatics, bad leg, or other ailments of its inmates, there was not the smallest sense of unusualness or awkwardness on either side; but it would have been a very different position for a visitor who had no previous acquaintance there, and was simply in *terra incognita* without any ostensible reason for the visit. It would be too detestably intrusive and ill-mannered for a stranger to set about a sort of house-to-house visitation to find out people's circumstances, and go poking unasked into cottages without knowing the names of the inhabitants or anything about them!

The difficulty of making a start seemed almost insurmountable, when there suddenly flashed into her mind like an inspiration the recollection of the Richards family. She had been to their cottage once already, so she had some kind of introduction to start from. She remembered quite well, too, how on the occasion of that first visit Ethel had told her she ought to try and do something to reform such untidy neighbours. She had not forgotten that, even though she had not as yet acted upon it. But she would do so now; it would be pleasant to be able to fancy herself working under Ethel's orders, whether the latter should ever come to know of it or not; and in such work she would have a sort of feeling of keeping her beloved cousin's presence continually with her. The Richards family seemed the very opening she was seeking, and not a moment would she lose in availing herself of it. And thus by the time the train rolled into Cwm-Eithin station, her mind was fully and firmly made up that she would go and see the Richards' on the very next day, come what would.

For several nights past there had been a sharp frost, and when Ralph made his appearance to welcome her soon after she had got home, he was carrying his skates in his hand. This was highly interesting to her, as skating was an amusement she delighted in.

'Oh, I *am* glad to see your skates out,' she exclaimed; 'there's been no skating near Carton yet, but this place is colder, I think. Is the ice bearing here? Papa's out, I suppose—I looked in his room, but he wasn't there.'

'Oh no! he's gone to old Sir John Smith's for a couple of nights, and doesn't come back till to-morrow,' replied Ralph, settling himself in front of the fire and beginning to inspect and grease his skates carefully. 'As for the ice, it's bearing all right enough, only unluckily it's lumpy and bad owing to a snowstorm that came on and spoilt it just as the water was freezing.'

'What an *awful* nuisance!' exclaimed Imogen, with the utmost feeling.

'Ain't it just?' returned her brother. 'But, however, it's some consolation that there's splendid ice over at Llantre, and so there's to be a no-end grand skating picnic there to-morrow. It'll be awfully jolly, with hockey and cricket on the ice, and all kinds of games.'

'Llantre!' said the girl. 'What's the good of that to us, unless papa'll let us drive? It's full ten miles, and that's too far to walk, and perhaps he'll want the horses for something when he gets back.'

'Aha! but I've thought of all that,' answered he. 'I heard before he went away that the picnic was to come off if the frost held, so I asked him if we could go to it. He was quite willing, and said we might have the dog-cart to take us. So you see that I've put the thing straight, and arranged all about it as well as possible. We'll have to get off early though, for the roads are desperately slippery, and I'm to play in the hockey match which begins at eleven.'

'All right! I'll be ready as soon as you like,' answered Imogen, gleefully. And then she suddenly recollected the plan she had already made for the next day, and which would be incompatible with joining the skating expedition; her tone changed as she continued, 'At least no—there's something I forget; I must cut Llantre to-morrow, I'm afraid.'

'Cut Llantre!' cried Ralph in surprise. 'Oh! rubbish! It'll be an awfully jolly day, and they say there's acres of the loveliest ice ever was. And besides,' he added, as an additional attraction occurred to him to bring forward, 'papa's bought a new mare this week, and she's to be put in the dog-cart to try to-morrow.'

'No! Is she really?' said Imogen, eagerly. 'What's she like, and how does she go? I wonder how she'll stand passing through that colliery on the way to Llantre? I should hate to miss the fun if she kicks up a dust.'

'Well; and no more you need that I can see. What on earth makes you say you won't go?'

'Oh, it's only that I've got some other fish to fry.'

'Fry 'em some other day then—they're bound to keep in this frosty weather; besides, a skate is so rare a fish in these parts, that it ought to be attended to before any others.'

'Well—that's true,' answered Imogen, hesitating. 'But no—I think I won't go. You see I'd made up my mind to do something else before I knew of the skating.'

'What's that got to do with it? You can unmake your mind as well as make it up, can't you?'

'Ah, but I hate weathercocks who never can stick to a thing when they've settled it. I shouldn't feel square if I were to go to Llantre to-morrow, so I guess I sha'n't.'

'What ever is this important business that you must stay for?' asked Ralph, impatiently.

'Oh, it isn't anything particular,' she replied.

'Then, what an idiot you are to make such a fuss about it! Let's hear what it is at all events.'

She had intended to keep her reason for staying at home a

secret; but he teased and chaffed her so about where she was going, that she thought she was making an absurd and needless mystery about the affair, and told him that she had determined to go and see Ann Richards.

'And who may Ann Richards be?' he inquired.

'Why, don't you know—she's the wife of the man they tried the other day.'

Ralph gave vent to a prolonged whistle of astonishment.

'And what the dickens takes you there all of a sudden?' asked he.

She hesitated a moment.

'It's not exactly all of a sudden. I thought of it some time ago,' she replied. 'It's partly because of something Ethel said; and partly because—oh, bother! What's the use of going into a long history of it when it doesn't make a scrap of difference to you, and perhaps, after all, you wouldn't just see what I mean? I'm going there to-morrow, and so that's an end of the matter!'

Ethel was an individual whom Ralph condescended to approve of, so the mention of her name as being concerned in his sister's plan made him inclined to regard it somewhat more favourably than before.

'Ethel!' grunted he, with several shades of otherwise-mindedness gone out of his voice. 'Don't see what on earth she can have to do with it! However, she's a good sort, and there's a fair prospect of reasonableness about any idea that *she* may have shoved into your nut. Does she want you to go and sniff after her jewels? By-the-bye—that just reminds me — you'd better wait and ask our parent's leave first. He'll think it'll look as if you wanted to share the swag, or patronise crime, or something of that kind. You bet he won't let you go.'

Imogen's sensitive pride was up in arms at this speech, which seemed to her an impertinent and unwarrantable attempt on her brother's part to interfere with her liberty of action. The idea of expecting that young women who were out, emancipated from the schoolroom and independent, had to ask leave, as he suggested, before going to any new place! Besides, this wasn't a new place, for she had been there before with her father himself. She tossed her head indignantly as she retorted,—

'Not let me go, indeed! I should hope I'm not such a baby that I can't settle for myself what he'd approve of in a trifle like that! Of course he won't mind my going; and of course he won't dream of my asking him first. He knows that I'm grown up now, and not a child any longer.'

'Humph!' growled Ralph, in a tone that was anything but convinced. 'I don't know so much about that neither. I don't believe he'll like it for a moment. I tell you you'd much better wait till you've asked him. You know he's cocksure as to Richards being the thief.'

'I don't see how anyone can be that when the jury found him innocent,' she returned. 'Anyhow, whether he is or not, 'tisn't him, but his wife and children that I'm going to look up. *They* had no hand in his misdeeds, at all events.'

'Who ever said they had?' he returned. 'Of course I know it's no use talking to you when you've made up your mind. You always were as obstinate as a pig! But, putting papa aside, still I don't see why you couldn't go just as well to-morrow, or the day after, or the day after that again, or not till the frost's over and there's nothing more amusing to do.'

It was all very well to repeat what she had already said about having made up her mind, hating weathercocks, etc., etc.; but still there was undeniably a good deal of truth in what he said. Indeed, a year ago she would have been entirely of the same mind, and would have thought that no mortal thing could be important enough to take precedence of a good day's skating. But during the last twelvemonths a considerable change had come over her. New ideas, new pleasures, new desires, new feelings of many kinds had begun to take effect upon her; and her notions of perfect felicity were no longer quite so exclusively tomboyish and wild as of old. At the present moment, too, she was fresh from the atmosphere of sincere (though perhaps somewhat conventional) benevolence which pervaded Carton House, and which she had been inhaling during the past week. The influence of that, of Ethel's tranquil example and society, and of her romantic admiration for her cousin, were still strong upon her and inclined her towards the cottage visit—not to mention that the warmth with which she had maintained her ground against her brother, had also some tendency to make her stick to the cause that she had espoused.

Yet notwithstanding all this, virtuous resolutions and all the rest of it, there was an attraction that was almost irresistible about the Llantre skating expedition, and the excitement of being in the dog-cart when the new mare was to be tried. The more she hankered after these things, the more clearly did she begin to perceive how much wisdom was contained in Ralph's words.

She said nothing to him of being disturbed by any inward waverings; but for all that she knew very well that her mind was not made up really finally as yet, and that it was still quite on the cards that he might have her company on the drive to Llantre next day.

It was not till late in the evening that she was brought to a final decision by the recollection of the two lines of Arnold's that she had read some time ago, that had struck her fancy, and that she had once quoted to him—

"Tasks in hours of insight willed,
May be through hours of gloom fulfilled."

That seemed to her just the very thing she had been wanting to help her to settle the momentous question of what she should do on the morrow. She had had her hour of insight; and what she had to do now, was to profit thereby. The hour of insight had come to her in the train when she had determined to go and see the Richards' next day; and she must stick to what she had then willed, and not let herself be tempted to give it up now that it did not appear quite so imperatively necessary as before.

So the end of the matter was that Ralph had to drive off alone to Llantre next morning, divided between almost awe-struck (though concealed) admiration for her heroic virtue, and indignation at such an inopportune fit of goodness. Which of these feelings should predominate he had been unable to determine, and so took refuge till his departure in a convenient grumpiness of manner which could not be considered as actually condemnatory, and yet served effectually to convey that events were not running altogether on lines that he approved of, and that their failure to do so was to be laid chiefly at her door.

It must be confessed that her eyes turned wistfully after the dog-cart as it rolled down the drive, and that she very nearly sighed regretfully at beholding some indications of skittishness on the part of the new mare. Imogen rather prided herself on her skating, and knew that she was the crack lady skater of that district. She thought how she would have liked to go and show off her skill—particularly if that Mr Sylvester were there, who so seldom seemed to think anyone could do anything worth noticing! She was still undecided whether to like him or not; sometimes when they met he only teased and piqued her, and sometimes again he was quite charming.

And then she dismissed all unheroic regrets for the ice picnic, and turned her thoughts resolutely to the improvement she meant to effectuate in Richard Richards' cottage. It should be like a transformation scene in a pantomime. There were the evil giants of dirt and untidiness to be overcome, and there was she to enact the good fairy and overcome them by her wand of soap and water—always remembering, however, that the potent weapon was to be applied vicariously and not with her own hands!

CHAPTER VII
A Sick Man

As Imogen was preparing to issue forth to begin the combat with the two giants that she intended to slay, a new difficulty suddenly presented itself to her. She had an idea that it would not do to go and pay a cottage-visit empty-handed, and at the same time, she was greatly puzzled to know what offering to take with her. The Richards' were neither sick nor in want, so far as she knew, so a gift of food might perhaps be deemed insulting—and to wound the feelings of inferiors was far worse than to offend equals in the same way, to her mind. But what was there except food, that they were likely to care about having? She had noticed that Ethel always took some kind of creature comforts with her when she went to a cottage, and that it invariably seemed to be acceptable. But then Ethel always had such a knowledge of the people's circumstances as to ensure her taking them whatever was the exact thing that they happened to be in want of; and Imogen was acutely conscious that she herself was totally deficient in that knowledge—which just made all the difference.

After debating this knotty point for a while, she came to the conclusion that the cottage susceptibilities could not possibly be hurt by her taking some dainty for the children. So she armed herself with a basket containing a pot of jam and some cake, and then proceeded on her reforming errand. Evidently it would be advisable to begin by coming to a good understanding with those whom she desired to reform, and she trusted that the contents of the basket would prove of service in attaining that object.

Having reached the abode of the Richards', she knocked two or three times without getting any answer, and began to think there was no one at home; but then hearing a voice within, she concluded her knocks had not been audible, so lifted the latch, and entered the house.

On crossing the threshold she passed into a tiny, unwindowed, and uneven-floored room, where if it had not been for the light that came in through the open door behind her, she could scarcely have avoided the Scylla and Charybdis of a sack of potatoes on one side and a pile of coals on the other, by which almost the whole space was filled up. A doorway so low that she had to stoop in going through it, led out of this into what served as the kitchen, and general living room. As this kitchen had only one small window, its illumination was not brilliant at the best of times; and on the present occasion it was even darker than usual, because half the window was stuffed up with old rags that were doing duty where the glass had been broken. The plaster had fallen off the ceiling in several places, and the rafters showed through. Beside the fireplace was a big four-post bedstead; and on this lay a wild-looking man, unshaved, and unwashed, with a filthy quilt, and sundry equally filthy garments piled over him. His thin face was flushed a deep red, his black eyes roved restlessly from side to side, and from time to time he muttered to himself, occasionally raising his voice excitedly. Little as Imogen had ever seen of sickness, she at once guessed that he was very ill, and light-headed. The only other live things in the room, were the child Sarah Ann, sitting on a low stool on the other side of the fire gazing stolidly at the man; and a lean, half-starved kitten prowling about the floor on a vain search for stray scraps of food. The child did not seem at all discomposed at Imogen's entrance, and merely remarked, 'Mother's gone for water.'

'Will she be back soon?' asked Imogen, whose shyness and fear of being considered as an intruder, were increased tenfold by this unexpected state of affairs, and who felt very much inclined to take refuge in an ignominious flight.

'She said as she'd be back now just,' answered the child, when a repetition of the question had made it penetrate into her brain far enough to produce a reply. Just then the man's excitement increased suddenly. Impatiently pushing back the things that were piled on him, he sat bolt upright, and began snatching at the ragged and dirty relics of a curtain that hung round the bed. This evidently greatly distressed Sarah Ann. She jumped off her stool, hurried to the bedside, and tried hard to pull him down again to a recumbent position. Finding that neither her strength nor height were equal to the task, she desisted, and looked appealingly at Imogen, as though wondering the latter did not come to her assistance.

'Mother said as he wasn't to get the clothes off of him for anything,' said the child, while two big tears trickled down her cheeks; 'and now he's all uncovered every bit! Oh dear! He '*on't* lie down.'

Imogen had not the most distant idea how to pacify a man in high fever. If only Ethel were there! Ethel would be sure to know! However, it was impossible not to make some effort to help poor Sarah Ann in this emergency, so the young lady deposited her basket upon a rickety table near the door, and went up to the bed. As the curtain seemed to irritate him, she told the child to pull it back out of his sight if possible; and then, putting her hand on his shoulder, she tried gently to press him down upon the bed. These endeavours he resisted strenuously, and, getting a bit of the curtain into his grasp, tugged at it with all his might. The stuff was too rotten to bear any strain upon it, and began to tear down from the top. Imogen was at her wit's end to know what to do. She felt that he needed restraint—that prompt action of some kind must certainly be necessary, and that she and the child were alike ignorant and unequal to the situation. The only idea that had been given her of the treatment he required was what Sarah Ann had said about keeping him covered. That constituted but a very scanty code of instructions with which to take charge of a sick-room; still, such as it was, it was better than nothing anyhow, and she proceeded to profit by it by taking up one of the dirty garments lying on the bed—which she could not touch without an involuntary grimace of disgust—and wrapping it round his shoulders. To this he paid no attention at all, and seemed to be quite contented in continuing the destruction of the curtains.

At this juncture the mistress of the house made her appearance to the immense relief of Imogen, who now felt that whatever happened, there was at all events a proper, responsible authority on the spot who would know the right thing to do, and be able to cope with the vagaries of the sick man.

'I'm so glad you've come!' she exclaimed; 'he *will* try and pull down the curtains, and we can't keep him quiet.'

Ann Richards at once took in what was the state of affairs.

'Stop you,' said she. 'He do get like this on spells; but he shall mind me better than some one else.'

So saying, she spoke to him in Welsh, quietly but authoritatively, and tried to unloose his hold of the curtains. Light-headed as he was, yet the familiar voice seemed to arrest his attention and tend to tranquillise him. He allowed the curtain to be disengaged from his hands; and after that, she had but little difficulty in making him lie down again, and let her pile the coverings on him as before. As soon as matters had been thus satisfactorily arranged, she turned reproachfully to the child, saying,—'Now, didn't I tell you not to leave the clothes off of him, not on no 'ccount? I did think as I could trust you that much while I stepped out for a drop o' water. But I never see such a stupit child as you—no, indeed!'

At this rebuke Sarah Ann's face puckered slowly up for fresh tears, and Imogen hastened to assure the mother that the child was in no way to blame for what had happened, that she had done all she could to prevent it, and that the man was too strong to be managed by a mere child. Ann received these assurances with the air of a person who reserved her own opinion, though she was too polite to contradict her visitor. To keep a patient covered up almost to suffocation, was in her eyes the first duty of a nurse, and it disturbed her greatly to think that this rule had been infringed. 'The doctor said to *mind* and keep the clothes on, and not let no draught come near him,' she informed Imogen.

'Well, he was only uncovered for such a very little bit, that I really don't think he can have done himself any harm. How hot and flushed he looks! If you were to put some eau de Cologne on his forehead and fan him for a bit, I daresay that might make him more comfortable. Haven't you got a fan anywhere?' said Imogen completely forgetting that the possession of eau de Cologne and fans was not the same matter of course amongst cottagers as it was in her own class of life.

Ann gazed at her in amazement.

'Er?' was her only response.

The woman's evident mystification showed Imogen the ludicrous mistake she had made; she could hardly help smiling at the comical idea of Ann's requiring scent and fans, but yet was quite cross with her own stupidity for having taken such a thing for granted.

'Oh no! I forgot—of course you haven't—never mind—it's nothing!' she answered with some confusion. 'But tell me, is that your husband? I don't know Richard by sight, as I've never seen him that I know of. And has he been long ill?'

'Yes, yes, 'tis Richard sure enough,' replied Ann. 'He have been ill for—how long is it?—oh, 'tis weeks back now. Only not quite so bad as this all the time, you know.'

'Do you know what's the matter with him?' asked Imogen.

''Tis the inflammashun, so the doctor do say,' answered the woman; 'and so I do believe myself too. 'Twas going about looking for work as he got ill. Getting wet through continual, he was, and too far off to come home and change hisself mostly. Then one bitter cold day he was get the blast; and ever since that 'tis here he have a bin—can't do a thing, and getting worser every day. And then he have bin worrying himself all along, what with not getting work; and not being a free member of his club so that there was nothing to come in; and one thing and another; and the worry do have kept him down, too, I do suppose.'

'Why, how came he to be out of work? I remember that when I was here before, in September, he was working at a colliery somewhere. Has the colliery stopped?' said Imogen.

'Stopped? No sure!' was the answer. 'But some other man got his place while he was in trouble about them jools; and then when he was free and went back to work again, the gaffer said something nasty about taking on a man as people said was bound to be a thief for all they couldn't prove it against him. And then Richard was a bit hot, and gave him words back; and after that he came away and said as he wouldn't work there no more—not if it was ever so!'

'And couldn't he get work anywhere else?'

'That he have been striving for, only he missed to get it. 'Tisn't no fault of his, and that's the truth. But, you see, when people keep telling as he's the man that took the jools, no one don't care to have him,—not so long as there's plenty of others to be had. And then he got daunted-like, and we was think to go right away somewhere else. But he's too bad to move now, whatever. Ssh! get away, cat!'

This last remark was addressed to the kitten, which, having scented the food in Imogen's basket, had scaled the table, and was endeavouring to raise the lid and get at a few crumbs to satisfy its voracious cravings.

Imogen's sympathies were by this time fully aroused on behalf of the sick man, whom she now saw for the first time in her life, and she listened eagerly to all that his wife told her about him. Having stood towards him—for however short a time—in the relation of a nurse, and having in that capacity touched him with her hands, and racked her brains to think what was to be done for him, made her feel interested in him with a queer sense of what was almost proprietorship. She made up her mind on the spot that he had certainly not committed the crime attributed to him, and that he and his family were very greatly to be pitied. Her compassionate zeal caused her to regard them as high-souled and persecuted innocents of stainless honesty, and it would have been a considerable shock to her had she known how far more lax their actual code of morals was than she imagined it to be. For, however touchy they might be at the charge of burglary, yet they did not consider poaching to be stealing, in any sense of the word; and furthermore, they would have been almost certain to keep for themselves any stray article picked up in the road, even if they had known who the rightful owner was. But then a burglary was quite a different matter. It was regularly going out of one's way to break the law, and as they felt no temptation to contravene it in that open and violent manner, they were naturally extremely hurt at being supposed to have done such a thing, and resented the accusation bitterly.

Imogen wanted to discover whether the family were badly off for money or not, but was very shy of making any inquiries on that head lest she should thereby wound the Richards' self-respect. Her bashfulness was, however, quite needless, for Ann had not the least hesitation in allowing that it was, 'poor times with us now,' or in receiving the few shillings which was all the money Imogen had with her, and which she laid on the table at her departure. It seemed to Ann quite the right and natural thing to accept any amount of money that might be given her—especially when the donor was one of the gentry, and therefore necessarily rolling in riches. Yet though ready enough to be greedy and grasping in some ways, the woman was free from the begging taint, and—unless under very extreme pressure of want—would have gone without pecuniary assistance sooner than humiliate herself to ask for it.

Imogen issued from the cottage glowing with pity for its inmates and with indignation at the accusation which had caused their calamities, and which, she felt convinced, was unjust. She longed to be able to help them in some way; but what was there she could do? Of course she would take Richard's part whenever she had the chance, and would never lose an opportunity of speaking a word in his favour; but it was to be feared that the neighbourhood would probably persist in sticking to its own opinion in spite of all her championship. No, the only really certain way of helping him would be to find out the actual criminal, and thus to establish her *protegé's* innocence beyond all manner of doubt. But, alas! How was that to be done? and what chance had she of being able to do it?

CHAPTER VIII
Poor Crambo

It happened that just after Imogen had left the cottage, chance threw in her way the very person whom she was so anxious to discover; though of that fact she had not the remotest suspicion. The sound of horse's feet coming quickly along the road behind her, made her look round; and there she saw Sylvester, mounted on his favourite Crambo, hurrying along to keep an appointment some way off for which he feared that he was already somewhat late.

Punctuality was a thing on which he particularly prided himself. It was his boast that he had never yet failed in keeping an engagement to the minute; and he believed that this rigid punctuality had been an important adjunct to his brains in pushing him forward in life. On the present occasion, however, notwithstanding his haste, he pulled up on recognising Imogen, and walked his horse beside her. The temptation to have a few words with this girl who had taken his fancy so strangely was irresistible. Crambo should make good the delay afterwards, no matter what the poor animal might suffer in doing so; for Sylvester was not a man who ever let himself be hindered in what he chose to do by such sentimental weakness as consideration for the feelings of any living thing.

The cause that makes one person like another is generally more or less inscrutable, and it would be difficult to account satisfactorily for what should have made Imogen so attractive to this thief, swindler, liar, and every way unprincipled individual. Probably, however, it was in no small degree owing to the perfect guilelessness and honesty that distinguished her, and that made her as strong a contrast to himself as could well be imagined. There was about her a joyous downright freshness and innocence that had struck him from the first; and it seemed as if he must have some unconscious appreciation for these qualities, notwithstanding his cynical disbelief in the existence of goodness. Anyhow, from whatever source it may have sprung, there the attraction was; and it was too powerful to allow of his riding past her with no salutation except a bow—as the urgency of his appointment would have otherwise made him do.

'Why, I made sure you would be at Llantre like everyone else, Mr Sylvester!' she exclaimed, when he pulled up at her side. 'How comes it you're not gone?'

'Well, I think I might say the same to you,' he replied. 'Business kept *me* from going. As for *you*,' he continued in a rather sarcastic tone, as he perceived the basket she had in her hand, 'I can see for myself what your occupation has been. You've been playing at providence in the matter of either soup or pudding. I know that all ladies delight in doing that sort of thing—more especially when the recipients are nice, tidy old people who talk prettily, and express their gratitude properly and effusively for the crumbs from the rich man's table that fall to their share.'

Imogen felt rather offended at the way in which he spoke. For one thing, she objected to the tone of superiority which he had assumed; and for another, she was particularly ready to resent any sneer at cottage visiting, now that she was fresh from staying at Carton, and inclined to think that everything done there must necessarily be perfect.

'Don't you think you may be mistaken?' she said dryly. 'Anyhow your facts are all wrong in the present case. Though I'm a lady, yet I *don't* love taking out puddings; and I hadn't either soup or pudding with me to-day; and there are no old people at the cottage I've just left; and as for talking prettily— well, a man who's light-headed and who was trying to tear down his bed-curtains till his wife came in and pacified him isn't likely to be *very* careful in what he says, is he?'

'I retract what I said,' replied he gravely, 'and apologise for having supposed for a moment that Miss Imogen Rhys was to be generalised about like other ladies, or to be expected to go and see any poor person less sensational than a raving madman. I conclude the gentleman has some kind of fever? probably an infectious one?'

'Poor fellow!' returned she. 'I fancy it's quite as much worry as actual illness that's put him off his head. It's the man who was accused of stealing my cousin's jewels; because of that, people wouldn't give him work, and of course he took it to heart when he found himself looked upon everywhere as a thief; then as he and his family began to get badly off that made matters worse. And altogether he got quite down in the mouth and was thinking of going to live somewhere where he wouldn't be known when he fell too ill to move. For my part I'm quite positive he's not the thief, and that the jury were right in acquitting him.'

Mr Sylvester was very much amused. Imogen's coming straight from the company of the false to that of the real criminal was a quaintly romantic incident, and the absurdity of it was enhanced by her beginning to champion the former to the latter in utter ignorance of the real state of affairs. He delighted in that sort of discrepancy between things as they were and things as they would be if all were known; and he enjoyed it all the more when he could feel that there was not a soul except himself who was able to take in and appreciate the oddness of the situation.

'Yes?' replied he interrogatively; 'if you are so sure of it, far be it from me to contradict you. I didn't trouble my head very much about the case, as it was no concern of mine. Still, I fancy that a good many people who ought to know, have grave doubts of Richards' innocence.'

'I know that well enough,' she answered eagerly; 'but now that I've seen the man I feel quite positive he's not guilty— somehow I seem to know it instinctively! If only he could be cleared by the real burglar being found, that *would* be a good thing!'

'What a credulous fool the girl is!' was the thought that rose naturally in his mind. Yet something about her—perhaps the contrast between the guilty secrets of his own life, and the absolute state of having nothing to be found out, that was expressed in every line of her face and every tone of her voice— influenced and checked him in spite of himself. He felt that for some unaccountable reason or other he could not look down upon her unreasoning enthusiasm with the contempt that he would have bestowed freely on anyone else; and was rather annoyed at that feeling.

'It all depends upon what you mean by *good*,' he said. 'If it was good for Richards, it would be ill for the other man, wouldn't it? And why should the one be favoured rather than the other?'

'Justice must always and necessarily be good,' she answered loftily; 'so whatever's unjust must equally necessarily be bad. And it's a manifest injustice for a man and his family to have their lives made miserable on account of a crime with which they had no more to do than you or I had.'

This impulsive, unreasoning belief in the innocence of Richards was extremely irritating to Sylvester. He wanted to try and upset it, to show her her folly, to recapitulate arguments that he had used scores of times before tending to encourage the popular feeling against the accused man. But somehow he could not do it now. The words seemed to stick in his throat, as though

untruth stood abashed in her presence, and all he said was,—
'Well; perhaps he's only unlucky then. Some people have good
luck, and some have bad; I suppose he must take his chance of
that like all the rest of us. But I must say I don't understand why
you should take his troubles so greatly to heart, seeing that you
had no hand in them, and can't be affected by them in any way.
Is it that you are so anxious to get rid of your happiness, that
you intend hunting out all the grievances in the world on
purpose to worry yourself about them?'

She coloured indignantly at this imputation of absurd folly.

'No—I'm not quite such a fool as that!' she replied. 'But it's
a different thing to want to give a hand to redress the wrongs of
some one of whom one happens accidentally to have some
special knowledge. When a man's one's near neighbour, and
circumstances bring one in contact with him and his belongings
so that one knows all about them, it seems to me as if that must
be almost a call to try and help him. Troubling oneself over a
case like that is quite another pair of shoes from getting excited
about the concerns of utter strangers. However, whether I care
or not, I'm afraid it'll make no difference to poor Richards. The
only practical good I could do him would be if I could lay hands
on the real thief, and that's just what I haven't a chance of, alas!
But, oh! I'd give *anything* to find him if I could. To set right a
grievous wrong like this, and to rescue an innocent man from
being crushed by a false accusation—that would be work that
one might feel proud of—something that would be well worth
the doing!'

Her enthusiasm had a strange effect upon him as he listened.
First he thought of how little she suspected how easily he could
have procured her the satisfaction she desired. But suddenly
that thought changed into an unaccountable longing to give her
pleasure at all costs, and to find out if she could feel any interest
in him as well as in this boor whom she was so full of. He was

conscious for a moment of a wild impulse to reveal the truth to her—to immolate himself that she might be contented—to say, 'I am the man you want; what will you do now?' The next instant he recoiled with horror at the idea of such a thing having occurred to him. Was he in his sober senses? It was impossible! He must be either drunk or light-headed, and he must seek safety in immediate flight, lest the temptation to such madness should return. Before, however, he could carry out this resolution, the interview came to an end naturally, as by this time they had reached a field-path, which was Imogen's shortest way home. Here they separated, and proceeded on their respective roads in solitude, each occupied with reflections of a very different nature.

We will follow Imogen's first.

What a curious man that was, she thought, and how much more pleasant at some times than at others. She didn't like him when he had a sneering fit on, as he had had to-day. She felt half puzzled and unsafe, somehow, when he was in a humour like that; and yet it piqued her pride too, and seemed almost like a challenge to show what stuff was in her. A person who was going to enact the part of good fairy, and slay giants as she intended doing, could certainly not be the silly, insignificant child that he now and then appeared to consider her! That reminded her of the original purpose of her expedition. She was disappointed to think that she had not yet done anything whatever towards advancing it, and that the Richards' had not yet heard one word of the soap-and-water doctrine that she designed to inculcate. However, she would be sure to take the very first possible opportunity for introducing it.

Here her train of thought was abruptly interrupted by the sight of a pool of water covered with ice—which, of course, she was not going to pass without having a few slides. She did not continue long at this occupation, however. Sliding was but slow work compared to skating, particularly when the sliding had to be done alone, and she could not help thinking wistfully of Llantre; of the numbers of people skating merrily there at that moment; of the fun they must be having; and of how dearly she would like to be with them. She did not exactly grudge having given up the picnic for the sake of what seemed to her right; but she could not resist an undefined and depressing doubt as to whether, after all, the game had been worth the candle— whether the good effectuated by her staying at home, had at all corresponded to the extent of her self-sacrifice. She was but seventeen, with plenty of the frailties of human nature; and remembering the keen zest with which a day's pleasure is enjoyed at that age, is it very wonderful that she should have felt somewhat quamp, left-out-in-the-cold, and dissatisfied ?

She pondered disconsolately on what she should do with herself for the rest of the day till Ralph's return, and finally determined to get out the entomological books, and try to find the names of some of the moths caught last year that had not yet been named, and arrange them in their proper places in the cabinet. Naming moths was not a very lively occupation— indeed, it was the only thing that she disliked connected with mothing. Still, it had to be done sooner or later, and, at all events, it would help to pass the time on this dull day; so she set to work at it resolutely as soon as she got back to the house, little dreaming of the episode by which her labour was to be varied before it came to an end.

Sylvester, meanwhile, was galloping away at full speed, to save his character for punctuality, and be in time for his appointment. Removed from the disturbing society of Imogen, he quickly recovered his equilibrium, and was able to reflect upon what had passed in his usual frame of mind.

There was a grim comicality about the way in which she had been confiding, without knowing it, in the very man whom she abhorred, and telling him how she longed to bring him to punishment. He could almost laugh at the recollection of it. For all that, however, it was certainly very needless and provoking that she should have gone and got herself thus mixed up with the burglary inquiry. Whoever had to suffer for the crime, it could make no possible difference to her; and so why couldn't she let the matter alone? Had it been any one else, he would have unhesitatingly pronounced all this interest about a poor man to be mere sham—got up in order to make her appear in the charitable-angel light, or something of that sort. But the unmistakable candour about her, and her perfect genuineness, had impressed him against his will; to attribute any kind of cant to such a girl as her, was a thing which he recognised to be impossible.

And so she was eager to discover the real thief, was she? Well! Let her do her best then! He had been too crafty to leave any clue by which he could be traced, and had not much fear of detection. Still, it was always well to be on the safe side; and if she went about championing Richards and trying to persuade people he was innocent, it would be prudent for him, Sylvester, to pursue an exactly opposite course. No doubt he had just now experienced a strange difficulty in doing this to her face; but that was no reason why he should not do it in her absence; he could manage it then well enough, he knew.

He used whip and spur to his willing steed relentlessly, and by that means reached his destination in time for his engagement, and with just one half minute to spare. But the handsome, high-spirited Crambo paid the penalty for his master's haste; the horse's strength and wind had been over-taxed, and he was a mere wreck of an animal from that day forth. Sylvester was vexed at this, not for the sake of his poor steed, but because he had been proud and, in a way, fond of it, and knew he would have some trouble in replacing it. Yet he had not the generosity to care longer for a creature when it had ceased to be able to minister to his wants. It then became, in his eyes, merely so much live lumber to be got rid of with as little loss as possible. Therefore the past faithful services of Crambo were as though they had not been, and the poor animal was sold for a few pounds to a cab-proprietor. Under this new master it dragged on a few weeks of weary and painful existence; and then, every spark of work and vital energy having been knocked out of it, it was at last mercifully consigned to the knacker. Sylvester must have known that such would be its miserable end when he parted with Crambo—but that was a matter to which he was profoundly indifferent. He had made all he could out of it, and that was all he cared for. What else is to be expected of a man who ridicules the idea of owing duty to any one or thing save himself?

CHAPTER IX
An Unexpected Proposal

The non-appearance of Imogen at the Llantre skating picnic was a sore disappointment to Sir Charles Dover, who was head over ears in love with her, and had fully resolved to take that opportunity to ascertain whether or no she would accept and return his ardent affection. For the last few weeks she had acted upon him as a sort of magnet, from the vicinity of which he found it impossible to tear himself away. Being a good-looking, good-natured, young fellow, with the further recommendation of owning a fine estate, he was very generally popular, and invitations flowed in upon him freely from all quarters. Hitherto he had been in the habit of accepting these invitations without regard to locality, and was perpetually rushing about from place to place, north, south; east, and west; but of late his travels had suddenly become astonishingly limited, and there had been a marked coincidence between the attractiveness which any house possessed in his eyes, and its proximity to Llwyn-yr-Allt. His amorous condition naturally made him anxious to remain in that part of the world where there was the best chance of meeting the person for whom he sighed; so, with the wiliness of the serpent, he applied himself sedulously to cultivate all his acquaintances—even the most casual ones—who resided anywhere within the reach of Cwm-Eithin. They, poor deluded mortals! attributing his attentions solely to their own charms, and feeling greatly flattered at the evident desire for their society entertained by so popular a young man, vied with each other in asking him to visit them. And thus it came about that by staying at first one house and then another in the neighbourhood, he had never been altogether out of reach of seeing Imogen since the occasion of her first ball, and had met her continually at whatever parties and social gatherings had taken place.

This happy state of things had been interrupted by her week's absence at Carton House. Never in his life had he found seven days such a dreary and interminable period; and before it was over he had made up his mind that the existing state of things was a mistake, that he would endure his present suspense no longer, and that he would propose to her and learn his fate at the first possible opportunity. He had, of course, taken care to be on the most friendly terms with Ralph, and by that young gentleman he had been informed that there could be no doubt whatever as to her being at the skating party. She was to come home certainly on the day before, and Ralph declared that she was sure to be wild to go to the ice picnic—it was just the sort of thing she loved, and he would answer for her in this matter as confidently as for himself.

The people with whom Sir Charles was then staying were also going to Llantre, and he had promised to accompany them; he could reckon absolutely on meeting her there, and he promised himself that before the day was over he would somehow find an opening for what he wanted to say. What her answer would be he could not guess. He was too blindly in love to be able to judge at all in what way she regarded him. He knew that she always seemed pleasant and sociable with him; and he thought that it was just possible she might vouchsafe to accept him, even though he felt himself to be quite unutterably inferior to her great merits. But, at all events, he was too impatient to wait any longer in uncertainty, and would put the momentous question without delay. For a whole week he had been separated from her, and had had to get on as best he could without either seeing or hearing from her, and now he was in a fever for their next meeting! Under these circumstances it may be imagined how his spirits fell at the sight of Ralph driving up to Llantre without her.

'Hullo, old fellow!' he exclaimed, as Ralph descended from the dog-cart and extracted his skates, boots, and other etceteras. 'What have you done with your sister? You said she was coming. Didn't she return home yesterday?'

'Yes; but she's not coming here to-day for all that,' was the answer.

The lover took quick alarm.

'Nothing wrong, is there?' he asked anxiously. 'She's quite well, I hope?'

'Oh yes, she's as right as a trivet. Only what's kept her at home is that she's got a fad about going to see some poor people or other. Just as if she couldn't have done that every bit as well some other day! I call it absurd nonsense of her— particularly when I wanted her to come here with me, and had taken the trouble to think of everything beforehand, and arrange with papa and all, so that there might be no hitch. It's the mere perversity of women, I suppose. She's devoted to skating, and I'm positive she'd have enjoyed herself here, no end.'

During the whole drive over, Ralph had been feeling desirous of blowing off steam on the subject of Imogen's unaccountable behaviour, and he was now pleased to have met with someone who was likely to sympathise with his annoyance. But he soon found that Sir Charles was by no means to be relied upon to afford him this satisfaction. The extremely spoony condition in which the young baronet was, made him inclined to see fresh cause of admiration in whatever she did or did not do, and it seemed to him that she had performed an act of uncommon self-denial. How noble and unselfish of her thus to relinquish her own pleasure for the sake of the poor, and how entirely worthy of love and devotion she was! It would be quite wicked to let oneself be provoked at such virtue merely because it interfered with one's own selfish wishes, and it would be far better to try and learn self-sacrifice from her example.

These elevated sentiments made him struggle valiantly against his natural irritation at not seeing her, and he began to take her part against her brother zealously. But, unfortunately, the lower and more earthly part of Sir Charles soon insisted on asserting itself in spite of all the fine feelings that tried to keep it down, and presently his habitual good-temper seemed to have deserted him almost entirely, and whoever happened to speak to him found him in a state of unprecedented snappishness.

A good day for skating? No! He thought it anything but that. There was a deal too much wind for one thing, and then besides that there was such a raw, nasty feel in the air. Skating was always a mistake, unless one had exactly the right weather for it. Was he going to play hockey or cricket? Certainly not—it was far too much trouble; and also he thought them very slow amusements on the ice.

For a little while he skated about with other people; but soon came to the conclusion that that was dull. Then he tried looking on—and found that both dull and cold. He really did think that this was about the most senseless way of spending a day that had ever been invented.

As he was yawning, and wondering discontentedly how ever he should get through the time till evening, it suddenly occurred to him that he was being victimised very needlessly. He knew Imogen was at home; what was to hinder his going straight away to Llwyn-yr-Allt to ask that momentous question for the answer to which he was so impatient? Having ridden over to Llantre from the house where he was staying, he was independent of the rest of his party as far as conveyance was concerned, and would have no difficulty on that score.

This idea considerably restored his serenity, and having taken off his skates he went to his hostess with an excuse about a telegram he had only just remembered, that must positively be despatched on that day. He had ascertained that Cwm-Eithin was the nearest telegraph station, and, with her permission, he would at once ride there, send off the telegram, and get back to the house by dinner time.

Was there no help for it, and must they really lose him for the day? What a pity that was, and how dreadfully he would be missed. And what would he do about lunch? and would he not find it difficult to know the way?

To all this he replied with a laugh that he had no fear of being lost whilst he had a tongue in his head, and that he hoped to be able to pick up sufficient food at some shop in Cwm-Eithin to save him from starvation. So as he was prepared dauntlessly to encounter the perils conjured up by his hostess's imagination, there was no difficulty about having the matter arranged as he wished, and in due course of time he arrived at Llwyn-yr-Allt.

He had no intention of applying for leave from the young lady's father to woo her, before he had found out what her own sentiments might be—for it seemed to him that in affairs of this kind the principals should always treat together directly from the beginning. But he knew that it would be considered highly incorrect if he were supposed to have gone calling upon an unmarried young lady; so, having rung at the bell, he inquired if Mr Rhys were at home—reflecting meanwhile on how absurd the social tyranny was which made it thus necessary for him to ask for someone whom he did not at all care about seeing, instead of for the person whom he longed with his whole soul to have even a glimpse of.

The master of the house had only just returned after his two days' absence, and had found an accumulation of letters awaiting him; consequently he was immersed in correspondence when the servant informed him that Sir Charles Dover was in the drawing-room. Though Mr Rhys was one of the most hospitable of men, and had a decided liking for Sir Charles, he wanted to stop and finish his letters for the post in peace and comfort, did not at that moment feel at all in the humour to go and make conversation for company, and wished he had taken the precaution of saying that he would not be at home to any caller that afternoon. However it was too late for such regrets now, so he reluctantly quitted his writing, and proceeded to welcome his visitor with the cordiality that belonged to his hospitable instincts, even though all the time he was inwardly hoping that the intruder would not stay long.

The baronet, on the other hand, could think of nothing except the object of his visit, and turned his head at every sound in hopes of beholding Imogen enter the room. Both host and guest being thus preoccupied, they were anything but lively company for one another, and the conversation languished in a deplorable fashion. Long pauses occurred, during which Mr Rhys wondered how much longer the young man intended to stay, whilst the latter, struck for the first time with the possibility of Imogen's not appearing at all, reflected with dismay on what was to be done in that case. Somehow he had quite forgotten that he might perhaps not see her, even though she was in the house; and he felt his calculations being completely upset by the turn affairs were taking.

The minutes dragged on, and no sign of her coming was visible or audible; and at last in despair, he suddenly bethought him of departing from his original plan, taking her father into his confidence, and asking for the parental consent for his wooing.

This proceeding effectually recalled Mr Rhys's wandering thoughts from his letters, roused his attention, and at once caused the conversation to become interesting. He cordially approved of the idea of Sir Charles as a son-in-law, and not only gave his consent readily, but—seeing the young man's impatience to learn his fate—facilitated matters by despatching a servant to summon Imogen.

The young lady was at that moment in her own sitting-room, absorbed in entomological manuals, by whose aid she was vainly striving to ascertain whether a moth was rare, or only a variety of a very common and variable species. The question was a difficult one, and she had been puzzling over stigmata, patches, spots, dots, elbowed lines, subterminal lines, longitudinal and transverse markings, and similar technicalities, till she was beginning to get rather tired of the subject, and would have certainly let it alone till she should get Ralph to assist her, only that that seemed like being beaten, and shirking work meanly. Under these circumstances, her father's summons was a very welcome interruption, and she appeared promptly in the drawing-room on hearing that he wanted her there.

Her arrival was the signal for his departure. Delighted to be released, and free to go back to his letters, he jumped up, telling her that he had some business to attend to, and that he wanted her to take his place in entertaining Sir Charles. And then he bustled off to his study and resumed his writing—pausing more than once, however, to wonder how affairs might be progressing in the drawing-room, and what sort of an answer his daughter would give to her suitor.

Now that Sir Charles had at last succeeded in obtaining the interview for which he had been in such a desperate hurry, and now that the critical moment was close at hand, he found himself in a much greater state of trepidation than he had expected. He wished to goodness that he hadn't been driven to tell Mr Rhys about it. Making a proposal was always a nervous sort of business—not at all the thing a man wanted to do in public. Yet really it was very nearly as bad as having an audience, to be *tête-à-tête* with a lady on purpose to propose to her, knowing all the time that a third person was perfectly aware of one's intentions.

'I'm so sorry you should have been disturbed on my account,' said he apologetically; 'I hope you weren't doing anything very particularly interesting?'

'Oh, it didn't matter at all,' she answered graciously; 'I was only naming a moth, and there's not the least hurry about it.'

'Mothing seems to be a most delightful amusement,' he observed, thinking meanwhile how best to turn the conversation towards the point he wished; 'I've a great mind to take to it myself.'

'Well, you'll find it awfully good fun. It teaches one a lot about natural history too, in one way and another, so it isn't all wasted time—if you're one of those people who want to be always improving themselves, and all that sort of thing, you know.'

'Are you one of those people?' he asked.

'I don't exactly know. Sometimes I think I am, and sometimes not. The fact is, I believe one can't get on without some object to live for, in the long run; and though collecting moths mayn't be anything very exalted, yet it's better than nothing at all events.'

Sir Charles's thoughts began to turn vaguely towards the appropriateness of suggesting a husband as a more satisfactory object of existence than an entomological collection. He did not as yet quite see his way to clothing the idea neatly in words; but he believed it might be done for all that.

'Ah, but you think of something higher than that, too,' said he, looking at her with sincere admiration; 'you help the poor, and whoever does that has found a noble occupation. You see I know what kept you from the skating to-day—Ralph told me.'

'Oh, did he tell you I was gone to see Richard Richards?' she exclaimed eagerly. 'Do you know people will persist in thinking that he's the man who stole Ethel's jewels, in spite of his having been acquitted. He's very ill indeed, poor fellow, and his wife declares it's all along of this affair. I call it no end of a shame to go on suspecting the man after the case has been fairly tried, and the jury has said he's innocent. Why have a trial at all if you aren't going to accept the result? Here's a man and his family being nearly, if not quite, ruined on account of a charge that has been pronounced to be false. It seems to me it's most awfully hard lines on him. Talk of work to do in the world—if one could get a poor fellow like that out of the mess he's in and set him straight in the eyes of everyone, *that* would be work worth doing if you like!'

She found Sir Charles a much more satisfactory person to talk to on this subject than Mr Sylvester had been. For one thing, it was his nature to abhor the idea of any kind of injustice being done, and to feel a chivalrous pity for, and desire to defend, whoever was weak and oppressed; and for another thing, a cause advocated by her was decidedly likely to find favour in his eyes just then. Richards' case was discussed at length, and she was delighted at his strong expression of opinion as to the hardship of suspecting an innocent person, and at his cordial agreement as to the desirability of detecting the culprit.

'Yes,' observed she; 'of course that would be the real way to help Richards—no one could say a word more against him then. Ah! if only I could lay hands on that burglar, I should feel as if I hadn't lived altogether to no purpose—as if I had managed to do at least one bit of good in the world before I die.'

Sir Charles wanted to get the conversation away from Richards, and back in the direction that he wished it to take, and saw an opening for doing this here.

'No doubt it would be a great pleasure to think you had cleared an innocent man,' said he; 'but even if you don't manage to do that, still it doesn't follow that there's any necessity for you to live "altogether to no purpose," as you call it.'

'Do you think not?' she answered; 'well—yes—I suppose you're right. But it must at all events be a great probability that I should do so—such lots of people's lives seem so absolutely good-for-nothing that I don't know why I'm to expect mine not to be the same. One seems to have so much spare energy that there's nothing to utilise! A case like this would be just the thing to turn it on upon, if only one had a chance of profiting by the opening—which I haven't, unluckily!'

He was tired of beating about the bush, and resolved to go straight to his point without delay.

'I can tell you of an even better opening, if you like,' he said, boldly. 'I know of an object for your energies who would afford them ample scope, and whose life you have the power to make perfectly happy. You say you want work that shall do good in the world, and make a real difference in it. Well then! Will you let me show you such a work lying ready to your hand?'

Her thoughts were running entirely upon Richard Richards, she had not noticed the peculiar earnestness of Sir Charles's manner, and she took it for granted that he wanted to tell her of some poor person in distress, on whose behalf he wished to enlist her sympathies. Of his real meaning she had not the slightest suspicion. She liked, and got on capitally with him, just as she liked and got on with any other pleasant companions. But matrimony was an idea that had never entered into her visions of a possible future for herself; and having always felt perfectly certain that she should never want to marry anyone, it did not occur to her to suppose that he or any other person was likely to be regarding her as a possible wife. Therefore she answered frankly and readily,—

'Oh yes! I'll be delighted to do whatever I can, only I'm afraid you've overrated my capacities, and that I sha'n't be able to help as much as you think I shall. Whom do you mean? Is it any one near here?'

Sir Charles got up, and came and stood close in front of her.

'I mean myself,' said he; 'I am appealing on my own behalf. I love you with my whole heart, Imogen; do you think you could care about me enough to marry me? Will you keep to the "yes" that you uttered just this instant before you knew whom I was asking you to take pity on?'

Not a word did he say to protest unchanging love and fidelity, or to promise to do all in his power to ensure her future happiness; his youthful devotion deemed all that sort of thing too obviously included in the mere fact of asking her to be his wife to be worth alluding to separately. And, indeed, no one could see him and doubt that his whole soul was in the words he had just said, as he stood there, waiting for her answer with his handsome, honest face expressing most genuinely earnest love and anxiety.

Imogen looked up at him in utter astonishment and dismay. 'Oh, I'm awfully sorry!' she exclaimed; 'but I really can't do that! I never dreamt *that* was what you meant! I shouldn't do at all well as a wife, I know, and I shouldn't like it either. I don't mean ever to marry!'

'Make an exception just for once in my favour,' urged the young man; 'then I'd promise not to ask it of you again! You'd do capitally as a wife, I'm sure,—only let me judge for you about that! And think how effectually you would then be supplied with the object to live for that you're anxious about! No woman need ever fear not being of use when she's married, you know!' This was a very unfortunate string for him to have touched upon. The girl knew well enough that the popular idea of woman's mission in the world is that she should be married; but as it was an idea which she greatly resented, she was sure to fire up immediately on hearing it mentioned.

'She can be just as much use when she's single, to my mind,' retorted Imogen rather sharply, her indignation at the idea that offended her making her forget her dismay at being proposed to, and her concern for the poor suitor whom she was rejecting; 'that's one of Ralph's pet notions that we women are all failures if we don't marry! *I* don't intend to, at all events; and yet I hope to fulfil my destiny just as well as I could if I were a wife!'

Sir Charles combated this assertion and pleaded his cause vehemently, saying everything he could think of to get her to change her mind. But it was no use, for she was immovable; and at last he rode off to Cwm-Eithin in a melancholy and dejected frame of mind to despatch the telegram which should make good his ostensible reason for having deserted the skaters. Its contents were the immediate result of his rejection. It was addressed to his own home and ran thus,—'Expect me home to-morrow.' Cwm-Eithin was no longer so charming in his eyes now that he had had that interview with Imogen for which he had been in such a hurry. But for all that, and though he perceived that he had no chance with her for the present, he nevertheless did not give up all hope for the future, and determined that he would try again by-and-by for the prize that he coveted.

CHAPTER X
Vexations

When Mr Rhys and Ralph heard of Imogen's refusal of Sir Charles, and when furthermore she communicated to them her unalterable resolution never to marry at all, they felt a good deal annoyed with her. Sir Charles was an excellent match in a worldly point of view; and besides that, they both agreed in considering him a thorough good fellow, and one whom they would have welcomed heartily into the family circle. As for this notion of hers about never marrying, it was simply ridiculous, preposterous nonsense, and they could not imagine what had ever made her get it into her head.

Ralph had, of course, heard her say the same thing before; but he had not attached any importance to it at the time, thinking it was a mere whim, and not fancying that she could possibly have been in sober earnest in what she had said. Being young and inexperienced, he would not let the matter alone, but kept on harping upon it continually, arguing about it, and endeavouring to convince her that she was foolish and unreasonable, until it became quite a raw[1] between them, and she thought it was almost a relief when his departure to read with a tutor for the army prevented her from having the subject perpetually dinned into her ears any longer.

Mr Rhys, on the contrary, adopted a very different line of treatment. He was aware of the tendency of human nature to cling with increased affection to a cause that it has had to defend, and believed that opposition was more likely than not to confirm her in her ideas. He perceived, too, the absolute futility of attempting to reason with a girl of seventeen, in the best of health and spirits, who was quite convinced that she should always prefer a life of single blessedness. Therefore, he had the good sense to conceal his annoyance, and to appear to acquiesce entirely in her decision. He merely told her that he was disappointed at her not being able to fancy Sir Charles, whom he regarded as a very excellent and estimable young man, but that, of course, if she was resolved not to marry at all, then there was necessarily an end of the matter, and it was no use saying any more about it. As he said this there was a funny expression twitching about the corners of his mouth which seemed to contradict his apparent seriousness. But fortunately she did not notice this look of amusement, and without doubting that his words had been spoken in literal earnest, felt grateful to him for not desiring to interfere with her plans as to her own future life; and meditated sagely upon the silliness of young men in general, and brothers in particular, and upon the vastly superior wisdom possessed by such a person as her father.

There was another matter, however, in respect to which she and he had more trouble in coming to a harmonious agreement. Mr Rhys, regarding Richard Richards with the utmost abhorrence as a certain poacher and possible burglar, had been quite horrified to hear that she had entered the cottage of such a notorious scoundrel, and had at first sternly forbidden her to repeat the visit. But before long her urgent entreaties to have the prohibition removed, and the picture which she drew of the man's illness and state of destitution, made him relent.

His bark was generally worse than his bite, and where sickness was concerned he was especially soft-hearted; so, after a good deal of humming and hawing, he informed her that, upon careful consideration of the circumstances of the case, he had changed his mind, and would make no objection to her doing as she pleased about going to the cottage.

Having received this permission, she used to go almost daily to see poor Richards with supplies of soup, milk, eggs, arrowroot, and whatever other delicacies he required; thereby, to say the truth, saving her father from what would otherwise have been a weight upon his mind—only he did not choose to have that fact known. It would have been intolerable to his kindly nature to think that there was some one sick and in want of proper food and medicine, just outside his own door, so to say; and yet it would have been a very hard struggle to go in person to see to the well-being of an individual so obnoxious to him as was Richard Richards.

But this difficulty was wholly obviated by Imogen's having taken upon herself to look after the man, as then Mr Rhys could feel easy in his mind as to the invalid's having all that was necessary, and yet was spared the necessity of shocking his own prejudices as he would have done by entering the house of such a bad character in the part of a benefactor. It was a trial to him to have to allow any kind of communication to pass between his own house and the cottage; but it would have been still worse to be himself the medium of communication—indeed he would probably in that case have felt as though giving a direct and reprehensible countenance to evil-doing.

It was not long before Imogen had the satisfaction of seeing Richards begin to mend, and his progress to recovery, though slow, was steady. A little experience soon taught her to hit off his tastes in catering for him, and she rarely failed to tempt his fanciful appetite with the various kinds of food she brought with her. Ann's favourite commendation when any especially acceptable delicacy made its appearance out of Imogen's basket, was,—'Indeed, and he shall enjoy hisself now just with this!' And this remark came to be made with a frequency that was highly gratifying.

Imogen was not, however, quite equally successful in the endeavours which she made occasionally to provide dainties for Sarah Ann and the rest of Richards' offspring. She supposed that her own taste in such matters was an infallibly safe guide to theirs; and one day it came into her head that it would be both pleasant and amusing to see the astonishment and delight with which their uneducated palates would receive French *bon-bons* and sweets of a *recherché* nature that must of course be far superior in niceness to anything they had ever tasted. But when she tried the experiment, its result was not what she had expected. In the matter of 'loshengias'[2] (by which term all sweets of all kinds were designated), the children were thoroughly conservative, and thought the ones to which they were accustomed were far superior to most of the strange new flavours and substances to which she introduced them. Chocolate, indeed, was received with some favour; but a rank peppermint drop, or a bit of coarse hardbake[3], were infinitely preferred in the cottage to the most delicate morsel of nougat, or to caramels, pralines, abricotines, and such like.

The greatest failure of all was a box of sweets filled with liqueurs that Imogen took with her one day, and which proved so wholly un-swallowable that no sense of politeness could save them from being spat out again immediately by the recipients. The mother, who had not herself tasted the sweets, was scandalised at this breach of good manners, though in her secret heart she entertained but little doubt of its being justified by the nastiness of its cause. Still, she felt it incumbent on her to make a show of rebuking the proceeding, if only to appease Imogen, who might perhaps feel mortified at so unceremonious a rejection of the gift that she had meant to be a pleasant one.

'Oh, fo' shame, Sairerrann!' exclaimed Mrs Richards, singling out the eldest, as the natural victim to be made an example of for the benefit of the rest; 'Miss Rhys 'on't bring nothing nice for you no more, and you so rude! I am quite shamed for you to do such a thing—yes, indeed. I don't know where you do get it from, not I— you never see such manners with *me*, whatever!'

Here Imogen interposed. She did not perceive that this displeasure was merely assumed out of compliment to her, and felt unhappy lest her present was to be the means of getting the luckless Sarah Ann into a scrape.

'Oh, never mind,' said the young lady good-naturedly; 'don't scold her; she was quite right not to swallow it if she didn't like it. I'm fond of these sweets myself, and I thought she'd have been sure to like them too; but, of course, it's all a matter of taste. Have one, Ann, and see what you think of it yourself.'

With these words, she put one of the *bon-bons* into her own mouth to prove the truth of what she had said, and offered another of them to the woman.

The latter was completely taken aback. After what had just passed, and the blowing up she had given Sarah Ann, she thought that for the edification both of her visitor and children it was indispensable for her to accept and eat the proffered dainty. Yet in her heart of hearts she longed to refuse it, for she had far more confidence in the good taste of her offspring than in that of Miss Rhys. And what if the thing were to be so abominably nasty as to force her to treat it as they had done in spite of all her efforts? She wished heartily that she had been less prompt in finding fault with them for the sake of producing a good effect. Taking the sugar plum into her hand, she contemplated it with secret misgivings.

'It do look beautiful, sure enough,' said she, hypocritically; 'I never was much of a one for loshengias myself, but I daresay as I shall enjoy this.'

The children were staring at her with looks wherein she read clearly their doubt of her accomplishing the enterprise before her. She had gone too far to recede, and, concentrating all the strength

of her will upon swallowing the sweet, and keeping it down—
however nauseous it might be— she boldly put it into her mouth,
and gulped it down in grim silence. No expression of either
pleasure or pain crossed her face, and as she did not volunteer any
opinion as to the merits of the morsel, Imogen did not like to ask
what she thought of it. But in spite of Ann's heroism, Imogen had
an uneasy sense of having made a blunder, and she began to realise
more vividly than before that it was a mistake to take it for granted
everyone else would like just the same things as she did herself.

It must not be supposed all this time that she had forgotten her
original object in going to the cottage. On the contrary, she
endeavoured to inculcate cleanliness and tidiness whenever she
saw what she thought a good opportunity of doing so, either
directly or indirectly. But perhaps she did not go the right way to
work, or perhaps the family may have been unteachable, for certain
it is that she was no more successful in this line than she had been
in trying to educate the children's taste in the matter of sweets. By
the time that Richards at last regained his health, the cottage was
not one whit less of a pig-sty than it had been when first she had
gone there. Not one corner had been touched by the soap and water
wand with which she had intended to perform miracles; and the
giants she had purposed slaying were in the most hearty and
thriving condition possible—which things were naturally
somewhat discouraging to a young person who had set out full of
reforming zeal, and with no doubts as to her own ability to play the
part of good fairy which she had chosen to undertake.

It happened, too, that just about that time she had two or three
other small contrarieties to endure; and as she was not of a patient
disposition, she easily became depressed, and inclined to think that
the whole world had got out of joint, and that nothing was
going right any more.

For one thing, Ethel was unexpectedly prevented from
coming to Llwyn-yr-Allt as she had promised to do; and this

was an immense disappointment to Imogen, who had looked forward greatly to her cousin's visit. Another thing that annoyed the girl was, that there was still no clue to the mystery of the burglary. It excited her; she tried to find some person in authority whom she could irritate into infusing fresh vigour and energy into the search after the criminal; and she made valiant attempts at persuading others to accept the fact of Richards' innocence, as unhesitatingly as she did herself. But it was no use; no trace had been found of the jewels or of their robber, and she had not managed to convert one single individual to her way of thinking; everyone was too prejudiced, cold, hard-hearted, lazy, and indifferent, as she told herself, indignantly, when meditating over her failure. A third thing that contributed to her general state of dissatisfaction, was a sense of having found even her beloved entomology a little wanting of late. Hitherto she had invariably had recourse to it as an unfailing source of consolation for Ralph's absence; but somehow she did not now find solitary mothing quite as charming and all-satisfying an occupation as of old.

The fact was, that she needed constant employment of some kind or other, either work or play, to absorb her restless and superabundant energies. An intuitive sense of that need caused her to make schemes in order to supply it; and when those schemes declined to prosper, and ended in collapse, it was inevitable for a person of her temperament to have an attack of the blues and to feel disgusted with things in general.

When in this frame of mind, and reflecting discontentedly over the failure of her efforts to find satisfactory occupation, it was impossible not sometimes to remember what Sir Charles had said about the opportunities for usefulness possessed by married women, and to feel qualms lest this should really be true. It would be too provoking if he and Ralph and the majority of mankind were to be in the right after all!

That made her think again of Sir Charles's proposal, and of the absurdity of her having said, yes, to it at first without knowing what she was doing; for she had never dreamt of his meaning himself when he had asked leave to show her what work to do, and she had assented so readily. Poor fellow! He had looked very handsome and manly as he pleaded for himself, and it really was a very great pity that she didn't care about him. But, there the fact was, and couldn't be altered. She knew quite well that she wasn't, and never would be in love with him. Even had she been one of those who believe woman's destined sphere to be matrimonial, yet the idea of *him* as a husband didn't seem any more peculiarly appropriate than that of anyone else—Mr Owen, say, or—or—Mr Sylvester.

Now-a-days she seemed always to be meeting this last wherever she went, and many an argument had they had together over the thoughts and schemes that she got excited about. Was he not, she asked herself involuntarily, a more interesting man than either of the other two, whose names had just occurred to her? Perhaps so—she hardly knew; but then she didn't feel as if she ever really got to know him any better, however much she saw of him, she couldn't make him out, and at times he would say things that made her downright angry; it seemed almost as if he and she could hardly be belonging to the same world sometimes, so utterly apart did what he say seem from anything of which she had any comprehension! Well! Whatever he was, luckily it didn't matter to her in the least. It was a great comfort to have thoroughly made up her mind never to marry, for she certainly didn't know any one who would do for a husband. And what a triumph it would be if some day or other she should manage to bring Ralph round to her way of thinking, and to make him allow that an unmarried woman was not necessarily a failure! Meanwhile though, it was very provoking to feel so hipped[4], with Ralph away; and Ethel not coming to stay as she had promised; and none of her little plans turning out as she wished. Why should she feel so much duller this year than before? she wondered.

A quite unexpected innovation now suddenly took place in the routine of her life. Her aunts, in their zeal for her interests, urged strongly upon her father that he would by no means be performing his duty by his daughter if he did not bring her out in London; and, moved by these representations, he announced to her one day, that he meant to take a house somewhere in Belgravia for the season.

He had never doubted but what Imogen would approve of the idea, and was quite astounded at the outburst of opposition with which she first received it. Her old childish wildness and hatred of forms, ceremonies, and conventionalities had been lying partially dormant since the time of her coming out, but it blazed up afresh at the idea that she was to be presented at Court, and regularly taken out in London. What was the good of it? She did very well as she was. She was sure it would be odious to have to live in *any* town, and was not London the very towniest of all towns? Was not the real meaning of taking her to London that they wanted to try and make her into a regular fashionable young lady—just the sort of silly conventional creature on whom she had always looked down with the greatest contempt?

At first, therefore, she made a fuss, and opposed the idea of going to London vigorously; but her resistance was less whole-hearted than it would have been formerly, and sprang rather from the recollection of an old aversion than from the actual living feeling itself; it was not so much that she was conscious *now* of any insuperable objection to what was proposed, as that she was instinctively trying to act in the manner that her un-come-out self would have expected her to do. She knew that in old days she had regarded certain things as altogether abominable, and she had not yet realised the possibility of a change having taken place in herself, and of there being a difference between her present and her former selves which would now make her judge the afore-mentioned abominations more favourably than of old. Whether she knew it or not, however, none the less was the change there, and certain to tell upon her. Consequently her first violent outburst of opposition soon became greatly modified; the London scheme assumed a more inviting aspect; and by the end of a week she was so far reconciled to it, as to make no further attempt to persuade her father to give it up.

Mr Rhys then proceeded to take a house in Lowndes Square, to which they removed in the beginning of May. The situation pleased Imogen particularly because of its proximity to Belgrave Square, where Mr Carton's town house was; so that she was able to see her cousin much oftener than had been possible in the country.

Riding in Rotten Row, too, theatres, operas, places of amusement, and parties, all proved far more delightful than Imogen had expected. And by the time the Rhys's had been established for a month in their new abode, as she looked one day at the plentiful supply of cards and notes lying in the big china bowl which was the receptacle for invitations, she confessed to herself honestly that London was by no means such a bad place as she had expected, and that there really were some redeeming points about it, after all.

CHAPTER XI
Lady Elise's Failure

By the time that the London season commenced, and the Cartons made their annual move to their town house, Lady Elise Bolyn had seen enough of the difficulty of striking up that solid, permanent friendship which she had desired to establish with Ethel, to make her anxious to meet with some equally wealthy but more impressionable individual to whom to attach herself. Her efforts to establish herself as confidante and bosom friend to the heiress had been baffled by the curious mixture of openness and impenetrability, simplicity and shrewdness which characterised the latter; and Lady Elise was beginning to recognise the fact that she neither had, nor was ever likely to have, any strong hold on Ethel's affections. Outsiders who judged from the length of Lady Elise's visits at Carton House, and the unwonted familiarity of intercourse to which the heiress appeared to have admitted her, might very likely have pronounced a different opinion. But Lady Elise was too much behind the scenes to be thus deceived, and knew only too well how one-sided were these marks of apparent intimacy.

There is a French saying that in all friendships, '*il y a toujours l'un qui baise, et l'autre qui tend la joue;*'[1] and however unwilling she might be to own it, she knew nevertheless in her secret heart, that that saying was an accurate description of the state of affairs existing between herself and Ethel. The one made advances to which the other never responded, though she was too indolent to do anything to check them. And that was not at all the sort of thing to satisfy a young woman like Lady Elise, whose great ambition was to establish herself somewhere comfortably with a prospect of permanence.

To be merely supposed to be Ethel's especial friend had, of course, some slight advantage, as it ensured her receiving a certain amount of deference from those who thought it expedient to pay court to the satellite in hopes of thereby securing her good word with the heiress. But Lady Elise aspired to something far more substantially advantageous than that; and she had arrived at the conclusion that the benefits to be derived from the Cartons were insufficient to compensate for the weariness of spirit which she had to undergo in order to keep up her present footing at their house.

The atmosphere at Carton was uncongenial to her in many ways notwithstanding its golden hue. There were radical diversities of disposition between her and Ethel of which she was aware, and which prevented her from ever feeling at her ease in Ethel's company.

Lady Elise was continually suppressing her natural self lest it should clash against that of the heiress and incur the latter's serious disapproval, and this involved a constant watchfulness lest some unguarded word or action might betray the want of harmony between them, which was very irksome. When in society and amongst a crowd of other people, it was not difficult to keep the strong dissimilarity of their natures from becoming apparent; but it was much harder to accomplish this in long daily *tête-à-têtes*; and Lady Elise was tired of the self-restraint which it imposed upon her. She was destitute of Ethel's kindly, charitable instincts, and though she accompanied the heiress in cottage visits because it was evidently considered the right thing to do at Carton, and for the same reason joined readily in discussions about the concerns of cottagers and benevolent schemes for their welfare, none the less was her interest in such matters purely artificial. In reality they bored her horribly.

Furthermore, she had a great weakness for a flirtation, and was never really contented without having some cavalier at her beck and call. Ethel, on the contrary, though by no means averse to the attentions of the other sex when they chanced to come in her way, had yet never found her happiness to be sufficiently bound up in male society for her to trouble herself about it if it did not come to her naturally. During the prolonged visits that Lady Elise had paid at Carton House since last summer, there had been various parties assembled there for hunting, shooting, lawn-tennis, and dancing purposes, and all these social gatherings had been delightful to her. But then, unfortunately there had been other, and more frequent periods, when the company in the house had been confined to herself, Mr Carton, Ethel, and Mrs Grey, the chaperon; and poor Lady Elise had found these other periods intolerably dull. There was not a young man to talk to, and nothing to do save to go pottering after stupid poor people! The want of amusement and of some one to flirt with, had been almost more than she could stand, and in her desperation she had once even entertained a wild idea of setting her cap at Mr Carton. But his absorption in his copying machine invention had rendered him wholly impervious to any such attacks, and she had speedily abandoned her project on perceiving its absolute hopelessness.

The result, therefore, of her experience of Carton House was that she had found herself greatly bored there, and did not see any sufficient prospect of advantage to make her care about subjecting herself to a repetition of the boredom. Having failed either to captivate the master of the house or to set up an intimate and devoted friendship with his niece, she could not flatter herself on having done anything towards securing that permanent foothold which had been her object. And thus, though far too prudent to give up the Cartons and cut herself adrift from her present anchoring ground till she saw a fair chance of securing another elsewhere; she was when she commenced the London season in a restless, unsettled condition, and keeping a sharp look-out for some more satisfactory individual or family to whom to attach herself.

CHAPTER XII
Thyatira Batis

Upon mature reflection, Sir Charles Dover came to conclusion that he had been too hasty in his proposal to Imogen; that he ought to have made his advances with more circumspection, and devoted more time and consideration to the important matter of trying to find out the best way of recommending himself to her before he spoke. And this conclusion made him determined to act more prudently before venturing on that second attempt for her hand which he fully intended to make.

After her refusal of him, he did not again see her till after she had arrived in London, and at their first meeting she was somewhat confused, and evidently inclined to be shy of him, and to take alarm at any indication of an intention to renew his suit. His behaviour, however, was a model of discretion, and she speedily recovered her equanimity in his presence. Then, as she began to feel satisfied that he must have abandoned his former absurd ideas of wishing her to be his wife, her confidence was soon restored, and she fell back naturally into the old *bon camarade*[1] way of regarding him. He perceived this with much satisfaction, and resolved to be careful that he did not a second time disturb their good understanding prematurely. Still, he thought that he would like to manage in some way to produce in her mind a pleasurable association with himself which should be a little different from that relating to other people. It seemed to him that if he could succeed in this, he could not fail thereby to advance his interests, and that the best way to attain this object would be to hit upon something to give her which she

216

would be certain to like, and which should be different from any ordinary gifts she was likely to receive. The difficulty was, however, to settle what the offering was to be, and for a while he puzzled himself vainly to find an answer to this question. Thing after thing occurred to him only to be rejected as too commonplace, or in some other way unsuitable. But at last he cried Eureka! He believed he had found the very idea he wanted, and proceeded to act upon it without delay.

One day, not long afterwards, when Imogen returned from riding in the park with her father, she found awaiting her a small, square parcel, registered and done up very carefully, that had just arrived by post. She took it up eagerly, and began to break the multifarious seals by which it was secured, saying joyfully as she did so,—

'Oh, papa! what can this be? Doesn't it look exactly like a jewel-case? How jolly if anyone's sent me something nice! It must be something very precious at any rate, to be so carefully packed up. Do look! here's cotton wool under the outside paper—and more paper again—and string—dear, dear! What a lot to undo! Who ever can it come from?'

Mr Rhys, also, felt his curiosity aroused upon this point. She had not thought of noticing the post-mark, and had flung the outer covering carelessly on the floor, so he picked it up and inspected it. Thence he quickly derived the information he wanted; he made no comment upon his discovery, however, but looked on silently whilst she continued to unpack the interesting parcel. After the cotton wool and one or two paper wrappings had been removed, a small wooden box with string tied round it was brought to light. She began untying the twine with impatient fingers, remarking,—

''Tisn't a regular jewel case, I see; but of course whatever's inside must be uncommonly choice to be done up like this. Bother these knots! Am I never going to get to an end of them?

Hooray! There goes the last one. Now we shall see what the treasure is!'

Full of pleasant anticipations (for she had a great weakness for jewellery of all kinds) she drew back the lid. But when her eyes fell upon what was beneath it she uttered an exclamation of mortified and indignant disgust.

'What a *horrid* sell!'[2] she cried. 'Why, after all this excitement here's nothing but a couple of *Thyatira Batis*!'

And so saying she turned the box so as to exhibit two prettily-marked moths, dead and reposing side by side on a bit of cardboard to which they had been pinned.

There was an amused smile on her father's face as he examined the insects which she held out towards him.

'I can't see why you should be so put out about them, my dear,' he observed. 'You're always wanting moths, and I'm sure these are very handsome ones. Of course no one would expect most people to care for such things; but they're all in your line, you know.'

'All in my line to want *Thyatira Batis*, indeed!' she returned contemptuously. 'Why, it's one of the commonest moths that there is—a thing that everyone gets directly he begins to have a collection at all! No one in their senses could suppose that I haven't already got as many specimens as I want of such a moth as that. And just look how clumsily these are set! It certainly wasn't anyone that knew much about mothing matters who sent them. I do wonder what stupid person it can have been!'

'Here's the address and post-mark on this,' said Mr Rhys, handing her the piece of paper which he had picked up; 'will they give you any clue?'

'So they may,' she answered, taking the envelope and beginning to scrutinise it. 'I'd forgotten that—it's lucky you thought of it; I must say I should like to spot the duffer who's been so silly. The handwriting's no help, though; I don't recognise it at all. Let's try the post-mark. Quendle — Quendle — I seem to know the name somehow, but I can't for the life of me recollect where I've heard it.'

Mr Rhys watched her. He remembered very well who lived at Quendle, but he did not tell her, as he was curious to see whether she would manage to solve the puzzle for herself, and how she would take it when she should have done so.

'Do you think it's the name of a place where some one you know lives?' he suggested, by way of assisting her efforts at recollection.

'Quendle,' she repeated again doubtfully; 'yes—perhaps it may be.' Then suddenly she flushed crimson as she remembered who lived there, and guessed who the sender of the moths was sure to be. 'To be sure! that's where Sir Charles Dover comes from—I suppose it was he who sent them. Well! I *do* think he needn't have imagined that I should care for such rubbish as these!'

So saying, and emphasising her words so as to express a withering degree of scorn, she hastily gathered up the box and its wrappings, and marched out of the room to take off her riding-habit. Her father looked after her with a quiet chuckle of enjoyment of what had just happened, and speculated secretly as to whether or not the signs which he had seen augured favourably for Sir Charles's future chances. Mr Rhys honestly desired nothing but her happiness, and was prepared to welcome with open arms any eligible son-in-law whom she might present to him—or none at all, if she chose eventually so to settle the matter. But though he would in nowise interfere with her choice, he certainly had a partiality for the good-looking, good-tempered young baronet, and would have preferred him in the capacity of Imogen's husband to any other young man of his acquaintance. He would have given a good deal to know whether she was still as resolutely determined never to marry as she had been two or three months ago; and also whether these *Thyatira Batis* would prove an additional stumbling-block in Sir Charles's path, or the reverse. Certainly it was an unfortunate circumstance that the moths which he, in his ignorance, had pitched upon to send her, should have happened to be such common ones. If only they had been great rarities, who could tell how they might not have softened her heart towards the sender!

CHAPTER XIII
Does She Like Him?

Sir Charles was, as may be supposed, very anxious to learn whether his moths had arrived safely, and how they had been received; but on each subsequent occasion of meeting Imogen, he failed to screw up his courage to the pitch requisite to enable him to allude to the subject. Knowing, however, that her brother was soon coming to London for a couple of days' holiday, he resolved to make him the medium through whom to discover whether the entomological offering had been acceptable, and to postpone, therefore, for a few days the gratification of his curiosity.

The two young men were excellent friends, and Sir Charles had already confided to Ralph his intention of making another attempt for Imogen's hand. Ralph cordially approved of the design; though to say the truth it seemed to him a somewhat undignified eagerness about a trivial matter, and caused his friend to sink just a tiny degree down in his esteem. The eighteen-year-old philosopher was inclined to think that no woman could possibly be worth asking more than once, and that one would do very nearly as well as another as a wife. Consequently he beheld with a delightful sense of superiority the spectacle of the older man who was so foolish as to imagine that his happiness was dependent upon securing the affections of this one particular girl—a mere every-day girl, too, who had no hidden romance, mystery, or anything of that sort to make her attractive. Though Ralph was extremely fond of his sister, none the less did he consider her to be slightly inferior to himself, who had the advantage of sex and of a year's seniority, and was on both those accounts clearly entitled to patronise her. And as besides this, he had known her all his life, and was convinced that he knew everything that there was to know about her, he could by no means comprehend how she should appear to anyone else in a more romantic, and un-matter-of-fact light.

The morning after Ralph came to town, his father and sister went to ride in Rotten Row as usual, but he could not accompany them because there was not a third saddle-horse to mount him on. Therefore he betook himself to the Park on foot, and lounged about under the trees, watching the riders. In this occupation he was presently joined by Sir Charles, who happened also on that day to be amongst the pedestrians. He was pleased to see Ralph again, but was otherwise in anything but a happy frame of mind, and they had not been together long before he made apparent what was troubling him.

'I can't think what your sister can see in that fellow,' he ejaculated discontentedly, as the Rhyses rode past them in company with Mr Sylvester, who was talking eagerly to Imogen.

'Sylvester, do you mean?' asked Ralph. The other nodded assent. I don't expect she sees anything particular in him,' answered Ralph; 'what makes you think so?'

'Because he's always about with her, and she don't seem to want to get rid of him,' grumbled the baronet.

'*Always*?' queried his companion. 'Come now! Are you sure of that?'

'Well, pretty nearly always, at any rate. Look at him sticking to her and your father to-day—it's been just the same other days, too! And then he was at the opera with them one night, and at the theatre another; and she dances with him ever so often at balls.'

'Come, that isn't quite *always*, after all,' returned Ralph; 'and I don't see why a man shouldn't speak to her when he happens to meet her if they get on together. Do you know him at all?'

'Never spoke to him in my life, and don't want to—that's more!' replied Sir Charles, moodily. 'I can tell by his face he's the sort of fellow I should abominate.'

'Nonsense! He's not at all bad-looking, only you're jealous of him. I don't care about him very particularly one way or other myself, but he can be amusing enough when he chooses, I can tell you. You should just hear him and Imogen go at it hammer and tongs sometimes when they get into an argument—she furiously in earnest generally, and he quite cool, and saying such queer things. You bet he's a clever chap. 'Tisn't for everyone's benefit that he chooses to make himself pleasant, though; no doubt that makes him all the more taking to whomsoever he *does* honour with his full powers of agreeability.'

'I wonder if he cares for mothing,' said Sir Charles, 'amongst his other attractions. By-the-bye, I sent her a couple of moths the other day. Do you know if she got them all right?'

At this speech Ralph suddenly burst out laughing, to the astonishment of his companion, who could not conceive what there was ludicrous in what he had said.

'Stop a bit—don't look so surprised, old fellow; I'll tell you in a minute,' exclaimed Ralph, struggling to regain his gravity. 'They came all right enough, but—oh, dear! I can't help laughing as I think of it—what on earth induced you to send her a couple of *Thyatira Batis*?'

'They were *Thyatira Batis* or *Thyatira* anything else for all I knew about them. I took no end of trouble about setting them and packing them up and all, because they were so uncommonly pretty that I thought she would like to have them. Didn't she?'

'Like to have them!' repeated Ralph contemptuously. 'Who's going to care about having beasts like that, which are as common as mud? I wish I'd been there to see their arrival, and her disgust! However, she told me what had happened, and then we did have a good laugh over it together. It was such a splendid sell for her! First the arrival of the package by post, all done up and registered as if it had been a jewel-case—then her opening it, thinking she was going to discover something very fetching inside—then the awful come down of finding nothing but two specimens of *Thyatira Batis* after all! She couldn't think who'd sent them at first, but afterwards guessed from the post-mark. *Thyatira Batis* indeed! Why, they're a perfect pest at sugars some nights!'

Sir Charles looked slightly crestfallen.

'How was I to know that?' asked he. '*I'd* never seen the brutes before, at any rate.'

'Very likely not,' answered the other, with an air of superior wisdom, 'and that just shows the foolishness of meddling with things about which you know nothing whatever. Precious little chance of doing yourself much good with anyone that way! There goes Lady Elise Bolyn. Who's that perky-looking fellow talking to her?'

'That? Oh, it's Guelph Crœsus-Hogg. Son of the man who was nobody till he made such a pot of money by contracts.'

'Is it? Well, I don't think much of Guelph's appearance, at all events. Has he got St Vitus' dance, I wonder? Do look how the chap grins and ogles, and mouths his words—giving his poor eyes and lips double the work they need have. And even when he's standing in one place and not talking he can't be still, but must needs keep poking his cane into the gravel, fidgeting his feet about, and playing with his watch-chain and eyeglass all the time. He looks as if he wanted to be thought fifty times wider awake than the rest of creation—don't you think so?'

'Ah—yes—' replied Sir Charles abstractedly, and evidently without taking the faintest interest in what had been said.

Ralph did not notice this inattention, and continued to criticise the unconscious Guelph Crœsus-Hogg.

'Why, the fellow don't look much older than me,' said Ralph; 'yet there he is having no end of flirtation with Lady Elise, who must be twenty-eight if she's a day! Look at 'em walking up and down together, and looking as pleased as Punch with one another! There! now they've gone and got two chairs and sat themselves down side by side. And I do declare he is sitting almost in her pocket, and grinning like a Cheshire cat, and she's looking as if that was precisely the thing she most enjoyed. I say! isn't it just absurd?'

'Ah—yes,' replied Sir Charles, as absently as before.

Ralph looked round at him, and perceived that his head was turned in the direction where Imogen had last disappeared, which was diametrically opposite to where Lady Elise and her juvenile admirer had established themselves. The fact was that the poor baronet was straining his eyes in hopes of seeing his lady-love re-appear without the obnoxious Sylvester being at her side, and did not exactly know what Ralph had been talking about, and had only ejaculated 'ah—yes !' because aware that some kind of remark was being expected of him.

His companion watched him for a minute or two with a mixture of amusement and pity; then, guessing rightly that there was just then only one subject in which it would be possible to excite his interest, Ralph gave up attempting to force the conversation into other channels, and returned to what he knew to be the congenial theme.

'I say!' he said, 'Here's a new idea for you, that's just occurred to me as I saw Ethel Carton drive past. Why don't you go and confide in her, and get her to give you a lift with Imogen? I daresay she could, for Imogen thinks an awful lot of her, I know—or used to last winter, at any rate.'

Sir Charles pricked up his ears hopefully at the beginning of this speech, but the conclusion disappointed him. Ethel was in his eyes far too formidable a personage for him to venture upon confiding his love affairs to her. He knew he should never muster up courage to do it, and marvelled how Ralph could have thought such hardihood possible. Still he thought it would look foolish to make known the degree of awe with which she had inspired him, so he did not at first put forward his real reason for objecting to the plan suggested.

'Oh no!' he replied, shaking his head, 'I don't the least think that would be any use.'

'Don't you be too sure of that!' persisted Ralph, who took credit to himself for the new idea he had struck out, and thought it ought to be at once adopted. 'It *might* be, you know, and, at any rate, you can't tell till you try. *I* believe it would be a first-rate spec! '

But Sir Charles did not seem to be convinced.

'You may be pretty sure,' he said, 'that Miss Carton would not thank me for troubling her about my concerns, and I don't see what right I have to do it either.'

'Oh, bless you, Ethel wouldn't mind one pin; shouldn't wonder that she wouldn't rather like it than not.'

'You forget that she is not *my* cousin, though, and that I only know her very slightly.'

'What a one you are to make difficulties! One would think you were afraid she'd eat you!'

'To tell you the honest truth, I think I am,' said Sir Charles, laughing, as he saw that his excuses were unavailing.

Ralph whistled.

'You don't say so,' he exclaimed, again feeling himself immensely superior to the older man. 'Well, *I* ain't afraid of any woman, and don't mean to be either. A man should never knock under to any of them like that, to my mind. And afraid of Ethel, too, of all people in the world! She's a thorough good sort when you know her, and nothing whatever alarming about her, I can tell you. Well, if you won't take my advice, you won't; but it's the best I can give you, and you know I'm all for you as my brother-in-law, if only it could be fixed.'

'Yes, yes; I know you're no end of a trump, and will do all you can for me,' returned Sir Charles gratefully; 'and look here, you can do one thing if you will, I think. You might put a spoke in Sylvester's wheel somehow for me, mightn't you? I don't want you to tell lies, or do anything unfair, of course. But tell her to be careful not to get entangled with any one before she knows what she's about; or tell her that he's a snob; or ask her why she lets him be always dangling after her; or—or say whatever you think best that would make her snub him, you know.'

It was now Ralph's turn to object to what was proposed. When on a previous occasion he had tried his hand at advising his sister in matrimonial affairs, he had been nettled at the ill-success of his efforts. The worst part had been too, that when he had tried to produce an impression upon her by assuming airs of incipient manhood (as he thought himself fully justified in doing at his age, and with some hairs of quite an inch long beginning already to shade the corners of his mouth), she had detected the intention at once, and laughed at it in a way that was most unpleasant to his youthful dignity. He was aware that she had had the best of the encounter, and did not feel at all inclined to provoke another battle on the same subject. Still he did not want to confess this after the boast he had just uttered about never being afraid of any woman, so he took refuge in excuses.

It was a ticklish thing to speak to a girl about this kind of matter. He believed Sir Charles was mistaken in thinking there was any inclination to a spoon[1] between her and Sylvester. Needless, fussy interference was simply ridiculous; the chances were it would only do more harm than good by setting her to think about what she wouldn't otherwise have thought of at all. Finally, being pressed further and driven into a corner, he declared, with some show of indignation, that, *of course*, he should speak to her at any time if he saw signs of her behaving indiscreetly, and getting into a scrape; but that at the present moment he could see no reasonable cause for alarm. As he appeared to be getting touchy, Sir Charles thought it best to be content with this declaration, and to say no more on the subject just then. He had the felicity of seeing Imogen ride past once without any companion save her father; and then the popular hour for lunch having arrived, they all followed the example of the rest of the world, and quitted the Row in search of that meal.

When lunch was over Imogen wrote a few notes that required answers, and then went across to Belgrave Square to see her cousin, whom she found at home.

'I saw you this morning in the distance,' said Ethel after greeting her; 'and I couldn't make out who you were riding with besides your father. Was it anyone I know?'

'No, you've never met him; it was Mr Sylvester,' answered Imogen, and her cheeks flushed a little consciously as she mentioned his name. 'I didn't see you sitting under the trees in the victoria with Mrs Grey, till just after we'd turned our horses' heads the other way. I asked him if he knew you, and he said he'd never had the honour of an introduction, so I offered to introduce him to you as soon as we got near the trees again. He would have liked it very much, only then unluckily before we came back to that end of the Row, he saw some one whom he wanted to speak to about business, he said; he rode off, saying he should rejoin us directly; but I expect he must have got kept, as we didn't see anything more of him afterwards.'

Ethel had heard her cousin's name coupled once or twice—though only vaguely and speculatively—with that of Sylvester, and was curious as to whether or not the rumour was likely to prove true. Imogen's slight blush in speaking of him had not escaped her notice, and now that he happened to have been mentioned thus accidentally, she thought she would pursue the subject, and try and discover some indication of Imogen's opinion of him.

'Never mind,' said Ethel, carelessly; 'you must introduce him to me at some other time. I shall be very pleased to make his acquaintance since he is a friend of yours. Tell me what he's like, and whether you think he and I shall get on together? Ah! You can't now, though,' she continued, as a violent peal at the bell of the front door announced a visitor; 'for there's some one come to call—I wonder who it is.'

Imogen was sitting by the window, and peeped out cautiously from behind a corner of the blind.

'Tremendous swell turn-out whoever it may be,' she observed. 'Coachman and two flunkeys in powder and calves. Horses; harness; carriage; liveries; coats-of-arms; crests and all the rest of it in the highest style of magnificence. Must be the Lady Mayoress at least, I should think! Only one person I know in the carriage, and that's Lady Elise Bolyn. Ah—she's getting out, and the others have driven off. What a bore! Just when I thought I was going to have you all to myself! She's *always* with you, I do believe; and no one else has a chance of a quiet chat with you, ever!'

Ethel looked amused.

'I haven't seen quite so much of her just lately,' she replied. 'She's been spending a good deal of her time with some new acquaintances that she seems to be making great friends with—the Crœsus-Hoggs.'

Imogen's face on hearing this was a study of contemptuous astonishment. In her dealings with people of the labouring classes, she was free from the smallest tinge of pride, and never for an instant dreamt of considering herself to be really their superior, simply because she chanced to have been born in a higher rank of life. But she was by no means equally democratic in her sentiments regarding those who did not naturally belong to the class of what she deemed ladies and gentlemen, and yet who assumed to do so merely on the strength of having quantities of money.

Towards such people she was greatly inclined to be fine and exclusive in her behaviour. She considered them as being pretentious, and pretentiousness was a thing which she abominated. What was mere money, that it should be supposed able to elevate a person above his own rank of life, and make him equal to those who were his superiors by birth? It gave her quite a shock to find that an earl's daughter, like Lady Elise, should be less fastidious than herself in such matters; and it seemed to her still more surprising and outrageous for anyone to be disposed to exchange the society of Ethel Carton, for that of mere plebeian *nouveaux-riches* such as these Crœsus-Hoggs.

'*Those* people!' exclaimed Imogen, in a tone of supreme disdain. 'What on earth can make her take to them? Every one says they are awfully vulgar snobs! I should have thought she would have had better taste.'

Before Ethel could reply, the door was thrown open by a servant announcing Lady Elise Bolyn; and the entrance of the lady in question put an end to the conversation for the time being.

VOLUME III

Contents

CHAPTER I
The Crœsus-Hoggs

Very momentous and unexpected were the results following indirectly from that call of Lady Elise's in Belgrave Square, which hindered the attempt Ethel was just about to make to sound her cousin upon the subject of Mr Sylvester. But before setting forth the object of Lady Elise's visit, it is necessary to introduce the reader to her new friends, the millionaire Crœsus-Hoggs.

The Crœsus-Hogg family was five in number, and consisted of the father and mother; two daughters, named respectively Guinevere and Victoria; and one son, named Guelph. Whatever charges might be brought against these people, over-refinement was certainly never likely to be one of them, as their appearance and manners would effectually give it the lie. Indeed, some persons thought that their standard of breeding was hardly near enough to that which generally prevails amongst ladies and gentlemen to allow of their being admitted to the society which esteems itself to belong to the upper ten. But then it was only a narrow-minded and prejudiced minority who took that view, and in the eyes of the majority of the world, the enormous wealth possessed by the Crœsus-Hoggs was sufficient to atone, almost, if not altogether, for any deficiencies of birth or breeding on their part. Never was seen such an establishment as theirs; such troops of gorgeously apparelled servants; such sumptuous liveries; such magnificent horses and carriages; such splendid furniture; such superb flowers; such valuable plate; such pictures; such statues; in short, such a lavish display of wealth in every direction! It was notorious throughout all London that no visitor of any kind—be he tradesman, servant, messenger, or individual, however insignificant—could spend a minute within the Crœsus-Hogg doors without discovering that luxury pervaded every corner of the house, and that something gratifying to the five senses of humanity was to be met with at every turn. And how enviable must be the condition of people whose lives were passed wholly amongst such delights, and who could enjoy them to the very fullest extent.

Whatever good thing money could buy, that the Crœsus-Hoggs would have, cost what it might; and throughout their establishment they would tolerate nothing less than as near an approach to perfection as it was possible to have. For instance, the artist who presided in the kitchen was a real genius, a cook such as is but rarely to be met with in this fallen world of ours. He was a Frenchman, rejoicing in the name of Gaston Leblanc, an enthusiast for his profession, which he regarded with a chivalrous love and veneration as being the only thing in the world deserving of unswerving constancy. Religion, morality, women, amusements—all these did very well to take up or leave alone for a while, according to the fancy of the moment. But not so his art; that possessed his heart too entirely for him to be guilty of fickleness towards it for so much as a moment; and to do anything that could bring it into disrepute seemed to him a heinous crime. He maintained that, inasmuch as every kind of food had its own natural and peculiar flavour, therefore those who destroyed that flavour—whether by over-saucing, careless cooking, unskilful mixing, or any other way—were little short of murderers, in that they deprived the food of the individuality which constituted its life, and whereby it was to be distinguished from all other foods.

The well-known saying to the effect that God sends meat and the devil sends cooks, was one day rashly alluded to in his hearing. His horror and indignation at the idea of the mere existence of such a heresy were so great that he nearly had a fit. When he had somewhat recovered from the first shock, he began seriously to consider the propriety of challenging to mortal combat the daring person who had been so wanting in delicacy of feeling as to give utterance to the fearful slander in his presence. The more he thought about it, the more convinced he felt that it was incumbent on him to take vengeance on some one or other; and that since the unknown author was unattainable, the only thing to be done was to chastise whoever had ventured to repeat the calumny. But then, fortunately, it all of a sudden struck him that the miserable English language had but one word to express cooks of either sex. That made him see the matter in an altogether different light. The offensive saying had doubtless been aimed only at female cooks—in which case he had not a word to say against it, and could certainly not resent it as a personal insult. And as on reflection this appeared to him to be evidently the correct view to take, his ruffled dignity presently subsided, and he recovered his wonted serenity.

Be it said to his praise that he was every bit as particular over the cooking of a mutton chop as over that of a truffled ortolan; and would no more allow a boiled potato to issue from his kitchen in an ill-prepared condition than he would the most artistic and showy *entrée* that the heart of cook ever devised. Of course, the fact of such a man being *chef* anywhere was a sufficient guarantee that in that house everything eatable would be first-rate of its kind, and so the Crœsus-Hoggs had engaged him at a tremendously high salary. And in every other department of their household there prevailed the same rule of conduct, viz., that no kind of excellence was to be wanting if it was procurable by money.

Now it has been already mentioned that the relations existing between Ethel and Lady Elise Bolyn were by no means to the liking of the latter. Firstly, because she was tired of keeping herself continually in check lest the worldly, selfish, hard, petty part of her disposition should become too apparent, and shock the more noble nature of the heiress. Secondly, because she had no love for the occupations and amusements of country life unless they afforded plentiful opportunities for flirtation, and therefore considered Carton House a dreadfully dull place to stay long at, and did not care about going back there. And thirdly, because she perceived the great difficulty of ever surrounding Ethel with tendrils of friendship strong and holding enough to be safe to rely on. Altogether, therefore, she had arrived at the conclusion that Ethel was a bad speculation; and that though she would be unwise to relinquish the intimacy to which she had already advanced before she should have found some more promising one to substitute for it, yet that it behoved her to search about for some other rich house at which to become a tame cat— some person to whom she could attach herself whose pecuniary advantages should be equal to those of Ethel, and who should be in other ways more satisfactory.

Under these circumstances the Crœsus-Hoggs presented themselves to her mind as being not unworthy of attention, and she easily induced her mother to make their acquaintance. The more she saw of them, the more plainly did she perceive, that here was the very opening that she had been desiring. That they were by no means all that could be wished in regard of birth and behaviour, was no doubt a drawback. But experience had taught her, long ago, the vanity of expecting to have everything exactly to one's mind; and it was quite evident that if she chose to consort with these people, she would be welcomed with effusion, and neither pains nor money would be spared in trying to please her. Was it not wiser to be a little thick-skinned, and to make friends with Guinevere and Victoria Crœsus-Hogg, than to continue to attach herself to a person like Ethel? The latter had no doubt the recommendation of being a lady; but then how wearisome it was to feel always obliged to be on one's P's and Q's, and to take trouble about making oneself agreeable lest one should lose innumerable luxuries and enjoyments which could only be reached by means of intimacy with their mistress's! With the Crœsus-Hoggs, on the contrary, Lady Elise need not give herself the very slightest trouble in order to be acceptable. Having no ancestors, they naturally adored the peerage, and ardently desired the privilege of associating with any of its members. Consequently they were every whit as anxious to have the favour of her company, as she could be to bestow it upon them. In their opinion, whatever she said or did was necessarily charming. Everything belonging to them was entirely at her service, and nothing could possibly be considered too good for her. They thought her affable, graceful, fascinating, the most enchanting of human beings, and were quite enraptured to find themselves gliding into terms of familiarity with an earl's daughter.

At a very early stage of the acquaintance, Guinevere Crœsus-Hogg had one day hazarded the remark, what a happiness it would be if only her brother Guelph, could manage to please Lady Elise's fancy, and persuade her to marry him. At the time, the idea had been pooh-poohed by the others as a thing too good to be possible—a joy too unattainable to be worth reckoning on. A woman like her would of course be the very *beau ideal*[1] of a wife for him; but then it was no use setting their hearts on such a piece of luck as that, because they would be so sure to be disappointed. But as Lady Elise's willingness to respond to their advances, and accept the invitations and other attentions which they offered her, became more and more apparent, the idea began to seem less unlikely after all; and they were now looking forward with ever-increasing confidence to the glorious possibility of her one day becoming an actual member of their family.

Whether Lady Elise herself ever contemplated such a thing or not it was impossible to say. At all events she was continually in their company, partaking freely of all the good things they had to offer, and doing her best to shut her eyes to whatever peculiarities of manner, speech, or sentiment jarred against her aristocratic sense of what was fitting. She reflected that it was absurd to be over-particular about trifles with people who meant really well by one. Still it would certainly be a comfort, considering how often she dined with old Mr Crœsus-Hogg, if he were not so *very* fond of putting his knife into his mouth— and such a long way in too—almost down his throat sometimes! It was a thing to which she had an especial objection, because she never saw it done without being in an agony lest the hand should slip, and the mouth be slit open; and that fear always communicated to her own lips a series of involuntary, smarting thrills of sympathy which continued till the misused knife had again returned to a place of safety. She would make heroic attempts to argue herself out of this weakness—reminding herself that even if the knife-sucker's hand *did* chance to slip, no one but himself could possibly be the worse for it; that she could look another way during the performance; that it was absurd to let a fad like that interfere with her enjoyment of Leblanc's exquisite cooking. But however well aware she might be of her own folly, she nevertheless could not wholly succeed in reconciling herself to her host's manner of eating; and if he happened to be away on any of the numerous occasions when she was at his house at meal-times, she invariably hailed his absence with a feeling of grateful relief.

This was far from being the only way in which her natural prejudices were continually offended by her new friends, though as she was too philosophical and worldly wise not to be able to tolerate what was unpleasant when it was to her interest to do so, she gave no sign of the discomposure that they again and again caused her. But that did not prevent her from having often a secret sensation of annoyance—a sort of rising of the gorge in their company; and she always experienced an especial feeling of refreshment and content when once more mixing in the society of her equals after an unwontedly large dose of the family of the Crœsus-Hoggs.

CHAPTER II
Ethel's Whim

'Dear Ethel! How *fortunate* to find you at home!' exclaimed Lady Elise, gushingly, as she followed the footman into the room where Ethel and Imogen were. 'Mrs Crœsus-Hogg brought me here in her carriage, and I made her come early on purpose, because then I thought there might be some chance of catching you before you went out for the afternoon. It's quite an *age* since we've seen each other, isn't it?'

'Quite;' rejoined Ethel, gravely; 'two or three ages at least, I should say. I think it really must be a whole week since you were here last. Do you find me much altered? or do I seem to be wearing pretty well?'

Lady Elise laughed rather affectedly. She could not quite make out whether this speech was mere harmless chaff, or whether perhaps Ethel's making fun of the exaggerated expression she had used, was meant ill-naturedly. For she did not feel very certain as to whether or not Ethel might be inclined in some way to resent finding herself deserted in favour of the Crœsus-Hoggs—and that uncertainty prevented Lady Elise from being altogether at her ease just now.

'Ha, ha!' said she; 'what funny things you *do* say, Ethel! But I'm *too* delighted not to have missed you, as I want to ask a great, a particularly great favour of you. Only tell me something about yourself first. How are you? and have you had any news as to the stolen jewels yet?'

'Thank you; I'm quite well,' answered Ethel. 'I've not heard a word as to the jewels. When last I did have a communication on the subject, it was to the effect that the police had no further clue whatever.'

'Dear, dear! How terribly provoking!' replied Lady Elise. 'Isn't it *too* wonderful where that man Richards can have hidden them? I think it's really *too* stupid of the police people not to find them out, or make him tell, or at any rate do something to punish him.'

'Why so, when he'd nothing whatever to do with the robbery?' said Imogen, firing up indignantly on behalf of the man whom she believed to be a persecuted innocent. 'I think it's very wrong of people to go on speaking of him as if he'd done it, when the jury have expressly said that he didn't. I should just like to see a few of them prosecuted for libel! That would soon teach them to be more careful.'

Lady Elise coloured at this blunt attack; and Ethel, knowing Imogen's uncompromising way of defending her own opinions, and fearing that a squabble was about to ensue, hastened to interpose before Lady Elise could reply.

'By-the-bye,' said Ethel, addressing her cousin, 'is the poor man well again, now? He was very ill, wasn't he, in the winter?'

'Yes, he was; but he's all right now, as far as health goes. Not in other ways, though, for all this bother about the burglary is driving him out of the country, and he's off to America next month. He and his wife hate going like poison, but there's no help for it. Lies and slanders have made this country too hot for them, and they can do no good staying in it any longer.'

'Going to America, is he?' said Lady Elise, endeavouring spitefully to aggravate the girl who had as good as told her she was libellous. 'Ah, then depend upon it, that's where he's managed to send the jewels to. It's all a pretence that he doesn't like moving, and, of course, in reality he's looking forward to the fun he means to have there when he's disposed of his booty.'

A storm was inevitable if the conversation continued to

relate to Richard Richards; so Ethel, with much presence of mind, promptly introduced a fresh topic.

'Pray do leave that wretched burglary alone,' she said; 'if you only knew how tired I am of it, I'm sure you wouldn't inflict it on me any more. Tell me instead about these grand amateur theatricals that the Crœsus-Hoggs are going to have, Elise. Of course you know all about it—what will be acted, and who'll act, and all the rest of it.'

'Well, I think I *do* know pretty much all that is settled, so far,' returned Lady Elise. 'I assure you it's to be a *quite* too awfully tremendous affair.'

'So everyone seems to expect,' said Ethel. 'Mr Scriven declares that on that occasion all such adjuncts as dresses, decorations, scenery, flowers, supper, etc., are certain to be so splendid as to make it a very unimportant matter what the actors are like. Even if they were the veriest sticks that ever breathed, yet the performance cannot fail to be a success, he says. In fact, I suppose, it'll be like a picture whose setting and frame are sufficiently magnificent to carry off any short-comings on the part of the artist. Who are going to act?'

'It is not altogether settled yet. Mr Trevor Owen is to act for one. I met him there at lunch to-day, and we've all been having a tremendous theatrical talk. By-the-bye, he gives me the idea of being quite wonderfully smitten with the eldest girl, Guinevere. She is to act also—though I fancy she's rather made a mistake in the part she's chosen; they say her natural turn is for comedy, but unluckily she's taken it into her head to try melodrama this time, and I'm too dreadfully afraid that perhaps she won't succeed. There are to be two pieces acted, and she insists on being the leading lady in the second one; and as soon as he heard that, he made quite a *desperate* fuss to be let to play hero to her heroine; no one objected, so that much is arranged definitely, at all events.'

Then Trevor Owen also had gone over to the Crœsus-Hoggs! Ethel very well understood that this was what had happened, just as clearly as she had comprehended the meaning of Lady Elise's less frequent visits of late, and general diminution of attentions; for Miss Carton's passivity did not hinder her from being observant enough to have a very good idea of what went on around her. Not the faintest wish had she, to retain either the lady or gentleman as worshippers at her own shrine, and their ready transfer of allegiance to the Crœsus-Hoggs, caused her no little amusement, untinged by the smallest particle of resentment. It was a matter of profound indifference to her whether Lady Elise and Trevor Owen might think it worth their while to continue to court her or not. But her indifference in this respect did not make it altogether agreeable to her to be shown thus plainly how very little her friends esteemed her for herself, and how entirely for what she was worth in L. S. D.[1] She did not much relish having that fact brought home forcibly to her, however willing she might be to allow that it was no more than the truth. Therefore her self-love was a little bit wounded by what she had just heard. A hazy notion crossed her mind that she would like some day or other to exert herself for once; to show people what sort of stuff she was really made of; to try and discover what she was really worth apart from her heiress-ship. Only then the worst of doing that would be that it would be sure to involve a dreadful amount of trouble. And besides, it would be utterly inconsistent with her favourite masterly inaction policy!

'I can't say I've ever seen Miss Crœsus-Hogg, but no doubt she and Mr Owen will make an excellent couple,' she remarked sweetly. 'And who'll they have to act with them?'

'Well, there's a singing part which Lady George Quaver has half promised to undertake,' answered Lady Elise, 'and if so, it's sure to be a success—she has such an altogether *delicious* voice, you know. But there's another important male part besides the hero's in the piece, and their great hope is to get that Mr Sylvester to do it—the man who is with Messrs Glass at Cwm-Eithin. They say he's a capital actor, and quite to be depended upon to make up for any unsteadiness in the leading couple. They've asked him to take the part, but he hasn't answered yet for certain. He says it must depend a good deal on his business engagements. Just now he's employed up in London. I believe he's going to be taken into partnership in a few weeks.'

'But you've only told us about the second play, yet,' said Ethel. 'Who are to be hero and heroine in the first one?'

Lady Elise looked a little bit conscious as she replied,—

'Oh, Mr Guelph Crœsus-Hogg is to have the chief man's *rôle*; and as for the woman's—I don't quite know—they are very anxious that I should see what I can do with it. Perhaps I may—indeed, I've almost as good as promised that I will. But there are *two* principal female parts in that piece—one almost as important as the other—and they pressed me so hard to find some friend of mine for it, that it seemed quite ill-natured to refuse. And that's the especial object that's brought me here to-day. I didn't say a word to them about my idea, which is this: it suddenly occurred to me how awfully nice it would be if *you* were to take it, dearest Ethel. Now do pray say yes—it would be so quite *too* delightful if you would!'

'I am much obliged for the offer,' answered Ethel, laughing; 'but I'm afraid I must decline; I'm sure I should be too nervous for one thing. And besides, I distrust my acting capacities, and don't at all believe they'd be equal to such a great occasion.'

'Oh! now that's only your modesty,' returned Lady Elise, eagerly. 'I saw you acting once last year, and I remember you did it *quite* too capitally.'

'But then I don't know your friends,' objected Ethel; ' that's another reason against it.'

'I assure you that's *perfectly* immaterial,' said Lady Elise, who was very anxious to get as many people of her own set as possible to take part in the theatricals, in order to keep her in countenance. 'Not only would *any* friend of mine be welcome, but also I know that you are a person whose acquaintance they would be only too *enchanted* to make. Now *do* let me persuade you, there's a dear!'

Ethel was about to refuse absolutely, when all of a sudden it struck her that this would be an opportunity for her to carry out that fancy which had just now come to her for showing what she could do, and finding out people's real opinion of her. Acting was an amusement for which she believed herself to have some turn. Why not appear incog. and see what reception she would meet with from an audience who had no knowledge of who she really was? It was a sudden, wild idea, very unlike her usual prudent and indolent self, and doubtless owing its origin to that little sting which her self-love had just received.

'Well, perhaps it might not be bad fun, if no one knew it was me,' she returned, after a moment's consideration. 'Do you think that could be managed? Could I alter myself in dressing for the part, so as not to be recognised?'

Imogen stared in surprise at this utterly unexpected reply, and almost doubted the evidence of her own ears. What could the tranquil and aristocratic Ethel be thinking of, to condescend to join in the revels of these vulgarians? As it was Ethel who contemplated this freak, there must doubtless be some good reason therefore; and it was very certain that Ethel herself could not become in the slightest degree tainted by contact with their vulgarity, whatever she might do. Still—it was extremely incomprehensible.

Lady Elise was astonished also. She had thought there was enough chance of securing the heiress to make the attempt not altogether a hopeless one; yet she had not much expected to succeed, and was delighted to see such ready signs of yielding.

'Oh dear, yes!' she exclaimed; 'you can alter yourself as easily as *possible*. It's the part of an elderly woman; and what with doing your hair differently, and the dress and get-up altogether, there wouldn't be the faintest difficulty about making you unrecognisable. Only there's the name on the play-bills,' she added; 'you forget that that would tell who you are.'

'Not if I took some other name,' said Ethel. 'I might adopt my second name, and appear as Miss Percival, you know. I don't suppose there would be any harm in doing that.'

'Harm!' rejoined Lady Elise. 'Why, what harm *could* there be in it? Of course not! Then let's consider the matter settled, shall we? Oh! this is quite *too* delicious!'

'Well, I can't say for certain till I've asked my uncle,' said Ethel; 'but if he makes no objection, you can send me the part. In that case I shall learn it by myself at home and not with the other performers, so as avoid being Miss Percival as much as I can. I don't know that I shall altogether like appearing under false colours, and it'll be quite enough to have to do it on the day of the performance without multiplying the occasions needlessly.'

'There'll be the rehearsals though,' observed Imogen. 'Won't you have to go to them?'

'I don't see that would be necessary if I work up my part alone thoroughly. At any rate I should think I might manage not to want to attend more than one. Mr Owen is the person who would be most likely to recognise me amongst the other actors; but as he acts in the other piece, and as I shouldn't stay a minute longer than was absolutely indispensable, I daresay I should be able to keep out of his way.'

'Oh, no doubt you would!' cried Lady Elise. 'And I'll use all my influence with the Crœsus-Hoggs to make everything smooth for you, and to keep your secret from them and everyone else. *Do* go and ask your uncle, dearest Ethel! I'm quite *dying* to feel that I've actually secured you. I'm convinced you'll have no difficulty with him, and that he won't object to *anything* you wish to do.'

'I don't quite know about that,' said Ethel, smiling. 'If I were to wish to have a finger in the construction of that machine he's making, I've an idea he'd object very strongly indeed. However, I'll go and see what he says to the acting scheme.'

So saying she went to his room, leaving her two visitors to turn over photograph books, remark that it was a fine day, and preserve an armed neutrality till her return.

'Well?' exclaimed Lady Elise, eagerly, as soon as Ethel reappeared.

'He says I may do as I like; so I'll try what I can do with this *rôle* of yours, provided you and Imogen promise faithfully not to breathe a syllable that can make anyone suspect Miss Percival and Miss Carton to be identical. Absolute incog. is the condition upon which alone I'll act, remember.'

Her cousin and Lady Elise readily promised secrecy; and when the latter met the Crœsus-Hoggs that night she told them that she had induced a friend of hers named Percival to act in the same piece as herself in the approaching theatricals.

Little did anyone anticipate how those theatricals were destined to end, and how much difference would ensue from Ethel's sudden whim of appearing incognito in them!

CHAPTER III
Sylvester and Love

How did the land lie between Imogen and Mr Sylvester? Was there any real cause for Sir Charles's disquietude?

Mr Sylvester was a man who generally made a very definite impression of some kind on whoever had much to do with him—his identity marking itself strongly on the memory something like that of a scent, which whether pleasant or not, is too powerful to be easily forgotten by anyone who has once known it. It was only natural, therefore, that Imogen should think a good deal about him, and that he should occupy in her mind a niche of his own which was quite apart from that of anyone else. Dangerous symptoms, no doubt! The man who is much in a girl's thoughts, and has secured a special niche in her mental furniture, is not unlikely to finish by gaining possession of her heart. But though Imogen liked Sylvester, she had not yet got any farther than that. She was dimly conscious that his powers of attraction were counterbalanced by occasional glimpses of something in his nature that seemed almost terrifying and mysterious. And it was probably owing to this vague consciousness that she had so far escaped falling in love with him.

She fancied that there was an alteration in him now from what he had been when first she made his acquaintance. Then he had seemed much the same sort of person at all times; but of late he had grown more uncertain, and it was impossible to reckon beforehand on what sort of a humour he would be in. One day he would be fierce, reckless, hard and cynical; and on the next, perhaps, almost like another man; gentle, and giving her a strange sense of pity for she knew not what, and of being in the presence of something sad, of witnessing some repressed and terrible trouble of either mind or body. Sometimes she would fancy that his old cynicism and hardness were diminishing; and then again would tell herself that it was not so in reality, and that what made her think so was only because by this time she had become accustomed to these things, and did not therefore always notice them now as much as she had done at first. Anyhow he was a sphinx to her—a being whom she had no key to understand. And, fearless as she naturally was, yet there were times when she was by no means sure in her secret soul that she was not a little bit afraid of this man.

When she speculated (as she did occasionally) on the way in which she regarded him, there was one point that especially exercised her mind, and seemed to her unaccountable. It was a favourite opinion of hers, and one which she had often maintained hotly in discussion with him, or anyone else who happened to talk about the reasons for people's liking one another, that likings were impossible between persons who had nothing in common, and could not thoroughly trust each other. Now she could not deny that she certainly did like Mr Sylvester in a way; and yet when she asked herself whether he and she had anything in common, and whether he was a man in whom she felt confidence, she had very considerable doubts of being able to answer in the affirmative. How was that? Was her theory an unsound one then? She knew that in respect of all the other people whom she liked, she could say unhesitatingly that she had points of sympathy with them, and would not hesitate to trust to them. Take her father, for instance, or Ethel, or Ralph, or—or—Sir Charles Dover. Though she did not want to marry this last, yet she did not for a moment deny that she liked him; but then it was quite according to her theory that she should do so.

He knew nothing about moths, it was true, and had even been so stupid as to suppose she could want a couple of *Thyatira Batis* (poor fellow! he had meant it kindly all the same; and what trouble he must have had about the setting of them!); but still she had not the faintest doubt that most of his tastes, occupations, and amusements would be congenial to her, and such as she could sympathise with. She had discovered, too, that he had high principles, and an honest desire to do right. She knew it intuitively, though he never said much about it; and, as for trusting him—why, the idea that anyone who did that would ever find their confidence misplaced, was an absurdity too great to be contemplated seriously! Oh yes; it was the most natural thing in the world to like such a person as that, and there was no difficulty whatever about understanding it. But why should she care at all for Mr Sylvester, who was so absolutely different? Had he some strange power—she hardly knew whether to call it attractive or repellent—which was peculiar to himself? Some power that could even dwarf, overshadow, and make to appear as of comparative unimportance, the virtues to which other people owed their likeableness, so as to enable him to be independent of such things?

But whatever doubt there might be as to the state of Imogen's sentiments towards Sylvester, there was none at all as to his towards her. She had attracted him from the first moment when he had heard her voice, and that attraction had gone on increasing at every successive meeting till it had at last taken possession of his whole nature.

It must not be supposed that he gave way to this feeling without a struggle. It gained insidiously upon him for a while without his realising what was happening to him, and when at last it one day dawned upon him that he was beginning to fall seriously in love, he became alarmed, and made up his mind at once to crush a weakness that might prove prejudicial to his interests. He meant to live alone, to concentrate his energies wholly on pushing himself on in the world; and had long ago determined never to let himself be hampered and kept down by a wife and family clinging to his heels, expecting to share his substance, and to be provided for. A pretty idea for such a man as him, indeed!

But Imogen had a charm for him that was more potent even than his schemes of ambition and calculating selfishness, and presently he was forced to confess to himself with amazement that he had been encountered by a power that was strong enough to conquer even him—invincible as he had hitherto believed himself to be.

What was to be the end of it all? He had lied, cheated, embezzled, committed burglary. If anyone had ever stood in his way, or seemed to threaten rivalry, he had not hesitated to get that person removed from his path by either fair means or foul; he cared nothing for right or wrong, and had lived only for himself—fighting his way upwards in the world boldly, unscrupulously, and successfully, though often at great risks. And she—how utterly different to all this she was with her ignorance of evil; her quaintly-earnest, though somewhat spasmodic unhappiness at not knowing how to set to work in order to advance the general good of humanity; her ready belief in others without suspecting them to be less sincere than herself; her downright honesty; her delight in innocent pursuits and amusements; her freedom from desire for any other position of life than that in which she found herself; her horror of injustice, falsehood, and wrong. How enormous was the contrast between them, and by how deep a gulf were their real selves separated from one another! Would it ever be possible to bridge over that gulf, the full magnitude of which could be known to no creature save himself?

If she had been only more like him! But there he stopped short. Was it not a profanation to imagine her as false, faithless, hard, with dark secrets that would, if known, make her unable to show her face openly, and go about like other people? Would her charm for him ever have existed if she had been such a one as that? Would he not, in that case, have probably been indifferent to her, or perhaps have even regarded her with disgust? Yet no! It must be mere folly to suppose that; for why should one dislike in another person the qualities that one most approved of and cherished in oneself. Ah! But then the question was whether he *did* approve of them in himself? Was there no mistake in thinking that? Was he absolutely certain that he was as well satisfied with himself as he had imagined—and that he would not be glad, were it possible, to alter the past in order that he might now be more like her?

Such were the questions that forced themselves upon him with a rush of passionate longing for her affection, and a bitter sense of the width and depth of the formidable gulf dividing him from her. Next moment he was fiercely indignant with himself for being thus troubled. Was he a mere weak fool to want to undo what he had done?—to become ashamed of himself and of the life he had led? It was hardly likely, indeed!

But no amount of resentment could alter what was the real state of the case. Whether he liked it or not, none the less was it the truth that the influence of his love for Imogen had begun to take effect upon him, and to undermine the foundations of the evil stronghold that had seemed to be planted so securely. Had it not been for that, he would not have hesitated about what to do in regard to trying to marry her, and would have avoided a difficulty that now tormented him.

Here was the dilemma in which he found himself. Should he let her see the gulf between them, and then ask her to be his wife? Or should he give her up? Or should he try to get her to marry him without giving her any inkling of what he really was? To tell his secrets seemed impossible. Not only would he have to fly the country if they should be known; but also, what chance was there that she would consent to be the wife of a man with such a past life as his? Yet to resign all further idea of winning her was a thing that he certainly could not bear to do. The only course remaining, therefore, was not to tell her anything, and try to make her his wife all the same. There could be no reason why a man with no principles should object to that course; yet somehow the idea of it was revolting to him—in some way or other it seemed most especially villainous, and he could not manage to reconcile himself to the thought of adopting it, in spite of all the arguments urged by reasonable selfishness in its favour. Look at matters how he would, there was that past life of his with its evil deeds rising up sternly to shut him off from her, and he bitterly realised the truth of two lines in *Felix Holt*:—

> "And having tasted stolen honey,
> You can't buy innocence for money."

With passion swaying him to and fro, and his newly awakened conscience struggling for its proper place at the helm, he kept veering from side to side according as conscience succeeded or failed in its struggle; and this caused the alterations that Imogen had observed in him of late. The powerful passenger, Love, having come on board had disarranged everything and deprived him of the command of his own ship. At one moment he was ready to give the whole world to make her care for him; and then, again, he would ask himself what good that would be when, even if he were to succeed, he would not know what to do next. He felt, vaguely, that he was changing—that a conflict whose issue he could not foretell was going on within him—that his will seemed to have lost its former strength; and he would get angry, sometimes almost maddened, at the doubts and passions that distracted him.

He thought of Tennyson's lines:—

"Tis better to have loved and lost,

Than never to have loved at all ;'

and wondered that anyone who had ever loved should have written them. As far as he could see, it was impossible for love ever to lead to anything but misery and disappointment. Supposing it not to be returned, then how pitiable was the state of the poor lover who was doomed to find that his patient waiting, devotion, dreams, and hopes had been all in vain; and that the thing he most longed for in the whole world was hopelessly unattainable. Or, take another case, suppose that the love were returned after a lukewarm and half-hearted fashion, with none of the warmth and energy that inspired the lover. Was *that* likely to content the poor wretch? Would he not be tormented by restless jealousy, and wistful cravings that pride would perhaps forbid him to show? And when at last he should come to realise the truth—to realise the futility of his longings, and perceive that he could never hope to receive such deep, true, affection as he had himself given—would not the pain of unrequited love be an enduring, gnawing ache that would be worse to bear than any transient bodily pang? Much happiness *that* man would have derived from love! Or say, again, that the affection given were returned with equal ardour, so that it might seem at first sight as though here, at least, love must have brought satisfaction. Yet could that really be the case when the state of bliss would be marred by the knowledge of its liability to be broken in upon by death and separation? The more perfect the happiness—and perfect indeed such happiness would be—the more terrible would be the dread of losing it. Its destruction could leave only broken hearts (if such things really were), and a dreary, blank future that would be one continual regretful retrospect at past joys that could never come again. Who was to be called happy with the possibility of such a fate as that hanging over him? And since these were the necessary consequences of love— a mysterious power that when once it took hold of a man so altered his whole nature as to prevent his ever again being the same as before—how could anyone speak of it as the poet did? It was nearly enough to make one suppose that he did not know what he was talking of, and had never truly loved in his life— only then it was impossible to read the rest of *In Memoriam* and think that.

That Sylvester should have reasoned in this way was but natural, for it would have been absurd to expect of such a man as him that he should perceive any possible good to be derived from love apart from the gratification of self. If he had been told that love was far higher and better than what he imagined it to be; and that its beautifying, elevating, and purifying tendency was capable of benefiting people even whilst causing them anxiety, sorrow, failure, loss, and disappointment, he would have jeered at the notion as fit only for a lunatic asylum.

In considering this man's character, be it remembered especially that it was not altogether his own doing that he was what he was, and that he would probably have been far different and better had he had some one to love him and be good to him when a child, and save him from concentrating his affections wholly upon himself as he had done. Now at last, however, they were being shaken by a still more powerful magnet that attracted him elsewhere, and his whole system was thrown into commotion by their movement.

Yet the magnet knew nothing of its own power. Imogen, with faults, follies, and virtues blended together according to the wont of humanity, never dreamt how she was revolutionising his nature; how likely any chance word of hers was to give it a bend or straighten it; what power, for good or for evil, she had over him.

Ethel's unconsciously-exercised influence over herself ought perhaps to have taught her the possibility that she, in her turn, might also be influencing some other person without knowing it. But the lesson had not come home to her yet, and she had not even begun to realise what an amount of work—both good and bad—is performed in this world of ours by unconscious influence.

CHAPTER IV
Picnicking

It was one morning about a week after Miss Carton had consented to take part in the Crœsus-Hoggs' theatricals, that Sylvester sat in his room considering the same question as regarded himself. He had been asked to act with the most flattering urgency, but had postponed replying until he could be sure what would be required of him in respect of some business arrangements. Now, however, he had just ascertained that they need not stand in his way, and was about to accept the Crœsus-Hogg invitation, when it suddenly struck him that before doing that, he might as well try and find out whether or no Ethel would be at the party.

Of course he was quite prepared for the very probable contingency of having to make her acquaintance at some time or other; he did not anticipate evil consequences from that event, for he believed there was no chance whatever of her identifying the voice, manner, and appearance of his natural self, with those that he had assumed as a burglar. Still, as there could be no use in running any needless risks, he meant to keep out of her way if possible, and had hitherto contrived, without exciting suspicion, to avoid the various opportunities of being presented to her that had occurred through his attachment to Imogen's society.

If he had thought it a wise precaution thus to shun meeting Miss Carton under ordinary social conditions, still more would it be prudent to do so when he would be disguised as a man of the lower orders, which was the part he was requested to take in the theatricals. Under those circumstances there would evidently be an increased danger of the sight of him awakening awkward recollections in her mind; so he came to the conclusion that he would decline the Crœsus-Hogg invitation if she were likely to be present at the performance. He was pretty sure that she was not acquainted with the Crœsus-Hoggs, but would easily be able to ascertain the fact for certain from Imogen; therefore he would postpone answering the invitation till he should have found out what he wanted to know from her. The delay this would involve would be only trifling, as he was to meet her on that same day at a picnic up the river, to which he knew that she and her father were going.

The giver of the picnic was Lady Gough, wife of the member for Cwm-Eithin, and amongst her guests on the occasion was another of Imogen's admirers, viz., Sir Charles Dover. The party was composed of about a dozen or so of people, who had been invited to assemble at Putney. There, boats were in waiting to convey them up the river; and a very merry and contented set of people they were, as they rowed along in the bright sunshine, except Sir Charles, who was anything but satisfied with the situation which Fortune (as represented by the hostess, Lady Gough) had assigned to him.

He had been in the very act of following Imogen into the boat where she was taking her seat, when he had been recalled by the voice of Lady Gough, telling him off to another boat, in which he found himself placed next to a Miss Smith, who was going through a course of cookery lectures at South Kensington, and could talk of nothing else. In the most liberal spirit she endeavoured to impart to all other people—partners, casual acquaintances, visitors, or whoever she might happen to meet— the instructions in the culinary art which she was herself receiving. She never by any chance remembered the quantities, proportions, or length of time required in preparing the various dishes she described, so that, perhaps, her well-meant endeavours to promote useful knowledge may have been less efficacious than she intended. But then, as she said herself, those little finikin matters were mere matters of detail, and would soon come afterwards—the grand thing was to know what ingredients to use. The art of manufacturing *beurre noire*[1] and *matelotes*[2] was at present occupying her mind; and butter, pepper, nutmeg, anchovy, button mushrooms, button onions, tarragon vinegar, capers, and similar things were the sole topics of her conversation. Cooped up beside her, in a boat, the poor baronet could not help himself, and had to endure her perforce; but the first use he made of his legs, on regaining dry land and liberty, was to fly beyond reach of her voice.

A clump of trees, standing in the midst of a large, uneven common, was the spot fixed upon for that feeding process, which is the essential point of a picnic; and though the trees were some distance off from the stream, it was not long before the materials for the feast were transferred thither from the boats by the servants and some of the gentlemen of the party.

At lunch Sir Charles was more fortunate than before, and managed to secure the place next Imogen; but afterwards his luck seemed to have again deserted him. The party broke up into small divisions as soon as the meal was over, and dispersed in various directions, to flirt, smoke, walk, sit still, sketch, botanize, or snooze, according to the bent of their several inclinations; and his ambition naturally was to attach himself to his lady love. He was, however, shy of doing so without being invited, or receiving some mark of encouragement; for the consciousness that he was a rejected lover made him always very much afraid of boring her, or of appearing to want to force himself upon her against her will.

Whilst he hung about near her, hoping that she would ask him to join her, or that he might find some colourable pretext for doing so, Sylvester stepped in and carried her off. Having entered into conversation with her, he managed by degrees to get her away from the people by whom she had been standing, and they were soon wandering off together alone. Sir Charles looked after them enviously, and had half a mind to go and join them unasked. But thus to intrude himself on two people who were evidently agreeable to one another, and perfectly contented without a third person, would be both ill-natured and ungentlemanlike, so he resolved to keep out of their way. As long as she was happy, he had no right to interfere, he knew very well; but that did not make it any the pleasanter for him, when he felt that he was being left out in the cold, and that his rival was having everything his own way. He might, if he liked, have consoled himself with someone else, as one or two of the other girls of the party would readily have taken him in tow, and been agreeable to him if he had been at all disposed to accept their ministrations. But his head was far too full of Imogen to make that possible, and he moved about disconsolately without in the least perceiving the gentle indications which they gave of their benevolent intentions.

Really, it was too bad for that Sylvester to be eternally in her pocket—it didn't give anyone else a chance. And yet Ralph had declared positively that he was sure it didn't mean anything. Sir Charles would like to know what the boy would say about it now, if he were here to see what was going on! What awfully stupid things picnics were. Might do well enough, and too well, too! for spooning purposes no doubt, but otherwise there could be no possible satisfaction to be had out of them—unless one happened to have a taste for ants and other insects with one's food, and for little caterpillars crawling about the back of one's neck! There was nothing to do, and one had to go on all day talking to the same stupid people, and all saying the same stupid sort of things.

In this discontented frame of mind he was discovered and taken possession of by Lady Gough, who was the only other companionless member of the party. Being a social humbug of the first water, and most conscientious, she proceeded immediately to do her duty both by this waif and herself according to her lights: that is to say, she endeavoured to get through the time with as little *ennui* as possible, and to convey to other people the impression that it was by deliberate selection and preference that she and her cavalier were walking about together, and not at all because of their having happened to be the only two members of the party who had been left alone by the others, and had no one else to fall back upon.

And to her care we will leave him whilst we follow Imogen and Sylvester, who had by this time seated themselves comfortably close to a heap of stones, on a sloping part of the common, some distance off from the clump of trees.

'Have you yet made up your mind whether or not to act at the Crœsus-Hogg party?' she was saying.

'Not quite,' he replied; 'I suppose that if I do, you will look down on me with contempt. I know very well what an aversion you have to those poor people, and that in your secret heart you consider it a mean truckling[3] to money on the part of anyone who goes near them. Now, isn't that true? And don't you mean to despise every soul who goes to their party?'

Imogen looked as if she did not altogether relish this question.

'Well—no—not altogether,' she answered, with some confusion. 'The fact is, I believe I shall be there myself after all.'

'*You!*' said Sylvester with surprise; 'I certainly did not think anything would have induced Miss Rhys to condescend to be entertained by a Crœsus-Hogg! What can have caused such a change of purpose? Is it that an exalted personage is said to be likely to be there, and that you think wherever the prince goes it would be unbecoming of his subjects not to follow him; or in other words, that you won't be out of the fashion? '

He knew well enough that she would scorn the imputation of being influenced by a motive which she would consider snobbish, and was prepared for the indignant denial with which she met it.

'Most certainly not!' she exclaimed; 'what he chooses to do has nothing whatever to do with me. It may be all right enough for him to go. As a farmer's rent comes from all his animals, it may be that he's bound to visit them all alike, and include the pig-sty in his rounds. But it doesn't follow that the horse, dog, cow, and nobler inmates of the farm-yard need follow his example.'

'Well, but a week ago you declared that you did not know, or wish to know these people; and yet now you say you are going to their house. How is the transformation to be accounted for?'

'It's no doing of *mine*; you may be very sure of that,' she answered rather crossly; 'and I'm not at all pleased to have to go. The way it came about was this. A few nights ago we met these horrid people at dinner, and it happened that Mrs Crœsus-Hogg fell to papa's lot as a partner. Unluckily he made a favourable impression on her, I suppose, for she couldn't be satisfied without pressing him to come to the bit of a party she was "going to 'ave," making him introduce her to me after dinner, and saying she should come and call on us if he had no objection. You know that dear good father of mine can't bear saying "No" to anyone; and what's more, I really do believe he was rather amused with the vulgar old thing, and thinks it'll be fun to go to her "bit of a party," so he just said yes to whatever she wanted, and promised faithfully to take me to the theatricals. So next day she came and called in due form, and left us a card of invitation. I don't think I ever saw such a hideous thing of the kind before! An immense big affair with a gorgeous crest and elaborately ugly letters standing out in solid gold; a border wonderfully illuminated in the rawest and most ill-matched colours; and a smell of scent that's enough to knock one down! I had to go and wash my fingers ever so often to get the smell out after merely touching it. And papa insisted on accepting, and declares that we are to go; so we shall have to, I suppose.'

Her voice and looks showed how intensely aggrieved she considered herself to be. Her companion could not help being amused at it; yet it gave him a pang, too, to be thus reminded of her intolerance of whatever she disapproved of, and he would have preferred a tendency to leniency of judgment which might some day prove to his own advantage.

'After all,' he said with a half sigh, 'I think you should remember that there *may* be some good in people and things even although they do not entirely correspond to your standard of excellence. By-the-bye, that reminds me of your cousin Miss Carton, whom I know you admire. Is she as particular as yourself? Does she admit the Crœsus-Hoggs to her visiting list?'

Imogen had not forgotten that no hint was to be given of Ethel's intention to be one of the actors, and shook her head. 'No,' she returned; 'they're not there yet, to my positive knowledge. But I do wish you knew Ethel; I'm sure you'd like her—she's so awfully nice. I really *must* introduce you to her. You know I've meant to do it several times already, only something or other has always just happened to prevent it. There's been quite a fate against it!'

This was not quite so unaccountable to Sylvester as it was to Imogen, since he had himself on each occasion, contrived the obstacle which had interfered with the introduction. However, he did not mean her to suspect that, so he replied hypocritically,—'Yes, I certainly have been wonderfully unfortunate in that respect hitherto, but I must hope for better luck in the future. It won't be at the Crœsus-Hoggs' I'm afraid though, as I think you said that she won't be there, didn't you?'

Imogen would not tell a lie about it, nor would she betray the secret entrusted to her, so she evaded giving a direct answer.

'I know positively that they are complete strangers to each other,' she replied; 'they've never met, called, or had any communication together. But to go back to what I asked you at first. I wish you'd make up your mind to act as they want you to do. I'm interested in the matter myself, now that I shall be there. I should like to see you perform—do say yes.'

It was sweet to him to be asked by her, and he looked earnestly and longingly at her.

'Consider it done, then,' he said softly. 'If a thing pleases you, that is reason enough for it in my eyes. It would need a weighty argument indeed that could prevent my endeavouring to gratify your lightest wish.'

Gesture, voice, and look are often more expressive than words; and Imogen was suddenly conscious of a deep wistful tenderness about her companion that made her feel uneasy, and think she would like to rejoin the rest of the party, though she did not exactly know why. Her embarrassment was terminated, however, almost before perceived, by a startling cry which was now borne down the wind to their ears, and made her forget about everything else. That cry was 'Mad dog! Mad dog!'

CHAPTER V
A Mad Dog

Few people care to sit still with a mad dog loose about somewhere close by, and the shout that Imogen and Sylvester had heard, brought them to their feet in a moment. On looking round they saw a large dog, at some distance off, running towards them with a couple of men in full chase after it.

'Let's make for those trees where we lunched!' cried Imogen. 'There are plenty of low branches there that we can climb into, and be safe.'

'They're too far off!' returned Sylvester, anxiously. 'We shouldn't have time. If the dog keeps on as he's going now, he'll be past the trees, and meet us before we could possibly get there.'

This being evidently the case, they looked about the great common for some other place of safety, but could see nothing more promising than the rough heap of stones near which they had been sitting.

'Those stones are our best chance!' exclaimed Sylvester. 'We must crouch down there, so that the brute won't see us, and will pass straight on. Let's get out of sight as quick as possible! Whatever you do, keep quiet, so as not to attract his attention.'

As he spoke, he drew her towards the heap, where they squatted down, and concealed themselves on the side opposite to that from which the dog was coming.

Sylvester felt a thrill of passionate joy at the thought that he and she were exposed to the same danger, and that there was no one but himself to protect her. He would have given much for an efficient weapon at that moment; but, unluckily, he had nothing more formidable than a penknife about him. A penknife might be better than nothing, however, so he took it out of his pocket and opened it, kneeling beside her with the determination that not one hair of her head should be injured, whatever it might cost him to defend her. Her safety was of the first importance to him, while for his own he gave not one thought—so inconsistent with his selfish natural self had love made him.

'You are as safe as if you were in your own drawing-room,' he whispered to her earnestly. 'Even if the dog *should* see and attack us, I swear that he shall not touch you—that my body shall barricade you from him as effectually as any walls could do.'

At this moment something fresh appeared upon the scene, and caused Imogen to make an effort to spring up, which intention of hers was, however, promptly frustrated by her companion.

'Oh, look, look! What shall we do to save them?' she exclaimed in horrified tones, pointing towards what had so disturbed her.

A little distance before them, and exactly in the direction that the dog was taking, there was a rise on the common, and over the brow of this hillock there suddenly came in sight a lot of school children out walking with their teachers, and all unconscious of the approaching danger, which they were making for in a direct line. Imogen's impulse was to start up instantly and to wave them back, without thinking of the peril that she might thus incur by making the dog notice her; but Sylvester was alive to this danger, and when she tried to move, he held her down by main force.

'Keep quiet, whatever you do,' he whispered; 'you can't help them, and will only be exposing yourself to danger for nothing. Let them mind themselves—they're not *our* look-out.'

'Yes they are! They're everybody's look-out! Poor little souls—let me go!' she exclaimed breathlessly as she redoubled her vain efforts to free herself from his strong grasp. Then suddenly desisting from her fruitless struggles, and remembering that shouting would warn them equally well, she cried triumphantly,—

'But you can't stop my mouth at any rate!' And then, without heeding his remonstrances, she began shouting out,— 'Mad dog! Get out of the way! Run!' as loud as she could.

The school heard her, and stopped in alarm; looked blankly this way and that, and then—seeing no safe refuge anywhere— took to its heels in all directions, tumbling and shrieking as it fled. In this stampede was plainly to be seen how widely the natures differed from one another; for while some of the teachers and bigger girls made off as fast as their legs could carry them without a thought of anyone else, others, of a more chivalrous disposition, stayed to catch up some one or other of the tinies into their arms, or to give it a helping hand in the race.

'Oh, *do* let us go to them!' cried Imogen, struggling with her jailer. 'Surely we could help some of those poor little tots!'

But Sylvester was immoveable.

'No, no,' said he, coolly; 'you needn't suppose I'm going either to let you run into danger, or to go myself and leave you here unprotected on account of a lot of strange brats like that. All I care for is to look after you, and nothing shall make me stir from your side till you are safe again. Jove! what a *sauve-qui-peut*[1] it is amongst them. Hullo though! There must be something new going on. What's making them all stand still, and stare back like that? and what can that fresh shouting be about that I hear now?'

Evidently something exciting was to be seen in the direction whence the foe was advancing; for first one and then another of the fugitives looked round, stopped running, and began gazing behind them, till they were all at a standstill.

The explanation of this apparently incomprehensible behaviour was as follows:—

The dog had got very nearly abreast of the clump of trees already mentioned, when a man who was safely ensconced amongst them emerged from their friendly shelter, armed with nothing better than a shawl, placed himself straight in the animal's path, and deliberately awaited its approach. As soon as the dog was within reach, the man, without letting go the ends of the shawl, dexterously flung the middle part so as to entangle the dog's head and blindfold it for a moment. Profiting by this momentary check and blindness, the man sprang astride upon the dog's shoulders before it could get itself free, and there he gripped it firmly with his knees and twisted the shawl as tightly as he could round its neck so as to bewilder and half throttle it. The dog, which was large and strong, naturally disliked these proceedings, and showed its resentment by growling, snapping, trying to bite its rider, and doing all it could to disentangle itself. The rider, however, was not to be dislodged, and managed—though with considerable difficulty—to stick to his place on the back of the blinded and floundering creature, and to avoid its teeth, till the men in pursuit arrived to his assistance and put an end to the dog's life with their sticks.

Public safety being thus re-established, people ventured out from hiding-places in all directions; the scattered school assembled together again (with the exception of a few of the swiftest and most cowardly who were by that time clean out of sight and hearing); and things in general speedily returned to their ordinary condition.

Only the last part of the combat between the man and dog had been witnessed by Imogen and Sylvester, as during the beginning of it they had been crouching down behind the stones out of sight. Consequently they did not know that the man had voluntarily left a place of safety in order to engage in the fight. They had seen quite enough, however, to excite Imogen's admiration for his bravery. She was very angry with Sylvester for having prevented her from going to the rescue of the school, and fully intended to expostulate with him on the subject; but for the moment she could think only of the exciting battle that had just taken place and of her anxiety lest the hero of it should have got hurt.

'What a plucky fellow that is!' she said, 'and how splendidly he managed the dog! I couldn't quite see whether he got bitten or not; I do hope he didn't. Let's go and see.'

Without waiting for an answer she set off quickly towards the trees, and Sylvester followed her rather sulkily. He did not like to think that she owed her deliverance, after all, to someone else than himself; and he felt irritated and jealous to hear her bestowing praises upon this other man, whoever he might be— for they had been too far off to make out if it was anyone they knew or not. The conqueror of the dog was surrounded by a group of people who hid him from sight at first, and it was not till Imogen was quite close that she discovered him to be Sir Charles Dover.

'I do hope you aren't hurt!' she exclaimed, hurrying towards him in evident anxiety for his safety. 'Did the dog bite you at all?'

If Sylvester had hitherto been to be envied for securing her society, now, at least, whilst Sir Charles saw that he stood first (though it might be but for a moment) in her thoughts and interests, he would not have exchanged places with anyone else in the whole world.

'Oh no, thanks!' he replied, flushing with sudden pleasure, even though for an instant he felt almost regretful at having escaped unhurt. For if he had been bitten, would not that have procured him the felicity of remaining interesting to her for a yet longer period? 'The brute never quite managed to reach me; he only got his teeth as far as my coat and tore that a little.'

'I'm so glad,' returned she; 'it looked much too close quarters to be pleasant from where I was. But I don't quite understand how it all happened, for I didn't see the dog's first attack on you. I almost wonder you couldn't have got out of the way, being so close to the trees.'

'Close to the trees!' echoed Lady Gough, 'why, my dear Miss Rhys, he was actually in perfect safety. When the alarm was heard he and I were together, and both of us climbed safely upon a bough. And then all of a sudden down he jumped, and went out to fight the dog armed only with a shawl of mine that he had been carrying. It was the bravest, coolest thing possible. I'm sure he deserves a medal, or a Victoria Cross, or something, as much as anyone ever did in this world.'

'By Jove! I forgot your shawl, though, Lady Gough; I'm afraid it's all to rags!' exclaimed Sir Charles, who, though not afraid to face the mad dog, was made extremely bashful and uncomfortable by the commendations that Lady Gough and others were beginning to bestow upon him freely.

He did what he could to turn the conversation into some other channel; and Imogen, seeing how it annoyed him to talk about his performance, forbore to say anything more about it just then when everyone else was talking and listening to him. There was something she wanted to know, however, and by-and-by, when he and she and Sylvester happened to be standing a little apart from the rest of the party, she said,—

'Then you were in safety and there was no actual necessity for you to have meddled with the dog at all, Sir Charles, only you went out of your way to do it. I want to know exactly what made you do that, if you don't mind telling me.'

'Oh, well—you see for one thing—I—I—I wasn't quite sure about you,' answered he with a little hesitation. 'I knew you were somewhere about, and I didn't know whether you were safe or not. And then besides that there were all those poor children you know. It would have been shameful for a great strong fellow like me to sit still and see a dangerous brute go running a-muck with a lot of women and children about and not try to stop it. And then there wasn't really any risk to me either; for if one gets bitten it's easy enough to be made safe by being cauterised, you know.'

'Thanks for telling me your reason. I'm so glad you thought the poor children worth caring for,' said Imogen, glancing meaningly at Sylvester; 'I'm sure you did perfectly right. It would have been horrid to leave them to themselves.'

Sylvester perfectly understood the rebuke conveyed to him by her glance and speech. She had not expostulated with him as she had at first intended, for not letting her go to help the school; but she had evinced her displeasure instead by taking no notice of him since rejoining the rest of the party. He knew very well what caused her avoidance of him, and chafed internally at being thus punished for what he could not understand her regarding as a crime.

He had been ready joyfully to sacrifice himself on her behalf if need were; no cowardly thought had crossed his soul for an instant; and he felt sure that she was as well aware of these things as he was himself. What more then, could she want? And what right had she to be vexed with him because he did not bother his head as to what became of anyone else—especially a parcel of stupid children and their teachers? He could not conceive what should have inspired her with the desire to succour such absolutely uninteresting creatures, who were no concern whatever of hers. If she had been one of the school mistresses, or monitors, or a person in any way responsible for them and liable to get into trouble if they came to grief, then it would have been a different matter altogether, and he could have understood her display of anxiety for their welfare; but, as it was, the thing was a mystery to him.

And then, by some unlucky accident, this Sir Charles, this mere long-leggit lad, must needs be moved by the same craze, and thus secure her attention and approval. Sylvester eyed him with a sinister look as she continued to laugh and talk with the delighted baronet, whilst she would only respond coldly to his own endeavours to make himself agreeable, and be admitted to a share of her favours. It was intolerable to suppose that he, Sylvester, could be snubbed on account of a mere long-leggit lad! But before long, fortune supplied him with a means of diverting her attention from Sir Charles, and recalling it to himself.

'Excuse my interrupting you, Miss Rhys,' he said, 'but as you care about moths I want to show you one that I have found sitting on a tree close by. The insect isn't a big one, but it's very handsome, and looks uncommon to my ignorant eyes.'

Her eagerness to see the moth made her forget that she was just then out of charity with him who had found it.

'Where is it?' she exclaimed, looking all around at the trees near. 'I don't see one anywhere.'

'No, it's a few yards to the left,' he answered. 'Come this way and I'll show it you.'

He led her to the place, and Sir Charles followed, angry at the interruption and hoping that the moth might prove as valueless as the ones that he had posted to her with such care. Consequently he was disappointed to hear her exclaim, joyfully,—

'What a little beauty! He's a *Tortrix* of some kind, though I don't know which.' At any rate he's one I've not got yet. I'm so glad you found him!'

With these words she produced from her pocket a small bottle, which she habitually carried with her, and in which there was a small piece of cotton-wool, with a few drops of chloroform on it. This bottle being carefully placed over the moth as it sat on the tree, the insect was stupefied by the fumes immediately, and borne away in triumph.

Thus the baronet's pleasure came to an end, and the offending Sylvester was restored to favour for the time, very much to the disgust of poor Sir Charles, who regarded the harmless moth almost in the light of a personal enemy. *Tortrix* indeed! He'd like to know why a *Thyatira Batis* shouldn't be as good as a *Tortrix* any day? It was bigger at any rate; and showier besides; and much the handsomest of the two, in his opinion. It was all that fellow Sylvester's luck! Directly he spotted a wretched, insignificant little moth it must needs turn out to be one she wanted; whereas when any one else found one for her—even one covered with lovely, round pink spots—it was only laughed at, and pronounced as common as mud! Oh, it was really too bad.

Notwithstanding this *contretemps*, however, the day's events had, on the whole, been more favourable to him than he imagined. The incident of the mad dog had given Imogen the consciousness (one not disagreeable to any woman) that there were two men who would not hesitate to jeopardise themselves on her behalf, and with either of whom she would be secure against any bodily harm from which they could save her. So far both the young men were on the same footing in her mind. But then in respect of their conduct towards the children, Sir Charles had decidedly the best of it. Sylvester's behaviour to them seemed to her quite extraordinary. If he had been a coward it would have been easy enough to understand; but of his courage she entertained no doubt, and for a brave man to act as he had done was simply inexplicable to her.

Sir Charles's actions, on the contrary, had corresponded entirely with her own ideas of what was right and proper; and she felt more than ever sure that it was impossible not to respect and admire him, and feel satisfied of his being a person eminently to be trusted—whatever one might think of him in other ways.

Thus did she review what had happened after she got home that evening. Meanwhile Sylvester, confident from what she had said that there was no likelihood of Ethel's being a spectator at the theatricals, was writing to the Crœsus-Hoggs to inform them that he should be happy to take the part that they had offered him.

CHAPTER VI
The Theatricals

As the time appointed for the theatricals drew near, the public curiosity about them rose to a high pitch. A theatre had been erected for the occasion in the garden at the back of the Crœsus-Hoggs' mansion, and was reported to be quite a marvel of artistic effect; the acting was to be followed by a ball, and the whole entertainment was to be even more gorgeous and magnificent than any previous ones that had ever been given there—which was saying a good deal. Invitations were sought after eagerly, and—immense as the house was—it would evidently be crammed. The rumours as to what the affair was to cost mentioned sums that seemed incredible. There were to be acres of the rarest flowers—fountains of champagne—icebergs of ice—miles of delicate gauze stuffs to simulate snow and give a cool effect. What the supper would be like, no one ventured to conjecture who knew the inexhaustible fertility of Leblanc's genius. Both the actors and those before whom they were to perform—but especially the former—grew more and more excited as the eventful night approached.

It being Ethel's whim—as may be remembered—that no one should discover the identity of Miss Carton and Miss Percival till after the theatricals should be over, she did not go to rehearse as the other performers did, but studied her part at home with a most unwonted amount of industry.

Her non-appearance naturally caused a good deal of uneasiness to the Crœsus-Hoggs, who had never seen this Miss Percival whom Lady Elise had enlisted, and knew nothing of

275

her; but Lady Elise managed to calm their anxiety—always finding some good reason or other for her friend's absence, and assuring them that she and Miss Percival had gone through their parts alone together, and that the latter was progressing famously.

On the day before the performance there was a final rehearsal which everyone, without exception, had to attend, and to this Ethel went. But she kept away from the rest as much as possible, did not stay to watch the rehearsal of the second piece (in which Sylvester appeared), and departed directly her own share in the acting was over. Owing to these precautions, and to the fact that the costume in which she acted was one that disguised her thoroughly, she was successful in preserving her incognito.

Neither Trevor Owen nor any of the other people present who knew her, had any suspicion of who she was; and it thus happened also that she never saw anything of Sylvester, who did not act in the same piece as herself.

And now at last the important time had come. The theatre was filling rapidly; some of the actors were beginning to feel qualms of nervousness that made them wish earnestly the night were over, and themselves well out of what they had undertaken; and the quantity of champagne that became imperatively necessary in the green-room was something positively alarming.

In due course arrived, amongst the other guests, Mr Rhys and Imogen—the latter in a rather mixed state of mind, as she was divided between displeasure at being there at all, and natural enjoyment of the party and all the fun going on. She would like the ball after the theatricals, as she loved dancing, and knew that plenty of her regular partners would be there. The acting might very possibly be less amusing, she thought; but then of course it gained greatly in interest by the circumstance that two people whom she knew as well as she did Ethel and

Sylvester were to take part in it. She had some curiosity, too, to see how the other actors would acquit themselves, and what the whole affair would be like, so that altogether there certainly seemed to be a reasonable prospect of her spending a pleasant evening.

But then against these arguments in favour of her present position, was to be set the disagreeable thought that she was being in a way humiliated by receiving hospitality from people against whom she was prejudiced as ineffable snobs and outer barbarians. The mercenary spirit that admitted such people, merely because they had money, to associate with ladies and gentlemen, seemed mean and disgraceful to her hot-headed youth. To be present at this entertainment was evidently giving countenance and encouragement to that objectionable mercenariness, and therefore she had an internal conviction that she and all the people about her ought to feel ashamed of themselves. What made the situation additionally galling, was to recollect how openly she had declared her opinions on this subject, and how resolutely she had made up her mind to avoid making the acquaintance of these Crœsus-Hoggs. Yet here she was after all; and it was in the power of anyone to twit her with her sudden change of views, and to suppose that she too had been affected by the mercenary considerations that she had hitherto condemned! Oh, it was *too* bad of papa ever to have made friends with that old woman! If only he had kept her at a distance instead of being pleasant and chatty all through that dinner to which he had taken her down, then Imogen need never have had anything to do with these dreadful people whose acquaintance was such an offence to her juvenile sentiments of exclusiveness and indignation at whatever was mercenary!

It was, however, to be remembered that her being there was no doing of her own, and that she would not have come if her father had not insisted on it. There was some comfort in this thought, and it enabled her to feel that her conscience was sufficiently clear to allow of her getting as much amusement as she could out of all the events of the evening. Consequently there was a rather mischievous twinkle in her eye that betrayed her readiness to make the most of any opportunity that might occur to pick holes in the Crœsus-Hoggs, their house, arrangements, and style of doing things. As, on her father's arm, she proceeded through the corridors and saloons to the theatre, she unconsciously expressed her disapproving and protesting condition by carrying her head a little further back, and her nose a little higher in the air than usual.

This unwontedly stiff bearing presented a ludicrous contrast to that of her father, who never for a moment dreamt of troubling himself as to the amount of right his entertainers might have to their social position, and was in a thoroughly contented frame of mind, intending to enjoy himself, and nodding, smiling, and how-do-you-doing with sociable vigour, to whatever acquaintances he saw in the throng.

At the entrance to the theatre stood Sir Charles Dover, watching for the arrival of the Rhys's as the most interesting event of the evening to him. His hopes had been reviving considerably recently, as at several balls where he had met Imogen since the day of the adventure with the mad dog, she had not only danced with him more than she had done for some time past, but had even sat out a dance with him once or twice. The exaltation of spirits caused by this amount of condescension had not been altogether quenched even by the damping reflection that that brute Sylvester had had quite as much favour shown him on the same or other occasions. Provoking as this was, yet the baronet derived some comfort from the thought that any marks of encouragement vouchsafed to a man whom she *knew* to want to marry her, must certainly mean more than they would do in any other case; and whereas, he, Sir Charles, had spoken out plainly and told her what he wanted; he did not for a moment believe that that other fellow had done anything of the sort, so that the chances were she was quite ignorant of his intentions—if he had any.

Be that as it might, however, Sir Charles had looked forward cheerfully to the theatricals. Whilst they lasted, Sylvester would be out of the way on the stage at all events, and there would be a chance for someone else to make the running without being interfered with; so Sir Charles meant to make the most of the opportunity that night, and had come early and waited patiently in hopes of being able to sit next his lady love in the theatre. Her unusual haughtiness of demeanour as she entered was a little alarming at first sight; but he speedily regained his equanimity on perceiving that he, at all events, was not the object of her displeasure. Her face relaxed visibly as she recognised him; he even fancied that he detected a momentary gleam of pleasure in it—yet then again he feared that was but a fancy—probably merely the effect of some reflection from the brilliant lights that glittered in all directions, and no solid source of happiness.

But at any rate she spoke to him quite graciously enough to encourage him to follow her to her place, and seat himself next her tentatively with a casual, no-intention-of-remaining-permanently sort of air, which would make it easy for him subsequently to betake himself elsewhere, if she should show signs of preferring his room to his company.

No such signs, however, did she show; but rather the contrary, for she said as he took his seat, 'Are you going to establish yourself there? That's all right, for I want some one to help keep an empty place by us for a lady who won't be here till presently. I promised I'd do it if I could, and you'll help, won't you?'

'Certainly,' answered Sir Charles; 'shall I bandage one of my legs with a handkerchief, stick it up on the empty chair, and assure anyone who wants to sit there, that I have a broken leg which must on no account be let to hang down?'

She laughed.

'No, I don't think you need quite do that,' she answered; 'but you must sit as big as you can, and spread yourself out well. When you and I and papa all do that, it'll be odd if we don't manage to hide away a fourth seat somewhere or other amongst us.'

'Very good,' returned Sir Charles. 'I'll do my best to assist you, regardless of the violence that I shall thereby do to my feelings of justice, though, certainly, you are about the last person whom I should have expected to ask such a thing of me.'

'Why? Where's the injustice?' she asked.

'To an unknown individual in the audience,' was his reply. 'Consider that if you succeed in your unlawfully secretive purpose, some unfortunate mortal will be doomed to stand who need not otherwise have done so. Really, I'm quite surprised at you! I did not think you could have been so unkind.'

This attack upon the morality of her proceedings was whimsical no doubt, yet not wholly without reason. But she was ready with her defence.

'Oh,' she rejoined promptly; 'but then against the discomfort of that one person, you must put the advantage that all the rest of the audience will gain by having more air. A person less will give them ever so much extra, you know—what with the extra space for it to occupy, and the quantity that another set of lungs would have consumed, and that will now be at the disposal of everyone else. Even if one individual should be a little uncomfortable in consequence of our conduct, yet a great many people will be much better off for it, don't you see? and of course we should always consider the good of the greatest number.'

'I'm convinced by your argument,' returned the baronet, 'and now, please, show me how to spread myself out and look big, in order that I may obey your behests.'

It need scarcely be remarked that after this he felt no hesitation about retaining the position which he had taken up by her side.

CHAPTER VII
Recognition

The theatre was crowded, and numbers of people who could not be contained within it had to content themselves with wandering about in the great house instead, and admiring its superb appointments, size, and magnificence, till the acting should be over and the ball should begin. But Imogen was successful in reserving a spare place for Ethel to occupy, notwithstanding the crowd.

The bell rang, the curtain rose, and the first play commenced. In this the hero and nominal heroine were represented respectively by Guelph Crœsus-Hogg and Lady Elise Bolyn. The chief interest of the piece, however, was by no means confined to these two; for the female part, that afforded most scope for fine acting, and was altogether of most real importance to the piece, was that of a hard, worldly, crafty, scheming adventuress, whose sole redeeming point lay in her passionate love for a good-for-nothing son, who repaid her affection with cruel ingratitude and baseness. The part of this sinned-against and sinning mother had been given to Ethel, who, stimulated to unaccustomed energy by the fancy that had seized her to discover for once what sort of verdict she could obtain for herself when unsupported by her heiress-ship, had thrown herself completely into the character, studied it carefully, and bestowed on it a good deal more labour than she was in the habit of giving to anything. By dint of this, joined to the strong turn for acting which she possessed naturally, she achieved an unmistakable success, stirring up people's emotions in spite of themselves, and surprising even the most *blasé* of the audience into an unexpected thrill of sympathy and interest. The host and hostess were besieged with inquiries as to who Miss Percival was? To all of which they could only reply that they had no personal knowledge of her, but that they had an ample guarantee of her being all that was desirable, inasmuch as she was a friend of the charming Lady Elise Bolyn, who had persuaded her to undertake the part, and made herself entirely responsible for her.

Imogen's affectionate admiration for her cousin made her rejoice as heartily at this success as if it had been her own; but it cannot be said that she was able at that moment to give her mind to it as thoroughly as she would have wished; for her attention was being distracted from her immediate surroundings by a moth that had got into the theatre, and was flying round and round the lights, high up out of reach.

Wherever the insect went, her eyes followed it involuntarily, and Sir Charles had no difficulty in guessing what was passing through her mind, as he saw the wistful looks she turned upwards from time to time whilst answering the remarks of some people she knew who began to talk to her after the first play was over. The species and nature of that moth was evidently the one question of really paramount interest to her for the time being, and he took the first opportunity, when she was not engaged with anyone else, of answering her unspoken thoughts.

'You needn't excite yourself about it,' he remarked quietly, with the air of one who thoroughly understands what he is talking about; 'it's only a *Thyatira Batis.*'

The observation was so *à propos* to what she was thinking about, that for a moment she forgot the entomological ignorance of the speaker, and the two moths that he had sent her.

'Oh no! indeed I don't think it can be,' she said eagerly. 'I'm almost sure the wings are too long and narrow, and—'

Here she suddenly recollected herself, and paused, looking a little shy.

'What do you know about *Thyatira Batis*?' she asked.

'A little bird has told me all about them,' returned he; 'I know that they're mere worthless rubbish. I know what sort of reception they met with when some one sent them to a certain young lady, and what an uncommon fool the sender was deemed for his pains.'

It was the first time that he had ever mentioned the subject to her, and though he tried to appear as if he were only chaffing, there was a shade of annoyance in his voice that smote her with compunction.

'No, *indeed* he wasn't,' she said earnestly; 'she thought it very kind of him to have taken so much trouble about catching, killing, setting, and packing them for her.'

'Oh, no doubt she got some gratification out of the present, for at any rate she could laugh at his stupidity in having bothered himself like that about things that she would only throw into the fire. It's always amusing to see people show their ignorance!'

'She *didn't* throw them into the fire,' said Imogen, with a slight blush.

'Well, into the waste-paper basket then,' returned he.

'She didn't throw them into the waste-paper basket either.'

'I suppose the fact is that by this time she doesn't the least know what she *did* do with them,' observed he.

'Yes, she does.'

'What was it then?'

Imogen did not answer for a moment, and then said,—

'Oh, look ! there the moth has found his way to get out at last.'

'So he has. Miss Rhys, are you going to tell me what you did with that brace of moths you got by post one fine day?'

'Why—what did you suppose when you sent them would be done with them?' replied she, hesitating a little in her answer, and feeling as if she were called upon to make the best of a thing which she ought perhaps to be ashamed of.

'There had seemed to me a possibility that they might be thought acceptable and kept.'

'Well, and so they were kept. One generally does keep a thing that someone has had a lot of bother about getting for one; doesn't one?'

That his present should have been treated with this amount of respect was a blissful and unexpected hearing to Sir Charles; but before he could reply, the conversation was interrupted by the advent of Ethel, who having resumed an ordinary evening costume and come round unnoticed to the front of the theatre, had made her way to the Rhyses to take possession of the seat they had reserved for her. Now that the object for which she had for once chosen to exert herself was accomplished, she was relapsing speedily into her normal condition of indolence.

The admiring comments upon Miss Percival's acting which she heard on all sides as she passed through the crowd, assured her of having achieved a success; and she would have been more than human if she had not felt a great and genuine gratification at the sensation which she perceived she had been able to create as an unknown individual. Yet all the time there seemed to be present in her mind a consciousness of '*Le jeu ne vaut pas la chandelle*.'[1] In her secret soul she doubted whether the satisfaction were enough to repay the trouble it had cost her to earn it; whether the best part of the whole affair were not the having got it over; and whether it could ever be worth while to do anything one was not absolutely obliged to do.

Then the second play began. The heroine of this was a sighing, love-lorn damsel who was impersonated by Guinevere Crœsus-Hogg. The part was one for which she was in no wise well adapted, either by appearance or natural talent, inasmuch as she was a large-boned, buxom, jovial-looking, young woman who excelled in broad comedy. But as few people have the sense to limit themselves to what they understand and can do, therefore it had come to pass that nothing would please her save trying her hand at a highly sentimental and romantic part. That sort of thing should, in her opinion, be played with much turning-up of the eyes, sighing, shaking of the head, and languishing; and to this conception of the part she kept true pretty steadily, except once or twice when she forgot herself for an instant and indulged in some familiar gesture of the broadly comic kind—even going so far on one occasion as to give a prolonged and ostentatious wink at her lover!

Altogether, therefore, her representation of the heroine was a somewhat incongruous one, both ideally and in appearance. The hero, her lover, was played by Trevor Owen. His barristerial practice had given him enough self-confidence, facial control, and power of pretending to be in earnest when he was not, to make him a fair mediocre actor, though he had not got it in him ever to rise higher than that in the histrionic line. The theatrical manager had perceived that with two leading performers of this calibre, it was evidently prudent that there should be some one strong in the cast supporting them, so as to cause any little short-comings that might occur in the chief parts to be overlooked; consequently, Lady George Quaver, with her magnificent voice, had been secured for one of the parts which had a song in it; and Mr Sylvester—who was reputed a first-rate actor, quite as good as a professional according to some people—was to represent the villain of the piece. On this individual much of the interest centred; amongst other things it fell to his lot to be mortally offended by the heroine in the first act, and to plan out a scheme of desperate vengeance, for the execution of which it was necessary in a subsequent act that he should join a gang of poachers, and pretend to be one of themselves. At this point, in order the more thoroughly to play his part, he rashly assumed just the same coarse speech, accent, and tone of a man belonging to the lower orders, as he had previously done in committing the burglary. Had he had an idea of the possibility of Ethel's presence, he would, of course, never have been guilty of such imprudence; but he believed himself to have ascertained with certainty that she would not be there, and imagined, therefore, that he might, with perfect safety, do what he liked to heighten the effect of his acting, and display his talents more fully.

At his earlier appearances in the play, Ethel watched him without any particular feeling of recognition, beyond a vague idea that she had heard his voice, or one very like it, somewhere or other before; but when he came on disguised as a poacher, and began to speak in his disguised voice, it was a very different matter. For a minute or so she listened to him with a queer, nightmare sort of sensation, wondering what disagreeable association had suddenly begun to press upon her memory, and clamour importunately to be given a definite form and name. Then all at once the truth flashed upon her, and she knew where she had seen that actor before. Voice, manner, accent, hand with a finger missing—the part he was playing of a ruffian to be dreaded—all recalled to mind her burglar exactly, and she felt, beyond all possibility of doubt, that the very man himself was there before her!

Full of horror and astonishment at this discovery, she was just about to impart it to Imogen, who was sitting next her, when she suddenly recollected the rumours she had heard in relation to her cousin and Mr Sylvester, and checked herself. What if there should be any foundation for those rumours? What if her cousin's affections were really set upon this man? Terrible as such a misfortune would be, Ethel could not shut her eyes to its being a possible contingency, and therefore it behoved her to act with caution, so that in case of the worst, Imogen's feelings should be saved as much as might be. Under the circumstances, to blurt out to her the appalling truth concerning Sylvester in a public place like this, would be a most brutal and injudicious proceeding she thought, and the very last thing that ought to be done!

It has been already said that Imogen's romantic attachment to Ethel was a one-sided affair, and that the latter had no idea of its existence. But though she did not reciprocate an affection of which she was ignorant, she nevertheless liked her cousin much, and had a very friendly feeling for her, and this—joined to her natural kindliness of disposition—made it impossible for her to contemplate the distress that seemed to her to be but too probably awaiting the girl, without taking it greatly to heart. She would have given worlds to be sure that Sylvester was nothing to Imogen. Certain knowledge of any kind as to how matters stood between the two would be of the utmost assistance in determining her as to what steps she should take in the present emergency. She felt it was most important to her to know whether Imogen liked him or not, and yet, unluckily, the state of her cousin's affections was a matter as to which she was profoundly ignorant. She knew that Sylvester had been a good deal in her company of late, and that people said something was to come of it—and that was all she did know; whether or not he had really succeeded in making any impression she had not an idea. Even Sir Charles himself (with the recently-acquired consolation of knowing that his *Thyatira Batis* had not been thrown away) was not at that moment more anxious as to what might be to be read in Imogen's heart, than was Ethel, as she sat watching the performance. Though outwardly as quiet and placid as usual, she was inwardly more worried than any one would have supposed it possible for her tranquil nature to be, as she perplexed herself to no purpose, in endeavouring to discover what she ought to do.

Perhaps she could find out something to give her a clue, even at this eleventh hour, to what she was so anxious to know. With that view she addressed fishing questions as to Imogen's opinions regarding the merits of the various performers, and especially of Sylvester's. But there was nothing in the smallest degree definite or satisfactory to be arrived at by that means. Then she watched her cousin narrowly to see if she could detect any special signs of interest when he was on the stage. But that attempt was as unsuccessful as the other. So Ethel fell back in despair on her memory for assistance—trying to recall whatever she had ever heard or seen that could guide her to the information she wanted. The more she reflected upon the subject, the more inclined she became to believe that her cousin really did care about the man. Various mere trifles that she remembered, assumed unnaturally large proportions in her present state of anxiety, and appeared significant circumstances. Words, tones, looks, that had been absolutely unmeaning were distorted by her fear into the very shape which she dreaded their wearing. The more horrible did it appear to suppose that Imogen could have given him her heart, so much the more probable did it appear also. And in her distress at the possibility of such a thing, she did not notice how very slight was the basis on which she was founding her conjecture. Then there was another question also to be considered in regard to this business and that was: who ought first to be told of the unpleasant discovery that she had made? there could be no doubt that she ought to announce it without loss of time, and she must make up her mind to whom the announcement was to be made. Perhaps to one of her uncles, as being her nearest relatives; or perhaps to Mr Trevor Owen, who had appeared for her when the case had been tried? She had a kind of idea that it was due to society that it should be immediately put upon its guard against the villain in its midst, and that therefore she ought to reveal his true nature there and then.

But then there was Imogen to be considered. Should she keep silence till she could have an opportunity for seeing the girl alone, and making a grand, final effort to find out whether or no Sylvester had contrived to insinuate himself into her affections? If not, then everything would be easy enough. But supposing—miserable possibility that it was!—supposing the contrary, and that she should have been so unfortunate as to fall in love with him, what would Ethel do then? Would there not be laid upon her the direful necessity of breaking to Imogen that she had set her heart upon a scoundrel? and would not that be as odious a task as could easily be imagined?

It seemed to Ethel that a terrible calamity was about, through her means, to descend upon her cousin; and then she began endeavouring to think of some way of mitigating it. If only Ethel could accomplish that, she felt that she would willingly surrender the punishment of the man who had robbed her, and all chance of ever recovering her precious jewels again also. Would it soften the blow, she wondered, if she were to offer Imogen to let him have time to get out of England before she gave any information against him? What a pity it was that she could not conscientiously let the whole matter alone and say nothing about it! The loss of the jewels was but a trifling ill compared to these bothers and perplexities that now distracted her and from which she saw no escape.

But there was no blinking the fact that it was her clear duty to unmask this detestable thief and hypocrite who enjoyed public esteem and confidence; who passed everywhere for an honest, upright, trustworthy man; and whose employers had placed him in a position given only to people of the strictest integrity. Besides, it would be no true kindness to let Imogen remain in ignorance of his real character and be perhaps led on to love him in course of time even if she did not do so already.

No! there was evidently no possibility of shirking the impending fuss and unpleasantness with a clear conscience—which was just the thing that sometimes made it so awkward to have a conscience at all, as Ethel could not help reflecting with a quaint, half-humorous ruefulness. Ah! why had she not stuck to her favourite policy of masterly inaction, she thought dolefully. Then she would never have got mixed up with these theatricals which had first interfered with the tranquillity she loved by stirring her up to work hard at learning her part, and now, by revealing to her who Sylvester was, threatened to lead her into a fresh and far more disagreeable state of commotion. It would have been so much better to have let the acting alone altogether!

CHAPTER VIII
Ethel and Sylvester

Ethel was still in this unsettled state of mind, and unable to resolve what she had better do, when the acting came to an end, and a general move was made to leave the theatre, and go back to the house, where dancing was now to take place. Mr Rhys offered his arm to his niece to conduct her to the ball-rooms, and Sir Charles followed with Imogen, whose hand he had secured for the first dance.

As they traversed the garden between the theatre and the mansion, a sudden impulse moved Ethel, whose habitual placidity was not so imperturbable as not to be now and then disturbed by some unexpected freak of fancy. She would stand face to face with Sylvester herself—would speak once more with this villain whom she had had to do with before in such a very different situation, and whom it was impossible to think of without aversion. Her uncle knew the man, and he should help her to carry out her intention.

'You know Mr Sylvester pretty well, don't you, Uncle Rhys?' she said. 'What sort of a person do you consider him to be?'

'Sylvester—eh?' returned Mr Rhys; 'oh, he's a very clever, go-a-head, young fellow, in my opinion. Just the sort of man who doesn't do a thing at all, unless he does it well. He'll always be either first or nowhere. Didn't he act capitally to-night?'

'Yes, no doubt he did,' answered Ethel. 'But I've never been introduced to him, and I'm curious as to what he's like when one talks to him. So I want you to introduce him to me by-and-by, when he comes round from the stage in the guise of an ordinary mortal again. Will you?'

'Introduce him to you?' replied her uncle; 'be delighted to, if you'll give me a chance of doing it; but mostly there's no getting near you young ladies when once you begin dancing—it's one partner after another all night long—I'm sure when I take Imogen to a ball, I hardly ever set eyes on her from the time we get into the room till the time we leave it. 'Pon my word, there she is gone off to dance with Sir Charles already! What the skin of her toes can be made of, I can't think—*mine* would be all blisters with a quarter the work, I know.'

'Ah! but then I'm older and more sedate than she is,' returned Ethel, laughing, 'and you may rely that I will be within reach presently for you to introduce me to Mr Sylvester. However, I must go now, for I am engaged for this dance, and here's my partner coming to fetch me.'

Sylvester was, on that night, in a moody, unhappy frame of mind, which had recently often affected him, and was out of spirits notwithstanding the numerous congratulations and compliments he received on his acting. Under any circumstances, he would have done that well, for in whatever he undertook he despised mediocrity and failure as unworthy of him, and was certain to have been successful even without the extra stimulus which Imogen's presence had supplied on the present occasion—the stimulus of desiring to show her what he could do, and make her think well of him if possible.

What tormented and depressed him was this. Whilst an ardent, intense desire to please her was more and more taking possession of him, at the same time he felt also a constantly increasing doubt as to whether it was within the bounds of possibility that he should ever be able to do so. He knew that he had talent and strength for her to admire—but what was the good of that if she were perverse enough to prefer virtue— which article it was certainly not in his power to offer? That she *did* prefer virtue—that her nature was one that was not to be

contented without it—was a conviction which impressed itself
more and more strongly on his mind every time he saw her,
and vexed him almost past bearing. It must be *that* that made
her want to help other people, be they who they might, and
made her take to heart injustice and wrong of all kinds. Hence
it was that she had been so anxious to clear Richard Richards
from the false accusation brought against him—on which
subject she had discoursed so much that Sylvester, in his mad
longing to please her, had once thought wildly even whether
he would not sacrifice himself for her contentment by making
known who the real culprit was. The idea had been promptly
dismissed as preposterous and nothing had come of it; yet
when not long afterwards he had heard her quote her
favourite—

> "Tasks in hours of insight willed,
> May be through hours of gloom fulfilled,"

he had been conscious of a passing wonder whether she would
have regarded as an 'hour of insight,' the romantic possibility
of self-condemnation that had crossed his brain for a moment.
She had subjugated him so completely that he felt as if he could
hardly oppose her will in anything, and as if it were even
imperatively necessary for him to conform himself to whatever
standard of morality pleased her. But how was that possible
unless he could undo the past, and alter his whole self? As
George Eliot says,—

> "You can't turn curds to milk again,
> Nor now, by wishing, back to then."[1]

And yet was there not, perhaps, some remote chance that he
might even yet become such as she would approve of, if only he
could have her presence always with him?

When the acting was over and he had changed his things,
he went to the ball-rooms and looked round for her who was to
him the only one human being worth considering besides

himself in the world. He wanted to have the bliss of dancing with her again and to be able, for that brief space at least, to give himself up to the present enjoyment and forget all irritating subjects. Forcing his way with difficulty from one to another of the crowded rooms, he searched for her for some time in vain. At last, however, he spied her sitting in a small, flower-decked boudoir alone with Sir Charles Dover, with whom she appeared to be carrying on a very interesting conversation. Neither of them saw Sylvester, who watched them for a minute full of angry disappointment at finding her thus engaged, and debated whether to go and interrupt the *tête-à-tête* or not. Jealousy prompted him to do so; but he was withheld by the melancholy forebodings that filled him of the futility of his passion. Supposing he chose to look upon himself as the representative of talent, then Sir Charles might fairly be considered to be that of virtue. And if she would persist in liking virtue best, what chance of success was there for talent if it could not compass the other attribute also?

Anyhow he would in no wise advance his cause by disturbing her at present, and he must put off till later in the evening the dance with her on which his heart was set. Therefore he retired from the room noiselessly, and, retracing his steps to the place where he had seen that Mr Rhys was standing, stationed himself in the vicinity of that gentleman to await her re-appearance.

Here he was quickly perceived by Ethel. She was still of the same mind about desiring to have an interview with him, in spite of the horror and almost fear with which he had inspired her. He certainly could not do her any harm here, in the midst of this throng of people; and it was now a favourable opportunity for carrying out her plan. So she pointed him out to her uncle, and suggested that the latter should at once perform the promised introduction.

Mr Rhys bustled off immediately to execute her wishes.

'Come along, Sylvester,' he said. 'I see you're not dancing, and I want to introduce you to a partner. One, too, who'll be envied you by half the men in the room. Lucky fellow, you are, that she's taken a fancy to dance with you! You know her well enough by name; everyone does that, I think, since she had half her jewels stolen when she was staying with me last September. It's my niece, Miss Carton.'

No more unwelcome name could possibly have passed Mr Rhys's lips.

'Miss Carton!' exclaimed Sylvester, with a feeling of overwhelming and unpleasant surprise. 'Why, I fancied she did not know the Crœsus-Hoggs, and would certainly not be here to-night.'

'Oh dear no !—how can you have made such a mistake?' replied Mr Rhys genially; 'there she's been this ever so long, admiring your acting like all the rest of us, and declaring it to be capital. Indeed, there couldn't be two opinions about that. However, come along, and be introduced—there she is sitting by the pillar of yellow roses.'

There was no escaping the ordeal. As he was led up towards Ethel, Sylvester swiftly reviewed his acting of the poacher an hour or so ago, and compared it with his performance of the burglar at Llwyn-yr-Allt last September. The entire similarity of the two assumptions of character made him shiver, and he hardly ventured to hope that she could have failed to know him again; still, there was just a chance of it, for it was wonderful how unobservant some people were. But this hope was destroyed when he reached her, and asked her to dance. In her unwontedly excited condition of mind, she was unable wholly to control the expression of her face; and though outsiders, who had no clue to its meaning would not have been able to read what was written there, yet in his eyes recognition of him, and hostility were visible too plainly to be mistaken.

What was to come next? he wondered, internally. Truly their relative positions were completely reversed from what they had been at his former meeting with her. Then he had had the upper hand, but now it was her turn to dictate to him. She could talk to him, dance with him, keep him at her side, do with him exactly as she chose; he dared not resist or try to slip away lest she should call out stop thief! and have him arrested on the spot.

She accepted his invitation to dance, and bowing politely, he presented his arm to lead her away just as he might have done to any other lady in the room. It was a strange sensation to her to realise that this was the same person who had put her in fear of her life a few months before; and to think that out of all the crowd of people around, she alone knew the villainy of which this seemingly respectable and worthy young gentleman was capable; she alone knew how dangerous a monster was in the midst of them, in an innocent, fleecy covering to make him look like the rest of the flock. She felt an involuntary thrill as she laid her hand on the proffered coat sleeve, and for the moment almost repented of her whim to be introduced to him. What she wanted or expected to gain thereby she would have been puzzled to say exactly. Had she been questioned on the matter she would probably have replied that she had fancied, perhaps, she might find it easier to settle what to do, when she had some personal knowledge of what he was like.

The fact was she had been moved partly by curiosity, partly by sudden caprice, and partly by a peculiarity to which some natures are liable, and which, when a situation occurs so extraordinary as to render it impossible to discover any guiding landmarks of precedent, will sometimes make even the most well regulated, Mrs-Grundy-ridden of females give herself up recklessly to follow the fancy of the moment, and resolve, as it were, to have a sudden frolic for once, and see what comes of it. But an idea of that kind never occurred to Sylvester, who, little used to feminine caprices, forgot to take their likelihood into account, and was consequently extremely puzzled as to what could possibly be Ethel's object in her present proceeding.

He felt that she was master of the situation entirely, and that he had no choice but to obey her pleasure, and wait and see what she intended to do. But what that would be he was burning to know.

In one respect she was out in her calculations, however. That he was sure to fear her recognising him she was quite aware; but she did not mean to let him know that she had really done so just yet, as she did not want him to be frightened away before she could determine her plan of action, and choose when to have him arrested. But she had forgotten the possibility of her face betraying her, and therefore he had the advantage of a fuller knowledge of how matters stood between them than she had reckoned on.

It was not dancing with him, but conversation that she desired; so after taking one short turn in the valse that had just commenced, she declared it was too full for there to be any satisfaction in attempting to dance then, and that, as she was a little tired, she should prefer finding a cool place to sit down in. Accordingly, Sylvester obediently took her to one of the smaller rooms. Here there was an alcove, in which was a window, with a luxuriously-cushioned settee, affording just room for two people to sit down comfortably. The superb, delicately-scented flowers surrounding it were stirred lightly by the soft night breeze coming in through the open window, on the sill of which stood a large block of ice, cooling every breath of air as it entered; and in this comfortable nook the oddly-matched pair— mutually fearing and detesting one another—seated themselves as though on the best of terms together, and were commented on by an irreverent Eton boy as 'a couple of beggars going to spoon; don't disturb the poor coves.'

They had but just sat down when Sir Charles and Imogen came in on their way to the ball-room and caught sight of them. There was a new look of elation and hope in Sir Charles's face, as though he saw a prospect of great happiness very near at hand, which gave Sylvester a sharp pain at heart. Of course, now that all was about to be revealed, and he was going to be arrested for robbery, there would be no more chance for *him* with Imogen, he thought; but it was none the less bitter to have to witness the triumph of someone else, and to reflect that talent had been beaten by virtue upon equal terms, and even before the former had been handicapped by the bringing to light of its past iniquities. And yet he loved her so! No one could love her better, he felt sure. And his love grew yet fiercer and more painful now that prison walls seemed about to shut him out from her hopelessly.

'So you two have actually made acquaintance at last!' cried Imogen, stopping for a moment, and coming towards the couple in the window-seat. 'And you've accomplished it without my assistance after all! Well, I'm delighted the spell has been broken, for I really began to think that there must be a fate about the way in which I invariably failed to bring you together. But do you mean to say your going to sit still during the *Manola*? *We* aren't at any rate, so good-bye for the present.'

And so saying she and her cavalier passed swiftly on to join the dancers.

'Certainly it is no fault of hers that we have not met before, for she was very anxious to introduce us to one another, I know, only there was always something or other in the way,' began Ethel, with a vague idea that it would be a good thing to lead the conversation to the subject of Imogen as a preliminary to finding out something about the state of affairs existing between her cousin and Sylvester.

The latter hesitated for a moment. He was quite positive of

Miss Carton's having recognised him; there were no witnesses, so that whatever admission he might now make would not tell against him hereafter in a court of justice, as it would be easy to deny it all then if needs be; and he was consumed with anxiety to know what plan she had in her mind in regard to his fate. What, therefore, was the good of wasting time in mere empty fencing?

'It pleases you to speak as though this were our first meeting, Miss Carton,' said he, 'and all the better for me if it were so indeed! Yet I can hardly believe that the one occasion when we met before has escaped your memory so readily.'

Ethel was somewhat taken aback at this frankness, and it needed all her self-control to prevent her betraying her discomposure to her antagonist.

'You are right; I have not forgotten it,' she replied calmly. 'But how did you know that I had recognised you?'

'By your face,' he answered; 'I read it there the moment you looked at me when your uncle introduced us; but of course I knew you could hardly help doing it after seeing me play that cursed poaching part just now, which you may be very sure I would not have done unless I had believed your absence a matter of certainty. And so now that we can speak openly, will you condescend to tell me what you intend to do?'

'What do you expect that I should do?' she inquired with some haughtiness.

'Give me up to the police.'

'You are perfectly correct in your supposition.

He laughed bitterly.

'And perhaps also you will be so gracious as to inform me how many more minutes of liberty you intend that I should enjoy first?' he inquired.

Ethel now fully realised the mistake she had made in letting her recognition of him be apparent. Her liberty of action was to some extent fettered by this premature showing of her hand. No doubt he would hurry off and make his escape immediately if she let him leave her before she had given him into custody; therefore she was no longer free to do as she had originally intended, and to postpone his denunciation till such time as it should be most convenient to herself.

Ah, if only she could know whether or not there was any kind of understanding or affection subsisting between him and Imogen! She would see if she could not discover something then and there by questioning him as to this most important matter.

'That depends,' she returned cautiously; 'of course I do not wish to behave with any needless harshness. It has been rumoured that—that—in short that you have an affection for Miss Rhys, and it occurred to me that in that case it would be kinder on my part to endeavour to spare the feelings of both you and her by contriving so that your arrest should not take place under her very eyes. Perhaps, however, the rumour to which I allude is false?'

Though despairing, miserable, half-maddened by the utter downfall of all his hopes that was impending, he felt no wish to deny or seem ashamed of his adoration for Imogen. Rather it gave him a sudden sense of pleasure to be able to acknowledge what bore testimony to her supreme excellence and power.

'No, it is not,' he replied, almost defiantly; 'I care more for her than for the whole of the rest of the world together.'

Ethel was surprised and a little bit moved at this abrupt and evidently genuine confession of love; it was impossible not to feel some slight compassion for the man who had been driven to make it.

'Does my cousin know this?' she said, speaking somewhat more gently than before.

'No; I have never told her of it.'

'Do you think it likely that she suspects it, though?'

continued Ethel, anxious to profit as much as she could by his unexpectedly confidential humour; 'or should you say there was any disposition on her part to reciprocate your attachment?'

'How can I tell? But no, I fear not.'

He paused. Never before had he spoken to another person of that love which was the one thing good, true, and honest about him. Now that he had begun to do so, when already excited and overwrought both by the discovery of his fatal secret, and also by the conviction that Imogen was being won by his rival, the violence of repressed emotion at last let loose, broke down his habitual self-control, and carried him on in spite of himself; he forgot the position in which he stood, the ruin that was threatening him, and felt only an unconquerable impulse to try for once in his life to impart to a second person something of the real heart and soul within him.

Ethel's knowledge of his being a criminal made it easier to unbosom himself to her than to anyone else; and after hesitating for a moment he went on again, speaking with a passionate intensity of feeling that made his voice tremble in spite of all he could do to control it, and that fairly startled his hearer.

'I said that I *feared* I was nothing to her. Yet why should I fear it, seeing things are as they are? You at least, knowing what you do, are able to perceive that hidden incompatibility between her and me which has been a barrier rising up again and again to hinder me from paying court to her as another man might have done. Ah! the barrier will not be a hidden one much longer. She, and the whole world too, must see it plainly the instant that it pleases you to draw back the veil now concealing it. But *I* have known it always. Look at the utter dissimilarity between her nature and mine—she, good and innocent, with her heart set on being of use in the world, full of all kinds of noble and elevated aims (or what the world calls such at any rate), and thinking that every fellow-creature has a claim upon her; whereas I—!

Why, before I knew her, I neither cared for nor believed in any goodness at all. And though now I have grown so to love her that I can no longer remain wholly indifferent to or incredulous about anything that she holds in honour—anything that is inseparable from herself—yet still I *cannot* change my nature, I *cannot* cancel the past, I *cannot* make myself such as she approves. What chance then is there that she would care for me if she knew what I really am? I could never hope for such happiness—never—never!'

It was not in Ethel to listen to this outburst of long-pent-up strong love and misery finding vent in words at last, without being touched by it. The power which the man possessed came out in his great emotion to its full extent, and she, like Imogen, became vaguely aware that there was something singular about him, and that either to attract or to repel he had a faculty that was peculiar to himself. Her compassion was aroused for his sufferings, and tended to mitigate the extreme aversion she had felt for him at first. However evil he might be he was surely not irredeemable; and her immediate instinct was to help him by trying to turn his mind in the direction where she knew she would herself find hope and comfort in whatever trouble might come upon her.

'It is true that you cannot alter the past,' she said, speaking very gently and pityingly; 'but yet you can alter yourself, if you will. Do you not know how gracious our Father is to all who turn, and repent of the evil they have done? Have you not any kind of religion or religious faith at all?'

On no lesser occasion could she have spoken thus openly about religion to a stranger. But ordinary habits both of thought and speech are sometimes discarded on great emergencies, and the man's startling and terrible earnestness made her feel instinctively the necessity of being utterly real just then—of saying out the true thing within her, be it what it might. As for

Sylvester, having begun to come out of his shell he could not immediately force himself back to it again, for he experienced a strange sense of relief in thus revealing himself for once as he really was to another person. He replied with the same abrupt straightforwardness as before:—

'Some time ago I should have answered "No!" to that question unhesitatingly; but now I am less positive about it than I was. Possibly some stray glimmers of light may have reached me by means of your cousin—though whether, if so, they came *from* or *through* her I cannot say. She may have been the sun whence they issued, or else perchance but the pane of glass that admitted them into a dark room—how can I tell?'

Ethel leant her head upon her hand and mused. The duty of unmasking Sylvester had at first seemed specially hateful to her on account of Imogen only; but now she was beginning to dislike it on his own account also. The unreserve with which he had shown her what was passing in his mind had not resulted from any deep laid plan for appealing to her feelings; he had, for the moment, forgotten himself too entirely to have any thought of that kind. Yet such an appeal, no doubt, was the effect that his outspokenness produced upon her. It would have taken a far harder heart than that of Ethel to listen to him unmoved; and the more interested in him she became, the harder she found it to decide upon what course of action to pursue. She had an inkling that his nature was one of those that need much sorrow to make them learn—to whom the purification of great suffering is indispensable; yet for all that she would rather it should be imposed upon him by means of anyone else than her. It was her bounden duty to proclaim what she had discovered in order that the world might be on its guard against the impostor, and that the innocent might be saved from unjust suspicion. Then this man would be put in prison—where he would be safe from further temptations, where he would have time for repentance, where it would be impossible for him to hold any intercourse with Imogen. Yet, obviously desirable and advantageous as all these results of his imprisonment would be, still Ethel felt a growing repugnance to speak the word that was to bring them about.

'I am so sorry for you, so *very, very* sorry,' she was beginning, when her speech was cut short by a sudden and alarming interruption which caused all other considerations to be merged in one of paramount and urgent importance to both of them—i.e., the securing of their immediate personal safety.

CHAPTER IX
Amongst Flames

A sudden cessation of the music, a hasty trampling of feet, and an outcry of 'Fire, fire!'—this was what caused Ethel to stop abruptly in the midst of what she had begun to say, whilst she and her companion looked at each other in horror. Then they started up with one accord and hurried to a small door of the room they were in.

A great square staircase with a gallery surrounding it occupied a large portion of the middle of the house, and the door to which they now hurried opened immediately on to this gallery, and was, therefore, the most direct way of escape from the house. But on reaching the door they found it impossible to get any further. All egress from the room where they were, in the direction of the gallery at all events, was cut off by a dense mass of frightened, struggling men and women, who blocked up the passage outside in wild confusion.

The first alarm has made every one anxious to get at once to the front staircase, and there is a general, simultaneous rush made towards it throughout every room on the first floor. But speedily there is a check at every doorway, where the outpouring stream is met by another one composed of those who got first to the staircase, and have there discovered the vanity of hoping to escape in that direction. For, alas! the lower part of the grand staircase is the very spot where the fire has broken out, and it is spreading rapidly up the sides by means of the gauze decorations of the bannisters. Going down the stairs, therefore, is simply rushing into the middle of flames; and it is evident that the gallery running round the top will shortly be also on fire. A most dangerous place, consequently, is that gallery which was just now struggled for so eagerly, and one to be by all means avoided.

What is to be done? Surely there is a back staircase to have recourse to—no house of this size can be without that convenience—who knows where it is?

Yes, there *is* a back stairs, and a good many of the guests know the way to it. Unluckily, it is somewhat out of the way, and the approach to it is narrow and inconvenient; still, it means safety at this moment, and thither does the stream flow with such speed as is attainable by a closely-packed, terrified mob of people, all shoving and struggling to get to the front, and moving along a tortuous corridor where every doorway brings fresh contributions of panic-struck human beings in deadly peril. For time is everything, and those who are last will inevitably be lost. The back stairs are not broad, and the crowd can only empty itself off thereby at a pitifully slow rate; and meanwhile the ravening flames will not wait; but, aided by all kinds of decorative fall-alls of thin materials, come leaping up the front stairs in fearful haste. Red tongues begin to shoot out through the bannisters into the gallery, which has not yet had nearly time to get cleared of the people, who rushed thither before the seat of the fire was known. Ill is it now for some of those who were first in that rush. The solid mass of humanity pressing towards the other staircase is a barrier keeping them prisoners in the fatal gallery, and it is hard to recoil far enough to keep out of the way of these cruel fiery tongues that leap higher and nearer at every minute. Ah! one of them touches the dress of a girl, and in a moment she is in a blaze; for a ball dress is of all things most inflammable. Instinctively turning to her fellow-creatures for protection in her mortal agony, she tries to press yet closer to them, and yet further away from the dreadful enemy, without remembering that in her present flaming condition, contact with her means death to all clad in thin dresses, and that she is now to be regarded as a fresh centre of danger—as a torch to spread the conflagration wherever she goes. But if she has forgotten this, others have not; and from out of the frantic, shrieking crowd are extended hands, fans, opera-hats, bouquets, anything that can be laid hold of, to keep her at a distance. Still, she will not be repulsed, and continues trying to approach; so the end of it is that a strong arm in a coat (since cloth does not catch fire easily) advances from out of the midst of the people nearest her, and gives one violent push that precipitates the poor, screaming girl headlong downstairs into the fiery gulf below. Inhuman and horrible as the act may seem, is it not perhaps the only thing to do? It is one life against many; to save her was impossible, and she had at all hazards to be kept away from this crowd full of women in tulles, gauzes, and muslins. Ah, well! her sufferings are over by now; but for us who remain—what is in store for us? Shall we escape or not?

How terribly fast the red tongues advance, gaining and spreading in all directions each moment! And how miserably slow is the rate of exit by the back stairs! Is there no other outlet? no other chance of getting away from being burnt to death? There are the windows, it is true. But the rooms of this magnificent dwelling are so lofty that the distance to the ground is far too great to jump; and the balconies are boarded in to-night, so that the pillars are not available as a means of descent even for those who can climb. Confused, shrieking, gasping, mad with terror, the people fight, jostle, and push almost without knowing that they are doing so; and many of the weaker ones, thrown down and trampled under foot, find in suffocation an escape from the fiery death that they are dreading. And all the time the foe goes on gaining and gaining with the swiftness of the wind, has swallowed up some more tulle-attired victims, and is beginning with fierce triumph to enter one or two of the rooms.

But it is time to go back to Sylvester and Ethel, whom we left when the first alarm had reached them, and they had run to one of the doors leading out of the apartment where they were sitting. As soon as Sylvester saw what was taking place, and that the passage was completely choked up, he exclaimed,—

'The private way to the theatre! Few people know of it, so it's sure to be free from crowd. If the fire hasn't touched it yet we can get out by that!'

'I didn't know there was such a way,' she returned; 'where is it?'

'Follow me,' was his answer, as he hastened to a door on the opposite side of the room. This led to a small, winding side-passage, through which they reached the conservatory; and on getting there, they found that there was no one in it, and that it was still clear from fire.

When the theatre in the garden had been erected, Guelph Crœsus-Hogg had taken it into his head that he should like to have a private way of his own for going to and fro between the house and stage. Therefore, some planks had been thrown across from a corner of the conservatory to the upper part of the theatre, roofed in, boarded at the sides, and carpeted and lined, so as to construct a tiny wooden passage, which, though extremely frail, and not broad enough to contain two people abreast, was yet quite sufficient to satisfy his whim.

This private way was known only to the household and to a few of the male actors who had been taken backwards and forwards along it occasionally by Guelph at rehearsals; and in this number Sylvester had fortunately been included. The entrance to the passage was concealed by a heavy velvet curtain, which he lifted up for Ethel. Then he said, pointing down the way as he spoke,—

'That'll bring you into the right hand gallery of the theatre. From there you will easily find your way downstairs and get out.'

'Are not you coming too then?' panted Ethel, breathless with the haste of their flight.

'Not till I have seen to your cousin's safety first,' was his answer, as he turned away from her and hurried across the conservatory again.

At the door he was almost knocked down by coming into violent collision with Guelph, who was hurrying along with Lady Elise.

'Jove!' cried the former when he saw who it was; 'where are you going, man? Have you forgotten my little passage? Everything else blocked—only chance left!'

'I'm coming directly,' cried Sylvester, 'but must find some one first. Don't hinder me!'

'I say! it won't hold many! Give us time to get off before you tell other people of it—don't be in too much of a hurry—keep it dark till we're safe,' Guelph hallooed after him; but Sylvester was already out of hearing.

There was a perfect network of side passages, small rooms, and ins and outs in the millionaire's great house, and as Sylvester had learnt a good deal of its geography during his attendance at rehearsals, that knowledge now enabled him to pass round from room to room without coming in contact with the crowd, through whom it would have been impossible to make a way.

Heartrending screams and cries filled the air. Everyone was striving wildly to gain the only known outlet—the remote back staircase; and every approach to it was crammed. Perhaps Imogen might be amongst the fortunate ones who had already escaped down it and reached a place of safety. If so, well and good; but if not! He was almost maddened at the idea that she might be perishing at that very moment in this terrible place whilst a means of escape was within easy reach. To the woes of the rest of that great company he was callous, and it never entered his head that there could be any necessity for imparting to a soul amongst them except her the secret of the private way. Why, if he did, the knowledge would spread like lightning, and a crowd would rush to the passage, choke it up, and break it down; and then how would he be able to save Imogen even if he found her? His theory had always been that people must take care of themselves or else go to the wall; and his conduct—both as regarded himself and others—had invariably been regulated in accordance therewith. It was true there flashed across his mind an uneasy recollection that the theory was one which Imogen had protested against indignantly; and that she had been delighted with Sir Charles for acting exactly contrary to it, and putting himself in danger for the sake of a lot of strange school children. But there was no time to consider things like that now. The one thing necessary was to seek for her high and low, and rescue her if she was not already safe.

Glancing hastily from the outskirts of the throng over the dense mass of humanity crushing and striving to get to the back stairs, and not seeing her there, he hurried off to explore elsewhere. The doom of all who were in the dreadful gallery was sealed irrevocably, as it was by this time all on fire, and he shuddered with horror to think of the possibility of her having been amongst them.

The first room into which he looked contained nobody. In the second were only two women. One was a very old lady, whose age and infirmities had made it wholly impossible for her to try and save herself in the rough, surging crowd; and the other was her middle-aged daughter, who—though world-hardened, painted, and frivolous—would not desert her old mother in this extremity, even to attempt to secure her own safety. The cheeks of both were rouged, and the fixed bright colour contrasted strangely with the ghastly white of their quivering lips, and with the scared expression of their faces as they clung together in despair; the daughter, helpless as she really was, yet striving to impart some sense of comfort and protection to her feeble mother by kissing and stroking her with infinite tenderness.

It was a pathetic little scene that might well have touched him with sufficient compassion to make him show them the way by which they could have escaped. But no such thought occurred to him, and he only uttered an exclamation of disappointment, and hurried on quickly to explore a third room for Imogen.

There, to his inexpressible relief, he perceived the object of his search. She was standing with her father near a window, and he and she together were endeavouring with frantic haste to construct a sort of rough rope out of the cords of the window-blinds, loopings of curtains, and whatever else they could lay hands on that could possibly serve their purpose. But the materials were not very suitable; their fingers were unskilled at the labour; and the rope was still deplorably far from completion. There was only one other person in the room besides these two, and that was Sir Charles Dover, who was lying back in a big arm-chair and evidently insensible, if not dead. If dead, then *he* would not be able to have the happiness of winning Imogen, at any rate, was the thought that crossed Sylvester's mind, not unpleasantly, as he advanced across the room.

But the baronet was only stunned—not dead. He had been dancing with Imogen when the alarm was first given, and as they had happened to be near Mr Rhys at that moment, the three had subsequently kept together. In the commotion it happened that a large and heavy marble bust close to where they were, became loosened and began toppling over. Sir Charles saw the great weight just as it was in the act of descending on the heads of the solid crowd below, and sprang towards it, making a desperate effort to seize hold of it, and keep it in its place. He failed, however, and the bust crashed over upon the living mass, one corner hitting him on the temple as it fell. Had he been at the time in the thick of the crowd, he would have inevitably been trampled under foot; but as he was fortunately at the extreme edge of it, he had been able to stagger into the next room before falling down insensible.

By the time this happened, Mr Rhys had discovered how extremely small was the chance of getting to the back staircase soon enough to escape by it; and it suddenly struck him that it might be possible for him and his daughter to make a rope strong enough to bear the weight of a man, by means of which they might let themselves down from a window—and Sir Charles also, if he had not recovered by the time the rope was ready. The only doubt was whether there would be sufficient time to execute this scheme. However, as far as he could see, it was either that or nothing for them all; so he drew Imogen with him into the room where Sir Charles had fainted away, and set her to work with him at rope-making as fast as possible.

But the time was becoming fearfully short, and the advance of the flames was hand-over-hand faster than was that of the rope.

This then was the position of affairs when Sylvester at last found the girl of whom he was in search. As she saw him approach, she pointed to their work, and made signs to him to come and assist them at it. Speaking would have been useless, for she could not have made her voice reach to as far off as where he was, on account of the terrible din that prevailed.

The extremely elementary appearance presented by the rope convinced Sylvester that it could not possibly be finished in time to be of service.

'The rope'll do you no good!' he shouted, going close to her and her father, and making himself heard with difficulty. 'Come with me—I can save you.'

There was no time for explanations, so they desisted instantly from the rope-making, and Mr Rhys turned to lift up Sir Charles, while Imogen shouted into Sylvester's ear,—

'Will you and papa be able to carry him alone? or shall I give a hand too?'

There had certainly never occurred to Sylvester the possibility of this. To be expected to linger when every moment was of inestimable value, in order to help save his rival—the man whom it would be more congenial to his feelings to send out of the world than to keep in it! It seemed to him more than human nature—or *his* nature anyhow—could bring itself to do; and his first impulse was to refuse absolutely to lay a finger on the unconscious young man.

'Never mind him!' cried Sylvester; 'you must leave him, and save yourselves while you can!'

But neither Mr Rhys nor Imogen were of those who will consent to desert a friend in extremity, and to leave Sir Charles to his fate was not to be thought of for an instant by either of them. So she merely shook her head in response to Sylvester's impatient adjuration, and prepared to assist her father in raising the baronet. As she stooped over him, she cast a reproachful and appealing glance at Sylvester.

The mute request for his aid was more than he could resist, coming from her. Besides, his knowledge of her character told him that if he continued to refuse his assistance, it would only end in Mr Rhys and her carrying Sir Charles by themselves as best they could.

That would cause delay now, when time was so inexpressibly precious; for of course her strength was far less than that of a young and vigorous man like himself, and she and her father would bear the burden much more slowly than if he were in her place. Overcoming, therefore, with a great effort, his intense distaste for what he was about to do, he seized hold of

Sir Charles by the shoulders, leaving the feet to Mr Rhys, and with Imogen at their heels they sped along towards the conservatory by a side way that he knew of; it was not the most direct route to take, but it was one that enabled them to skirt round the fearful confusion going on in the principal passages, without coming in contact with or being hindered by it. His two companions accepted his guidance blindly, not knowing whither he was taking them nor how he intended to escape, till they found themselves in the conservatory. Here he hurried across to the covered entrance to the private way, drew back the curtain that concealed it, and made Imogen go on into it in front of them—for its construction was so frail that he did not feel quite certain whether it would not break down under the weight of two men carrying a third; and if she went first, her safety would be ensured whatever might happen.

Meanwhile the hubbub and turmoil all around seemed to grow continually greater, and the confusion worse confounded. By this time one fire-engine had arrived at the house; and what with the shrieks and groans of the miserable people cooped up inside, the shouts of the crowd outside, and the hissing of the water poured upon the flames, the Babel of sounds was in truth appalling.

Just after Imogen had got inside the tiny passage that led to safety, a sudden thought struck her and she stood still. Hitherto she had followed Sylvester without reasoning upon what they were doing, but now she all at once perceived of what value this means of exit might be to numbers of other people, if only they were aware of its existence.

'More lives could be saved if this way were known about!' she cried. 'People think there's nothing but the staircase. I'll go back and tell them of this.'

The mere idea made Sylvester's heart well-nigh stand still with horror. How greatly did he then rejoice at having made her enter the narrow passage first, for now it was impossible for her to make her way back past him and Mr Rhys, however much she might desire to do so!

'You shall *not*!' he exclaimed. 'You shall *not* pass back. Don't you see how mad it would be for you to do the thing you propose? A woman—in a dress that a spark might set on fire at any moment! Hurry on—and don't linger here!'

She had no choice but to obey, for the path behind her was entirely filled up by the two men and their burden. Yet it was unwillingly that she continued her progress, and in spite of what Sylvester had said, she would most certainly have flown back to do what she could for her fellow-creatures if she had been free to do what she chose.

At that moment there arose a sudden fresh clamour of screams, groans, and cries that was more appalling than ever, and pierced her ears and heart anew.

'Oh, this is horrible! horrible!' she exclaimed; 'can *nothing* be done for them? Let me go back, and tell at least some few of this outlet! Do let me go!' Her distress affected Sylvester powerfully. It seemed impossible that he should witness it without attempting to relieve it.

And then, suddenly, there came upon him like an inspiration, the idea that such an opportunity as he could never again have lay before him. Yes, for once in his life, at all events, he had now a chance of doing something that would meet with her thorough approval, and he must not let the unlooked-for chance slip. He would himself do this thing that she was so anxious should be done; he would himself return to the fiery house, and see if he could not rescue some more people by means of the little passage whilst it was still available. He would first help Mr Rhys to deposit Sir Charles, who was beginning to show signs of returning consciousness, in the theatre, which was a place of comparative safety. Thence Mr

Rhys and Imogen could easily complete the escape of all three without his further assistance, and he would go back to fulfil her pleasure. After all, the expedition would not be quite so dangerous for him, as at first sight it might appear. Though as soon as the flames should reach the conservatory, the planks of the private way would, of course, quickly be alight, and the retreat cut off, yet that had not yet happened. No fire had yet extended so far, and there might be minutes and minutes still before the conservatory would be touched. Therefore the way was at this moment safe and open. A man's costume was not of the inflammable materials of a lady's ball-dress. To a person like him, naturally brave, knowing the ins and outs of the house well, and having all his wits about him, the undertaking offered a very reasonable prospect of success, and of a safe return from it.

Besides, he was just then in a state of unnatural excitement, which made him unusually reckless of danger. He knew himself to be detected, and on the verge of being ruined, and hopelessly cut off from the woman he loved passionately. Soon she would know all, and turn from him with loathing and disgust. But she did not know yet; and now—this night—for once, at least, she should think well of him, come what might. There should be at least one memory of him to approve of whenever she might happen to think of him in the future; outcast and criminal though he might be.

This thing, too, whereon her heart was set so strangely—this desire to help others—must it not really possess some actual good of its own which he had never been able to discover? Else why would one like her care so much about it?

And in a sort of way there thus came to him through her he loved, some approach to sympathetic compassion for the miserable creatures perishing in the fire, to whose sufferings he would otherwise have been indifferent.

There was no time for many words, even had it been easy for a voice to make itself audible in that wild uproar. The instant he was beyond the passage, Sylvester laid down Sir Charles, and hurriedly pointed out to Mr Rhys the way by which he would have now to proceed in order to get into the open air again through the theatre.

Meanwhile he still occupied the entrance to the passage, so that there might be no possibility of Imogen's rushing back, and carrying out her intention in spite of him. Then he turned to her.

'Not you, but me!' he shouted. 'I'm going back to do what you wish. Will that please you?'

It was more than she had expected of him. A sudden expression of gladness, surprise, and admiration rushed into her face, and showed clearly what she was feeling.

'Oh yes!' she exclaimed; and then added simply, 'I'll pray for you meanwhile.'

Never before had her eyes rested upon him with the look of trust and cordial approval that shone in them at that moment. He was almost intoxicated with the delight that it caused him. His heart throbbed with wild joy as at some great honour conferred on him, and he desired ardently to deserve it, while yet at the same time he had a consciousness of being very different from what she imagined him to be, which abashed him in spite of himself.

Acting on the impulse of the moment he seized her hand and kissed it. 'Thank you,' was all that he said. But the words could not have been uttered with more sincerity and profound, real, gratitude by the most earnestly religious of human beings. And then, feeling strangely exalted, glad, and aided by the knowledge of her prayers on his behalf, he flew back to the Pandemonium he had just quitted.

There, matters were growing rapidly worse. The fresh

outbreak of shrieks that had wrung Imogen's heart had been caused by the flames spreading to the foot of the back staircase—all crammed and packed as it was with fugitives. In honour of the grand entertainment of the night it had been swathed from top to bottom in gauze, gracefully festooned and draped; and the fire, catching the gauze like so much tinder, ran up the sides like lightning and enveloped all who were on the steps in one blaze. For these poor creatures no escape was possible. But those who had not yet reached the staircase might still have some faint hope of saving themselves, so there was a sudden check in the stream of people who were pressing eagerly towards it as their last chance of salvation. Stopping short and turning sharp round, they struggled frantically to fly in the opposite direction; and as those in the rear were still ignorant of what had happened, the confined limits of the passage became the scene of a short but furious conflict before the receding throng could prevail over the advancing one and turn the current backwards again.

Wilder and wilder grew the tumult as soon as it was realised that the only known means of exit was in the power of the foe. The panic-stricken mob took refuge in the rooms and fought for access to the windows. Some shouted to those below to bring blankets for them to jump into—imploring them to save them somehow—anyhow—for the love of God. A few leaped out recklessly without heeding what might be beneath to alight on—whether road, garden, pavement, or pointed rails; possessed by an agonised terror of death by fire they thought only of avoiding that, and cared nought for the risk of being bruised, maimed, impaled, or killed in their fall. And now a fire-escape arrives at the window of the second drawing-room. But everyone cannot get to that at once—and there is the floor of one room fallen in with a fearful crash already! The fire gains so fast, so terribly fast!

This then was the state of things prevailing when Sylvester returned. Close to the conservatory door he met a group of people half-dazed with fright and roaming about distractedly without any definite object in their movements. By dint of gestures, words, and some violence he got them to the entrance to the private way, and made them understand that they must go along it. The sight of this unexpected means of deliverance out of the fiery prison seemed to restore their scattered wits, and they fled down the passage without further hesitation, whilst he went back in search of others.

As he entered the room adjoining the conservatory there came a great puff of spark-filled smoke that startled him and showed the enemy to be closer at hand than he had imagined. For an instant he paused in doubt.

Would the way back be passable a little longer? Had he not better return now while escape was certain? But the kindly look that he had seen on Imogen's face a few minutes ago was before his eyes, and he was yet glowing with the enthusiasm and happiness it had given him. Would he merit her favour if he should leave so many victims to perish miserably, while there was still a fair chance of rescuing some of them?

Hardly, he thought; and, so thinking, rushed back for one last effort to save life. The fire had as yet only just appeared in the room in which he was, and before it could spread to the conservatory there would surely be time to dash once more into the body of the house and get back again with yet a few more men and women snatched from the jaws of destruction. Without losing an instant he rushed into a room where a number of people had taken refuge.

'Safety! a way out! follow me!' he roared at the top of his voice, gesticulating and beckoning at the same time to attract the attention of those who could not hear his words. There was a tumultuous rush to accompany him on the part of those who partly heard what he said and partly guessed at his meaning, and he led the way back in furious haste through the blinding smoke that rolled more and more densely through every part of the house. There was still time—surely there was still time!

Alas! some of those fatal decorations of muslin and gauze had been put up in the conservatory also. These having caught fire led the flames with fearful speed all round the glass building; by the time Sylvester returned there with his companions the place was all ablaze. The wooden passage had caught fire and he was shut in hopelessly to perish with those for whose deliverance he had sacrificed his last chance of safety.

Ceilings and floors having once begun to go are falling in rapidly. The sparks fall thicker and thicker—the smoke grows more and more unendurable—the only fire-escape that has yet arrived is far away—and the end cannot be very long in coming.

Well, at all events he has done his best to please her, and to act for once according to the principles in which she believes—even though it *was* unfortunately wholly beyond his power to attain to that state of general virtuousness that she would persist in admiring. He has done all he can for her, and he thinks that he wishes she could know that, at any rate. But though that is impossible, yet somehow, and in some strange way, he does not feel so absolutely severed from her now, as he has always done heretofore. He remembers that last look she bestowed upon him as they parted. Besides, does he not know what she is doing at this very moment? She is praying for him—she promised that she would, and she always keeps her promises. Who had told him something about the prayer of a righteous man availing much? He seems to have heard it or read it somewhere or other, but he can't remember where. Anyhow it makes him very glad to be certain that she is praying for him.

Ah! what a fierce, scorching gust came then, and how difficult it is to breathe in this suffocating smoke! And suddenly there flashes across his recollection the cool, dewy freshness of the air that early morning last September when first her voice and merry laugh rang in his ears. Cool—dew—freshness! can one understand that such things can exist when one is in a burning, horrible atmosphere like this?

Still she is praying for him—and he has done what he could to save the people as she wished. Oh, this terrible feeling of choking! air! air!—is there none? but she is praying for him all the time—he knows that with certainty, and it comforts him strangely somehow, though he knows not why.

Not until the whole house was burnt down was the conflagration extinguished, and amongst the numbers who perished in the flames was Sylvester—noble and heroic in his death, however evil and criminal in his life. Neither the misfortunes of his early training, his faults, nor his follies had ever managed wholly to quench the latent power for good that was within him, and that had been quickened to life by the unconscious influence of one whom he loved. Little had that love ever brought him from first to last save exceptional pain and unhappiness; yet who shall say that he was not really the gainer for a suffering that was able to purify his nature from so much of the evil in which it had become encased?

CHAPTER X
An Ungracious Task

Terribly long was the list of people who perished in the great fire at the Crœsus-Hoggs', and rarely had London been so deeply shocked and moved by any event.

Amongst the victims, however, Mr Rhys and Imogen and Sir Charles were fortunately not included. After Sylvester left them, the girl and her father had managed to carry and drag Sir Charles out of the theatre. Once outside, the open air had helped to revive him and he had been able to stagger along with their assistance till they were beyond reach of danger; then he had been taken as soon as possible to his rooms and put under the care of a doctor, who ordered him to bed immediately, and enjoined a condition of strict quiet for some days at least.

Ethel also had escaped unharmed. When she saw in the next day's paper that Sylvester was amongst the victims, she felt at the first moment as if a great weight was taken off her mind. Villain though he was, he had saved her life, nevertheless, and she was glad to think that there was now no necessity for her to make known his crime, since he was dead, and there was no longer a danger of his harming anyone. Poor Imogen! how sad for her if she had indeed cared for him—yet less sad now, perhaps, than it would have been if he were still alive. And Ethel's anxiety on this point was so great that she at once put on her bonnet and walked across to Lowndes Square— ostensibly to see how her cousin was after the fearful events of the night before, and really to try and ascertain if the girl were mourning over a lost lover. If so, Ethel thought she might be able to comfort her with the account of that ardent love for her which he had expressed—the knowledge that he had been devoted to her to the last, would surely be some consolation to the poor girl.

So completely had Ethel, by this time, worked herself into the belief that her cousin had fallen in love with Sylvester, that it was an immense relief to her to perceive, by the way in which Imogen spoke, that she was evidently heart-whole about him. In Ethel's satisfaction at this discovery she said nothing about what had passed between her and him at the last interview they had had together—for why, thought she, should she trouble her cousin with the thought of having been loved by this man? Anyhow she would not do it in a hurry, but would take time to consider whether it would be wise to impart that piece of information or not.

From Imogen she learnt what had not had time to get into the newspapers, and what she did not therefore yet know; and that was, how heroically he had gone back to save others, and thus met with his death.

As the heiress returned to Belgrave Square, she could not help pondering over the short glimpses she had had of this man whom she had seen but twice in her life, and thinking what a strange character his must have been. Her disposition, feelings, and principles were all thoroughly antagonistic to such a criminal, and prompted her to think of him only with abhorrence—yet somehow she did not feel inclined in the present case altogether to obey this prompting. When first she had discovered that he was the person who had robbed her, she had regarded him with the utmost possible horror and aversion, supposing him to be nothing less than an utter scoundrel. But the revelation of his real self that he had subsequently made to her, had touched and moved her, notwithstanding her prejudice against him, and that favourable impression was now increased by the knowledge of the self-sacrificing manner of his death. As she thought about him she recognised the fact that she had been brought face to face with a nature of by no means an every-day kind, and that he who had been able thus to wring some sort of esteem from her, almost in spite of herself, must have had some force of character distinguishing him from the common herd of men. To have to proclaim him a robber would have been most distasteful to her, she thought; she had at first only hesitated about it, lest Imogen should have been so unfortunate as to set her affections on him, but now other reasons also made her unwilling to make known his iniquity, and Ethel was rejoicing to think that she would not have to do so, when suddenly the recollection of Richard Richards came to her and filled her with dismay. The poor man was about to leave his home, driven away by the popular belief that he was guilty of her burglary, and nothing save the production of the real offender could remove that suspicion from him. To consider the living before the dead, and the innocent before the guilty was a manifest duty. Was she then to come forward, now that Sylvester was dead, and to strip off the veil of ignorance under cover of which his memory was held in respect, admiration, and honour? Surely he who had saved her life, merited better treatment than that at her hands; it seemed as if there would be something especially ungenerous, mean, and ungrateful in a denunciation of him coming from *her*. Yet, alas! what else was there for her to do? However ungracious the task might be, there was no other possible way of exonerating Richards from a false charge, and restoring his character. So she overcame her great reluctance to speak, and revealed the secret of Sylvester's burglary.

Of course such a startling piece of news produced an immense sensation. Society was quite in consternation to find that a man of this kind had been living in the midst of it, and going about like anyone else without anybody's having ever dreamt of supposing there was any harm in him. Why, Good Heavens! who could one venture to feel sure of after such a discovery as this? How were Brown, Jones, and Robinson ever again to dare to put faith in one another? Would they not henceforth be perpetually looking askance at each other, and mutually suspecting themselves of being forgers, pickpockets, incendiaries, and perhaps murderers, in disguise? Then, too, in the chorus of indignant exclamations were to be heard the voices of a few of those people of the prophet-after-the-event class who are never wanting when any surprising event takes place. These declared that they had had more insight than the rest of the world, and had always been convinced that there was something queer about Sylvester, and that he was not a man to be trusted further than you could see him. It was an opinion which they had, as they averred, stated repeatedly to other people; and this statement it was of course impossible for anyone to contradict, though it certainly did seem rather odd that it should receive no corroboration whatever from the memories of even those friends who were most intimate with them, and therefore most likely to be acquainted with what they had said. But then some people are so unaccountably forgetful!

On the whole, however, his memory was not harshly dealt with, and the comments made upon it were far more kindly and charitable than they would have been if he had died a natural death. The manner in which he had lost his life restrained and silenced idle and venomous tongues in spite of themselves. For death for the sake of others compels all men to admiration whether they will or no—it seems as though some shadow of the Divinity of the crucifixion must rest upon it for ever.

Little as Ethel had seen of Sylvester, and little as their two natures had in common, she had yet understood him sufficiently to be sure that there was nothing he would have more ardently desired than that Imogen should do him justice and think kindly of him now that he was dead. Therefore Ethel no longer now hesitated to relate faithfully to her cousin what had taken place between them at that last interview before the fire. She resolved to let the girl know the good that had been in him, the passionate love that he had borne her, and the suffering which it had entailed upon him. In doing this Ethel felt that she would make the only reparation in her power for the obloquy that she had been the unwilling means of bringing upon his memory, and it seemed to her almost like a dying man's message that had been entrusted to her to deliver.

It happened that several days elapsed before circumstances were propitious for her to make the communication that weighed upon her conscience; but at last a favourable moment occurred one day when she found herself alone with Imogen in the Rhys's house in Lowndes Square, and she profited by the opportunity immediately. Truth to tell, she had a sort of lingering, unexpressed fear, lest perhaps Imogen might have drawn the man on by flirting with him unfairly, but she was made easy on that score by the genuinely innocent surprise and concern which the girl's face showed when she heard of his attachment to her.

'Oh, how sorry I am!' she exclaimed. 'I never dreamt of all this! I only knew that he seemed rather to like to dance with and talk to me, and never suspected that anything deeper lay behind. Lots of couples do that much together without the least meaning anything more serious, and I supposed it was just the same between him and me. I do wish he hadn't cared for me so! It makes me quite uncomfortable to think of it.'

'I don't wonder at that;' answered Ethel. 'You find that you had enormous power over him of which you knew nothing, and of course you naturally feel anxious as to how you may have used that power. The influence exercised by people who are loved over those who love them is so important a factor in the world's concerns, that I sometimes think it's almost enough to make us all shrink from being loved because of the responsibility which that love lays upon our shoulders.'

It was quaint to hear Ethel delivering herself thus without in the least suspecting the extent of her own power in this way over Imogen, and the great weight attached by the latter to all her utterances and opinions.

'Yes, indeed it is,' returned Imogen, heartily; 'I'm sure I'd far rather that he hadn't cared for me at all. The wonder to me is, whatever can have made him do it? I know *I* shouldn't have!'

The wonder thus naïvely expressed was perfectly sincere and free from all intention of being a bait for a compliment, as Ethel easily perceived.

'I daresay that some one will explain that to you some day or other,' she returned, smiling; 'wait till you get married, and then see!'

'Married!' cried Imogen. 'I don't ever mean to get married. I've said so over and over again, and stuck to it, too, in spite of all the stuff Ralph talks. His favourite saying is, "Every woman intends to marry if she can; and quite right too, for if she doesn't, she's a mistake." But I shall just show him the contrary. What does a boy like that know about us?'

'Ah, well,' replied her cousin, 'perhaps you will, and perhaps you won't—you know possibly you may change your mind some day. If ever you do, at all events you'll have one satisfaction that will be denied to me in similar circumstances, and that I confess I envy you.'

'What's that?'

'The satisfaction of not being forced to think that you are probably sought for your money, and not for yourself. You know that is a fear that I must have continually before my eyes. I shall never be able to feel sure that anyone likes me really.'

'Oh, I don't think you need be unhappy about that!' rejoined Imogen. 'I'm sure lots of people like you ever so much! Look how welcome you are everywhere; I've sometimes thought that I wish I were half as popular as you are—it must be very pleasant.'

'Well—yes—so I find it generally, I believe,' answered Ethel, reflectively. 'Only then the pleasantness is rather spoilt now and then, when it suddenly occurs to me that probably it is only the owner of so much wealth that is wanted and welcomed, and that whether that owner's name be Carton or Crœsus-Hogg is a matter of profound indifference to the person welcoming. I very rarely think of such a thing, for of course there's no use in making oneself miserable about what is inevitable. Still, when the idea *does* happen to cross my mind, I naturally don't find it a very agreeable and soothing one. Sometimes I fancy that it must be in vain for me ever to hope to be liked quite disinterestedly—that the esteem in which I might be held by even the honestest and most unselfish people, would always be to some degree affected by the fact of my money.'

It was at the tip of Imogen's tongue to reply,—'*I* like you for yourself, at all events.' But she checked herself before the words had passed her lips. They would sound like a mere empty protestation; and for mere empty protestations she entertained a profound contempt. Better to wait, and let time show whether or no her friendship was a real and enduring one. Therefore all she answered was,—

'Yes; I suppose it must be a horrid bore never to be able to trust to anyone's caring for you in earnest. But, after all, I don't think you find the position of an heiress altogether intolerable—do you, Ethel? You can't say honestly that you want to change it—now can you?'

Ethel laughed.

'I never said I did,' she returned. 'But I must be off now, or I shall be too late for an engagement. By-the-bye, have you heard lately how Sir Charles Dover is getting on? They say he was a good deal hurt.'

'He's getting better, I believe,' answered Imogen; 'I shall hear for certain how he is before long, for Ralph is up in town again for a couple of nights, and said he should go and see how Sir Charles was to-day.'

And so Ethel departed to keep her appointment, and Imogen was left to her own meditations.

CHAPTER XI
A Sensitive Conscience

Imogen's meditations after her cousin's departure were not of a particularly agreeable nature. She was somewhat more upset by all that had just happened than she would condescend to show. First there had been the shock of the horrible fire, of her own narrow escape, and of Sylvester's gallant death. Then came the startling discovery that the man with whom she had associated, and who had saved her life in the conflagration, had been a thief and evil-doer, so base and unprincipled as to have had no scruples about letting someone else suffer in his stead, and encouraging the idea that another man had committed the crime of which he was himself guilty. And now finally came this fresh revelation of his having loved her.

To find that he had cared for her in earnest was a complete surprise to her. She was a girl who was remarkably free from the common female attribute of vanity, and was not at all likely to imagine any admiration of herself as existing, unless it were expressed very plainly indeed. He had never told her right out that he cared for her, nor had he in any other way made his sentiments evident enough for her to perceive them.

Since the time of her coming out, her life had been amply filled by the business entailed upon her by this new phase of existence—the business of assimilating some things to herself and herself to others, by which process her character was being unconsciously transmuted and formed whilst still retaining its own original individuality as the foundation. In all that appertained to this, she had been too fully occupied to have time

331

to trouble her head with speculations as to whether any particular person liked her or not, or to what extent the liking might go. She had always supposed that Mr Sylvester must think her tolerably agreeable because he seemed to like to be with her; but she attached no further importance than that to his fondness for her society. She had generally found him pleasant, and had learnt to recognise that he possessed a strange power of attraction that was peculiar to himself. But to regard him as a lover was a very different matter, and she had never felt inclined to do that. Had she been saved from such a misfortune by the firmness of her conviction that she should never want to marry anyone at all? Or had she perhaps had some kind of intuition warning her of that invisible gulf between them of which he had been so painfully conscious?

Ethel had spoken of the responsibility of being loved; and the words now came home to Imogen not only with the force due to the undoubted truth they conveyed, but also with the additional weight which they derived in her eyes on account of the person who had uttered them. Imogen was disquieted as well as surprised to think of the power that she had had over Sylvester. She could not help asking herself uneasily how far she might have been responsible for his moral condition since she had known him? and whether, perhaps, some of his subsequent lack of goodness or actual wickedness might not lie at her door? When in her best and highest moods she had often been troubled by an impatience of the uselessness of her life, and had felt eager cravings to be able to benefit the world somehow—to do something that should make a real difference in it for good. And now that it appeared that the very chance she had longed for had come to her without her perceiving it, she felt by no means satisfied of having made the most of it, and profited by it, as she might have done.

To think that she should have had the opportunity of influencing another human being, a soul, a clever, strong man who might in turn have influenced perhaps numbers of other people also—what a tremendous responsibility that was! Had she always spoken and acted as she would have done if she had known of this responsibility? as she wished she had done now? Had she not, perhaps, sometimes done harm by careless, foolish words which, though not exactly wrong in themselves, had yet fallen short of what they ought to have been, and had certainly not been such as she would have uttered if she had had an idea that there was anyone likely to attach especial importance to them? Or even if she had not done any actual harm by her conversation, yet had she done all the good that it had been in her power to do? Possibly if she had been altogether a better person than she was—more consistent, more earnest, more true to the highest standard, then she might have been able to assist him effectually, and might perhaps have been the means of reforming him altogether. The immense responsibility of influence had never before been so deeply impressed upon her mind as it was now. For all she could tell the making or marring of a man's life might have been entrusted to her hands, and her conscience would not let her feel altogether satisfied as to the manner in which the trust had been discharged.

A sensitive conscience pricks its owner for sins of omission as well as commission, and she had presently worked herself into a state of considerable self-reproach and unhappiness. She imagined that she would like to talk the whole affair over with some one else and find out how the eyes of another person would regard it. That thought led naturally to the consideration of who would be a satisfactory individual to confide in, in a case of this kind, and she began to pass her friends in mental review. First she considered her father. No—he would not do. She felt she needed some one with a capacity for youthful enthusiasms, and as he must certainly have out-lived his by this time, therefore she was sure it would be no use to expect him to understand her. Her next idea was

Ralph. It was not unlikely that he might be able to look at the thing from pretty nearly her own point of view *if* he chose to do so; but then it was quite likely that he would not so choose unless he should happen by luck to be in the right humour just when he was talked to about it. That would never do; for she was sure that she could never confide what was troubling her to anyone unless she should feel perfectly certain of meeting with a sympathetic reception—so Ralph, also, was dismissed from the list of possible confidants. Then there was Ethel; would not she do? Well—yes—perhaps; yet she, too, did not seem to be exactly the ideal confidante that her cousin was hungering after at that moment; possibly the extreme admiration which Imogen felt for her imparted a sense of awe and restraint that prevented her from appearing absolutely satisfactory in the confidante capacity.

Then Imogen began to wonder when Ralph was coming back from his expedition to see how Sir Charles was getting on. That suggested the thought of the baronet as a possible recipient of the history of what was disturbing her; and, to her surprise, it somehow or other seemed as if he would be the very person she wanted. She believed he would be sure to comprehend her meaning even if she had a difficulty about putting it very exactly into words—he always did seem to have a faculty for comprehending people who were wanting to do right, she had noticed. Then she was convinced that his opinion would be worth having, because he had always seemed to her to know by instinct what was the best thing to do, without any fuss, bother, or uncertainty, on all occasions. And he was not a person who was ever likely to judge anyone harshly or sternly, which was a yet further recommendation to her when she felt as sore and shaken as she did at present. Quite a childish disinclination to be scolded and longing to be comforted had taken possession of her, and she felt an instinctive conviction that he would be the very ideal comforter whom she desired. Strong, gentle, reliable, and sympathetic, what more could she want? and she was sure that he would neither be amused at her as her father might be, nor yet snub her as there would be a chance of Ralph's doing.

Then suddenly a new and startling idea that came into her head made her blush hotly. Was there not something odd and unnatural in her feeling such a thorough confidence in a stranger as to cause her to be inclined to turn to him as a comforter rather than to any of her own family? Was this curious preference to be attributed purely to friendly esteem, or could it be the result of a warmer feeling having crept in unawares? Could she, who had always regarded herself as destined to be a champion of single-blessedness as the natural condition of women—could *she* have actually gone and fallen in love? It was surely not possible that she should so readily have departed from her principles! and yet—and yet—and yet—the more she thought about it the more firmly convinced she became that there really was no one in the whole world to compare to him!

Was she indeed, then, forced to confess to herself that she was in love—and she not yet eighteen! Oh, what a speedy and ignominious come-down from her loftily independent ideas, and oh how Ralph would laugh if he knew it! He didn't know it though—not yet, at all events; perhaps it might be that he never would, for it must all depend upon whether or no Sir Charles were to make her a second offer. She couldn't ask him, if he didn't ask her—that was quite certain.

Was it likely that he would try again? Well—when she came to think of it, she had a kind of idea that such a thing was not wholly impossible. If he did—why then her answer would be somewhat different from what it had been before; only of course he would have to find that out for himself. How provoking Ralph would be when he found himself triumphant, and how he would crow over her! Indeed, so strongly did that consideration weigh with her, that she began to ask herself whether she could make up her mind to face his ridicule, and whether she would not almost rather remain single to the end of her days. Yes—*almost*, perhaps; but then *almost* is by no means the same thing as *quite*. After all, it would not so much matter being laughed at and crowed over, if she could hope always to be consoled by the only person who appeared to her thoroughly qualified for the office of comforter!

And if he did that for her, would not she perhaps be sometimes able to help him in return? Anyhow he must have thought so when he asked her to marry him, because he had described himself as work for her to do, all ready to her hand. He had declared that a woman could make more difference to the man who loved her than to anyone else in the world, and all this that had happened about Mr Sylvester certainly seemed to confirm that theory.

Only then again there was such an enormous difference between the two men in question, that perhaps they could hardly be judged by the same rule. Mr Sylvester had needed help in a way that Sir Charles certainly did not. She was sure that the latter was ever so much better than she was, and that it was only his modesty that had made him fancy she could be an assistance to him. Rather it was just the contrary; it was he that could help her, she believed, and not she him. Yet no doubt he had *said* that he wanted her help—and she did not think he told lies.

How silly she had been not to have appreciated his merits properly from the first! Perhaps, after all, he might never give her this second chance which she had been anticipating; perhaps he would take a fancy to marry some one else—some one who would be too wise to reject such an opportunity of a paragon husband. Well! if so Imogen felt that she would have to bear the disappointment as best she could, knowing that she had only herself to thank for it. At any rate, Ralph would lose his chance of a triumph in that case; for as it was most improbable that such another paragon as Sir Charles could be in existence, therefore there could be no likelihood of her being again tempted to give up her original determination of remaining an old maid to the end of her days.

Here the door opened suddenly, and two people came in whose entrance put an abrupt end to her meditations.

CHAPTER XII
How Ralph Will Crow Over Me!

People sometimes give indications, which may be interpreted by a close observer, of feelings which they are not themselves conscious of possessing, and this had been the case with Imogen. Though she was quite unaware of drifting into falling in love with Sir Charles, there had nevertheless been a slight, indefinable alteration in her manner to him of late, which had not escaped his observation and had raised his hopes greatly. He had thought the alteration especially noticeable when he met her at the theatricals, and had esteemed it of such good omen to find that the moths he had sent her had not been thrown away, that he contemplated renewing his proposal to her on that very night if he should have a favourable opportunity for doing so. The tragical termination of the party had of course made it impossible for him to execute his purpose, and since then illness had kept him prisoner and prevented his seeing her.

Tossing feverishly on his bed, he had gone over again and again in his mind all that had passed between them, recalling and dwelling upon words, looks, and tones, and trying to draw good auguries therefrom. Was she really changed towards him? or was he merely a ridiculous, presumptuous ass for venturing to think so? Then again he would be depressed at the thought of how very little reason he could discover in himself to make it likely for anyone to fall in love with him; for he was by no means conceited, and had but a low opinion of his own powers of fascination. But still his hopes reverted hopefully to the difference he had noticed in her recently, and he longed to be able to see her again and to put his luck once more to the test. Being laid by the heels was at that moment most especially annoying, and he daily besieged the doctor with entreaties to be allowed to go about as usual.

When at last the happy day of emancipation from the house arrived, his first thought was to go and call upon the Rhyses. Perhaps she would be at home and alone, and if so, he would surely ask his question. And anyhow he could not rest without making an attempt to see her, whether alone or not, for it was a whole ten days since they had met, and his eyes hungered for a sight of her again, and his ears longed after the sound of her voice. He was on the point of setting out, then, for this call, when Ralph came to see him.

'Hullo!' exclaimed that young gentleman, meeting him on the threshold of the door; 'glad to find you well enough to go out! Don't turn back on my account—I'll come and see you another time! Where are you off to?'

'I was just going to call on your people,' rejoined Sir Charles; 'shall I find them at home, do you suppose?'

'Don't quite know,' answered Ralph. 'I fancy my father's out, but Im may be at home perhaps. Tell you what! I'll go back there with you, and then we can go on together somewhere else afterwards—unless you don't want me, that's to say?'

Sir Charles declared that he would be delighted to have Ralph's company, and then they started for Lowndes Square. On the way there it did occur to the baronet that it might tend to facilitate his seeing Imogen alone if he were to confide the object of his visit to his companion. But then he was deterred by recollecting how grievously on the previous occasion he had been oppressed and hindered in getting to his proposal by the consciousness of some one else's knowing all about it all the time. So he held his tongue now, and gave Ralph no inkling that there was anything particular in the wind.

Ralph's presence made the servant, who admitted them at Lowndes Square, think it needless to announce the baronet's arrival to Imogen, who was sitting in the drawing-room; thus the two people who suddenly disturbed her in the train of meditations which had led her to discover that she cared about Sir Charles Dover, were none other than that gentleman himself and her brother. This unexpected entrance of the very person she had been thinking about discomposed her considerably; and her cheeks burnt almost as though she had imagined him able to see into her mind, and know the place that he was occupying there.

'Oh! here you are, Im,' observed Ralph, airily; 'I thought perhaps you'd be at home. It's the first day this fellow's pill has given him leave to go out. I found him just starting to call here when I got to his diggings, so I came back along with him, you see.'

'I'm glad to see you so much better, Sir Charles,' said Imogen; 'I hope you'll soon be altogether out of the doctor's hands.'

She tried hard to master her confusion so as to appear exactly the same as usual, and had an internal conviction that her attempt was a signal failure—which naturally only increased her discomposure. That there was anything wrong about her passed unnoticed by Ralph, but was immediately apparent to the finer perceptions of a lover. Sir Charles knew that there was a change in her voice and manner, and felt somehow puzzled to account for the novelty. What did it mean? Was it stiffness? Could he have displeased her in any way? What was it?

'Thanks for your good wishes,' he replied. 'I've no doubt that I shall pick up in no time, now that I may go out again. Fresh air always agrees with me better than anything else, and I find I don't get on at all well without it.'

'No more do I,' she answered. 'Unluckily it's an article that's decidedly scarce in London. It's one of the few things that no shop keeps in stock, or undertakes to be able to supply you with by the day after to-morrow at latest—as they do in respect to almost every other thing one can possibly require. I suppose you'll go to get it in the country somewhere, or by the sea, now that you can move.'

There was a mingling of sweet and sour in this speech as it seemed to Sir Charles. On the one hand it was satisfactory that she should take an interest in his well-being; but then again he did not at all admire this prompt suggestion that he ought to go away where he would be out of her reach—especially just now on this first occasion of meeting after such an immense time, no less than a whole ten days having elapsed since he had last seen her!

Here Ralph interposed with a bit of news that he had picked up and was anxious to impart to his sister.

'I say, Im,' he said; 'there's a new wedding just given out. Guess who the parties are that mean to get spliced?'

'Guess ? Not I!' she returned. 'What's the good of wearing out my brains with trying to guess something that you can tell me all the time? Who is it?'

'Well, I'll tell you the lady's name, and you must find out the gentleman's for yourself,' he replied; 'it's Lady Elise Bolyn.'

'And is the other, young Mr Crœsus-Hogg?' asked she.

'The very thing itself,' answered Ralph. 'Perhaps she thought herself bound in common gratitude to accept him after his getting her safe away from the fire; or perhaps she admired little Guelph; or perhaps she admired little Guelph's money; who knows? At any rate they've fixed it up; and the old Hoggs are quite enchanted, and inclined to think that the acquisition of such a daughter-in-law is ample consolation for the burning of any number of mansions. What a thing it is to be rich! They say those Hoggs think no more of the loss of their magnificent house with all the splendid pictures, furniture, plate, statues, and etceteras, than anyone else would of losing an old carpet-bag.'

Ralph was in a conversational humour, and went on cheerfully retailing and commenting on whatever gossip he had heard, without suspecting how greatly Sir Charles would at that moment have preferred his room to his company. Meanwhile the baronet was trying to find some pretext to get rid of the loquacious youth, or in some way or other to secure a private interview with Imogen. Presently a bright idea occurred to him.

'Miss Rhys,' he said, 'I have a great fancy to look at those two moths I sent you. Will you think me very troublesome if I ask to have my whim gratified?'

Imogen blushed. She felt rather shy on the subject of those moths now that she had discovered the tender sentiments that had been developing unsuspected within her, and led her to set store on a worthless gift merely for the sake of the donor. As for Ralph, he entertained no doubt whatever that the insects had been thrown away long ago, but thought that she probably would not like to say so to Sir Charles, and therefore was annoyed at the baronet for requesting to see them.

'Deuced stupid of him, after I'd told him what rubbish they were, and how she laughed at them when they came,' grumbled Ralph to himself. 'I didn't think he was so tactless—of course it puts her regularly up a tree.'

'Oh no!' replied Imogen readily, in answer to the baronet's request. 'They're in a drawer in the little boudoir on the back stairs. I'll bring them to you directly.'

Ralph stared in astonishment, for it never entered his head that the moths in question could really be there. Yet she spoke with the utmost confidence. Certainly he had not thought she could lie so like truth as that—however, she was blushing pretty considerably he could see. What did she mean to do? for after what she had just said, she was of course bound to produce two moths of some kind or other for the baronet's inspection. It would have been easy enough to arrange the thing if she had had her entomological cabinet in reach, for then she could have fetched out a couple of old specimens of *Thyatira Batis* to be looked at. But he knew that the collection of moths had been left at home, so she certainly couldn't get out of the difficulty in that way. Would she trust to the chance of Sir Charles's not remembering what the moths he had sent were like? and show him a couple of some other kind, and try and palm them off upon him as being the same?

Imogen's answer was just what Sir Charles had hoped for, as affording an excuse for him and her to go into another room alone together.

'I couldn't think of troubling you to bring them here,' he replied, 'but I should like extremely to go and see them in the boudoir, if you'll take me there.'

He was, however, mistaken in thinking that he would thus get rid of Ralph's presence; for that youth was becoming very curious as to what his sister would exhibit as Sir Charles's *Thyatira Batis,* and had not the remotest intention of being left behind. Sir Charles looked imploringly, meaningly, at him, as he rose to accompany them; but the look passed unnoticed. Sir Charles took advantage of Ralph's being a few yards behind them as they went out of the room, to affect not to perceive his intention of coming, and shut the door in his face. Then when Ralph pushed it open and followed them, the baronet exclaimed,—

'Hullo, old fellow! what on earth makes *you* want to see these moths?' with an air of surprise so exaggerated that it might really have given Ralph a hint to stay behind. But all such hints were completely thrown away upon him, for he never noticed Sir Charles's behaviour at all, being too much occupied with wondering how his sister intended to extricate herself from the scrape in which she had, as he believed, got entangled. Never once did the possibility of her having kept the insects occur to him, till she opened the moth-box, and he saw within it a couple of ill-set, unmistakable *Thyatira Batis.*

Glancing at her in utter amazement, he was struck by an unusual look on her face, which seemed to express embarrassment and softness, mingled in a way that he had never before seen there. Sir Charles, too, was looking at him strangely, he thought; and then all of a sudden, there began to dawn upon him a perception that he was perhaps in the way.

Sir Charles, meanwhile, who recollected Imogen's interest in Richard Richards, and her anxiety for his innocence to be proved, was asking whether he and his family had yet left their home, as they had been going to do, or whether the certainty of his innocence had come in time to prevent the move.

'Yes, it was just in time,' answered Imogen; 'they were to have gone next week, but now they can stay on where they are, and Richard has been taken on at work by someone directly— people seem to feel that they are bound to do something to make up for their past unjust suspicions, and I hear that a subscription is to be got up for him. Ann—his wife, you know—must have been delighted to be able to stay, for she couldn't bear the idea of leaving home. However, she didn't indulge in any very extravagant demonstrations of joy on the occasion, for when she heard that her husband was cleared from the charge against him, I'm told that she only gave a sort of grunt, and remarked,— "Well; and there's fullish people was to be so long finding that out. *I* was know it all along." What a strange, sad business this has been about the burglary.'

'Yes, indeed,' he answered. 'Whatever Sylvester may have been, he behaved nobly the other night and saved us at his own risk. There would have been a poor chance for our lives then, if it hadn't been for him. And when I think how he helped to carry me out of that horrible place where I lay insensible, it seems perfectly odious to have to consider him as a thief. I feel as if I wanted to knock down anyone who ventures to suggest such a thing. I knew very little of him; but it's my firm impression that he must have been a fine fellow in some ways, at all events.'

Ralph had relieved them of his company a few minutes previously upon the pretence of a note which he declared himself to have suddenly remembered an immediate necessity for writing and despatching. Sir Charles and Imogen were consequently alone together, and the mention of Sylvester's name might seem to lead naturally to her confiding to the baronet that history of the relations between herself and Sylvester that had troubled her so greatly a short time ago. It had then seemed to her most desirable to have a confidant for her troubles; and now here she was, alone with the very person who had appeared to her as an ideally perfect confidant. She did not, however, avail herself of the opportunity, which was to be accounted for by a sudden shyness of her companion that had come over her in the last half-hour or so. Instead of continuing, as might have been expected, to speak about Sylvester, she rather nervously suggested that they should return to the drawing-room. But the young man meant to have his say first, and plunged into it boldly.

'Wait one moment first, please,' he said. 'I want to repeat a question, Imogen, that I asked you once before. Perhaps you will think me a mere vain fool for troubling you a second time with it—but—but—somehow I have dared to fancy that if I tried again I might possibly get a different answer from what I did before; and the prize I hope for is too precious to risk losing for want of a word. I sent you a couple of moths and you did not reject them even though they were but common and worthless.

May I meet with the same good fortune as they did? May I, too, not be rejected, even though I have no special merits to recommend me in your eyes?'

Her face was turned downwards, and her cheeks were crimson. Extreme nervousness and many conflicting emotions made her feel awkward, and she did not immediately reply. She felt half uncomfortable even notwithstanding a new sensation of gladness that was creeping over her. Suddenly she looked up at him with eyes shining with the strange, deep, hitherto unknown emotion that filled her; there was, too, upon her face a half-saucy smile that seemed a sort of final effort against yielding to that sentimentality of being in love which she had so often laughed at.

'Ah, well!' she said; ' I suppose it would be hardly fair to treat you worse than I did your moths. And after all, you are better than them in one way—for while there are lots of *Thyatira Batis* in the world, you know there's only one YOU. But oh, dear, just to think how Ralph will crow over me when he hears of it!'

THE END

Notes

Changes have been minimal, only where the original text was erroneous, for instance, Lady Elsie rather than Lady Elise. Punctuation changes have been made solely if comprehension was frankly unclear, grammar points such as 'to let to do' or 'next someone' have been retained, the vocabulary and slang of the period remain unchanged as have the older spellings, such as 'dulness' and 'chaperon' or attempts to reproduce certain accents via spelling such as 'nottice'.

Notes have been given only for the more unusual foreign, mainly French, words and expressions; it is assumed, however, that the more common terms such as 'penchant', 'ménage' or 'double-entendre' are understood. As for other words and references, notes have been confined to the explanation of the more abstruse literary and historical elements or of terms like L.S.D. (Pounds, shillings and pence), which might otherwise lead to some confusion!

Volume 1.
Chapter I.
1. p.2 Sir Wilfred Lawson – A Liberal politician and Temperance leader (1829-1906).
2. p.3 *mauvaise honte* – French expression which literally means 'bad shame' but could be translated as 'bashfulness'.
3. p.7 a mere tyro – just a beginner, novice or inexperienced person.
4. p.7 chippy - bad-tempered or 'hung-over'.
Chapter III.
1. p.17 pluming himself – congratulating himself in a self-satisfied manner.
Chapter IV.
1. p.21 Captain Mayne-Reid – An Irishman (1818-1883) who was a pastor, then a trapper, a journalist and a

captain in the U.S. war against Mexico. He became famous especially for his adventure stories involving Red Indians.

Chapter V.

1. p.28   *triste* – sad, melancholy, unhappy.
2. p.28   *abîmée* – ruined.
3. p.28   *désolée* – sorry, upset.
4. p.29   Silvio Pellico – An Italian writer, dramatist, poet and patriot (1789-1854).
5. p.29   Menzel's *Geschichte der Deutschen* – Reference to a German textbook: *Paradigms and Glossary to The German Reading Lessons from Menzel's Geschichte der Deutschen* (1838)
6. p.29   forrarder – further ahead
7. p.30   Mr W.D.Howells – A renowned Welsh-American editor, writer and critic (1837-1920), his novels written during the 1870s, ending with *The Undiscovered Country* in 1880 on the Shaker religious community, marked the transition between his adventure tales and his more celebrated Realist period.
8. p.30   *Huntingtower* refers to a traditional Scottish ballad for children from the early nineteenth century. Jeanie and Jamie sing a duet in which Jamie, who turns out to be a rich landowner and proprietor of Huntingtower Castle, promises riches to Jeanie although he has 'a wife and bairnies three' and admits, 'And I'm not sure how ye'd gree, lassie'.
9. p.32   *bouchées* – vol-au-vents or tasty morsels to eat.
10. p.32   Quotation from the first stanza of the poem *Morality* (1852) by Matthew Arnold (1822-1888).
11. p.33   plump – with a sudden or full impact.
12. p.34   quamp – apparently from the Gloucestershire dialect, meaning quiet or still.

Chapter VI.

1. p.40   a toady – a sycophant, a person who flatters or defers to others in his own interest.
2. p.41   nice – fussy, fastidious, particular.

Chapter VII.

1. p.52   Davingport brothers – Probably a reference to the American Davenport Brothers, known for conjuring

and spiritualism. They toured the States and
Britain with their escapology tricks when tied up in
a box. Later, from 1865, these tricks were exposed
as 'humbug' by the circus impresario, P.T.Barnum.

Chapter X.
1.   p.76   a Paul Pry – an inquisitive person (character in a U.S. song
              of 1820)

Chapter XII.
1.   p.96   drams – tubs of coal hauled by ropes.

Volume II.
Chapter I.
1.   p.115   a rood – a quarter of an acre of land (0.10 hectares).
2.   p.116   backstone bread – bread (or scones) cooked on a
              griddle at the back of the kitchen range.

Chapter II.
1.   p.126   Bradamante – Fictional heroine of Italian
              Renaissance literature, created by Ariosto, known
              for her warrior-like qualities.

Chapter III.
1.   p.131   *beauté du diable* – literally the 'beauty of the devil',
              this could be translated as bewitching beauty or
              attractiveness.

Chapter V.
1.   p.155   a pink of propriety – a perfect example of propriety.
2.   p.160   Mrs. Oliphant 'just a long-leggit lad'– Margaret
              Oliphant 1825-1897 had a prolific literary career and
              was especially known for her novels on Scottish life.

Chapter X.
1.   p.202   a raw – a raw patch or sore spot.
2.   p.205   loshengias – probably from lozenges (sweets to be
              dissolved in the mouth).
3.   p.205   hardbake – a sweetmeat of boiled brown sugar or
              molasses, butter and almonds.
4.   p.209   hipped – melancholy, depressed.

Chapter XI.
1.   p.212   *"il y a toujours l'un qui baise, et l'autre qui tend la
              joue"*– Literally the expression means there is always
              one who kisses and the other who offers his or her
              cheek. Here, it shows that the affection is accepted
              but unrequited.

Chapter XII.
  1. p.216 *bon camarade* – good friend, chum.
  2. p.218 a sell – a deception or hoax.
Chapter XIII.
  1. p.227 a spoon – an example of amorous behaviour.

Volume III.
Chapter I.
  1. p.237 *beau ideal* – le beau idéal is the ideal of beauty but here probably means very perfection.
Chapter II.
  1. p.243 L.S.D – £.s.d. Pounds, shillings and pence, the monetary system in use in Britain before decimalisation.
Chapter IV.
  1. p.259 *beurre noire* – beurre noir is butter melted and browned, then mixed with vinegar or lemon and other seasoning.
  2. p.259 *matelotes* – a matelote is a fish sauce with wine, bacon, onions and mushrooms.
  3. p.261 truckling – being servile or obsequious.
Chapter V.
  1. p.267 *sauve-qui-peut* – a stampede or 'run for your life!'.
Chapter VII.
  1. p.285 *Le jeu ne vaut pas la chandelle* – The game is not worth the candle.
Chapter VIII.
  1. p.294 This George Eliot quote, like that on page 253, is taken from Chapter 17 of *Felix Holt*.